ARCADIA

ARCADIA

JIM CRACE

JONATHAN CAPE
LONDON

First published 1992
© Jim Crace 1992
Jonathan Cape, 20 Vauxhall Bridge Road, London SW1V 2SA

Jim Crace has asserted his right
under the Copyright, Designs and Patents Act, 1988
to be identified as the author of this work

A CIP catalogue record for this book
is available from the British Library

ISBN 0–224–02692–5

Printed in Great Britain by
Mackays of Chatham PLC, Chatham, Kent

"The tallest buildings throw the longest Shadows
(thus Great Men make their Mark by
blocking out the Sun,
and, seeking Warmth themselves, cast
Cold upon the rest)."

Emile dell'Ova, *Truismes*
Editions Baratin, Paris, 1774

PART ONE
THE SOAP MARKET

1

NO WONDER VICTOR NEVER fell in love. A childhood like the one he had would make ice-cubes of us all. He lived on mother's milk till he was six, and then he thrived on charity and trade.

On the day that he was eighty, Victor dined on fish. He loved fish best. As he had scaled and silvered with old age, so his taste for fish had grown. Ten live perch from his own stock pool arrived that morning at the station and were driven by cab in a plastic travel-tank to his offices. The kitchen staff were used to Victor and his coddled fish. They planned to cook them steeped in apple beer, and serve them cold with olives from his farm. There would be champagne too – the boss's own. And fruit, of course. All this for just five birthday guests. Greengrocers every one, spud traders, bean merchants, middlemen in fruit – and each of them, like Victor, old and slow and hard of hearing. There were – at his request – no gifts, no cards, no cake. He would not tax himself – or any of his staff – with speeches. What old men want is peace and informality, and the chance to talk amongst themselves like smutty boys.

He said he wanted a simple country meal. The fiction in his mind was this: that he would sit surrounded by his friends beneath a canvas awning. There'd be white cloths on a shaky trestle. A breeze. The guests would push off their slippers and rub their bare toes in the dust. They'd twist round on their

3

stools and spit olive stones in the air. Some cats and chickens would take care of crumbs and perch skins. With just a little teasing and some cash, the cook's fat son would play plump tunes on his accordion. That was Victor's ideal birthday meal. Simple, cheap, and attainable for country people living earthbound on a farm, say, thirty years ago; but a dream beyond the reach of cheques and fax machines for a man whose home is twenty-seven storeys and a hundred metres up, with views all round, through tinted, toughened glass, and tinted, toughened air, of office blocks and penthouses and malls.

Nevertheless, the man we knew as Rook had done his best to cater for old Victor's dreams. White tablecloths were easy to locate. Rook had the cats. The breeze was air-conditioning. The old men could shake their slippers off and rub their toes in carpet wool. They could spit their olive pips at waitresses. Why not?

They'd have to go without the chickens, reasoned Rook. Victor could not have free-range hens clucking amongst his halting guests. He was not Dali, yet. The accordions were booked. The agency had arranged a band of three, two sisters and a friend. Perhaps, thought Rook, he ought to spray the elevator with aerosols of field dung, or play recorded birdsong on the intercom. He'd have the boss in tears. He'd have the boss in tears, in any case. He had resolved to indulge Victor for the day. He planned to dress a birthday chair for him in greenery, just like they used to in the village where Victor was born. Just like the chair in Leyel's *Calendar of Customs*: Plate XVII, a fogged black-and-white photograph of a small boy from the Twenties, beaming, tearful, overdressed in breeches and a waistcoat, amid the birthday foliage of a high-backed seat. Victor could have the same. Office Security and Caretaking would disapprove – but, surely, Rook could decorate a chair without the building grinding to a halt. A little greenery would do no harm.

So that was Rook's day arranged. It made a change from simply standing by as the old man inked his mark on cheques and papers or pointed his icy nose at the latest trading journals or – more warmly – at Alkadier's *Illustrated Guide to Greenhouse Coleoptera* which was his bed and desk and lavatory companion. Besides, it released Rook onto the streets for a while. His greatest joy, to let his tie hang loose, to dodge and stroll amongst the people of the city. But earning wages all the time, bleeding Victor's purse, bleeding purses everywhere.

There was a city garden, at the heart of the crop market and not far from Victor's, where there were roses, laurels and all sorts of green-grey, stunted shrubs. It used to be the public washing square, and was known still to all the locals as the Soap Garden. With a logic more poetic than functional, the market which engulfed the garden was known, too, as the Soap Market, though soap was not on sale. The bludgeoned medieval scrubbing stones and the gargoyle fountains of the washing square were still there, though protected from the people by a fence. Seats and tables spilled out into the garden from the many adjacent market bars. And there were lawns, a cake-and-coffee stand, and shrubbery that would make a perfect dressing for a birthday chair. 'I could send a chauffeur or a clerk, it's true,' thought Rook. But on sunny days like this there were girls spread out across the grass – more and prettier than he'd ever meet in country lanes. 'Why waste such prospects on a clerk?'

He told Anna, the woman who ran the outer rooms, hired and fired the staff, and controlled the door to Victor's office

suite, that there were 'arrangements to be made' and that he'd
be gone two hours at the most. 'Bring back a cake for me,' she
said. She was no fool. She knew Rook well. She'd known him
hurry out before on urgent morning calls, then caught him
sitting idly in his room with nothing on his desk but crumbs.
He was not the sort to play the grandee if the staff included
him in their gossip or their pleasantries. He did not have a
reputation there for hard work, or pride. He was Victor's
buffer – and his fixer – that was all. Boss said; Rook did.
Though what Rook did and fixed was anybody's guess.

Anna liked the teasing mystery of Rook. Her pleasure
showed: her voice amused, her face a little flushed and kin-
dled. She wondered if she would dare to share a cake with
him, their mouths and tongues contesting every crumb.
They'd been so close to that a thousand times before – his
hand upon the waistband of her skirt or pinching at her flesh,
his breath upon her neck, as they stood in line at the coffee or
the copying machine; her hand, just playfully, on his, when
side by side each morning, when hip to haunch at Anna's
desk, they checked the agenda of Victor's day. If this was love,
then it was wise, not youthful love, not timid love, not blind
romance. And if this was simply passion and no more, then it
was in good hands, for Rook and Anna were both old – and
young – enough to make the most of passion while time was
on their side. For Anna there was pouching beneath her chin,
some lines and bruising at the eyes, a softness to her stomach
and her thighs, some parchmenting of skin along her inner
limbs, the loss of buoyancy, and more, to tell her daily, every
time she washed or dressed or ran, that she was over forty and
that she should dare to change her motto from the *Careful Does
It* of her youth to *Yes and Now and Here*.

For Rook the signs of ripening were much the same, plus
listless hair that was blanching at the temples and an asthmatic's prow-like chest as evidence that, underneath the lively tie
and shirt, his lungs were shallow and distressed. He saw
himself as lean and weightless. His mind was lean. The expression on his face was lean. But – naked in the shower or in
bed – his leanness was exposed as thinness. But still he was a
tempting, enigmatic man, not dry or beaten like the other men
she knew. Anna dared to look him in the eye and contemplate
the cake – and more – that they could share. 'We'll see,' she
said, not quite aloud, her fingers church-and-steepled at her
chins, her spirit moistened by the prospects of the day. Yes,
yes. Yes here. Yes now. Rook recognised himself in her. He
smiled at Anna and he asked, 'Just name your cake. What can I
tempt you with today?' She said she wanted a Viennese with
fruit and cream. That would go well with the best champagne
which she expected the boss to press upon his personal staff
so they could toast him at his birthday lunch. Rook promised
to fix it. What he'd do was this. He'd see to it that all the
people working in the outer rooms got cakes and drink.
They'd join the aged greengrocers in celebrating Victor's
eighty years. The staff could eat a cake, he thought, without
the building grinding to a halt, though buildings-grinding-to-
a-halt appealed to him.

Thus Rook, on that summer Friday in our city, was armed
with errands to gather cakes and greenery, as he descended
the hundred metres and the twenty-seven floors by Victor's
private lift and walked towards the open air through the
pampered, plastic foliage of the atriums which flared and
billowed from the building like quilted valances of glass. He
showed his face and his Staff Pass at the tasselled rope and

---

stepped between the wings of a revolving door. THESE DOORS ARE AUTOMATIC, announced the sign. It was a warning and a boast: These Doors are Greater and More Permanent than You. They simply swept him in a rotating triangle of processed air into the sun and breeze beyond. All security ended there.

You note he did not choose to take a car. There was a man on duty at the doors who would have been glad to summon one, a taxi or a chauffeured company Panache. Rook was valued there as much as Victor's perch – if not a little more – and he was not expected to take his chances on the street. But he preferred to walk. And who would know? Five minutes and he would be amongst the crowds, indistinguishable from all those other duplicates in office wear on worktime errands in the city. What could be sweeter than to pass unrecognised amongst familiar strangers, or to proffer half a nod, a shadow smile, to passers-by whose faces rang a bell? What democracy! – to dodge and jostle, tadpoles in the stream. But first he had to walk the hot and empty cloisters of the mall where the noise of distant traffic was waylaid by architectural water. It fell and fountained, day and night, with a rhythmic certainty no mountain stream could match. Rook did not pause, despite the heat and solitude, to sit beneath the award-winning lampposts on the mall, or to play elaborate hopscotch on the coloured marble flagstones.

He chose a route which freed him from the shadows. He fixed his eye ahead, upon the skyline, where the unaspiring towers of the ancient town competed for light and oxygen with the mantis cranes of building sites and the skeletal scaffolding of half-completed office blocks, draped for modesty in flapping plastic skirts. Rook said he loved to see the cranes perched overhead. He loved it best, at Summerfest, when all the cranes were hung with streamers and with lights and there were fireworks. Then, for once, the streets were duller, darker than the night sky. He liked his city noisy, teeming, dressed in black. He saw himself as lean and black, a cliché creature of the night. Indeed, that's partly why our Rook was known as Rook: the black clothes that he wore when he was young and on the streets. The rook-like nasal cawing of his laugh, too, his love of crowds, his foraging, his criminality. But more than that: the puff-chested, light-limbed posture of a bird.

They said he'd made his money out of Victor – that Victor, childless, heirless, treated Rook like a son and settled money on him in lieu of love. A cheque was Victor's version of a kiss. 'Money is the best embrace,' he said. But there the gossip amongst the secretaries and clerks was way off mark. Victor – for all his years and for all his understanding of the blandishments of money, of how people could be purchased and caressed by cash – paid Rook a salary, no more. And Rook was wise enough to keep his office fingers clean. He knew how frayed and slender was the leash which tied him to the old man's purse, and, indeed, how loosely that leash was now held, how easily his boss could let the leash go free. For two men who spent so much time together, they shared few sentiments or loyalties. Rook's cheerfulness should not be taken as fondness for his boss or work, but more as his device for filling in the silences which were the heavy furniture of their daily intercourse. Victor did not appreciate Rook's special knack of levity, his disregard of silence, his subversion of proprieties, his aggravating idleness. Victor's simple creed was this: until a man agrees to dedicate himself to work, then he will not be rich, or valuable, or admirable, or – best of all – at peace.

Yet Rook was rich, there is no doubt. A poorer man would not pass up the offer of a limousine. It takes a man who's certain of his wealth to choose to walk when he could ride. It also takes a man who's used to streets, whose heels have eyes, to know when he is being followed and by whom. As those dismissive, automatic doors rotated Rook into the unconditioned air, a fellow, hardly in his twenties, with a cream and crumpled summer suit, detached himself from the hard shadows amongst the quirks of a colonnade and followed him onto the mall, keeping, catlike, to the sunless walls. He sauntered like a truant, faking interest in the fountains, the street lights, avoiding joins and fissures in the coloured marble flagstones. Here is, his manner meant to say, an innocent abroad. It said, instead, here is a ne'er-do-well at large. Stay clear. Watch out. Protect your pockets when you walk.

Rook's ne'er-do-well was fresh in town. His nails were cracked like slate. His hands and neck were scorched. His eyes were streaming from the windborne grit and dust which pecked and spiralled at his face. He hadn't learnt the city trick of squinting as he walked. He was jubilant at being there and far from home, and lost, and poor, and free. He had in his pocket an old flick-knife that's spring was slow and temperamental. No cash. Sometime, on Victor's birthday, he'd come face to face with Rook. Who'd come off worse? He was an optimist, though in the end, of course – unless there was murder on his mind – a boy like him was bound to come off worse. At best, there would be poverty ahead, and drink, and crime, and selling sex and favours in the street. At least while he was young. And then just poverty and drink.

If we were looking for two poles-apart to represent good fortune and bad luck we could not better these two men, the fixer and his shadow, as they ducked into the walkers' tunnel and passed below Link Highway Red which separated the old town from the landscaped decks and platforms of the new. It was a tunnel built for beatings or for rape or for the urgent emptying of bladders or as a refuge from the rain and night for people without roofs. Pillars provided dark recesses for loiterers. Its low lighting winked and buzzed, failed at intervals or flared like photographic bulbs. The paper litter scooped and fluttered like a pigeon, trapped and fretful. The smell was urine mixed with street.

Rook thought his shadow might close the gap between them underground and there would be a tussle for his wallet, or he'd be cornered for 'a loan'. He walked a little faster then, and breathlessly. He wrapped his fingers round his keys, so that any punches thrown by him would be hard and heavy. He was glad to see the daylight spilling down the steps at the far end of the tunnel and to hear the pavement clack of women's heels, the vendor bells, the shop-front tannoys touting bargains for the town, the doors and horns and brakes of cars.

2

QUITE SOON HE WAS a different Rook, not yet the firebrand that he'd been when young, not quite the wagging spaniel of the office block, but someone more relaxed than both. His pace had slowed. He strolled. His tie was loose. His shoulders dropped. His bird-like chest no longer heaved for air. There was no tension here, in public space, except the amiable and congested tension of the streets which kept the traffic and pedestrians apart, which made atonal harmonies with honking motor-horns for brass, and news-stand yodellers as vocalists, and percussion from the beat of leather shoes on stone. Now Rook's main quests upon this street of salons, boutiques, and restaurants, were oddballs, cronies, pretty girls, anyone to stare at, or anything to buy. He was on the look-out, yes, but not for thieves and trouble any more, not for the fellow in the cream and crumpled suit. Rook no longer gripped his keys. Somewhere between the new town and the old his ne'er-do-well had disappeared, swallowed raw by the pavement multitude.

Untutored in the waltz, the simple quick–quick–slow of passing through a crowd, Rook's country shadow had been blocked by waiting cars and errand bikes, thwarted by citizens on opposing routes, stopped in his path by shopping bags, and kids, and snack-or-bargain carts. He'd been delayed by brochure touts and leafleteers, tackled at the knees and chest by rubbish cans, hydrants, signs, post boxes, newspaper stands. He'd been bumped and buffeted by the selective tidal chaos of the street which unfooted and swept away those newcomers who did not understand its current or its flow. This was a city at full pelt.

As Rook maintained his pace unerringly and blunderless, the young man in his suit – whose name you'll know before the day is out – was left, a stray, unable even to spot his quarry's browsing head amongst the unremitting throng of citizens. He stopped and window-shopped himself, waylaid by seagull flights of lingerie, by jewels thrown out across a bed of sand as carelessly as stones, by chocolate truffles displayed like jewels on satin trays, by terraces of boots and shoes, by all the sorcery of *Look, Don't touch*. He pressed his back against the window glass expecting eyes to look him up and down, and disapprove. But there were none. The only eyes that stared at him were in the plaster mannequins. They looked out, day and night, as if they dreamed the street, and all the passers-by were figments in the glass.

Who can resist the privacy of crowds? A crowd is people, freely voting for themselves. Rook's shadow joined the crowd and went with it along Saints Row, around the Tower Square, and back again, until it beached him amongst the pavement tables of a bar. He sat. He'd sit until a waiter came, and then he'd hurry off again. He was not bored. The street was cabaret, with mime, and all the spoken badinage delivered stagily, in a whisper or a shout. He'd stay there for a while, he thought, and then go back to where he'd spotted Rook, where there were never crowds, in the ill-lit tunnel under Link Highway Red. That was the perfect spot for the ambush that he planned.

Rook, meanwhile, had gone beyond the bustle of the

boutique street. He'd skirted round the boundaries of the Mathematical Park where flower beds were cut for every shape – an octogon of primulas, a perfect circle for begonias, roses in triangles and squares – and Pythagorean climbing frames and wooden seats designed impossibly like Möbius strips. Now Rook was walking through the neighbourhood where he was born and raised, the Woodgate district of our city.

Where were the wooden gates that gave the place its name, those medieval, oaken sentries to what had been an ancient town? Burned down, seventy-four years before, when Victor was a child of six. The incendiarists – so it was said – were city councillors who wanted to 'better' what had become a low-rent district of beggars, thieves and prostitutes. Their improving additions were terraces of five-storey blocks – one floor retail, one floor wholesale, two floors apartments, attic, cellar, stables, yard, high rent. In their haste, they'd followed, not replaced, the charred and muddled labyrinth of medieval streets. The Woodgate district was then, and still was on Victor's eightieth, best suited to the horse. Those narrow stable yards and *cul-de-sacs*, those twisting alleyways that locals called The Squints, were scarcely wider than a mare is long. No motor vehicle could turn about inside The Squints. They were too tight and modest for the cussed constipation of the car.

The Woodgate neighbourhood had its vehicles of course. A town must breathe, and there were straighter, wider ways which offered access to The Squints and provided Rook a fast, straightforward route to cakes and greenery. Now he was walking down the road, four mares in width, where he was raised. There were parking bays where he'd once played asthmatic ball-and-tag. The building where his parents had leased a flat was let to businesses – a barber on the pavement floor, an accountancy above, and then three floors of warehousing. The room which Rook had shared with a brother for ten years was wall to wall with mats and *phaga* rugs, and druggets from Kashmir. An asthmatic's fibrous nightmare.

Neighbourhood was not the word. There were no longer neighbours there. At night the barbers and accountants, and the warehousemen, went home by car and bus and train to suburbs out of town. At night The Squints were dark and dead. But still the buildings were the ones Rook had known when he was small. There were no demolitions yet. And still there was a faint smell in the air, beneath the odour of the cars and the scent of secretaries, of ancient fire. And rotting vegetation, too, as if the area had been built against-the-odds on the sweet and sour of a swamp. For these were the borders of the Soap Market. The smell, an airborne punch of cabbage stalks, figs, olives, beet . . . had belched and yawned along these streets and down these Squints for six hundred years. The housing bricks and paving stones, they said, could boil down into soup; the place was steeped in root, and leaf, and fruit. So, of course, was Rook. Rook soup would taste as much of fruit as meat. Just like the merchant's monkey in the song,

'His testicles were mango stones,
(Quite normal in the Apes);
His cock was courgette on-the-bone.
He   Shat   Fresh   Grapes.'

For all his coolness and his suits, Rook was a market boy, a Soapie through and through. His mother and his father made it so. His parents had rented a market stall and too frequent were the days when they'd encourage Rook to miss out school and help them stack and sell their wares. He did not know, perhaps, the shape of continents or algebra when he was ten, but he could tell – by smell, by patina, by shape (no easy task) – a Trakana cherry from a Wijnkers, and know, before he broke the skin, which aubergines were soured, which peas had greyed inside their pods.

So it was in a sentimental mood that Rook, on Victor's celebration day, walked the familiar hundred metres between his old home and the market rim beyond which, as yet, the colonising barbers, the accountants, and warehousemen, had made no mark. The canyoned pattern of the city ended here in a huge 0-shaped, cobbled court, which could not be circled – Rook could guarantee – by a shallow-winded boy on a bike in less than fifteen minutes. Except for those few low-rise restaurants and bars in the Soap Garden which formed the centre of the 0, all buildings in the court were wood and canvas market stalls. The place was open to the sky, and could have been a medieval harvest fair. Except that Big Vic – as Victor's office block was known – and the other high-rise monoliths of the new town cut off the market from the skyline hills, and fast and heavy traffic on the Link Highways beat drum-rolls across the awnings and the roofs.

Inside the oval, there were no parking bays, traffic lights or ordered flows. The marketeers parked where they chose, or where the Man in Cellophane (who took it madly on himself to block and beckon traffic) directed them. Their trucks and vans choked paths and access streets. Their barrows and their porter sleds were left where they were used. The wooden produce trays, the emptied sacks, the pallets, bins and panniers which had held vegetables and fruit were piled and stacked unevenly, discarded like the crusts and rinds and eggshells of an outdoor meal. It was safe haven for a sprinting criminal pursued by police in cars.

The odours here were less opaque than those which spilled out, windborne, into the streets beyond. To walk amongst the stalls, eyes closed, would be to test one's nose for all the subtleties of countryside and food. The practised nose – like Rook's – could tell when barrows of potatoes were pushed by or where the garlic nests were hung or whether medlar fruit had bletted long enough and now were fit to eat, or when (the softest, then the foulest scents of all) guavas were for sale, or durians. But why would anybody want to close their eyes? No gallery of modern art could match the colours there, the tones, the shapes, the harmonies and conflicts on the stalls.

The yellow stars were babacos; the Turkish turban was a squash; the pile of honeydews were rugby footballs begging for a kick; redcurrants, clinging fatly to their spindly strigs, burst and bled; zucchini from Sardinia retained their orange, tissue flowers and peeped out of their boxes like madly coiffeured snakes. And dead snakes, sometimes, as green and cold as water melons, could be found coiled thinly round mangoes or cantaloupes. And thrips and ticks and lice and grubs and flies, the living things that make a living out of market fruit and market crowds. The roaches, bugs and weevils that share our meals and beds.

The first traders, on the outskirts of the market, were the bananamen, the specialists in *musaceae*. They did not wish to penetrate too far into the maelstrom of the stalls. The snags of fruit weighed far too much to move around, ten, twenty overlapping hands perhaps, each with a dozen fingers to the hand, and each fibrous stem damp and heavy from refriger-

ation on the seas, from journeying, from ripening, from growing sweet. Bananas were mostly sold in bulk from off the back
of vans. They sold them by the hand, and not by number or by
weight. The bananamen stood by, foul-mouthed, lascivious,
and raucous with their yellow-penis jokes. Their fleshy plan-
tains were rewarded with the biggest laughs, the deepest
blushes. These traders were the butchers of the market place.
They each were ready with a knife, like senators at Caesar's
death, to cut the hand selected by the customer expertly from
the stem. Every knife, and every trader's tongue, was as sharp
as limes.

Beside them was the jackfruit van – one jackfruit always
sliced in half and cubes cut out so that anyone could test the
flesh for creaminess and age. And then the melons and the
yams, the gourds, the Herculean beets, the pumpkins, the
pyramids of cabbages and swedes. Each had its pitch, exactly
and invisibly marked out. God help the reckless cabbage that
strayed or rolled into the sovereign kingdom of the yam. God
help the greengrocer who scrumped his neighbour's space.

So old and honoured were the patterns of the trading
pitches that Rook, or so he claimed, could have walked as
sure-footed as a village cat between the produce and the stalls
to the Soap Garden at the market's heart without a glance to
either side or to his feet. But Rook was not the man to pass
unnoticed or unnoticing through such a place. His eyes were
Victor's. This was his boss's empire, the place that made him
rich. This market was the keystone to the solid arch of Victor's
wealth. Wealth can disappear unless it's watched and hus-
banded. So Rook was more alert than he had been all day. He
watched to see which soapies called out his name and waved,
which ones had customers and which had none, what new

faces were portering or helping out with sales, who scowled, who hid, who turned away as if they'd never seen his face before, who bid him wish the boss a pleasant birthday lunch, what fruits there were, what vegetables were new, who had no right to be there and yet was.

At times, Rook simply stood and stared in wonder at the wit and artistry for sale and on display – the plump, suggestive irony of roots, the painted, powdered vanity of peaches, the waxen probity of lettuce leaves, the faith implicit in the youth and readiness of onion sets, the senility of medlars (eaten only when decayed), the seductive, bitter alchemy of quinces which young men bought to soften women's hearts. Who could pass unfeeling through such splendour? Who could resist an orange from the pile? Not Rook. He pushed up against the paper trimmings of a stall. Before him were the peaks of citruses, the best, most flawless fruit built into perfect ziggurats with prices marked on flags. There were common blonds and bloods and navels – oranges from twenty nations of the world; Cuban green griollas, the yellowish valencias from Spain, the red sanguinas grown on the southern slopes of Atlas. Not just oranges in peaks, but foothills too of bergamots, lemons, limes, kumquats, and the infinite variety of mandarins. And all this summer landscape edged in boulders made from grapefruit, shaddocks and half-caste pomelos. The fruiterer had made a passing masterpiece of oranges. He'd added, too, a fringe and diadem of lights, the colour and the shape of citruses. No matter how they shone they were eclipsed. No light was bright enough to glow more cheerfully than fruit. No packaging could better them or sing their praises louder than themselves.

Rook made his choice and took an orange from the cheapest pile. Its peel, it's true, was blemished, dirty almost. There was a brownish lunar landscape on its outer crust. The price was low. But for Rook, who knew his oranges, such blemishes were marks of juice and sweetness. An orange so discoloured is an orange which has ripened in the heat, in countries or in seasons where the nights are warm and bruising. An orange so discoloured would have slaked its daytime thirst upon the perspiration of the moon. Rook held his purchase up, and searched for a few coins. The fruiterer just clicked his tongue and shook his head to signify there was no need for Rook to pay, that he should take this orange as a gift.

Rook scalped the orange at its pig with his teeth. He spiralled off the peel and ate, stepping back and stooping to save his shirt-front from the juice. The flesh left fluorescent lacquer on his lips and chin; the pith made anchovies of flannelette beneath his nails. He let the peel fall to the ground as he walked. The detritus of fruit, the husks and pods and skins, the blowsy outer leaves of salad, the blown parsley sprigs, were not considered litter there, but God-given carpeting for cobblestones.

Rook loved it all, this market world, this teeming concourse of cobbles. What good, he wondered, would it be to own this land, as Victor did, and yet not have the legs or lungs to browse amongst the smells and tints and sounds? Yet, don't be fooled. Our Rook was not at ease. The market boy was now a predator. What made Victor a millionaire – the rents on market stalls, the 'seeds-to-stomach' stranglehold on wholesale and supplies, the canning and bottling plants – had made Rook wealthy, too. His wealth was surreptitious, though. No penthouses for Rook. No limousines. No coddled fish for lunch. No Rolexes or La Martines. His money was the kind

you couldn't spend too openly and couldn't bank. It was the
kind that came in cash four times a year, slipped to him in a
paper bag with a mango or some grapes or handed over at a
bar, a cylinder of notes – all used – and held by rubber bands.

Compared to the trading rents which Victor charged,
Rook's 'service fees' were small, a modest tithe for peace of
mind from every market trader there. A guarantee against
eviction. A small amount to pay for Victor's ear. 'Pitch money',
it was called. A sweetener for Rook: vinegar for those who
paid. You could see it on the faces of the men who came to
Rook just then – his chin still damp with orange juice, his eyes
alight, alert – to make their summer payments for their
pitches.

One man peeled off his payment like a sinner giving alms.
Another passed his ransom concealed inside his palm. A
handshake did the trick. A third – the soapie known as Con –
shook openly and tauntingly a sealed envelope in Rook's face,
with Rook's name written large and red on it for all to see.
Others saw the payment as a trade. They paid, then men-
tioned problems that could be fixed, if only Rook would talk
with Victor. The price of olives was too high. The pears were
bruised by the new mechanical pickers that Victor used. The
contractors who hosed the market down at night were playing
games with the water jet and damaging the decoration on the
stalls. 'Please let old Victor know our troubles. He can't fix
what he doesn't know. And – please – wish Victor Happy
Birthday from us all.' What was unspoken but accompanied all
the cash that Rook received was this: Long may you rot in
Hell.

What should we make of Rook, then, as he, shame-faced,
proprietorial, pushed through the shoppers and the porters in

the medieval alleyways of wood and canvas, of trestles, awnings, stalls, and booths, of global colours, smells and tastes, and reached the bars and lawns of the Soap Garden? That he was bad? Or shrewd? Or simply, like the rest of us, a weakling when it comes to cash?

3

WHEN ROOK ARRIVED AT the sunlit respite of the Soap Garden, there were no seats. The bars were full. The lawns were packed with porters and with the low-paid women who weighed, wrapped and sold the city's purchases. Their bosses occupied the shaded chairs. Keeping a fruit or vegetable stall is not an unremitting task. There is free time.

At that hour of the morning, the soapies came for coffee-and-a-shot and to fix and chalk their prices for the day. Some turned away or sank into their seats when they saw Rook. Some watched him blankly. One or two – the older, more successful ones, the ones invited to Victor's birthday lunch – stood up and waved at him to indicate that he should join them at their table, that they'd be honoured if he'd drink a shot with them. But Rook had Victor's chair to decorate and Anna's cakes to buy. He'd join them later, when his tasks were done. He went first to the cake-and-coffee stand and chose a dozen cakes from their display – four fruit, four cream, four chocolate. Rook leaned against the stand and studied all the sales girls on the lawns and then the foliage of the garden while his cakes were gift-wrapped in a cardboard pyramid and tied with red and silver tape.

Of all the trees and bushes in the garden, the burgher laurels seemed the best for Victor's birthday chair. Their leaves looked supple, shiny, washable. Besides, their branches were within easy reach and, unlike the roses and the snag trees which lined the lawns, they posed no problem for the naked hand. Rook chose a laurel which grew against the railings of the medieval washing place and threw its shadow across the worn stone sinks, the emaciated gargoyles on the fountains, the cluster of grotesques which nuzzled at the basin rim. Rook, made devil-may-care by his passage through the market, was in no mood to be unnerved by rules or inhibitions. He simply grasped a slender laurel branch, and tugged as if he expected it to snap like celery. His hands slipped, ran free, and stripped the leaves, together with the fledgling buds which roosted at each node. What was that smell?

He took more care with the second spray. He bent it downwards at its base, and tried to twist and break it off. It snapped but was too green and sinewy to separate cleanly. He tore it free. He held it by its broken stem, satisfied that it would do for Victor's chair. Quite soon he had a thick papoose of laurel sprays resting on his arm.

Rook was bemused, not by the cussedness of laurels, but by the odour of the exposed wood, a cooking, kitchen smell both unnerving and familiar. He smelt his fingers and then put his nose to the fractured branch. 'What's that?' he asked himself, and sneezed. He walked across the grass to the group of traders on the patio of a bar. They were all men that he knew by name, and all about Rook's age, not old or rich enough to dine on Victor's fish. They'd all been market boys together, kicking turnip-balls amongst the lettuce leaves, made shrewd and tough beyond their years by labouring for dad. They'd all been comrades in the market strike a dozen years before. The noisy pair were brothers; bananas were their trade. The balding one was Spuds, a shapeless idle man with wife and kids to match. Another was the man called Con whose envelope of hard-earned cash was in Rook's jacket pocket and who now held court with his account of how, at dawn that day, he'd very nearly had his pockets picked. He stopped mid-sentence when he spotted Rook. He'd already seen the fellow once too often for the day, a thousand times too often for a life. This was the man, this Rook, who'd betrayed the soapies, who'd led the produce strike and then abandoned it for pay and privilege at Victor's feet, as if fine sentiments were not as fine as cash. 'That man'd barter every tooth inside his head,' he thought, but said, 'Watch out. Here comes the apple grub.' Con was not the understanding sort. He'd gladly throttle Rook. He'd gladly shake out every golden tooth. He'd pay to have it done.

The others were more forgiving. They might still have been Rook's intimates if it weren't that they were always in his debt. 'Pitch' payments had cost Rook a thousand friends. They smiled at his approach, but not with generosity or welcome. It was simply that their childhood friend looked rather foolish to their male, no-nonsense eyes: one suited arm weighed down by foliage; the fingers of the other hand entwined in the fussy, dainty packaging of cakes.

Rook leant against their table and he sneezed again: a clearance of the nostrils and a shout of matching force and volume.

'What *is* that smell?' he asked, wiping his eyes with his sleeve and placing the laurel amongst their cups and glasses. They passed the broken branch around the table and put their noses to the wood. They scratched their heads. Their noses knew that smell so well, but their tongues could not locate the name.

'Like coconut,' said one.

Another thought it smelt like cake. They called their favourite waitress to their aid. She hardly had to smell. 'It's marchpane,' she said, using the country word for marzipan. She handed back the laurel branch to Rook. Once more he held it to his nose. The girl was right. He smelt the eggs, the sugar and the almond paste as perfectly as when he was a child and helping mother mix and shape the birthday treats, the balls, the stars, the leaves of marzipan.

'That's it! It's marzipan,' he said, translating. 'I wonder if it tastes.' He put a broken laurel stem into his mouth.

The waitress laughed and said, 'That's poison, that is. Don't you know? You don't suck that.' She pointed at the beads of sap which were swelling like water blisters where the wood had snapped.

'How should I know? I'm not a countryman,' said Rook, and sneezed again. It was his boast that he would wither out of town. He wouldn't last five minutes away from traffic fumes or crowds.

The waitress was the sort to stand and talk, mulishly deaf and blind to summonses from older, less flirtatious men at other tables.

'Those spoonwood leaves', she said, using once again the country term, 'are poisonous. You'll run both ends.' Encouraged by their laughter, she embarked upon a tale of how the women in her village used once to boil the poison out of laurel leaves. They'd soak the poison into bread, she said, to bait the rats and mice: 'A woman my grandma knew made chicken soup with laurel seeds and laurel sap. They'd use it as fox bait. Or for killing crows. She fed it to her bloke by mistake. He had his bum and stomach pointing at the toilet pan for near enough a week, and then he died. The soup had poisoned him. Nice way to go.'

'I've eaten soup like that here,' said Con, and winked. This time their laughter was prolonged. They knew this waitress had a second job. She was the kitchen girl as well.

'Bang goes your chance of ever breakfasting with me,' she said to Con, and then pressed on with what she had to say about the laurel tree: 'My aunt, she had a neighbour who wanted to inherit a little apple orchard when his grandma died. Except she wouldn't die. The older she got the fitter she became. So this man and his wife, they asked the granny round for supper. She got the spoonwood soup. She was shaking like a cow with qualsy before she'd eaten half a bowl. But she was tough. Her heart and stomach were made of wood. They had to pinch her nose and force some second helpings down her throat. Then that was that. She'd gone. He got her apple trees.'

The waitress paused so that the point of what she said was not missed or weakened by the laughter that she caused or by the noise of Rook's disruptive sneezes. Then she said, 'And no one ever knew the cause of death. Though they took the body to a hospital and experts cut the old girl up to see what they could see. The reason is that spoonwood doesn't leave any traces. Except a rash inside the mouth.' She turned to Rook. 'You'd better watch yourself,' she said.

Rook did not hear. He sneezed again. He looked as pale as chalk. It seemed his tongue and mouth were drier, and more blunted, than they ought to be, though whether this was caused by laurel sap or by the juice of orange he could not tell. He helped himself to water from a jug on the traders' table and rinsed his hands. He took the shot they offered him, gargled with the spirit and spat it out into a drain. He rubbed the stinging corners of his lips. He wiped his tongue on the cuff of his jacket. His mouth was now his most self-conscious part. Rook cursed his luck. He knew the signs of asthma on the march. His sense of smell had failed. His nails – dug in his palms – left deep red weals which would not clear. 'You'll live,' the waitress said. 'It takes more than a lick of spoonwood to harm a man your size.'

Rook placed his pyramid of cakes beside him on the ground. This time the sneeze gathered in his upper nose and fizzed but did not detonate. He took deep nostril breaths to try and burst the bubble forming in his head. He started breathing through his mouth. He sucked in air. He beat his chest as if he'd eaten too much cheese and stomach wind was warring with his heart. The more he tried to let the sneeze go free, the more it burrowed into him, and spread. His sputum was like lard. These were the times he missed his parents most. They coped with him when he was small. They'd ignite an asthma firework for him at the table and let him inhale smoke, his head inside the cowling of a blanket or a towel. They'd massage him. They'd soothe his chest with balsam brewed from cloves and juniper and peppermint. They had been dead for fifteen years.

At first, the market men were unconcerned, amused that Rook was making such a fuss. They did not understand what asthma was or how the trigger of the laurel sap and smell had so alarmed Rook's lungs. His breathing now was panicky and spasmed. The tree of passages, the branches, twigs and sprays, which served the air sacs in his lungs, were swollen. They were almost blocked. He had to cough. His chest had shrunk. He did not understand what anyone was asking him.

He could have died. The waitress beat him on the back. She struck him with the rounded heel of her right hand between his shoulder-blades. She thought he'd got a scrap of twig or leaf lodged in his throat and that he should bring it up or choke. Her blow knocked Rook onto his knees. It marked his back. He coughed up pinkish phlegm. 'That's right,' she said. His lips, his fingernails, his tongue, his feet were turning violet. His face was mauve. She struck him once again. He had the sense, and luck, to roll this time onto his back so that, unless she took it on herself to punch him in the stomach or the ribs, or kick him on the ground, he was more safe. In fact, he found it easier to breathe flat out upon his back beneath the traders' table. The air went in and out more freely. The tidal ebb and flow increased. He pinkened, gasped a little less, then sneezed. His mind was clear. He understood. He'd been exposed. The grass. Some pollen. The orange juice. The laurel leaves. Some rural irritant had stressed his city lungs.

He felt his pockets in the hope that he had brought his nebulising spray. It was not there. He'd left it in the top drawer of his desk. He was too careless with himself. He should have known. The garden was no place for him. He couldn't wait to reach Big Vic and his nebuliser's balsamed mist. He would have hailed a taxi for the journey back, but there were none. No car or taxi, no ambulance, could ever reach the garden during trading hours. The market was impenetrable except by foot or porter's barrow. Rook took a napkin and wiped the beads of sap from the laurel stems and then he took the sheets of a discarded newspaper and wrapped them round the bunch. He held them downwards so that he did not share their oxygen.

29

'It's greenery for Victor's birthday chair,' he said. 'To decorate it.'

The traders watched him blankly, without warmth. Rook looked at the waitress, expecting that she'd understand. She was a country girl, after all. But no. Her eyes were just as blank. She'd never heard of dressing birthday chairs. Now Rook's discomfiture, his sense of foolishness, was changing from embarrassment to irritation and regret: irritation that the men were so open in, first, their mirth and then their coolness at his expense, regret that he was not where he belonged, sitting side-by-side with them, and laughing at the ink-stained stiffness of some other clerk on trifling errands for his boss, made paranoid and breathless by a dab of laurel sap. For what could be more foolish or banal than these tasks of greenery and cakes, which earlier had seemed to Rook to promise so much freedom and amusement? And what could be more demeaning than the panicked, public face of adult asthma?

Rook took his foliage and his cakes through the maze of market stalls. The journey back, out of the innards of the city, seemed less ordained than the route he had followed in, towards the Soap Garden. He wove a clumsy passage through the shopping crowds, hampered and encumbered with his gleanings and his purchases. He felt displeased, and fearful too. Already he was at the market edge. The banana and the jackfruit men were ready with their knives. The Man in Cellophane waved him on impatiently. Beyond, there was the district of his birth. Beyond, there were the boutiques of Saints Row, Link Highway Red, the ne'er-do-well, Big Vic. Rook walked, half dreaming, from the old town to the new.

4

ROOK'S NE'ER-DO-WELL WAS CALLED Joseph. His broken nails and weather-beaten neck and hands were all he had to show for three years of work on one of Victor's farms. He'd purchased the cream and crumpled suit from a catalogue. Its light, summer style was marketed as *On the Town*. The fashion model in the catalogue had been sitting on a bar stool with his sun glasses hooked inside the breast pocket of the jacket. One hand – the one with a single, gleaming ring – was resting on his knee, palm up. The other held the barmaid by the wrist. The gold watch on his arm showed the time as five to midnight, or five to midday. There was a bottle of muscatino on the bar and strangely, promisingly, three glasses, as if another woman had just left, or was expected soon. Or, perhaps, the glass was waiting there for Joseph.

When the parcel with the suit arrived, Joseph had cut the picture from the catalogue and put it in the breast pocket as if to equip his clothing with a pedigree and, more than that, an aspiration. The model's empty, upturned palm, the drama of the barmaid's wrist caught by the strong hand of the man, exactly matched Joseph's notion of the casual spontaneity of city life where day and night were all the same, where drink and wealth and women were within easy reach. What else was there to fill his mind each day? Trenching orchards, driving

31

tractors, mucking fields, cutting cabbages, boxing plums was not the work to satisfy a youth like Joseph. The muscles that had hardened in the fields had made him vain. And vanity is stifled in the countryside – the rain, the overalls, the solitary work for little pay, make sure of that.

The only chance he had to flex and strut was at the station every cropping day when he went to load the produce onto trains. Mostly they were goods and freight trains, passing slowly through soon after dawn or late at night, and Joseph's vanity hardly noticed in the dark. But once a week, at 7.10 on Thursday evenings, the Salad Bowl Express, as it was called, stopped at the station with passengers weekending in the city, on shopping sprees or love affairs or binges, or just touring the sights. On Thursday evenings rich women and their daughters pressed their foreheads and their noses to the sleeper-carriage glass to watch the men load on the trays of strawberries or cress or endives, fresh for the busy weekends of hotels and restaurants. Some passengers lowered the Pull-man windows to buy fruit in cornets of twisted leaves from country girls whose own weekend did not begin until the moon came up on Saturday.

This was the chance for Joseph, obscured and dramatised by the gelid mists of dusk which pirouetted on the platforms with the sweating vapours of the train, to take his work-shirt off and parade for them along the station like a boxer, bare and muscular and young. He'd rest the produce boxes on his head and steady them with his arms raised. He felt his body looked its best that way, his muscles stretched, his stomach as flat and hairless as a slate. Besides, in such a pose, his face was hidden by his arms, and Joseph knew his face was not well made. The noses and the foreheads at the glass were pow-

dered, painted, sweet-smelling. Their shapes were good, sym-
metrical, each ear adorned with rings, the hair poised for a
weekend in the city. Joseph's nose and forehead were not so
ornamental, not ugly but uncouth through work and poverty
and innocence. The corners of his mouth were cracked from
sun and sweat. His nose was pitted from the scabs he'd
picked. One central tooth was gone. One cheek was blemished
by a birth-stain, cherry-coloured, cherry-shaped. His chin was
far too heavy and his face too drawn to benefit from the thin
moustache that he was growing. His was a rural face. But his
body, give or take a scar or two, was smart enough for town.
He dreamed of the day when he would press his own nose to
the steamy glass and glide away on the Salad Bowl Express.
He worked, saved his wages, sent for his *On the Town* suit,
and planned his escapade.

He was not bright. He could not name exactly what it was
he sought in town. But it was *privacy*. In town he'd sit inside a
bar at noon, three-quarters full of drink, a woman on his arm,
his lighter lifted to her cigarette, and no one there would know
his name, or where he lived and worked, or who his family
were, or how he coped when he was just a metre high at
school, or that he had a magpie reputation there for theft. In
town he'd flourish in the privacy of crowds, in the monkish
cells of tenements, in streets. His neighbours would be strangers. They'd hardly nod. He'd be a mystery to them. They'd
only know the things he chose to tell. And – safely, without
fear of what the village folk would say – he could choose to tell
his city neighbours lies. In any case, the truth of Joseph did
not match the suit. He wore it for the first time on the
Thursday evening – the day before Victor's birthday lunch –
over his khaki working shirt, his black field-boots, and helped

33

to load the produce boxes on the Salad Bowl Express. The women pressed their perfect noses to the glass. This time he did not strip to show his working muscles. His suit was on parade. When the klaxon blew to mark the train's departure, Joseph lifted his final load – a plastic travel-tank marked URGENT: LIVE FISH – and stowed it in the corner of the goods car which carried Victor's name. And there Joseph stayed, as quietly as a slug in fruit, until the Salad Bowl Express set off for town. Smudge-suited, ticketless, naive, Rook's ne'er-do-well migrated from the world of plants and seasons to the urban universe of make-and-take-and-sell.

He found a cigarette to smoke, and there was fruit for supper. His couchette was four sacks of spinach leaves. He could not shift the sliding door to urinate upon the line. Besides, he did not want some cousin's tittle-tattle friend to look up from his hoe or spade to watch the train go by and catch a sight of Joseph hosing the dusk. He wanted just to disappear and be forgotten, not be remembered – immortalised – as the locomotive pisser in a village joke. But men have shallow, porous bladders which nag and leak. A shaking train is torture when they want to piss. Why suffer, Joseph thought. It crossed his mind to urinate onto the apples or the greens. But he had spent too many years attending to them in the fields to treat the crops like that. More fun, more logical, to add a little water to the fish. He unscrewed the cap which sealed the tank. He knelt, unzipped the trousers of his suit, and put his mushroom in the hole. The ten perch, used to hand-feeding with protein biscuits in Victor's stock pool, gawped and butted at his penis end, but when his bladder got to work they fled into the cooler, blander depths.

Joseph found blander depths as well. He dozed until the

countryside was gone and woke to find the last dregs of the night made watery by suburban lights. He shivered at the window of the goods car and looked for signs of poverty and waste, of power and indifference, of wealth and sex and violent energy, for signs of destiny. His eyes were sharp for tall and optimistic buildings, and tall and optimistic girls, for flashing neon lights and fancy cars. The suburbs, though, were fast asleep and, much like any habitation at that hour, showed little appetite for day. A few small cars were on the move, obeying the traffic lights and not the logic of the almost empty streets. A cyclist held the centre of a road. Once in a while, in houses and apartments, a curtain pattern was illumined from within by someone half asleep, and out of bed, and taking last night's final piss or their first coffee of the day. The lights in rows of private shops fell squarely onto pavements; their goods were on display for cats and bats.

Joseph was struck by all the stillness of the city night. A country night is just as busy as the day, but here there were no trees to bend before the wind. The signposts did not move. The clouds – if they were racing through the sky – were doing so invisibly, blacked out by streetlamps, put out of sight by electric light. Rain fell like country rain, but underlit, theatrically. It could not soak into the earth. It slid down tiles. It skirted round the angles of each brick. It raced through gutters, dropped down pipes, consigned itself to drains, turned roadside conduits into streams with discarded snack packets as the sails of its racing dhows. It ducked through iron sumps. It undernavigated roads in airless culverts and joined the curling traffic of water below the town, where sewers emptied into sluices and sluices discharged their flood into much slower and more muscular arteries of water. And thence into the mains. And thence into the reservoir, the treatment plant, the aqueduct, the pipe, the tap, the coffee pot, and down the sink as giddy waste.

It took a simple mind like Joseph's to wonder how it was that city rain was so enslaved. He was not bright enough to ask himself, as low-rise housing blocks and sleepy boulevards gave way to warehouses, shunting yards, high-rise offices, and morning's curdy light, how he could hope to soak into the city's ground, how he could stay afloat and unenslaved when so many young men, just like him, had been unfooted, swept away, down gutters, into drains, by the careless rapids and the all-embracing floods of city life. He did not have the time or temperament to care.

His train arrived at dawn. The van-doors were thrown back by porters. It was easy for Joseph – much used to being inconspicuous – to merge in with the workers there, three trays of lettuce balanced expertly on his head, and make his entry into town. And then? What then? He put the trays of lettuce with all the other produce in a market van. When it drove away through early breakfast traffic slower than a country cart, slower than a thaw, he followed it, through streets more futile and more aimless than even he had hoped for, to the Soap Market. Of course. Where else would such a hidebound country boy end up?

The time was six-fifteen. The bustle of the market as the traders fixed their pitches for the day was not the world of catalogues. But Joseph's mission was quite clear. City folk were easy pickings. Rich and careless. Weak. Those pampered noses on the carriage glass could sneeze banknotes. Those clerks and secretaries in their cars had gaping wallets, purses, cash to spare. He'd never had the chance to steal off strangers before. It would be easy, he could tell. He'd not be caught. He wouldn't have to turn his village pockets out for every city coin that got lost. He had no face. He had no name. He had no reputation. It was his lucky day.

He'd known such careless crowds at country fêtes and auctions, so all the bump and jostle of the Soap Market was nothing new to him. He was not lost, or overawed. The stalls and market paths had logic. That distant office building on his right gave him his bearings. He knew that empty barrows wheeled by porters led to the outskirt streets where produce vans were parked. The country boy is used to mapping routes, in hop plantations, forests, in the pleats of fields, in mazes made from furrows, fences, dikes. So Joseph stored and sifted signs – the stall that sold shallots, the music of a radio, the trader with the piebald beard, the man in cellophane, the diadem of coloured lights, the breeze – to keep a tab on where he was, and where he'd need to run, or hide, if he should chance upon some luck.

He was surprised, it's true, by such a city landscape, fashioned out of repetition and conformity, with matching buildings and matching streets and people dressed the same. He was surprised there were no gradients, no sea, no streams, no fertile land. Some fool had built this city on the flat between the pebble and the clod where nothing grew except the appetite. Some fool, in fact, had built this city on the worst of sites. Where was the fish-stocked estuary, the river bridge, the sheltered harbour, the pass between two hills, the natural crossroads in the land where ancient settlements were meant to be? Where was the seam of coal to make the city rich? Where were the hummocks and escarpments to make the city safe? Where was the panoramic view to make the city spiritual, a holy place? What made this thirsty, ill-positioned city – too southerly to benefit from hops, too northerly for grapes – so rich and large? The answer crowded him at every step. It caught his shins. It bustled him from side to side. The market place! A city with no natural virtues is reduced to trade. Seas, rivers, hills, coal seams, make fishing, farming, metal-bashing, tourist cities. But cities like ours have little choice except to buy and sell and deal, except to do what Joseph planned to do, to make a living out of theft.

If he had been a wiser man, he would have waited for a while before he embarked on his chosen trade. It was too early for the careless shoppers. The only people in the market at that time were marketeers. This was their habitat. This web was theirs. They noted him – not as a thief, but as a scrumper, one of those who came to breakfast *gratis* on the fruit. He was never unobserved. And so his luck ran out. He'd seen his chance. The soapie Con had moved an envelope with the one red word 'Rook' written on it to the back pocket of his trousers so that he could bend and lift more easily. It wagged invitingly as its owner embraced a sack of carrots. Joseph was fast and skilled, but obvious. His fingers wrapped round 'Rook'. He got the envelope – but not before three voices had called out a warning, 'Look out, Con!' Con's hand shot back and caught Joseph by his trouser leg. He fell. In seconds he was pinioned to the ground. A crowd had formed. His suit was stained by soil and fruit and leaves. He took the first kick of the day.

'You'll pay for this,' Con said, already seeing opportunities for cashing in on this young fool's misfortune.

So there was Joseph, a few hours on, paying for his short-lived, bungled life of petty crime by undertaking the 'contract robbery' of a man called Rook. Was this the big-time opportunity he'd dreamed about? Was this – so soon – his golden chance? As instructed, he'd first dogged Rook along the mall, to get to know his face. And now he waited for his return in the tunnel under Link Highway Red. He squatted on his haunches, smoking, and studying the picture Con had given him – a snapshot of a market stall. The man amongst the vegetables and fruit was a younger Rook, smiling, scarf unknotted at his throat, his clothes all black. Here was the man to ambush, frighten, rob. Con's promise was, as he dispatched young Joseph to do his business on the mall, that Rook – as he returned from the Soap Market to Big Vic, and not before – would carry money, hidden, maybe, but cash and notes in large sums. There would be an envelope as well, the one he'd failed to steal. Brown, sealed with tape, and marked in red with Rook's name. Con showed the envelope again to Joseph. 'Remember it,' he said. 'The man you're looking for will have this somewhere on him as he heads back to work.' All Joseph had to do was wave his knife and take the envelope, unopened, back to Con's market stall. Anything else he found on Rook was his to keep. If he did this task efficiently, there'd be no police involved. The pocket-snatching rashness in the market place would be forgotten. Joseph's Identity Card, which Con had confiscated as security, would be returned. Perhaps, there'd be a proper job for him as well. What job? Con wouldn't say, except 'a market job, a job where muscles like the ones you've got won't do you any harm'.

Joseph, now out of cigarettes and more hungry in the walkers' tunnel than he had been upon the streets, once more fixed Rook's much younger face onto his memory, and then bent more eagerly to study a second picture in the oscillating light – the illustration from the clothing catalogue. Now he and the model in their matching suits were cousins, at the very least. The longer Joseph stared at all its appetising detail – the suit, the upturned hand, the third and unattended glass – the more certain he became that soon he would be drinking at the bar.

Quite soon Joseph was tired of sitting on his haunches in the gloom. He was hungry, damp, and desperate for nicotine. He was embarrassed, too, by the way the elderly woman who had passed him in the tunnel did so with such nervousness and haste that she had missed the pleasant smile he'd given her. He'd never met a woman of that age before who did not know his name and family, who did not stop to swap a word or two. He called after her. At first a cheerful greeting. Then abuse. She did not turn. She did not seem to hear. Perhaps she was the sort that hates the young.

He was impatient now to prove himself a citizen. He walked towards the daylight spilling down the steps from the street in the hope of spotting Rook amongst the faces in the crowd. Much easier to follow Rook and rob him from behind. But as he turned to mount the stairs he saw Rook descending, in his path, three steps above. His victim was not looking well. He held his chest. The pallor on his face suggested fever or anxiety. He was breathless, too, from walking fast and from carrying through crowds what looked like burgher laurel branches and a ribboned box, a pyramid, which, thought Joseph, promised riches of some kind. That was the moment Rook and Joseph met. Rook, recognising who it was, alarmed and startled, stepped aside to let his ne'er-do-well climb past. But Joseph did not move. He let Rook step a pace or two into the stench and echo of the tunnel, then placed his left arm round Rook's thin throat and held him – plus a bunch of laurel

– as tightly as the model held the bar-girl's wrist. 'I've got a knife,' he said. And to prove that he was honest in his way, he held the flick-knife, last used to stop tomatoes at their crowns, in his right hand and sprang it open just a little distant from Rook's nose.

'Drop the box,' he said.

Rook let the pastries fall.

'Now empty all your pockets, one by one. The jacket first.'

Rook pulled out the envelopes with both hands, the rolls of banknotes, all the pitch money he had received that day. He held the money up and out, at arm's length, as unthreateningly as he could and as distant from the knife as his shoulders would allow.

'It's yours,' he said. But Joseph had no hand free to take possession. One arm was pressed against Rook's throat. The other held the knife.

'Just drop that too.'

Rook let the money go. The envelopes and banknotes, more money than Joseph had ever seen before, fell on the pyramid of cakes. Con's envelope was in the pile.

'The trousers now,' he said. Rook emptied both pockets and turned their innards out like a schoolboy caught with sweets. 'Let's see what's there.'

Once more Rook held out his hands at arm's length. He held a handkerchief, his staff pass, his keys and just a little change.

'Keep that,' Joseph said, and liked the sound of it, the style, the generosity. He released Rook from his grip, and stepped away. The laurel branches fell amongst the booty at his feet. 'Turn round. Back off.'

Rook turned to face the robber and his knife. He moved

two steps away and waited. The 'Keep It' spoken by the youth had told Rook what he had hoped, that the knife was for display and not for cutting throats or stabbing chests. The 'Keep It' meant 'Live On'. Rook's fear made way for irritation and for shame that he had let this ill-dressed, ill-shaped hick make such a fool of him on this of all days, when he'd already – unaided, uncoerced – made himself a public fool. He wrapped his fingers round his keys. He let the bevelled end of one long key poke out beyond his knuckles. He bit his lower lip – not fear, but anger on the boil. He felt a little sick, a little drunk, a little like a brute. It was not hard to take one long step forward as Joseph bent to gather up the envelopes and cakes, to fix his eye on that birthmark in cherry red, and strike this young man in the face with knuckles and with keys.

Rook meant to hit him on the nose or chin, but missed. He struck him on his forehead, just above the left eye's overcliff. The key's sharp end went in. It broke the skin and left a fleshy pit like those left by the beaks of jays in pears. Rook struck again. This time his fist caught Joseph on the ear. Again the jay had left its mark, but raggeder this time. A tear. A bloody one. The third blow came from Rook's right foot and left an imprint of the street on Joseph's suit and a crescent-shaped bruise on Joseph's chest. He toppled forward, winded, shocked. He crushed the cardboard pyramid. His face was pressed against the laurel leaves, though there was no marzi-pan to scent his fall. The laurel stems, in fact, no longer smelt. There is no permanence in plants. Their sap, their colours, and their odours drain, disperse. The only smell was tunnel-dirt. The taste was blood, and tears. He'd wake up soon. He'd find the blood came from a forehead wound. The blood was run-ning down his face. The tears were blood. The laughter-lines around his eye, his lips, his hair-line on one side, the lapel and shoulder of his suit, were marked in red. The picture from the catalogue and the photograph of Rook fell from his pocket, faces up.

Rook's final blow was to Joseph's hand. He kicked the knife away. That kick was delivered with a cough. Rook's throat and chest were heaving like a gannet's. Joseph got up and, empty-handed, ran up the flight of stairs, into the light and safety of the street. God bless the street.

Rook gathered up the things that he had dropped: the banknotes, the envelopes, his staff pass, the flattened box of flattened cakes. He picked up Joseph's knife as well. He closed its blade and dropped it in his pocket with his keys. The laurel branches were too battered now for Victor's chair. He kicked them against the tunnel walls. He was surprised at how calm he felt, despite his breathlessness. First, the restoration of his nebuliser. Then, champagne.

He felt no anger for the country boy. That scrap with him had been too short and undramatic for lasting animosity. The asthmatic turbulence that Rook had suffered at the table in the Soap Garden had done more damage than the fight. The mockery had hurt him more. If only those old friends of his – the greengrocers with whom he'd grown up – had seen the scuffle in the tunnel and how the street in Rook had put to flight the mugger with the knife. If only they had witnessed what he'd done. Violence is the perfect repartee, he thought. More dignified, more eloquent than words. He felt in touch again, with boyhood, streets, the town, the universe of labouring. He felt excited, eager for the day. He felt as tough and sentimental as a movie star. He couldn't wait to share a cake with Anna. He couldn't wait to use his fists again.

Rook stooped to recover one last dropped banknote from the tunnel floor. It was moist with Joseph's blood. Next to it was the clipping from the catalogue, covered by the photograph which Con had given Joseph. Rook looked at Rook, perplexed. He had not seen that photograph for years. How could it have fallen with his money there? Perhaps some trader, who had paid his pitch money that day, had put the photo with the cash. Why? Some arcane rebuke to Rook, no doubt. Some accusation from the past. It was the sort of petty rebuff he'd expect from bitter, unforgiving men like Con. Rook picked the photo up. The suit, the model and the barmaid, which had been hidden underneath, were now on show. He took a closer look. He recognised the bar, perhaps? The model's face? He put both pictures in a pocket with the knife. He knocked the detritus of laurel from his coat and trousers and headed for the steps.

Rook made his way back to Big Vic and, clumsy and encumbered though he was, he could not disguise the hint of hopscotch in his step as he walked across the coloured marble flagstones of the windswept, empty mall. Around him, out of sight, the bankers banked, expeditious every instant of the day; dollars became *lira* became *marks*; commodities and futures bobbed and ducked in value, unobserved; screens conversed in numbers on fibre-optic cables like gossips at a garden fence. Above, a restless matrix with its lights like traffic headlamps in the rush sent out its electronic information into town. The stock report. The city news. A flood in Bangladesh. A birthday greeting for the boss. A puff for Fuji Film. Traffic junctions to avoid. Fly Big Apple – Fly Pan Am.

Rook reached security at last. The automatic doors swept him into processed air. He showed his pass. He tightened his tie at his collar, and summoned the old man's private lift. While he waited for it to fall the twenty-seven storeys of Big Vic, he picked himself a fine bouquet of plastic branches from the gleaming, sapless, perfect foliage of the atrium. He did not have to tug or cut. Each leaf, each twig and branch, was fixed by sleeve joints. The real, reconstituted bark was stuck to moulded trunks with velcro pads. The soil was soil with nothing much to do, except to fool the people of the town.

5

ROOK PUT THE FINAL touches to the room, while the waitresses and kitchen staff prepared the settings and the food for Victor's lunch. His buoyancy had not been punctured by the tightening of his tie, by the dull proprieties of going back to work. He'd dropped the scuffed and battered pyramid of cakes on Anna's desk and simply said, in response to her surprise, 'I had to fight for these!'

Anna asked no questions. She simply filled her lungs with air and closed her eyes and said, 'Such gallantry!' Her persiflage was sweet. It was a tease. It was the kind of irony that Anna knew would work on men. Men were clockwork toys when it came to love and sex. You wound them up, you faked a phrase or two; they marched, they danced, they beat their drum. It was her plan to fake some satisfaction, if she had the chance, with Rook. Why not? He was not married. She was now divorced. She was only older than him by a year. He was not short of cash and might have fun if he could spend his money and his time with her.

Rook was an oddball, yes. But oddballs had their appeal for Anna. She liked the stimulation and surprise of men who lived beyond the grid. She liked Rook's secrecy. She was not fooled by his sardonic ways. What kind of man, with power such as his, would spend the morning on the streets and come back laden with squashed cakes and a bunch of plastic leaves?

46

A man worth knowing, she was sure. So Rook and Anna left it brewing in the air that their flirtations would bear fruit, and soon, before it was too late, before the heightened passion of the day, its sap, its colours and its scents had drained and dispersed for good. Let Victor have his birthday first. Let champagne loosen tongues and dilate hearts. Then let Rook and Anna stay on late, to sort out papers, say, to tidy up, to joust among themselves as the evening and the office blinds came down. They'd spoken not a word, but they were old and wise enough to comprehend the promise and the charge of 'Such gallantry!'

Rook took the plastic branches, a roll of sticky tape, some string, into the office storeroom and began to fix them to the back-rest of an antique wooden chair. The moulded twig ends protruded through the spindles of the chair and made the decoration amateurish, and rushed. Rook tried to bite off lengths of string so that he could tie the twig ends back. But the string was just as tough and artificial as the greenery. He searched the shelves for scissors – and then remembered the knife he'd picked up in the tunnel, the flick-knife that the clumsy, birthmarked mugger in that too-large suit had dropped.

The too-large suit! The thought of it, ill-fitting, grimy, badly made, was all it took to solve the mystery of the second picture Rook had found amongst the debris in the pedestrian underpass. So that was what he'd recognised. Once more Rook found the piece of catalogue and scrutinised the faces and the bar. No other recognition, now. Except, bizarrely, for that suit. Rook smiled at *On the Town*, at its frugal price and style, at the implication that the early photograph of Rook himself had come not with pitch payments as he'd thought, but from the pockets of the young man's suit. He'd been no chance encounter, then, but targeted. This lad had known, and God knows how, that he would carry cash in quantity between the old town and the new. But how the ageing photograph tied in with that he could not tell. Some opportunist soapie? Some maverick inside Big Vic? Some oddball with a pettifogging grudge? Who knows exactly who one's foes might be?

Rook held the knife out, sprang the blade and set to work on cutting string and strapping back the plastic twigs. It was then he spotted the eleven worn letters scratched inexpertly on the handle, 'JOSEPH'S NIFE'. He felt he'd like the chance to hand the flick-knife back, not to make amends for the kick he'd landed and the cheating fist of keys which had inflicted such a bloody face, but for the chance to find out who'd set this 'Joseph' up, and why. But for the moment he was glad to have the knife at hand, to put its blade to proper use for Victor and his chair. The decoration now was neater. Only leaves were on display. It looked as if the stained, antique wood of the chair, long dead, had undergone a resurrection of some kind, had put down roots and put out foliage, like the farmer's magic chair of fairy tales. A little spit and polish was all it took to finish off the job. The spit took off the office dust. The polish – a *Woodland*-scented aerosol – put back the colour and the sheen. Rook's handkerchief buffed up the waxen glimmer of the leaves.

He'd promised there'd be cats for Victor's lunch. They were a part of Victor's dream. The boss himself had three, to chase off pigeons from the roof. Rook had arranged that they should be brought down to the office suite. They'd settled in, two on the sofa, one underneath the desk. The tablecloth was white, exactly as required. The air-conditioning provided just sufficient breeze. In the visitors' lobby the three musicians of the Band Accord were practising the country dances they would play for Victor. The fruit and cheeses were in place. The champagne was on ice. Rook went through to the inner room and Victor's desk. He telephoned the chef. The perch were cooked and already steeped and cooling in the apple beer. The waitresses were standing by. The five old greengrocers were seated, subdued and patient, in the atrium below, waiting for the summons to the lift. Rook carried Victor's birthday chair into the anteroom. He placed it with its back against a wall, so that the tiara of leaves faced into the room, and the disenchanting clutter of plastic, string and sticking tape could not be seen.

When the call came that lunch was ready to be served and that his friends – his guests – were already waiting in his suite, Victor was in his rooftop greenhouse on the twenty-eighth, examining the yellow aphids which congregated in a ruly crowd on the underleaves and along the infant stems, a congregation of busy wingless females plus a single ant which feasted on their honeyed excretions. Victor hesitated with his spray. He almost cared for insects more than plants – but not quite. These aphids were too common to be lovable. He showered them with toxic milk. The ant, he spared. How high, he wondered, would he have to build to rise beyond the pigeons and the flies, to reach above the aphids and the ants? Forty? Fifty storeys? Would there be oxygen enough up there, for vegetables to thrive, for bees to come and pollinate his plants? He looked out through the lichened, mildewed glass, northwards, beyond the mall, the highway and the high-rise stores, towards the old town, and the suburbs, and the hills. Skyscrapers are the skyline optimists. They have the first light of the dawn, the final warmth of day. They get the flattened, cartographic view of towns, the neat geometry of north, south, east and west.

Victor knew his city like a hawk knows fields. The innards of the city were laid bare from the 28th floor, from what was once the Summit Restaurant of Big Vic but now, because the Summit diners could not stomach the swaying flexibility of skyscrapers in wind, was private garden. Innards are chaos and a mystery to any but the practised eye. In time, with study, Victor had got to know the spread-out entrails of the streets. He knew the bones and organs of the town – the university, the stadium, the graveyards and the parks. He knew the Bunkers where poor, delinquent townies lived in blocks as packed as hives. He knew the yellows and the ochres of the public buildings, the grand works of the eighteenth-century trading potentates, the book-end buildings of the police headquarters where once the low-rise slums had been.

The routes and patterns were quite clear. No river – but a line of pylons and the railway halved the town, and link highways made a rhombus as a frame containing both these halves. The rhombus, in the midday summer heat, dangled from the city's flight and swoop of motorways like a box which swings on ribbons. Beyond the box? The groundscraper mansions of the wealthy, crouching behind the thick masonry of security walls. The suburbs and their trees. Out-of-town commercial centres with fields of tarmac for the cars. A threatened *cul-de-sac* of countryside, earmarked as building land.

Victor liked the grey and green of boulevards the best, where lines of trees and central lawns plunged living splinters into the city's skin. He liked the city humming to itself: the cheerful plumes of smoke which came from rubbish tips and factories and crematoriums, the distant drone of traffic, the cadences of wind.

The suburbs of the city from the 28th through Victor's less than perfect eyes were patterned fabric, not quite alive, though shimmering like shot silk in greens and greys and browns. Nearer to the eye, the striped and garish awnings of the market, dignified only by the grey-green of the Soap Garden with its few two-storey trees, seemed capricious and unnatural, set at the centre of the old town's patterned stratagems of startled roofs with their exclamatory chimney pots.

Victor did not like the market place. He did not like its awnings and disorder. He did not like its crowds, so dense that taxis could not pass. He disapproved of truck-back trading, of noise and inefficiency, of waste. He'd not been to the market now for seven years – too old, too frail, too numbed by life – but he could see it every day, a garish blockage at the centre of the city which spurned both logic and geometry. He'd put it right. Why not? What else could old men do? He'd stood inside his greenhouse now for fifteen minutes at the very least. Three times enough for him to earn the money for a month in Nice, a car, a year's supply of clothes. His farms and markets, his offices and shares, his merchant capital crusading in a dozen countries, a hundred towns, earned fortunes by the minute. Thirty millions a month. Morocco's health and education budget in a year. Enough to build a dream in bricks. Or stone. Or glass.

His accountants and advisers had been working on him for a year or more. The market place, they said, was out of date. It did not earn enough for such a central site. It was – compared to canneries and bottling plants – a poor outlet for fruit. There'd been hints from the city government, that if he were to seek approval for a plan to renovate, or move the market elsewhere, say . . . then, there would be no fight. No fight, indeed! Victor was not so foolish as to think there'd be no fight if he were to tinker with the market place. He knew what soapies were, an awkward bunch, opposed to any change on principle. Well, that's Rook's job, he thought, to keep the soapies quiet. Yet Victor would not share his thoughts with Rook. He did not trust the man to hold his tongue. He did not trust his judgement or his loyalty. Rook was no businessman. What businessman would be so sociable? What businessman would settle for such a salary as Rook and for so long? What businessman could see the market operate and not be shocked at its trading nonchalance? But Rook, he loved the Soap Market. He loved its crowds. He'd said as much: 'It's paradise for me.' And Victor thought, If that is paradise, that regimented, noxious crush, that milling battlefield of chores and errands and anonymity, then that's the paradise of termites.

Old Victor took his stick and walked quite steadily between the pots of young peppers and tomatoes towards the lift. And lunch. He paused to rub out with his thumb the greenfly on the fessandra bushes which grew in sentinel pots at the roof-top door. He wiped the mush of bodies on the lintel, wheezed, coughed, and spat a practised splash of phlegm into the pot compost. It glistened for a moment like the gummy, silver residue of slugs. 'Good luck,' said Victor, to himself. That's what all good farmers said when they spat in the soil. The luck was for the soil and for the spitter, too. The luck that Victor wished upon himself was this: that he would live into his nineties, long enough to make his lasting, monumental mark upon the city. His age was not an enemy. In fact, the day that he was eighty seemed the perfect moment to begin the spending of his millions. He had no family to leave it to. He had no debts. What should he do then? Leave it all to charities, and tax, and undeserving skimmers-off like Rook? Or play the geriatric fool and plough the crop back in?

Eighty was the age for second childhoods, so they said. He'd never had his first. He'd never been a boy. He'd only been a baby and a man. So let's commence the childhood now, he thought. Let's be an old man full of impulse, prospects, hope. Let's lay the bitterness aside and die at peace. He spat again – more to clear his lungs than to win more luck than he deserved – into the compost of the second pot.

6

VICTOR'S SIMPLE DREAM OF celebrating eighty years in country style could not come true. The air inside Big Vic lacked buoyancy. It was heavy and inert. It was soup. Dioxides from the air-conditioning; monoxides from the heating system; ammonia and formaldehydes from cigarettes; ozone from photocopiers; stunning vapours from plastics, solvents and fluorescent lights. What oxygen remained was drenched in dust and particles and micro-organisms, mites and fibres from the carpeting, fleece from furniture, airborne amoebi from humidifying reservoirs, cellulose from paper waste, bugs, fungi, lice. The air weighed too much and passed too thickly through the nostrils and the mouths of the guests at Victor's lunch. They coughed and sneezed and grew too hot. Their eyes began to water, their heads to ache, the rheumatism in their knuckles and their knees to grumble. Big Vic was sick. Contagious, too. It shared its sickness speedily with these old traders, these outdoor men, as they waited for their boss. They blamed their wheeziness, their migraines and their lethargy on nerves. They blamed their dry mouths on embarrassment at the prospect of what had been described on their printed invitation cards as 'a relaxed birthday lunch for a few close friends'. *Relaxed?* Not one of them could be relaxed in Victor's company unless there was a deal to close or market business to be done. *Close friends?* Were they the closest friends that Victor

54

had? It made them smile, the very thought of it.

But then, who else could he have asked if not these five? He had no family, as far as anybody knew. There were no neighbours on the mall. This was not, after all, the country-side, where people lived so close at hand and in such sodality that they were free and glad to sit-in overnight to ease the passage of a corpse, to be the wedding guest, to aid with births or weeping, to help an old man puff his eighty candles out.

'We're here,' one ageing soapie remarked, 'because there's no one else.'

'We're here,' another said, 'because, these days, we have to do what Victor wants. We're here because we haven't got the choice.'

It was true they'd been more intimate, at one time, when Victor's empire was as small as theirs and his unbroken dryness had been seen as irony, his silences as only childlike, not malign. But now he was the ageing emperor and they the courtiers, obsequious, fearful, ill at ease. Indeed, the whole lunch had been arranged as if this old man were a medieval ruler, addicted to the indulgences and flattery of everyone who crossed his path. He'd been met, as he stepped out of the bright lights of his lift into his office suite, by quiet applause. A respectful corridor was formed for him, so that he could make his progress to the table without the hindrance of his old colleagues. Three accordionists accompanied him across the room with the March from 'La Regina', the bellows of their instruments white and undulating like the young and toothy smiles of the staff who had gathered at the door.

The snuffling trader guests closed in when Victor passed and formed his retinue. A waiter or a waitress stood at every

chair, except for Victor's. Rook stood there, like the Prince-in-
waiting or the Bastard Son in some fairy tale, clapping both
the music and the man. Even Victor felt emotions that, though
they did not show, were strong enough to make him sway and
lean more heavily upon his stick.

They begged, of course, that Victor should sit down, and
then they clapped some more. He asked for water, but surely
this was the perfect moment for champagne. Trays of it were
brought, for Victor and his guests, for all the workers in the
outer rooms. Even the accordionists were given glasses of
champagne, though hardly had their nostrils fizzed with the
first sip, than they were called upon to play – and sing – the
Birthday Polka. So Victor sat, the Vegetable King, surrounded
by employees, waiters, clients, acquaintances and cats, each
one of them dragooned to serve him for the afternoon, as two
stout ladies and their friend pumped rhapsodies of sound and
celebration round the airless room. Those few who knew the
words joined in. The others hummed or simply stood and
grinned.

There was an instant, when one of the three cats jumped
up amongst the cheeses and the fruits on the table and put its
nose into the butter dish, when it seemed that village ways
had made the journey into town. But Rook's raised eyebrow
and his nod brought that fantasy and the cat's adventure to an
end. A waiter, none too practised in the ways of cats, removed
the creature from the butter, lifting it clear by its hind legs as
if it were a rabbit destined for the pot.

The music ended. Rook nodded once again, and all the
staff, following the details of his memo to them earlier that
day, left Victor's room and returned to their screens, their
telephones, their desks, their manifests of trade in crops. The

Band Accord played – *largamente* – at the far end of the room. The guests sat down to the silent whiteness of the tablecloth, while the waitresses served the coddled fish. Rook, bidding everybody *Bon Appetit*, left Victor to hold court and joined Anna and her staff for flattened cakes – and more champagne – in the outer rooms. Later on, when Victor had been softened by the meal, he'd enter with the birthday chair.

The meal, in fact, was not as perfect as the cook had hoped. The perch, despite their freshness, were just a little high, a touch too bladdery. They had not travelled well. Only one guest, his palate bludgeoned by the pipe he smoked, dispatched his fish with any appetite. The rest concealed their daintiness by making much of savouring the olives and the bread, or filling up on cheese and fruit. They turned the perches' bones and mottled skin to hide the flesh they could not eat.

It was not long, of course, before the meal was finished and the waitresses had cleared the dishes, leaving the old men, freed by champagne and liqueurs, to follow the informal agenda of the birthday lunch and reminisce. There'd be no gifts or speeches. That was Victor's stated wish. His hearing was not good enough, despite his humming, temperamental hearing aid, for gifts and speeches. But stated wishes of that kind are only code for something else. No one demands the gift they want. Instead they say, 'No need. No fuss. I'm happy just to see you here.' So Victor's friends had done their best to translate the old man's code. What gift would please a frail and childless millionaire about to embark upon his ninth decade? Something you cannot buy, of course. They'd had grim fun, these five ageing traders, identifying all those things that can't be bought and which were lost as men got old. Good health. Good looks. Teeth, hair and waists. The pleasures of the bed. Patience. Energy. A fertile place in someone's living heart. Control of wind and bladder. All these were gone and way beyond the sway of credit cards. What then for Victor's birthday gift? A place in history? Esteem? These must be earned, not bought.

'A statue, then!' The suggestion had been meant in jest. A statue to the vanity of age. But the idea was better than the jest, and soon had the old traders nodding at its aptness. They'd place a statue with a plaque in the Soap Garden. They'd raise the funds through subscription. All the traders in the market place would want to give. A good idea. A public gift to the city to mark the old man's birthday. They'd had some drawings done by the woman who had cast a bronze statue (for the entrance of the new concert hall) of the city senators who died on lances in 1323. They liked her work. These senators were men in pain. Those lances were as straight and cruel as Death's own finger. The hands which sought to stem the wounds or pull out the lances by their shafts were hands like mine or yours, except a little larger and in bronze. This was no abstract metaphor. She was no artist of the modern school. She'd talked to them in terms they understood: payments, contracts, completion dates, the price of bronze. Despite his spoken wishes, then, there was a shortish speech, a gift. The five old men presented Victor with the artist's drawings. 'They're just ideas,' they said. 'You choose. We'll see your statue is in place before you're eighty-one.' Victor did not make a speech. He nodded, that is all, and put the portfolio of drawings on his desk.

'I'll find some time later for these,' he said, and joined them at the table once again to add his monumental awkwardness to theirs.

They tried in vain to open up some windows and let some town air in. But all windows higher than the second floor were double-glazed and safety-sealed and only activated by a call to the building's brain, the high-tech deck of chips and boards which regulated everything from heating to alarms. They tried to resurrect the country lunches that they had shared when they were younger, middle-aged, and vying for crops and produce at the small-town auctioneers. They tried to sing along with all the sentimental tunes dished up for them by Band Accord. They tried to grow animated rather than just sleepy with the alcohol they'd drunk. But the office suite was deadening. The headaches and the rheumatism which had made such progress, nurtured by the formal tension of the lunch, deepened their discomfort and the furrows on their brows. Their coughs could no longer reach and clear the tickling dryness in their throats. Their eyes were smarting. Their faces were as red and vexed as coxcombs. Conditions there were perfect for a heart attack or stroke.

Victor sat as deadened as his guests, not by the onslaught of the offices – he was used to that – but by the discomfort that he felt in company. He'd never had the conversation or the animated face to make himself or the people round him feel at ease. He had no repartee, no party skills, no social affability. What kind of city man was he that did not relish the light and phatic talk, the spoken oxygen of markets, offices and streets? He did not care. He did not need to care. A boss can speak as little as he wishes, and stay away from markets, offices and streets. Truth to tell, he did not even relish the joshing and the drink-emboldened flattery that his guests – between their coughs and flushes – were exchanging at the table. He mistook their talk for trivia. He took their wheezing and their creaking and the damp heat on their foreheads as the wages of their sinful lives, their drinking, smoking, family lives, their lack of *gravitas*. He looked on them with less kindness, less forgiveness, less respect than he had looked upon the yellow aphids that he'd killed that day.

Victor's own breathing – papery and shallow at the best of times – had become distressed by the cigarettes and the one pipe smoked with the brandy after lunch. His stomach too was just a little restless from the fish.

'Excuse me, gentlemen,' he said, and stood, his brandy glass in hand. His guests stood, too, as promptly as they could, expecting toasts.

'Fresh air,' said Victor, his sentence shortened by a cough. 'Let's go to the roof.'

He led them in a halting, single file across the room to where his private lift waited for his summons. The three accordionists, instructed to 'accompany' proceedings until instructed otherwise, tagged on, their instruments strapped on their chests like oxygen machines. The waitress with the brandy – dutiful, uncertain – followed on. And last of all, the cats. They crowded in as best they could. The lift was meant for one. It shook a little on its hawsers as the old men and accordions wheezed in unison, and stumbled intimately against each other on the ascent to the 28th. But when they had emerged beneath the arch of fessandras into the air and foliage of the roof-top garden, the greengrocers breathed deeply, swallowed mouthfuls of the dirty but unfettered air, turned their faces to the sun and wind, and looked out across the city and the suburbs to the blue-green hills, the grey-green woods, beyond.

The Band Accord stood at the door, their mood transformed. The new note that they struck was sweet and sentimental. They played the sort of joyful harvest tunes that make you dance and weep, their grace notes jesting with the melody. The weaving cheerfulness of the accordion could make a teacup dance and weep. It is the only instrument strapped to the player's heart. Its pleated bellows stretch and smile.

The guests spread out, at ease, delighted, cured all at once by the magic of the place, invigorated by the care and passion bestowed on every plant that grew on that rooftop. The centrepiece, so different from the sculptured water in the mall, was a pond surrounded by a path of broken stone. There were no fish, but there were kingcups, hunter lilies, flags, and – hunched over, like a heron – the shoulders of a dwarf willow, providing shade for paddling clumps of knotweed and orange rafts of bog lichen. There were shrubs all around, some in clay pots, some in amphoras coloured thinly with a wash of yellow plaster, some in raised beds. A wooden pergola, heavy with climbing roses, honeysuckle, creepers, led towards the greenhouse. The traders followed Victor there and rubbed the leaves of herbs and primped the seedlings like owners of the land.

The Band Accord was summoned to the greenhouse door. 'Play on, play on.' The waitress poured more brandy. The old men passed the glasses round like schoolboys on an outing, making sure they kept for themselves the fullest glass. They all found a place to rest or sit. Some upturned pots, a wooden bench, some low staging for the plants, made perfect seats. The cats made the most of the dry and practised hands, the bony laps, the strokes and preening that were on offer. The waitress was a little flustered by the flirting helpful hands which aided her with drinks. The two stout ladies of the band and their slimmer friend, on the other hand, were serenading this impromptu glasshouse gathering with the smiles and gestures of the most intimate nightclub. 'To Victor!' And someone added, 'May you grow new teeth.'

Everybody raised a glass and once again the band squeezed out the Birthday Polka. Everybody sang the words and passed their glasses for more drink. Victor stood to say eight words, no more, of thanks. 'Just like the village parties, gentlemen,' he said, promoting the deceit that he had sap for blood, that he was just a countryman at heart. 'Your health.' He looked out for the second time that day towards the garish awnings of the market place. Before he'd had a chance to sit, he added one more toast, 'Our town!' He swept his hand towards the market, as if to wipe the townscape clean. He would have said, if he had been a more loquacious man, 'Before I die I'd like to clear all that! To start afresh. A market place. A building worthy of our town.' Instead, he said (he could not help himself), 'To business, gentlemen.' Again they lifted glasses up, and drank. 'I trust your businesses are well. No problems that you want to talk about?' No one was in the mood to answer him. They shook their heads and laughed, as if the very thought of problems was a joke.

'Well, then,' said Victor. 'That is as it ought to be. Rook's paid enough by me to solve and settle problems . . .'

'By us as well . . .' The man who spoke had meant it as a joke. He'd never stopped to think before whether Rook's pitch payments were transactions that he shared with Victor. Too late to wonder now.

'By you as well?'

'It's nothing much. A gratuity for everything he does.'

'What does Rook do that is not already funded by his salary?'

Victor saw discomfort all round. He read it perfectly. No wonder Rook thought the Soap Market was paradise. The market termites droned for him. The man was taking bribes. Victor knew at once what he must do to this extortionist and how – a timely gift – it served his long-term purpose perfectly. A man like that, a man who served himself before his boss, a man, moreover, who could not be trusted should a market renovation plan be contemplated, could not expect to keep his job. There was no wickedness in that. It was a duty for a boss to let the shyster go, just as it was the task of gardeners to rid themselves of bugs.

'How much exactly do you pay?' he asked. Again, there were no volunteers to speak. They did not wish to seem the victims of dishonesty, or collaborators in deceit. Victor took a notebook from his jacket, and a pen. 'Jot down the size of payment that you make to Rook,' he said. 'I would not wish my friends to pay more than they ought.' Of course, they did as they were told.

Downstairs, one floor below, Rook and Anna judged – as all seemed quiet in Victor's office suite – that the time was right to seat their boss in his birthday chair, amongst the gleaming foliage, and to raise their glasses in a toast. The chair was carried from the anteroom. The drinks were poured. More champagne, naturally. The chair was placed at the centre of the lobby outside Victor's suite where they presumed the birthday lunch was – quietly – still in progress. Rook stood behind the chair, a smile composed already on his face. Anna knocked on

Victor's door, and entered. The only sound and movement in the room came from the air-conditioning.

'They've gone,' she said to Rook. He came and stood beside her at the door and looked where she was pointing, at the table, at the olive pips, the undrained glasses, the stubbed cigar, the detritus of orange peel and fruit skin and undigested fish. Anna laughed, and – doing so – she dropped her head momentarily onto Rook's shoulder.

'They must have doddered to the roof,' he said, and put his arm around her waist. He felt elated and uneasy. The empty room, the woman's reassuring waist, the birthday chair, unoccupied and foolish in the middle of the lobby, were not what he had planned.

'Let's drink the champagne anyway.' He turned his back on Victor's door and sat himself amongst the plastic foliage of the birthday chair, satirically, defiantly. He lifted up his glass until Anna, standing at his knees, was still and silent and composed. She raised her glass as well. 'Ourselves!' she said. 'Ourselves . . . ourselves . . . ourselves . . . ourselves . . .'

7

THE MARKET WAS AS good as gone, and so was Rook. Decisions had been made, that day. The skyline of our lives was changed. Five halting traders, a band, a waitress, and the boss took air and brandy on Big Vic's garden roof, while, on the 27th floor, Rook and Anna grew tipsy and engrossed with lesser things. There'd be a *romance* (How we love that word!), one *death* at least (We're not so keen); there'd be distress and devilment upon the streets, some fortunes made and lost – and all because a dry old millionaire, alive too long, a little drunk, had fallen foul of that ancient sentimental trap, the wish to die yet linger on.

When Victor offered up his glass and said 'Our town!' perhaps the toast was not for what there *was* but for what he *saw* in his mind's eye, the prospects and the dreams. His hand swept up across the distant cityscape. He wiped the market off, as if he was simply clearing steam from glass and looking on the hidden clarity beyond, his place in history.

The story, though, that was running through the city by that midnight was not the one that would change lives and landscapes – unless you were a fish. The story that amused the traders and the porters as they gathered in the Soap Garden for their final coffee-and-a-shot, that so obsessed the chatterlings, the social consciences, the bleeding hearts, the evangelists of social change who talked into the night, was the story of

Victor's coddled fish. The fish at Victor's party – or so the midnight edition of the next day's city paper claimed – were better treated than his guests. Ten fresh and living perch were taken from the station to his offices 'BY CAB!', was the report. Their plastic travel-tank was lifted by porters onto the cab's rear seat and the driver was instructed to go no faster than a hearse. Live perch, it seemed, could lose their sweetness and their bloom if sloshed about like lunchtime bankers in the backs of cabs. Their flesh would flood and stress and, no matter what the chef might do, would disappoint at table, clinging apprehensively to the bone and tasting faintly bitter.

The cabbie – a little stressed himself, and bitter too at what he took to be a joke at his expense – adjusted his rear-view mirror so that he could drive and watch the yellowed water in the tank. He was used to spying into women's laps that way. He'd earned a little cash a week or two before when he had spied a politician's hand rest briefly in a woman's silken lap. The woman was an actress, not the politician's wife, and the cabbie sold both names to me. You will not mind, I know, if briefly, after introductions, and having kept myself discrete thus far, I step back into shadow. This story is not mine, at least not more than it is every citizen's. I am – I was – a journalist. My byline was The Burgher. I was, at this time, the mordant, mocking diarist on the city's daily.

On Victor's birthday, the cabbie phoned me once again and sold the story of the fish tank too. 'By God,' he said, 'I swear the water smelt of piss.' Here was, I felt . . . The Burgher felt . . . an amusing illustration of the oddity of millionaires, but only worth a quarter of the fee – and half the column space – that The Burgher's budget could afford for hands in laps. The paper ran the story in The Burgher column, on the back page, with a cartoon – a cab completely full of water, bubbles, weed; a snorkelled diver at the wheel; a periscope; and at the street corner a well-dressed perch, fin urgently raised, calling, 'Victor's please – and hurry, he's expecting me for lunch!'

Nobody would have the nerve to show the piece to Victor. Such gossip and such jokes would only baffle him. But Rook was in the mood for gossip and cartoons. As usual, as a Friday treat, he'd bought the midnight paper from the operatic huckster on the street below his apartment. He had taken the paper back to bed with him, with coffee, brioches and cubes of melon, and had shown it to Anna as if the joke on Victor would wear thin, the newsprint fade, unless she woke and read the paper then. She'd left her glasses in her bag, and where her bag was, amongst the urgent chaos of their clothes, their shoes, their coats, they were not sure. So Rook removed his slippers and his gown and rejoined Anna in his bed to read The Burgher's words aloud. Their laughter led to kisses, and their kisses to the passion of the not-so-young in love. A breeze from the open window rustled and disturbed the pages of the paper which had been thrown carelessly and hurriedly upon the floor. Their faces reddened, their bodies swollen with embraces, their mouths limp and tenacious, they ended their working day much as a thousand other couples did beneath the roofs and chimneys of the town, their cries and promises soon lost amid the hubbub of the traffic and the revellers and the calls of traders in the alleys, avenues, boulevards and streets. The wind. The countless noises in the lives of cities. The climax of the night. The recklessness of sleep.

The market place was resting, too, though not silently. The stalls and awnings had been packed away – some in padlocked wooden coffins, five metres long; some decked and

lashed like rigging on a boat and riding out the stormless
doldrums of the night; some wigwamed carelessly and stacked
like bonfire wood. It looked as if a squall had struck, reducing
all the trading vibrancy of day to sticks and cobblestones. The
noise came mostly from the cleansing teams, the men in
yellow PVC whose job it was to operate the sweep-jeeps,
brushing up the vegetable waste, the paper bags, the scraps
and orts of the Soap Market like prairie harvesters, and then to
uncap the hydrants and bruise and purge the cobblestones
with sinewed shafts of pressured water. The quieter group –
men, women, kids – foraged for their supper and their bed-
clothes, gleaning mildewed oranges, snapped carrots, the occa-
sional coin, cardboard sheets and squares of polythene before
the brushes and the jets turned the market's oval benevolence
to spotlessness.

Quite soon the cleansing gangs would go. The night folk
of the Soap Market would secure their night-time roosts.
Dismantled stalls and awnings – once the water has run off –
provide good nesting spots for people without homes. Cellophane Man – his clinging suit refreshed and thickened by
the cellophane he found discarded in the market place – stood,
vacuum-wrapped, to watch and organise the final vehicles of
night. The drinkers had their corner. They did not sleep at
night, but sat in restless circles, sharing wine or urban rum
and fending off the dawn with monologues and spats. The
shamefaced women there, fresh out of luck and cash, kept to
themselves, and, desperately well-mannered, slept sat up,
their arms looped through their bags, their minds elsewhere.
Only the young stretched out – the youths who'd come to
make their marks away from home and had ended up as city
dips, or tarts, or petrol sniffers. Some – like Joseph – had just

arrived. The Soap Market was their first bed-sit, and still they hoped that day would bring good luck. Indeed – again – where else would Joseph be but here? Not sitting at a bar for sure. The pockets of his summer suit were empty still. *Emptier*, in fact. He'd lost his clipping from the catalogue. He'd dropped his knife. He'd come off worse with Rook. He slept – young, stretched out – with spinach as a pillow and a mattress made of planks.

At least he slept. For all the bad luck of the day he still retained the knack of easing tiredness, relieving disappointment, with a little sleep. At first he was unnerved by lights and noise; the engines and the headlamps of motorbikes ridden by spoilt young men drawn to the dismantled market by the fun that could be had at speed on cobblestones, and with the 'trash' who drank and slept there. But soon the town went quiet – no hoots or yelps to puncture night. He'd lain and watched the city darken as the last few lights in homes and offices had been switched off by insomniacs and caretakers and automatic timing switches. The only lights that did not dim were streetlamps and the silent conifer of silver bulbs which stood, unswaying, twenty-seven storeys high above the town. This Tree of Lights was Big Vic at rest. The block's computer told which bulbs to shine, and when. It was the perfect fir – except that those who cared to stare might see at night a firefly at the summit of the tree, as Victor – without the knack of sleep – wandered through his apartment and his office suite, marked as he moved from room to room by lamps and lights outside the fir-tree's grid.

It was his birthday night. He'd had too much to drink. One glass at his age was too much. His stomach growled. The pissed-on perch was drowning in champagne. Walking seemed to ease the wind which pressed against his chest. He belched to let the champagne free. He knew that in his office desk there were sachets of kaolin to still his gut. He found them, and he found the portfolio of drawings, too, the artist's working notes for the sculpture that his contemporaries seemed keen to force on him. He carried the portfolio to the water fountain in the lobby outside his office suite. He tipped the dry and powdered kaolin into his mouth like a child with sherbert and washed it down with water from the fountain. The coldness of the water dislodged the pains inside his chest. He belched again. He felt quite well at last. Not sick, at least. Not faint.

Victor put down the sheaf of drawings and looked at each. Romantic, formal pieces sketched in chestnut pastels. A market vendor weighing out his fruit. A girl with grapes and flowers. A porter with three produce trays on his head. And then – alarmingly – a drawing of his past: a beggar woman with a suckling child, her hand outstretched, the gift of apple balanced on her palm. He sat, he almost fell, into an aged wooden chair pushed in shadow up against the lobby wall. He looked and looked at what he took to be a drawing of his mother and himself . . . what, almost eighty years before? His head was flooded now, his face was drained. This was the statue that he'd have. He'd make his mother once again. He'd put her back. He knew exactly where she should sit and beg in bronze, between the Soap Market and the garden. At last, the implications of his sweeping hand that afternoon upon the roof became more clear. He'd start afresh, just as his accountants had advised. He'd build a market worthy of the statue. A market like a cathedral, grand and memorable. A market worthy of a millionaire. He would outlive himself in stone. His mother would outlive herself in bronze. It made good business sense, though no doubt Rook would not approve. He'd fight for Paradise.

What better time to start than then-and-there? Decide. Remove all obstacles. Proceed. Victor took his memo pad and wrote a note in pencil on it. For Anna. She could deal with Rook. A less generous man would call the police, and let them sort it out. But, no, let Anna do the job. That's what he paid her for.

Victor was glad – relieved – to have this task with which to fill his ninth decade and so engrossed by every touch and mark upon the artist's page, that he neither saw nor felt the plastic foliage pressing on his back.

PART TWO
MILK AND HONEY

1

THERE'D BEEN NO OTHER birthday chairs in Victor's life, other than the one that Rook had prepared for him when he was old, other than the one he'd sat upon yet failed to see. Victor was a townie almost through and through. He was not as soily or as leafy as he claimed. He'd fled the countryside when he was three weeks old, when this brusque, gymnastic century was also in its infancy. His dad had died. An epidemic of the sweats had seen him off before his son was born. His home village could barely cope with the sudden glut of widows, dotagers and orphans, all shaken from their tree before their time, all seeking charity at once. A widower could work and earn his keep. But who would go without to feed and clothe the harness-maker's wife, or her new baby, when it came? Her husband's skills had died with him. He had left no land or crops for her to sell. The workshop cottage and its yard was only theirs by rent. The landlord's agent let her stay until the child was born, and then – what choice had he? – he asked for payment for the weeks she'd missed. The money that she'd made from selling unworked leather, harness tools, her husband's horse, was not enough to clear the months of debt, and live. The mother and her wrinkled kid were as cold and poor as worms.

At least Victor's tiny gut was full. His mother's breasts were independent of all the hardship in their lives. But she was weak from loss of blood and milk and lack of food. The best she had for meals was half a block of pigeon's cheese and two jumps at the larder door.

What of the free food of the countryside? The mushrooms and the nuts? The stubble grain left over by the thresher and the harvesters? The berries and the birds? The honey and the fish? Life's not like that, except in children's books. The free food of the countryside is high and maggoty before it's ripe; or else it's faster than the human hand and can't be caught. What's free and good is taken by the bully dogs and birds. What's left is sustenance for flies and mice.

So Victor's mother had no choice but to pack a canvas bag – a bag her husband stitched for her before they wed – and set off with her baby to the town. She had a distant, younger sister there, a maid to some rich man. Her address was *poste restante* at the Postal Hall. Victor's mother asked the landlord's agent to write a note. It said, 'Sister, my husband's dead, and less than twenty-three years old. I have a child. His name is Victor. So we must come to you as you are all we have, and will be with you soon for love and help. Today is Monday and the 26th of June. God keep you well. Signed lovingly, your only Em.' She begged a postage stamp and left the letter with the village clerk. There was a mail train every other day. The letter would soon be in the town. Her sister would prepare to take the widow and the orphan in, for sure, and find them food and work.

Em made a sling for Victor and strapped him to her chest with her shawl. She tied the canvas bag across her back. She threw some grains of maize – for Thanks and Fare-thee-well – on the doorstep of her house. She lit a candle. She ought to carry light from their old home into their new, wherever that might be. Light is luck. You take it with you when you move. She lifted it and put it down again. Once. Twice. The flame drew back. It ducked and shrank. The light would have to stay. She was not fool enough to think she'd keep the flame alive out in the wind and night.

'We'll leave it here for him,' she told her son. 'Your father always loved the mummery of candle flames.' But Victor cried when he lost the sight of that low flame. It was his first and only toy. He wanted it. Em knelt and snubbed it then, with fingers moistened by her tongue. She let him grip the candle end, a nipple and a finger made of wax. It kept him quiet as they set off on their journey to the town, through valleys made patchy-blue that time of year by fields of manac beans. The sky and countryside were fabric from one cloth, and that the colour of the Caribbean Sea.

The baby Victor was content with little more than suck and blow. He was happy just to hold the candle end, to sleep or feed, made biddable by the rhythm of his mother's steps, kept warm and coddled by the sling and by her breasts. A child of three weeks old is built to bend and bounce and sleep throughout. And just as well, because his mother's hike to town took seven days and passed through storms and woods and fords which would frighten and dismay children of a greater age. Em feared wolves and chills and broken legs, but Victor filled his empty head with heartbeats from his mother's chest. She washed his soiled and heavy swaddle cloths in streams and let the wet clothes dry and stiffen, draped across her back. By the time they reached the outposts of the civic world, the cemeteries, the rubbish dumps, the gipsy camps, the homes of bankers, the abattoirs, the outer boulevards of town, Victor had regained his birthweight. His mother, on the other hand, was paler, thinner, colder than a cavern eel.

They left the fields behind. They reached metalled roads, and rows of houses with lawns and carriage drives. They came through high woods and found a measured townscape spreading out in greys and reds and browns, with a shimmering mirage of smoke which made it seem as if the hills beyond were chimney products of the city mills and that the sky was spread with liquid slate. This was a different city from the one we know. Less egoistic, more malign.

Em carried Victor down the causeway of trees and grass which split the city's outer boulevard in two, and conducted trams and countryside into the town. These were the days when foot and hoof and wheel were battling for the government of towns, and wheels – because the rich had motor cars – were winning every skirmish on the streets. For peace and quiet the walkers shared the causeway with the trams.

She asked an old man for the Postal Hall. 'It's far, you'll have to take a tram,' he said, pointing to the tallest part of town. He showed her where the tram would stop and waited while she joined the queue. But, once he'd turned away to dodge a path between the vans and carriages which thronged the road, she set off once again by foot along the tramway into the city's heart. She feared the other passengers. She feared the clanking trams with their winding, outside stairs, and their wind-blown upper platforms which shook and muttered like the devil's haycart. She trembled in the street. Yet surely these were women just like her, beneath their feathers and their ribbons, beneath their hobble skirts. What had she expected? That city people got about on hands and knees, as country wisdom claimed? She looked her urban sisters in the face, but could not find an eye to match her own. They seemed like modest girls – or sinful ones – who could not lift their eyes, who did not have the energy to smile. Em walked and smiled and sought a welcome from everyone she passed. How could she know how strange she seemed, how disconcerting was her upturned face and mouth? She kissed her Victor on the head. She nuzzle-whispered in his ear the chorus of the nursery rhyme: 'Townies, frownies, fancy gownies; noses up is; mouthies down is.'

The Postal Hall was not what she had thought. In her world halls were empty spaces defended against the weather and the night by bricks and tiles, and only full for meetings and for feasts. She'd thought the Postal Hall would be a covered clearing in the town. Her sister, unchanged from the young girl who'd emigrated there three years before, would be waiting at the door. Or else, Em thought, she'd simply give the number of the *poste restante*. Someone would press a bell or make a call to summon her sister from her work. If it was simple to find folk in country towns, then think how easy it would be in cities such as this where everything was done so quickly and so well. Instead she found a sandstone building with many flights of steps, and far too many doors. Her access was blocked by carts and trams. Opposing streams of people competed for the pavement and the road. Never had she witnessed so much speed, heard such urgency or encountered such confidence and hesitation all at once. Never had she seen so many horses: so at ease and so fulfilled, despite the brassy onslaught of the motor cars.

Em crossed with Victor in the wake of two fat men in uniforms. She chose the central entrance to the Postal Hall, and went inside, through giant columns and great bronzed

doors. At once, she took her hat from off her hair and held it
in her hand. She almost crossed herself and fell down on her
knees to pray. Here was a bloated, oblong hall, sepulchral and
forbidding. What light there was came through high windows
in a dome and from gas chandeliers which hissed like nuns,
and were reflected in the polished, veiny marbles of the floor.
There were a dozen mahogany counters and a score of metal
grills and at each one a jostling queue. All the men and
women there had forms or money or parcels or letters in their
hands and, even though they whispered as in church, the
hubbub of the place was louder, deader than the street. No
one seemed to see her there. Their arms banged into hers. She
held the paper out with her sister's number, but no one
stopped to help. She called her sister's name. Her raised voice
upset Victor who had mostly slept despite the city. He pushed
his chin against his mother's breasts, vexed by something.
Wind, perhaps, or by the taste of desperation in his mother's
milk. She pushed him to the nipple once again, but he only bit
it with his gums, and cried like old men cry, his face a contour
map of lines, his eyes squeezed tight. Again she called her
sister's name. But no one came except a Post Commissionaire,
who pointed to his badge and then the door and said that she
should leave or 'cut the noise'.

She joined a queue behind a line of people, most of whom
had envelopes or cards. They moved away from her, her
homelessness, her baby's noise, the smell of urine drying on
her clothes-line back.

'Is this the place?' she asked, and held her sister's number
up. They saw the two words, *poste restante*, and pointed to an
anteroom. Inside were ranks of metal boxes, each with slits
and locks, another counter and another queue. When her

chance came, Em held her sister's name and number up against the grill. The woman at the counter glanced at it and disappeared into a closed, back room without a word of greeting. She returned a moment later with a letter. It was the one which Em had sent – thanks to the borrowed literacy of the landlord's agent – two weeks before. The clerk said, 'That's all there is,' and 'Identification, if you please.'

Em was confused. She said, 'My sister, is she here?' She gave her sister's name again. She held a conversation that made no sense and made the people in the queue short-tempered and amused. The counter clerk put her sister's letter to one side. 'I can't help,' she said. Already she was serving someone else.

Outside again, Em could not find a place to rest and contemplate. 'So this is my life now,' she thought. 'I'm all the Bs – bitched, buggered and bewildered – and far from home!' At least young Victor was asleep again. His mother rolled the end of candle in her hand.

Em walked aimlessly while there was light. She hoped to see her sister on the street. On that first night they slept in stables near the railway yard, but in the morning dogs had sniffed them out and frightened Victor with their barks. Again she walked the streets and looked in all the faces passing by. If she saw women of her sister's age who looked like maids, she stopped them, mentioning her sister's name and asking them for help, advice or work.

'You'll not get work with that,' one woman said, pointing at the top of Victor's nuzzling head. 'What is it? Boy or girl? There's people in this town who'd pay good money for a kid like that. I can find you someone who will give this kid a proper life.' She held Em's arm. 'Come on,' she said. 'I'll take you to a place where you can eat and sleep.' Em had to shout and struggle to get free.

That second night they slept as best they could on sheltered benches at the tramway terminus. The lights were harsh and there was noise from work-gangs cleaning trams. The yardman said she'd have to move, but when he saw the child he let her stay. 'For just one night,' he warned. 'And then you'd better take the baby back to where your people are. A little dot like that won't last five minutes sleeping rough.' Em said she had a sister who would help. She told the man her sister's name and what had happened at the Postal Hall. He shook his head. 'You've no idea,' he said. 'Your sister's just one tiny country bean, buried deep down in the sack. You won't find her by sticking in your hand and pulling ten beans out. This city's big. You've seen the crowds. Your sister, she's as good as dead unless you've got the address of a house.'

Later, he came back. She woke to find him watching her. He had some cold fish and some bread.

'You're quite a pretty girl,' he said, looking more at Victor and Em's breasts than at her face. 'You'd better find some man to take you in. You'd better find a proper father for the child.'

Em shook her head and said she didn't want the bread or fish. She had no appetite. She feared the yardman wanted something in exchange for food. His eyes were flared and restless like a pig in heat. He looked – to use her mother's phrase – as if his heart had slipped below his belt. She closed her eyes and pulled her shawl across her chest. At last she heard the yardman walk away. He had not left the bread or fish behind.

Now, her third day on the streets, she did her best to keep her problems to herself. She did not try to match the gazes of the men and women in her path. She did not seek – or trust – their kindness any more. She sat with Victor in the sun on the steps of the Postal Hall. She'd tried the clerks in *poste restante*. This time a man behind the grill had asked for proof of who she was before he'd check the number that she gave. He had looked at her and Victor as if they both were pigeons of disease. She could not stop the tears. She could not stop them running down her cheeks onto her shawl even when she'd fled the Postal Hall and rested in the sun. What should she do? Seek out the yardman? Sell Victor for the highest sum? Head out of town and find her husband's village once again, beyond the sea-blue fields? Perhaps she ought to step beneath a tram. Or try her luck beneath the hooves and wheels of some fast cart. She was too tough to take these easy routes. In those days life was hard. All life was hard. They raised you then on work, debt, hunger, cold. Three days and nights without a bed in town was better than the seven they had spent walking through the fields and woods. So things were looking up and would improve each day.

She nursed the dream of meeting with her sister once again, but set her daily target low. The first task was to find a place of safety. Then to find a place where they might sleep without fear of men or thieves. And, then, a little food perhaps. A good crisp apple, sweet with sun, was what she most desired. This was the country treat for little girls with tears or for children who'd been good. 'Cheer up, dear Em,' her mother used to say. 'Go on. Go to the shed and get yourself a nice ripe apple from the tub.' Em smiled at this – the memories of her mother and of treats. It must have been the smile and the charm and snugness of Victor at her breast, that caused the two women passing by to pause and match her smile with theirs. They threw a few small coins into Em's spread lap, and smiled again, and walked away. They looked like sisters, plump, modest girls, with shallow caps pinned to their hair and shoes with little heels. The baskets that they carried – the country market kind, woven out of teased bark – were empty. They looked like rich men's maids, like country girls who'd made their lives in town. Em followed them. It seemed the wisest thing to do. They led her through narrowing streets, past mews, and squints and alleyways, beneath the medieval wooden gates, into the merriment of the Soap Market where they – and Em herself – were soon lost in the crowd. If her sister was a maid to some rich man, then surely she would buy her victuals there, thought Em. Besides, she felt at ease and safe amongst the country products and the smells. What could be more innocent than shopping in the market place for food? Ten, twenty times, she thought she saw the plump sisters once again. But all the women looked alike. They seemed to dress the same, and walk in pairs. These were the type of women, as Em had discovered, who would give coins freely for a widow with a child on milk. She knew that this was where her fortune would be made.

That night she joined the others without homes, scavenging for fruit and coins amongst the mats and panniers of the market. She sucked the laxative and discarded fangs of rhubarb stems. She dined on dates and green tomatoes, while Victor made supper out of milk. She knew what she would have to do. At dawn she woke, wet with Victor's urine, and disturbed by cold and the noise of porters, barrows, market girls. She turned her palm up for sympathy and cash. A market trader, fond of children, placed a perfect apple in her palm.

So Victor lived beneath a market parasol for eight, nine months. His mother found it thrown out. Some flower trader, at a guess, had given up on it and bought another. Its wooden pole had snapped in two. Its green and yellow canvas canopy was torn. She made repairs as best she could without materials or tools. She made the most of nothing. Women had to then. A bit of canvas and a broken pole were better quarters than the trenches that their men would occupy when war broke out. Em set up her umbrella at the centre of the market place, between two bars and near the scrubbing stones. There was the flat, damp trunk of a snag tree for back support. There was market waste and mulch to soften cobblestones. Her begging pitch was chosen well. The drunks, the mad women, the wretched ones, the innocents with visions, the dregs and cynics, assembled at the steps of churches, and begged for coins, alms, for Holy Charity, from worshippers, and peni-tents, and wedding guests. The ones with whistles, tricks with fire or balls, stayed on the busy streets and entertained the hangers-out, the tramline queues, the café clientele for cash. Em's kind of beggar, the kind that is the model of what could happen to us all, must be clean – and in the Soap Garden there was running water all day long. Crowds of people, too, with time to spare. The traffic there was mixed: market traders, bar-girls, their customers, the women and their washing, the men who came to drink and talk. No one came there without a little cash. The bars, the girls, the market stalls weren't char-ities. Gratitude was not the bargain that they sought.

So Victor's mother did more than beg. She traded smiles and peace of mind. She did it well. She had a baby to support. The coloured, broken umbrella was the perfect touch. It was what country women used to shield themselves from the rain and sun when they came in to town to sell their flowers or their garlic cloves. Passers-by would look down to see what this woman had for sale. Em's face was hidden by the parasol. Her breasts were on display – with Victor hard at work. The child in need. One hand – the one with a single wedding ring – was resting on her knee palm up. The other pressed the baby to her chest. She marketed herself. She felt no shame. Shame is a family, village thing. It doesn't count for much amongst strangers. Her only fear – and hope – was that her sister would chance by and look beneath the parasol. She did her best to beg with pride. It was not sin, like drink or bed, that had brought her there. She pinned a browning photograph of her husband to the canvas of the parasol with a black silk funeral rosette. It signified, Here is a widow and her child. Look at their man. His death has made them homeless, poor.

What of Victor at this time? Are kids of less than five weeks old so self-engrossed and innocent that nothing in the outside world makes any impact on their lives so long as they are fed and warm and free from wind? The truth is, yes. The only bonding that there is takes place between the nipples and the lips. Victor was the kind of child who bonded to his mother's breast with the tenacity and deliberation of a limpet on a stone. If he was sucking, he was well. Detach his gums, prise him loose with the gentlest finger, and he would imitate a seagull bickering for shrimps, his tiny call – not yet a voice – as querulous and fretful as a dirge.

Em thought this threnody would earn her cash, that Victor singing thinly for the breast would move the hardest passer-by to find a few spare coins. If her child could cry like that so readily she only had to pop her nipples free when people passed and she would earn a fortune in small change.

No one was mean enough, she thought, to close their ears to babies in distress. But she was wrong. We in this city are the sentimental sort. We don't like tragedy. That's why the drunkard at the railway station gates, singing bits of opera in fake Italian and French, and bothering the women with his arias, earned more from begging than the trolley man who'd lost a wife, his mind and both his legs in some forgotten war. To toss some coins in the drunk's old opera hat was to show one's liberality, one's worldliness, one's sense that all was well. To give cash to the trolley man – taken without a word or smile – was to price a life, a leg, a personality. At what? At less than one could spare. The coins clattered on the trolley floor. Enough small change to buy a rind of pork, a two-stop tramway ride, a piece of ribbon for your hair. The coins paid for guilt-free entry to the forecourt and the trains. Except, of course, the gateway where the trolley man lay in wait was the one least used. His naked stumps, his naked hopelessness, made people change their routes. The operatic drunkard got the crowd.

So it was with Em. When she took Victor off the breast, his protests cleared a space around their parasol. The shoppers did not look to see what was for sale. They knew. They heard the baby's screams and kept their eyes away from this private tableau of distress. It would not do to stare. Or smile. Or break the moment with some coins in Em's palm. Besides, what could a coin do for one so young? A coin would not change its life. What should they do then? Search their pockets for a little solid love? Hold out their hands and offer to this pair that spare room, rent-free? That job? That meal? That ticket home? No, Victor's tears – and, here, who will not pause to note the leaden candour of the words? – were of no worth. But what could be more appealing than a baby on its mother's nipple, the two most loved of natural shapes, the infant cheek, the breast? No need to look away from nakedness like that. You could study scenes more intimate in churches or in galleries. Madonna and her Child. The Infancy of Christ. First Born. Indeed, there was a sculpture reproduced on the lower-value silver coins of that time. A woman, Concorde, held an infant to her breast, her tunic open to her waist, her thighs becoming tree trunk, tree bole, the tree becoming undergrowth, becoming Motherland. Here, then, was the sentimental counterpart of comic, operatic drunks. Em and Victor made a wholesome sight when Victor was asleep and on her breast. Coins dropped into the mother's palm or on her shawl were tribute tithes for family life. Em understood. To earn the pity and the cash of citizens she had to seem respectable and, more than that, serene – a living sculpture labelled Motherhood.

2

FOR THOSE MEN WHO were not moved by
Motherhood, Em acted Eve. She wore a mask of gormless
innocence which was as challenging to them as the pouting
and the paint upon the faces of the bar-girls who sold real sex
for cash. The market traders who passed her frequently and
saw the way her expression seemed to fluctuate haphazardly
between Eve and Motherhood thought – preferred to think, in
fact – that Em was none too bright. They said she hadn't got
the sense that God gave lettuce. They labelled her 'The Radish'. That was the nickname that they used for girls red-faced
and odorous and from-the-soil like her. These traders had
good cause to doubt the sharpness of her intellect, besides the
permutations of her face. She muttered to her baby all day
long, and in those slow and well-baked country tones which
stretched the vowels and squashed the consonants and made
the language sound like morse. Yet there was cunning just
below the widow's skin. Alms-givers welcome gormless gratitude. They do not give to people who seem wiser than themselves, no matter whether it be Eve or not. No, Victor's mother
was no fool, despite appearances. A fool would have an empty
palm, but Em's was always slightly curled and buttoned heavily with the copper brown of coinage.

Her looks, of course, were helpful there. She was a radish
with a round and childish face. Her breasts were high and

firm with milk. Her throat and shoulders were vulnerable and bare. Her knees were spread to make her lap a cradle for the child. Her feet and lower legs protruded from her apron skirts with the unselfconsciousness of a small girl sitting in shadow at the harvest edge. Any man who paused to drop some coins in her palm had paid for time to stare at her – though if he stepped too close the parasol would block his view. She did not lift her face to look these men directly in the eye. A look from her would make them hesitate, or return the coins they had found for her in the pockets of their coats. For women, though, the radish turned its chin and caught their eyes and smiled. Most shopping women are too timid and too sociable to fail to match a freely given smile. And having smiled themselves at Em, what could they do? What else but mutter phrases about the weather or the child, and buy escape from smiles and platitudes with coins in Em's palm?

Sometimes the crowds which walked between the market and the garden were too dense for smiles to work. The shoppers simply dropped their eyes and let the beggar woman's beams slip by. But Em soon learnt the trick of targeting her smiles with words. 'God Bless the Cheerful Giver,' she would say. Or 'Lady, Lady!', spoken urgently, as if she'd spotted danger on the street or recognised a family friend. If Em could only stop the first one in a crowd and embarrass her to pause and give, then she could count on gifts in streams. The first fish leads the shoal.

So Victor and his mother lived beneath the parasol by day, and slept at night wherever they could find a place amongst the dozing market baskets or at the back of bars. They were not rich. Of course they were not rich. How could they be on gleanings? But they survived, sustained by charity, by the prospect of Em's sister chancing by, by the certainty that the city would provide abundantly, by the sense of awe they felt at being at the centre of such a boisterous web, by the dislocated optimism of those whose lives are trembling at the gate.

Was Victor happy? So far, yes. He fed contentedly. He slept. His domain was his mother's lap. Her nipples were his toys. But then the muscles strengthened in his neck and arms. He grew bored with suckling. He wanted to lift his head to look around at all the movement and the colours in the streets. He fell back startled from the breast when he heard Em calling out, 'Lady, lady', or when the hubbub of the crowd seemed more eloquent and urgent than the beating of his mother's heart. He found he liked those moments best when he was upright on his mother's knee and she was belching him, separating the suckling oxygen from the milk that he had swallowed and which was causing jousting mayhem in his gut. She had one hand flat on his chest, supporting him. The other tapped and played a gentle bongo on his back between his fragile shoulder-blades. Or else she beat her tune, not with her fingers on his back, but with the cracked and greying candle stub which she would only light again when she had somewhere to call home. Her son's short neck was creased in tidal ripples of baby fat. His mouth was hanging open, waiting for the upward storm of warm and milky wind. Some passing men made clicking noises with their tongues for him, or comic, pouting kisses with their lips. Sometimes a dog ran by. Or older children. Always the market offered entertainment to the child – a porter with teetering crates of onions on his wooden cart, an argument, a snatch of song, some shoving between friends, and, almost constantly by day, the casual, tangled flow and counter-flow of citizens in search of romance, fortune, pleasure, food. At times the street around the parasol was quiet and empty, but then Victor found a butterfly to watch or sharp-edged sunlight winking on a broken neck of glass or the flexing toes of his own feet, or spilt water – parting, joining in its halting, bulbous progress through the cobblestones.

Once he'd belched he would have stayed most happily, his head laid back upon Em's chest, his hands encased in hers, a dozing spectator. But there was money to be earned. His mother's breasts were Victor's lathe, his workbench, the family spinning wheel. Em put her small son to her breasts. She put his mouth onto her nipple and she held him there, whispering and pigeoning into his ear to make him calm. It was a hopeless task. A growing child will not stay calm and supine all day long. A child is put upon this earth to raise its head and stretch its legs and grab. Em sang him lullabies. She told him country tales. She reminisced about her husband, Victor's dad. But Victor did not care. The docile, suckling infant grew less tractable. His stomach became distended and would not clear with belches. His testicles and inner thighs became encrusted with a bitter rash, its scaling plaques and lesions made angrier by the baby's water and his stools. He cried when he was wrapped inside his swaddle clothes. He thrashed his legs and pushed his fists into himself.

Em knew what should be done. A nappy rash is not the plague. It only takes a little air, some white of egg, and patience for the rash to clear. She begged an egg and broke it into the half-skin of a discarded orange. She put tiny poultices of orange pith, glistening with albumen, onto her son's sore thighs and testicles. She stretched his legs and let him lie, naked from the waist down, across her lap. The sun and breeze were free to sink and curl between his legs. Young Victor – his flaming gonads patched in orange pith – looked as if the madders and the ochres of a peeling fresco had settled in his lap. So much for Eve and Motherhood. This sculpture was not good for trade. Em's outstretched hand was hardly troubled by the weight of coins now. Nobody caught her eye. The squeamish men no longer paid to stare at Victor on Em's breast.

The remedy was simpler than eggs. The problem was that Em was eating too much fruit. Her diet was the oranges, the grapes, the grapefruit, the tomatoes and the apples that the more familiar shoppers and traders tossed to her as they passed by. She dined on that. Then for supper she fed herself on what she gleaned amongst the cobbles, the fruit discarded, bruised, mislaid in the Soap Market. She fed herself on citrus, pectins, fructose. Her waters were as tart and acid as peat dew. Her milk was too. It passed through Victor acrimoniously. It turned his gut. It chafed and scalded his most tender skin. Feeding made him restless on his mother's breast. He tugged her nipples in his gums. He tried to bite. And then Em had a problem of her own. Her son had made one nipple sore. The nipple cracked, and was not helped to heal by all the acid in her milk. She would not let her child feed on that side. She only let him suck milk from the right. But he was bigger now and wanted more. One breast was not enough. He'd passed six months. His mouth and stomach were prepared for solid food – some mashed banana mixed with milk, some peas, potatoes, stewed apple, grain. But Em was frightened of the day when Victor would renounce the breast. She liked the way he clung to her to feed. She simply pushed her child onto her

93

one good breast and hoped his rash, her crack, would heal before the cash dried up.

Em's fruity undernourishment and her fatigue at coping with the child alone reduced her flow of milk still more. Again the baby lost all interest in the outside world. He sucked all day, but still he was not satisfied. He was tired and fretful now, at night. He would not sleep for long. He whimpered and he dozed. His mother's breasts were irritants to him. She would not let him suck the one; the other one was nearly dry. Em was in pain. Her cracked nipple had become infected through neglect. She was feverish. A nut-sized abscess had formed amongst the milk-ducts of her breast. It blushed and throbbed. The pain was memorable.

'I'm out of oil,' she told herself, picking at the peeling fossil slates which were her nails.

Together Em and Victor rocked away the nights and days. Em's careful presentation of her baby and herself was neglected. The radish face turned yellow-white. The good health of the countryside did not survive the hardness of the town. She had no plan to make a fresh escape. She sank into the shade beneath the parasol and called out above the fretful cries of Victor, 'Please help. Please help. My baby's dying.' She wept. She tried to seize the trouser legs, the skirts of passers-by. She mimed an empty stomach. She put her hand onto her heart. She tried abuse. She called out words she had not known before she came to town.

It did not work. The rich were blind to noisy poverty. The people hurried by. The crazy woman with the parasol would win no hearts like that. She had trembled at the gate. Now the gate was closing on them both. The city was about to lock them in a cell of hunger, sickness and despair. And then their fortunes changed. Em's sister, Victor's aunt, was sent by chance to rescue them.

3

SHE WAS NO RICH man's maid. She was a beggar, just like Em. And worse. The aunt had lost the kitchen job for which she'd come to town three years before. She'd not excelled at the skivvying which – when her widowed father died – the Village Bench had hoped would 'quieten' her. High hopes indeed for such a squally girl. Her face, and tongue, had not found favour with her employer's cook who had taken her teenage dreaminess, her wilful tawny hair, her lack of tact, her pockmarked forehead and cheeks, as insolence.

The hope had been that Aunt could – quickly, cheaply – be transformed from hayseed into scullion. But she was not the curtsy-kowtow kind and had no kitchen skills. 'She couldn't boil up water for a barber,' cook had said. 'That girl's as much use in this kitchen as a cat.' Instead, she was the sort who saw the city as a place for play not work. Unlike the country working day the city day was ruled by clocks. It had its shifts for work and meals and sleep. And there were shifts when Aunt was free to play. What did she care if cook found single, errant, tawny hairs entwined in dough or curling like a filamentary eel in 'madam's' soup? Why all the fuss? Nobody had died from swallowing one hair. And what if there were egg bogeys between the tines of breakfast forks? Or if the skillet smelled of pork? So much the better if the skillet smelled of pork! Anyone with sense or appetite would take a fold of bread and 'wipe the pig's behind'. She and her older, married sister, Em, fought for such a treat when they were young.

Aunt simply could not understand the odd proprieties, the niceties, of bourgeois city life where more was wasted than consumed, where laughter, yawns and stomach wind shared equal status, swallowed, hidden, stifled by a hand. She did not like 'indoors'. But she adored the bustle and the badinage of streets, the intimacy of crowds, the hats, the clothes, the trams, the liberty. She had it to herself once in a while – when she was sent by cook to purchase extra eggs or vegetables, when every second Saturday she had a half-day off, when – once, at night – she climbed the back-yard wall and walked till dawn in those parts of the city where lamps – and spirits – were rarely dimmed. On that occasion Aunt was met by her employer's dogs when she returned. They took her for a thief and, though they knew her well enough from all the times she'd favoured them with kitchen slops, they were too dumb or mischievous to let her clamber back into the kitchen yard. Their barking called the Master and the police. For cook this was the final straw. She did not find it likely that the girl had just been 'walking' as she claimed.

'You country girls are all the same,' she said. ' "Bumpkins do not good burghers make." ' She did not say what she had told her employers, that Aunt was mad, 'a leaking pot'. She paid Aunt off with the exact train fare – one-way – to the village of her birth, only fifteen months after she had fled it for the prospects of the town. Aunt spent the train fare on a hat.

She skipped around the bars and restaurants quite happi-ly. She wore her hat – a high-crowned, deep-brimmed cloche in straw with dog-rose sprigs in felt. It was the fashion for that year amongst young women of a cheerful disposition. It masked the pockmarks on her forehead and made her seem more winsome than she was. She doffed her hat at groups of men who sat on the patios of bars or on the terraces of restaurants. They seemed so bored and so keen to be amused. She only had to smile or comic-curtsy or spin her hat around upon her open hand, to earn a little cash. It was so easy to take money or a meal off men and still stay good.

There were a dozen country girls like her who worked the same neighbourhood of the city and who shared a two-room attic in a tenement near the Soap Market, in the Woodgate district. The Princesses they were called, sardonically, by the poor families and the labourers who inhabited the lower floors. They'd all lost jobs as maids or kitchen girls and had finished on the streets. Some stole. Some sold themselves to men. Some earned a little from the sale of matches or doing fetch-and-carry for the posh, frail ladies who took strong waters in the smart salons. Aunt stuck to begging. She was good at it. And soon she had enough each day to pay the pittance rent for a small corner in the Princesses' attic rooms. There was no proper light or water there, or any stove for cooking. But there was camaraderie and candles. We know that poverty's not fun, but if you are young and poor in company then shame, and lack of hope, and loneliness do not increase the burdens on your back. Sharing nothing or not much is easier than sharing wealth.

So Aunt was happy with her life. There was no washing up. No slops. No punctilious, grumpy cook. No silver breakfast forks. They shared – like only women will – their daily gains, their city spoils, their swag. The only privacy they had – if, say, they wished to sit unnoticed on the pot – was to hide behind the lines of washing, strung across the rooms, or to wait for darkness. But why hide away to pee, when peeing in full view of all your friends can cause such mirth and raucous joviality? 'Hats off,' they used to say to Aunt, whose cloche would rarely leave her head. 'It's impolite to pee like that in the presence of Princesses.' They'd wait until they heard the spurt of urine in the bowl and then they'd say, 'Hats off. Stand up . . . and take a bow!' Or 'Sing, sing! And show your ring.' The communal laughter of these Princesses was laughter with no victim and no spite.

Aunt learnt the tricks of begging from their attic talk at night, as each described the day they'd had; how men's brains were unfastened with their braces; how careless waiters were with tips; which restaurant chefs would give a back-step meal to any girl who'd volunteer to mop the floor. You'd eat the meal – then run; what places were the worst and best for palming cash from strangers. She learnt how just a dab of zinc and vinegar could make a girl look feverish. It didn't work with men, but women – older ones – would pay to make you go away. She learnt a gallery of beggars' faces, how to slide her tongue between her teeth and lips to look the simpleton, how to fake the single floating eye of the insane, how picking noses is just as good as picking pockets for getting cash if it is done on restaurant terraces and in a childish, not a vulgar way.

So she did well on city streets. She begged and importuned enough to count herself – by country standards – well set up. She was much plumper than the girl who'd skivvied in the kitchen. She had her hat as talisman and her Princesses for family. She did not think about the coming day – or much about the day just passed. She liked to place her hat upon her head and wander streets as if they were country lanes and she was simply searching for free fruit. She never tired of putting out her hand or challenging – this was her favourite trick – the drinking men in bars to toss and land a coin in the canyon brim of her straw hat.

Despite the drama of the hat, she was an ill-built, scruffy girl. The pits and craters on her face were blessings in disguise. They kept the men at bay. She did not have her sister's looks. But what she had was something better, rarer in those days than mere good looks. She had a sense of unembarrassed self-esteem. She liked the way she was. So when she heard her sister calling from beneath her green and yellow parasol, 'Please help. Please help. My baby's dying,' Aunt was not the least put out. She'd heard a hundred stories of the saddest kind of why and how her Princesses had fallen on hard times. Tough tales that made her wonder how animals, as frail as adolescents are, could surface with such buoyancy from depths so cold and bitter. She guessed that there was death in Em's own tale or illness or the loss of work. She was not shockable. It seemed to fit, not flout, the patterns of the world that Em, like her, should end up in this place. Fate – the fate of being born a country woman in those days – was not Coincidence, nor was it Chance. The poor take trams. They travel on fixed lines. It's only the rich that go at will in carriages.

Aunt stooped below the parasol and matched her sister with the voice she'd heard. They were the same, except that Em was poorer, thinner than a head of corn that had been stripped of ears. Aunt knew – from just one glance – that her sister was forlorn and ill and underfed. She heard the whimpers of the child. Her niece or nephew, she presumed. She felt content to have a sister once again, to be an aunt. She knew that she could help.

So Em became the oldest of the Princesses – and Victor was their little Prince. Most of the girls were glad to have a child at first. They passed him to and fro and petted him as if he were a cat. They teased him with their little fingers in his mouth and marvelled at the power of his gums and lips. They loved to belch him on their knees, his fingers wrapped so bonelessly round theirs, or to press their noses to his head and smell the honey-must of cradle cap. They kissed the baby dimples on his arms, his back, his chin, and called him 'Little rogue' and sang 'Dimple in chin, Devil within'. They made noises like you hear in zoos from those determined that the parakeets should talk. But Victor was in no mood for games. You see, already he was malcontent, and not because of his acid rash alone. He wanted food. Warm lips and murmurs do not serve supper. He tried to push his hand between the buttons of their dresses. He wet and creased the fabric of their blouses with his mouth.

'They're all the same,' a Princess said. 'Men only want one thing.'

Aunt found some floorboard for Em and Victor below the sloping attic roof. She scrounged a little matting and some cloth for blankets. Aunt carried Victor to the street, and within twenty minutes had returned with a topless conserve jar containing tepid mashed potato, manac beans and gravy which she had begged at a restaurant's back door.

'This kid's a gold mine.' She crushed the beans and made a mixture with the potatoes and gravy. 'There's plenty here for all of us,' she said, though softly so that 'all of us' meant Victor, Aunt and Em. She made stewballs in her palms, four large ones the size and shape of eggs, and smaller pellets for her nephew, Victor. His first solid meal. He was almost nine months old. His first milk teeth were winking through the gum.

Together they poked the food into his mouth. It was too dry for him. He coughed. And when he closed his mouth the food was squeezed between his lips and fell into his mother's hand. He did not cry, though. This was not distress. He simply did not have the knack of swallowing such lumps. Perseverance won the day. The sisters had a score of fingers to keep the food inside the baby's mouth. Fingertips are like enough to nipples for Victor to be confused and suck. The sucking did the trick. For every scrap that slithered out across his chin a small amount went down his throat. His sucking dragged the gravy from the mixture. He liked the smell and salt. He had his fill. He slept – for once – without his mother's breast.

Em told her story of how she'd come to town, and how the town had almost beaten her. Then Aunt replied with hers, and how the town was better than a friend. It took more care of waifs and strays than any village in the land. 'If that weren't so,' she said, 'the countryside would be the place for girls like us. The trees and fields would overflow with widows and orphans. But look around you, Em. Look on the streets. It's cities take us in.' And then she added, 'City air makes free.'

They talked like artisans at lunch, about the problems of the begging trade. Their jobs were like all jobs. Why should they be abject? They had their colleagues, rivals, clientele. They had their working rituals, too – and the pride and purpose that such employment brings. The problem was that Em's breasts were nearly dry, and still too sore for comfort.

Giving solid food to Victor might give them time to heal – but would the child return to the breast when he and Em were begging once again?

'When Victor isn't feeding,' Em explained, 'I don't make money on the streets.'

'If that's the only problem you've got, then you're the lucky one!' said Aunt. She took her sister by the hand. 'Just sleep,' she said. 'I told you, Victor's gold to us. A baby at the breast earns cash. You don't need milk for that. You don't need spit to stick your tongue inside your boyfriend's ear.'

At dawn, while Em and Victor were still asleep, Aunt put on her hat and went down to the bars where the traders, warehousemen and porters had coffee-and-a-shot before they started work. She found the comic angle for her hat. She wore her sweetest, daftest smile. She stood against the walls of bars and called for pitch-and-toss. She'd show the men her plump and mottled knees if anyone could throw a coin in her hat. The man who stepped up to her and softly dropped a coin in, imagined he had got the best of Aunt. She showed her knees. He departed poorer than he'd come, but she, quite soon, had earned enough for food. She bought a bruised banana, cheap. A fresh, warm turban of bread. A bottle of rootwater. A twist of honey. Cheese. She was a cheerful sight upon the street. She skipped like someone half her age. She took the stairs two at a time. She found a dancing path between the sleeping Princesses, and spread the breakfast on the boards. She broke the bread and cheese. She snapped the banana into three, and mashed one third with rootwater in a spangled cup until it ran like gruel and was thin enough for Victor to swallow.

She woke up Em and then woke Victor too. He was not ready for the day. He wailed like a damp yew log in fire. She pinched him on his arm until tears dropped heavily and he was wide awake and mutinous. Em tried to push her sister back, but Aunt was stronger. She lifted Victor by his arms and held him tightly at her side. He beat her with his wrinkled fists. She said, 'Now watch!' She undid the loops of her woollen top, and pushed her clothes aside. She put her index finger in the twist of honey and wiped it on her tiny nipple. The honey sagged like candle grease. Aunt pinched Victor one more time. His voice made pigeons fretful on the roof. Aunt put him firmly on her breast. The silence was as sudden and as comic as a burst balloon. He pressed his mouth and tongue onto her skin. He sucked and made the noises that children make when drinking juice through straws. 'You see? He doesn't need a knife and fork,' she said. 'Or milk.' She outlined how they would share the child. They'd work the boy in shifts. 'Four tits beat two,' she said. 'Ask a cow. And honey's got the edge on milk. Ask bees.'

Em watched her baby nuzzling at her sister's breast, as fickle when it came to food as adults are with love. He threw his head from side to side and tried to get a proper grip on this modest nipple, this impermeable and unswollen breast, this honeycomb. He was engrossed and sweetly satisfied and, for the moment, wanted nothing else. Em almost wished that she and Victor were still marooned beneath the parasol.

4

SO THIS WAS VICTOR'S life. Two lives, in fact. While other children learnt to crawl and pick up what they found as if the world was all a toy and theirs, he shared two women's breasts. His gums grew numb on honey. His nose was flattened by their ribs.

Em still preferred to work the market place. She knew the faces there and all the odours were the odours of the country-side, congested and compressed. She'd lost the parasol. Its pole had ended up on someone's fire. Its cheerful canopy was ripped and jettisoned. But she sat cross-legged for harvesting ('We're harvesters. We do not beg,' her sister had said) in the usual spot, between the garden and the market, her back against the flat trunk of her tree. It was a comfort when she saw crops of the class and quality that her birth village had produced – 'yellows' from the potato fields, carrot clumps, onion sets, the stewing roots, sweet dumpling pumpkins, the dusty shingle of the beans – all so familiar from the days when she and all the other village kids had been dragooned to join the harvesters so that the crop could be brought in quickly and at its best.

She'd known, she would know still, all villagers apart from the shape of their arses. A bean field when the beans were splitting was a field of arses facing bluntly upwards as villagers played midwife with the soil. A potato field was much the same. The horse plough turned the soil – and then the village bums were higher than the noses for the day as harvesters with trowels sought out the timid 'yellows' in the crevices and punctures of the soil. These townies only dined on such fresh crops because the country folk were not too proud or idle to stick their arses in the air. Em slowly had convinced herself – with Aunt's help – that coins given to her now were payment for the hours that they'd spent as girls, unpaid, with blackened hands and aching backs amongst the produce of their fields.

She harvested the market place, less passionately, less urgently, than she had done before her sister arrived. She had a place to sleep, a family, a group of friends, somewhere to wash and eat, a simple route to and from her work, free time. She felt no different from the other working women in the market place and garden, the waitresses and salesgirls, the prostitutes – that is to say, she felt as bored, inured and dutiful as anyone who has to labour for their pay.

While Aunt slept late, Em took the morning and the midday shift because those were the times when people came to shop for vegetables and fruit, the times when the Soap Market and the Soap Garden were most profligate and careless with their cash. She served her time, with Victor at her breast. She had a little milk and honeyed nipples to keep her outsized baby still. And if he tried to raise his head? Or twist to see the world pass by? She only had to wrap his head inside her shawl for him to quieten or to doze. The darkness was a drug for him. His pulse was slower underneath the cloth than when his ears and eyes were naked to the clamour and the city light. If he cried, Em simply hushed him with a dab of honey on her breast, and murmured country comforts to him with her lips

ARCADIA

pressed to his cheek or ear. 'The squeaky door gets all the oil,'
she'd say. 'The gabby cat gets cream.' She found rhymes and
games to put him on the breast. 'Ring the bell,' she said, and
tugged the wayward quiff of hair on Victor's head. Then,
'Knock the door.' She drummed her fingers on his forehead.
'Lift the latch': she pinched his nose and – that's the nature of
the nose – his jaw dropped down, his mouth agape. 'And walk
right in!' She placed her honeyed nipple on his lower lip.

In the early afternoon Victor's skipping aunt would come
with bread or cheese to share with any fruit or salad that Em
had harvested that morning. There was no food for Victor
then. He only fed at night. 'The hungry mongrel does not
bark,' Aunt said. She made these nonsense phrases up, to
mock her sister, to mock herself. She liked to play the country
muse for those foolish men in bars who'd pay for hollow
'wisdoms' such as that. She was not right about the hungry
mongrel – but she was wise to caution against feeding Victor
while he worked. A sated child will not take honey. A sated
child cannot be blackmailed by the promise of a meal. It's
hungry circus seals that sit obediently on tubs and balance
beachballs on their snouts. The more they are rewarded with a
fish, the more they flap and slither out of line.

When Aunt and Em had eaten, Victor was passed on. His
face was pressed against the younger breasts, where the honey
was not mixed with the blood-hot residues of milk, but where
the torso flesh was deeper, softer, less discrete. Aunt tied him
to her with a sash which passed around her neck and round
her waist. His body was not long, but long enough by now to
make Em's sister stoop a little from the toppling ballast of
his weight. Em was now free to walk back to their attic rooms
or buy a little food or bring the family washing to the

public washing square at the centre of the Soap Garden, or
sleep.

Her sister carried Victor to her usual haunts, the bars, the
restaurants, the tea salons, of the medieval streets to the east of
the station yard. She wore Victor like she wore her hat, an
accessory to her outfit and her act. She'd show her knees – at
least – to anyone who'd pitch-and-toss some silver in her hat
or place a coin 'on my baby's cheek'. If any man seemed slow
to search for change, she'd wink at all his friends and ask,
with the innocence of a music-hall soubrette, 'What's wrong
with him? Has he got a snake in his pocket, or what?' She'd
lean over dining tables with Victor gummed to her breast like
a bloated termite at a grape, and invite the diners – loosened
by the wine or beer – 'to place a silver coin on my baby's eyes
if you want fortune and good health'. It sounded like an
age-old rite. In fact, she'd dreamed it up. If young Victor
raised his head, to bare his honeyed teeth and scare off custom
with his cries, then Aunt would knock his head back to the
breast with the speed and firmness of a factory foreman, bent
on keeping working children's noses to the loom or press or
lathe. She was not hard. She simply liked the way she was,
and wished to keep it so. What sort of kindness would it be –
to whom? – if she behaved towards the boy as if he were a
rich man's son whose duties only stretched from play and food
to sleep? What money would she harvest on the street with
Victor in her care, if Victor were the normal child, allowed to
crawl and scream and play with stones exactly as he wished, if
Aunt was just another 'mother' in the town? Where was the
sentiment, the plaintiveness in that? Who'd pay for such
mundanity? So trading says, The child must suck the breast.
Six coins out of ten are lost unless the child is on the breast.

So, Child on Breast! That was the requisition of the working day.

It was not fair that Victor did not seem a willing volunteer in this. 'This kid's a gold mine,' Aunt had said. He kept the sisters fed and clothed. He kept them decent, free from sin. They did not have to steal or prostitute themselves or find thin comforts and escape in drink, while Victor was still small. They did not have to learn the trade of *dipping* – picking pockets, that's to say – while Victor's tiny grazing head was eloquent enough to make hard men and stony women pick their own pockets of small change.

They used the child as bait, it's true. Put crudely and unadorned like that, it makes the sisters less than kind. But *Less than Kind* is not the same as *Without Love*. He was their 'little blessing'; their meal-ticket, too. They loved him for the gift he gave them: he saved them from the grinding molars of the city which seized on women very much like Aunt and Em and made them old and sick and spiteful within days. Imagine Em and Aunt without a child. No need. Just think of all the country girls who lived and begged and starved alone in cities such as ours, across the world, in those dead days before the rich bred consciences, before the telephone, the car, the welfare cheque, the safety net, the thawing of the civic heart. The lucky ones kept jobs. They laboured over stoves. They scuffed their knees in cooling clinkers as they raked out grates at dawn. Perhaps they flirted with a stable hand or – more ambitiously – exchanged embraces with madam's chauffeur. Perhaps they fell in love and, if their half-days coincided with their sweetheart's – rare chance, indeed – they walked unfettered for an hour, embraced by city crowds and understanding all too well that this was the best that life in towns would offer them, that there was worse awaiting them, if they should lose their looks or tempers or good luck. They could be roofless, empty-gutted, and with no embraces to exchange except those given to their own rough knees, at night.

So why should Aunt and Em not count themselves as blessed in having Victor? Why should they not take care to put him to good use, and love him still, and love him all the more? They liked the independence that he gave. They did not know – he did not know – that they had robbed him of his liberty, that their ribcages were for him two sets of prison bars, their arms his warders, their breasts his sedatives.

They went about their business, dawn till dusk, and ploughed a life. Quite soon – within a year and a half, when Victor was three, with teeth – they had harvested enough to move downstairs, below the attic rooms where the changing cast of Princesses had made the sisters ill at ease. They rented one small room in a crowded family apartment. It was their own. There was a tap and a small coal stove that they could use in the raised courtyard at the back. There was a communal but a proper toilet too, in an outhouse. The sisters took their turn in emptying the 'honey can' when it was full. Was this the 'citizenry' that they sought? There was no time to ask. There was no time to sit like sisters, face to face, and knit a conversation from the warming wool of gossip, hope and love. Em had to be at work before the traders took their breakfasts in the bars. Aunt had to be at work until the restaurants had closed and all the rich and drunk had gone back home. So Victor grew weaker, older, a city child whose landscape was all ribs and cloth and honeyed, female flesh. The stones and mayhem of the street were ever at his back, a hidden world imagined only from its hums and dins and choruses.

What does a small boy know, a child that – by this time –
is barely four? A toddler who has yet to crawl? A little
smothered lad? A boy who is trained to do nothing but drape
and nuzzle like a bean-sized joey in its mother's pouch? How
could young Victor tell that this routine of facing flesh all day
was not normality? He was no revolutionary in bud, no mystic
with a notion of a patterned world. He was just worm – a
mouth, an arse, a readiness to bend. He sought the softest
earth, the warmest way, the stone that had no jags, the
twilight safety of the breast. He had no choice. They'd got him
trained, just like a dog. He knew that if his head went up and
turned towards the lights, a hand much stronger than his head
would push him back. He knew that if he spat the nipple from
his mouth and raised his chin to cry he would not get what he
was crying for, unless he wanted pinches on his legs or Aunt
to hold his nose.

He had no general sense of smell. The cloying odours of
the honey and the herby alkalescence of the breast blanked out
the city smells, the horses and the fruit, the men with pipes,
the scent, the woodsmoke, the urine and the puddled rain. His
eyes were clinkered with the grit of too much sleep. The
underlids were sore from lack of air and exercise. They did not
focus well in light – and streamed at night when he was fed
with solids in the oval, orange thrall of candlelight. His legs
and arms had not grown strong. They'd had no chance to
punch and kick the air. His hands were good for nothing
needing pull or grip. He lived for sound alone. His mouth was
sealed – but his ears were free and open to the world. He
knew the market cries, the trundle of a porter's cart, the curses
of the men weighed down by baskets of crops, the whistles of
a happy man. He knew the tucks and folds of Em's sweet

murmurs from the challenge and the bounciness of Aunt's street voice. He knew them, but could not clothe them with a shape or form. They were just sounds to him. Sound is air made tangible. No one flourishes on air alone.

As he got older, heavier, so Em and Aunt got tired of harvesting the streets. It was less fun, living in their shrunken home, away from all the toughness and the jollity of the Princesses above. The sisters got on well enough because they hardly met, because they hardly talked. And just as well. If they had met and talked more frequently they would have found what many siblings find when they have fled the nest, that sharing parents is no guarantee that temperaments are also shared. The only thing they did as family was sleep together, sharing mats, with Victor in between. Their bodies were the rails of Victor's cot.

Aunt took the boy onto the streets with less enthusiasm as he grew older, as he passed four. He weighed too much. His body was too long; when he was 'feeding' his feet found footholds on her knees. It made no sense to carry him, but Aunt was not prepared to sit with Victor on her lap all day, a fixture on some restaurant steps or at the entrance to a bar, waiting for the harvest to make its way to her. She was the sort who liked to move about, to have a stage, to work (she said) 'my mouth and not my bum'. She tried to keep him entertained, yet keep him also blind and nuzzling at her chest. She had not learnt the sentimental skills of entertaining kids. They liked crude noises, little nonsense rhymes, and songs with simple choruses. What kind of child would understand or like Aunt's running commentary on the world, the adult jokes, the cynicism of her words as she earned money on the streets?

'This one's a soft touch,' she would say, as she – with

Victor held aloft – approached a woman sitting, waiting, at a table in the garden of a tea salon. 'Look at that coat! She's good for a fifty at the very least.' And then, 'A twenty! God, she's tight. Look at her little walk. You'd think her bum was made of tin. Her boyfriend's out of luck tonight for sure . . .'

Or else, 'Hey! This fellow's giving me the eye. Suck, Victor, suck. It turns 'em on. Hold tight. I'll give my hat a little twirl. And show my teeth . . . Aha! He's got his rhubarb up. What did I say? Two fifties and a wink. I bet his wife don't know he's got "expenses" in the town like me. She'd have a fit if she could see her little chap's so loose with cash.' Or else, 'Oh dearie dear, here's a fellow looks as if he's wee'ed on nettles and doesn't like the pot-pourri. His lady's stood him up, I bet, or else his boss has stood him down. "Hey mister! Put some silver on the baby's eye. Whatever's wrong will turn out right!" Well, well, we're not surprised. He'd rather that we went away. It would appear he does not wish to give to charities like us.' Or (Aunt's step and manner quickened as she saw men outside a bar), 'Smiles on parade. This lot are drunk enough to spit cash in my hat!'

The truth is, Victor grew to like his aunt's brash tones, despite his inability to understand the words. He liked the way she walked the streets and joined in badinage and arguments and helped herself – and him – to uneaten titbits from restaurants. He began to lift his head more often now or find a sideways view onto the world of streets and bars. Aunt did not care enough to push him back to feed. She'd tired of having sticky honey on her blouse, of having this stretched infant invade her clothes. Life was more comic and more profitable if she just put him down inside a restaurant gate and let him topple under waiters' feet while she did routines with her tongue and hat. Here was an education of a kind. He learnt about the legs of chairs, and shoes. And once – the final straw – he learnt that tablecloths could move, if tugged. He learnt, too, what fun it was to have a bowl of lukewarm noodles smash onto the floor. He'd never had a toy so wonderful as noodles and the broken bowl. The mistress of the restaurant, of course, was not charmed by Victor's play, or by the mess of tablecloth and food. 'I do not care to see you back in here,' she told Aunt, as Victor draped the noodles round his fingers. 'Not unless you're eating *à la carte*. Get off our premises. Remove yourselves. Go back into the haystack where you belong. No beggars here. Understand? If you don't want to eat, stay on the street.'

She took Aunt by the arm and pushed her towards the doorway.

'And don't forget the kid,' she said. 'You shouldn't have a kid. It's not his fault. Look at the state of him! What kind of person lets their little boy crawl on the floor like that? You shouldn't even have a kid if you can't live respectably . . .'

'Alright,' said Aunt, to stifled laughter from the clientele, as Victor stretched the noodles in his hands, as Victor squashed the noodles on his legs. 'No need to work up blisters on your lips.'

'That could have been a bowl of soup,' Em said, when Aunt recalled their escapades that night. 'You could have scalded him!' The time had come, it seemed to Aunt, when her sister was a hindrance in her life. Victor, too. He had lost her more than she could earn if she were on her own. At four, at almost five, the boy was far too big for comfort. More frequently she failed to turn up at the market place to take the child off Em. Or else she said, 'Why don't you keep the kid and stay here longer? You'll get more. You're his proper mum, and people aren't fooled by me. Not any more.'

So Victor lost the chance he'd had with Aunt to lift his head more frequently, to glimpse the world with one eye shut, to study feet and floors. He was back, full-time, where he belonged, an outsized infant on his mother's breast. He was confined again.

5

AND WHAT OF EM? How did she feel? How did she fill her time? She thought of nothing else but getting home, though *home* was not the five-by-five she shared with Aunt, but the sagging country cottage with a yard and thatch and pigs where she herself was raised, or the saddle-maker's rented workshop where she had snubbed her husband's candle out. Just as Victor came to live on fictions of the countryside, so Em looked back upon the village she had known. She made a tinselled paradise of it. It was the market place transformed, the ranks of vegetables, the fruit, strewn loosely in arcadia. It was a world where everything was ripe and colourful and sweet and free. It was a buffed and shiny version of the village she had known before her husband had – both country phrases – *earth as eyelids*, and his *eternal freehold on a narrow strip of land.*

How wonderful the city had once seemed, how promising. But now she felt that she had reached her highest rung and that her city life was in descent. How long would it be before she was as blunted by the foraging for food and cash as those other mothers she had met? The ones who hired their children out. For what? They dared not ask. The ones who used creams and grease and face ointments to make their kids seem daft or ill or menacing. The ones who kept their ageing babies on the breast by stunning them with pods of opium or mandrax tea.

A country beggar such as her must have good looks or youth or, at least, a helpless infant to hook the passers-by. She'd lost her looks. Her hair was now as lifeless as the leaf tuft on a pulled beetroot. Her clothes sat on her like a saddle on a goat's back. Em was so thin – said Aunt, who had a phrase for everything – that her belly-button and her back-bone kissed, and squeaked. She'd lost her youth, as well. Five years and more of city life could take the paint off carriages or stunt a country oak, make flowers grey, drain country faces of their rosy brightness and etch in lines as ploughs put furrows in a field. She'd still got Victor. What use would he be when he grew? He was only helpless now because she and beggar-ing had kept him so. How long before he turned his back on her and said, 'Enough's enough. I've spent too long already in your lap. I'm going to open my eyes and stretch my legs and see this city for myself.'

Small children ran past Em when she was begging in her usual spot, children who were younger than Victor but already had loud voices and strong legs and who were never still. Yet Victor, as he aged, moved with less frequency, not more. He was inert, as if these years of falsifying on his mother's breast had robbed him of pluck.

Em knew that you could train or trick a chicken to lay down dead, as motionless as stone. She'd seen it done when she was young. It was a common village trick. You pushed the chicken to the ground. You held its wings. You pressed its beak into the dust, and drew a hard and short and rapid line in coal, or chalk, or channelled in the soil, out from its beak end. The hen was hypnotised. It was geometrically transfixed. It could not lift its beak clear of the line. You had to rap the chicken's beak to make it stand again and take part in the world. They said that without this liberating rap upon its beak the chicken would just fade away, pressed to the dust by weights that could not be seen or touched. What should Em do to lift the weights from Victor's head? She feared that he would fade away as well, made weak and thin by too much breast and too much mother's lap, his rigid, geometric life. Her only remedy – given that to stay in town meant begging could not end – was to retrace the journey out of town. To walk back down the boulevards until the tram tracks reached the turning gear, and metalled roads grew narrower and rutted, and drains were ditches, and gas streetlamps no longer held their sway amongst the stars or repelled the flimsy light of dawn.

'The first thing you'll see beyond the blue of manac beans,' she told her son, her palm outstretched, his hands both tucked and curled beneath her shawl, 'is how our village seems to have a mind that's all its own. The river there, it doesn't run fast and straight, not like the drains and culverts of the city do. The river takes its time. It's like a snoozer snake. That's the slowest snake there is. It coils between the fields so slowly that you never see it move. Or else it moves, but only when our backs are turned, at night perhaps, on days when it is raining pips and pods and we are kept indoors. Except your father never stayed indoors. He used to love the rain and stand in it. To get the smell of leather out, he said. He'd wash the leather and the tannin out of him with rain, and let it run off down the gutters of the lane into the snoozer snake, then downriver till the smell and dye on him was swept right out to sea. That's what he said, "Right out to sea," though we were nowhere near the sea. I loved it when your father spoke like that. It made the sea seem ours. It smelt like the saddles that your father made.'

Em told Victor what fun they had – would have – in fields, at harvest time, with all the fattest rabbits, the lizards and the snakes trapped in the last stands of the corn, how captured rabbits could be skinned and salted for the pot, how lizards could be raced or made to shed their tails, how harmless snakes could cause distress when dropped in people's laps or hidden in a grandma's drawer. She told him how the packers used to – for a laugh – put a snoozer in the top of apple barrels and send them both to market. 'To this Soap Market here maybe,' she said. They'd laugh themselves as wet as cress at what the market men would do when they dipped in their hands to pull out pippins and reinettes and found the fleshy, yellow fruit of snake.

She told Victor, too, some other time when he demanded 'Village Talk', how he had come about.

'We thought you up,' she said, 'one Sunday afternoon.'

It was September and the mushrooms on the beech cobs were getting high and tasty. 'Your Dad and me went out to fill a basket. And then – we'd only been married for two months – we had, you wouldn't understand, a kiss and cuddle there and then. It had to be that time because I know that when we took the mushrooms back we found a birth-bug in amongst them. That's a sign, for sure, that you'll get fat with child. Your Dad hung a key on a string above my tummy. It swung clockwise, that's how we knew you were a boy. Anticlockwise is for girls. We picked on Victor as your name straight away. You never were an *it* to us; you were always a *he*. You always had a name. Though your grandad on your father's side – he thought he knew a thing or two. He said it had to be a girl, anti-clockwise was for boys, we were mud-dled up. He got a pair of scissors and a knife. He hid them underneath two bits of cloth on two kitchen stools. He put the stools side by side right in the middle of the scullery. He called me in. He said sit down. Your Dad was there. Your aunt was? . . . no, she'd left already for the maiding job in town. Your grandfather said, "Select a stool, the one that seems the best for you, the one that's calling you by name. Go on, sit down." I sat down on the scissor stool. "That settles it," he said. "The baby's going to be a girl. The knife's a boy. The scissors are for girls." They neither of them got to see you born. Both dead. His father first, then yours. When you were born I saw the key was wiser than the stool. I dreamt one night your grandad came back from the dead to see the baby girl. He got a shock. He saw your little dinkle there. I said, "What kind of clockwise girl is that, she's got a knot between her legs?" I gave your thing a little push. "What's that then, Pa?" "I wouldn't know," he said, and then, "I wouldn't want it on my eyelid as a wart." '

She told these stories to her son. He took them in, eyes shut, laid out across her lap. He did not understand the half of what she said, a quarter of the words. What could it mean, the key was wiser than the stool? That knives are boys and scissors girls? And rain was pips and pods? And sea was saddle? A normal child of four or five would think it all a strange and – finally – a tiresome game, to bend words in a way that was confusing and not funny. Kids of that age would know the shorthand of the street, the beg and tell of play, the arrow accuracy of simple words. They'd know how smell and shape and distance made sense of sound, how words were rounded, focussed tools which served the moment, did the

job, and left no waste. But as we know, Victor was no normal
child. For him the words his mother spoke were two-
dimensional, a sheet of sound, a shallow wash of stories from
his mother's village and the past. He had no role to play except
to keep his head and body still, and listen hard.

He did not know – despite his age – the trick of speaking
sentences or how to make his mark with words. He had not
learnt to shout, or tease, or burble rhythmic nonsenses like
other children do. On those few times – at night or when his
aunt was minding him – when he was spoken to by strangers
or Princesses or by the family from whom they hired their
room, he could not form replies. He could not speak. He was
in that respect, and others, too, a baby still. He was comforted
by breast. He did not have the skill to feed himself. His
bladder and his bowels had open gates. Anything he chanced
upon – an apple core, a pin, a cockroach case – he tested with
his mouth. He was not happy on his feet. He never ran. He
could not dress himself or tie the laces on his shoes. You
would not guess he had a temper, or that he wanted anything
beyond the milk, the honey and the whispers that seemed to
keep him calm.

In one respect, Victor, in those years before our city was
hustled like so many others into war and weaponry, was more
adult than his years. He had, at least, a muscular and exercised
imagination; that is to say the tales his mother told confused
him, yes, but still they entered him and filled his mind as
music enters infants far too young to grasp its geometric
principles, its hieroglyphs, its rhythmic cunning. So when Em
retold Victor for the third?, the thirteenth? time how he had
come about – 'we thought you up amongst the mushrooms' –
he formed a picture in his head concocted from the wooden

tubs of mushrooms which he knew in the market place and
the single mushrooms which dropped and rolled from time to
time within Em's reach at her station on the approaches to the
Soap Garden. He saw himself a pink but ragged mushroom,
odorous, peaty, one day old. The basket was his crib. It was a
frozen fairy tale for him, an illustration from a children's book.
The tighter that he pressed his eyes together the clearer the
image was; the larger and the pinker the mushroom; the
rounder, the smoother, the waxier the forests and the fields
which were the backdrops to his 'thinking up'. The world of
passers-by, of market porters, trundling barrowloads of cauli-
flowers, fruit, which Victor saw when his mother did not talk
and he was tempted to turn his head and lift his lids a little,
was chaotic and without pattern when compared to that village world he structured from his mother's words.

The irony was this, the richness of his life was richness
second-hand. His mother's childhood and her adolescence in
the village landscape was made shiny and intense by distance
and by time. It was Victor's milk and honey now. He fed on it.
It kept him quiet and still and satisfied. He was a country boy.
The city was the dream. He opened half an eye to fall asleep.
He woke to find the nightmares crowding in. He dozed,
caressed by Em's refurbished better times, and by higher skies
and fresher winds and more magical conjunctions than any
city could provide. Imagine what an inner world – bright and
sanitised – a boy would make of all this country talk, curled up
as warmly and as darkly as a sparrow in a wolf's mouth. It
would be nowadays, what? a theme park marketed as Rural
Bliss? The film-set for a country musical? The sort of hayseed
Kansas encountered on the road to Oz?

How could a child not be charmed by rural nights when

skies were punctured by white stars, and dreams disturbed by falling fruit in orchards where the plums and pears and oranges grew side by side in such harmony that it would seem they shared the branches of one tree? How could he resist the baffling cussedness of grandpa's anti-clockwise cottage door?: Put the key upside down into the backward lock. Turn it the wrong way. And lift! What boy would not desire a village party feast, with a table placed outdoors, or set his heart upon a birthday chair decked and garnished in the finest greenery to be his country throne?

'I promise you,' Em told her son, 'that when the warmer weather comes we'll put our things into a bag and walk back home.' She rolled the candle stub across his cheek. 'We'll put a light to this. We'll lie awake at night and listen to the apples drop. When you are six you'll have a leafy birthday chair.' She meant it, too – though it was clear that Victor was not strong enough to walk much further than the market rim.

She could not carry him. He was too big and badly ballasted. But she was clear what they would do. At night the marketeers left wooden trolleys parked in the cobbled alleyways between the dormant trading mats and baskets. She'd help herself to one. The market owed her that. She knew which one to take. A trader who was kind to her and gave her fruit and greens when they were cheap possessed a painted cart which was not unlike a child's perambulator. It had solid rubber tyres and, when he pushed it, it seemed quite light and manoeuvrable.

'That's your carriage passing by,' she'd tell her son. 'It's full of winter melons now – but soon you'll be travelling in it like a little king.' Em smiled as sweetly as she could at her innocent benefactor and the means of her escape. It was not theft to take this cart from such a kindly man. She'd cushion it for Victor with all their clothes and they'd set off at night. She was not the sentimental sort, nor given to ungrounded optimism, yet at those moments when her mood was grey or stormy she could calm herself with just the thought of Victor in the cart at that point where the trams and city stopped and turned, and where blue fields began.

6

It WAS AT DAWN, in fact, in May, when Victor was a month short of his sixth birthday, that Em at last gained freedom from the town. More freedom than she'd bargained for. She was asleep, and warm enough to have pushed her blanket back and stretched her naked arms beyond the pillow and her head. Her forehead was red and wet with perspiration. Her nose was blocked and whistling when she breathed. She had not been well. A cough had kept her sitting up until the early hours. The floorboards and the blankets puffed stale air and dust. The room was heavy with the smell of damp clothes and candle smoke and sleep. If she awoke she'd find her head was aching, a ring of pain which was most fierce and unforgiving behind her eyes and in the shallow dell between the tendons of her neck.

Victor had slept, of course. Or lain still, at least, throughout the night. But when the morning light started to infiltrate the room's single whitewashed window glass, he sat up and crawled across the floorboards to the pot. He straddled it on hands and knees and spread his legs. He pissed like donkeys piss but with less steam. He had a donkey's aim as well, and wet the floor a little. He watched his urine sink into the wood and make dramatic grains in what had been a grey and lifeless board. He called for Em to wake and see the patterns that he made. When she did not wake he kicked the pot – in irritation

– with his heel, so that the triple waters of the night were spilled.

It was in part an accident, but one which suited him. He knelt and rocked upon his hands to watch the family waters as they sought the cracks and contours. The stewed apple smell of urine. The apple yellow-green of bladder juice. He let the fluid swell and flow and soak. He let it coil and curl round knots of wood. The snoozer snake again. He watched the stream gain power on the floor until it reached the impasse of a raised timber. It formed a pool; it leaned and strained and then set off at a new angle. It had almost reached Aunt's shoulder when Victor pulled her arm to wake her up. He called, 'Water down!' His words made Aunt sit up in alarm and look around, expecting ceiling leaks or Judgement Day. Em was too tired to wake for leaks or Judgement Day. The best that Aunt and Victor could do was watch the urine seep away, as Em slept on and coughed.

'We'd better wash it down,' Aunt said at last. 'Get the water can.' She dressed him in a pair of knee-length trousers and a jacket, no underclothes, no shoes, and put on her own coat and hat above her nightcloth.

'We'll see if we can earn ourselves a nice fresh loaf, as well,' she said.

Together they went down the stairs, Aunt first, then Victor, bumping on his bottom down each step. They left the water can beside the tap in the yard and went outside. They walked along the central street, nipped narrow by the district's pair of wooden gates, into a squint too rough and angular for carts or crowds. There was a bakery two streets away. The first loaves of the day were cooling in their tins. The men who sold them on the city streets from shallow raffia trays were gather-

ARCADIA

ing to load their merchandise and check that all the bread they took was free of pockmarks, burns, and splits. The loaves with blemishes would not be sold and so the traymen made the baker take them back into his shop. There'd be disputes. And sometimes, when a loaf was badly deformed or split enough to earn the name of Devil's Hoof, the baker would toss it to the pigeons or to the early vagrants waiting there. Most mornings all they had to breakfast on was smell, though even the odours of a fresh, warm loaf are more filling than the scents of other streets where there are riches but no food. As luck would have it that day, the ovens had not let the baker down. His yeast had risen evenly. His dough had not bubbled into caves, or cloven like a devil's hoof, or browned in patches. It all looked good and saleable and – with flour priced the way it was – expensive, too.

Aunt would not carry Victor, though he lobbied her for a piggyback. She made him walk, but let him hang onto her arm or hold her hand. He seemed unnerved to be out on the street and not pressed closely to his mother. He was free – if he wanted – to do what any other boy would do, that is to run ahead into the smell of bread which beckoned them. They moved through the almost empty, almost daytime streets, between two smells. The smell of loaves. And, now, behind them, out of sight, the smell of burning wood.

Which Princess knocked the candle over, or struck the careless match, it is hard to say. The girls themselves all blamed it on the one they liked the least, or else said arsonists (in the landlord's pay) or some spurned man or neighbours with a grudge, had set the attic room alight. Who said that candlelight was luck?

Why there should be matches, candles, arsonists in the

apex of that building at dawn no one could readily explain. But what was sure was that there was fire and smoke. By the time the first Princess had woken, the flames had found a carriageway of draughts and were unrolling like a lizard's tongue across the room. Less surreptitious, simpler flames climbed walls and snapped their lips at curtains and at paint. The smoke at first was almost white and then, when the fire had reached the Princesses' mattresses and their clothes and had brewed sufficient heat to peel the blackened paint off window ledges, the smoke became heavier and darker. It was laden with the ash and dust which had been buoyed and agitated by the flames. Its colour now was blacker than the worst burnt loaf. It smelt and tasted like a new-shod horse.

The Princesses, when they woke – or were woken with a shake – did not stop to check the cause of the fire. Already they could hardly breathe, and one or two, the screamers there, had singed their throats. They ran, not for water to put out the fire, but for fresh air and safety in the street. The stairs were narrow. There were falls, and breakages. A young girl broke her begging wrist (and made a fortune out of that for the nineteen months she kept the bandage and the splint in place). Another broke her neck, and almost died before she reached the bottom step. But not one Princess was licked by too much flame. Nor did any one of them get left behind, curled up in blankets, to suffocate in the airless caverns hollowed by the heat. They banged on doors as they went down into the lower levels of the building. They raised their neighbours out of bed, but no one took it on themselves to check in every room that there was not a pet cat or a sleeping child that should be saved. They simply passed the message on, and messages are bound to end when they reach deaf or hidden ears. Once the refugees had reached the street, and looked around to check the faces there and comfort those who were blackened or distressed, no one noticed Em was not amongst the crowd. In fact, some swore they saw her standing there, with Aunt and Victor, breakfasting on bread.

Em slept. She was so tired, and dreaming too. The noise and smoke, they said, must have been the scenery of dreams, so that they did not threaten her or make her wake. The smoke – they said, they said – would have sunk into her room from the attic and curled up where she lay and hugged her tight and dry before the flames came down the stairs. They said she would have dreamed her death and felt no pain. But who can tell? Perhaps the truth is this, Em woke. Who would not wake when there was so much noise and anarchy, when the timbers cracked and grumbled like Epimenides the Slumberer who woke, stiff and dry and fiery, from two hundred years of sleep? Her eyes were smarting; from dreams, she thought at first. But then the smell, the boiling vapours of the house, the smoke, the drumming hubbub of the flames, made confusions of that kind short-lived. She would have called at once for Victor, and gone down on her hands and knees to scrabble for him where she thought he slept. How long was it before she realised that he was safe? Or thought that he was dead? Or took the chance to save herself and all the rest be damned?

The smoke by then was far too thick and acrid for Em to see the window light, suffused by shadow and by whitewash even when there was no fire. She could only guess where the door was. Perhaps she found the wall and felt along it for the architraves. And then, empowered by some ancient sense of flight, found easy passage through her neighbours' rooms into the hotter, fresh-brewed smoke which furnaced from the few remaining timbers in the flaming, disappearing stairwell. Did she die there, gasping, gaping like a fish on land for moist and icy oxygen and finding only pungent, scalding gas? Or did she simply curl up to drown beneath the fervent, swirling blanket of smoke in her own room, her husband's unlit candle melting in her hand, her family's spilt and puddled urine holding back the flames for just a trice, because she did not wish to live without her son? These are the questions everybody asked – and answered – for a day or two. But no one volunteered the truth, or called the owner in for questioning, or wondered why Princesses should play with fire at dawn. And no one asked, of course, how it could be that sixty-seven people slept in this four-storey house that had been built for ten. Or how they lived with just three taps and no gaslight and just two toilets in the yard. Or where the singed and heated dispossessed had found themselves new 'homes'. Or why it was that no one came to name or claim the single blackened corpse.

Aunt should not take any blame. She and her nephew were moved away by policemen with the others in the crowd. The policemen did not care if those they moved were gawpers from the neighbourhood or residents. 'Move on, move on,' was all they understood, as if the drama of the streets was a private spectacle, cordoned off to everyone except those few who wore the ticket of a uniform. There were no firemen there or fire appliances. In neighbourhoods like that all epidemics, rioting and fires were left to run their course. The buildings, bodies, laws were not worth keeping thereabouts, it was thought. In fact, a city councillor had said the week before, that the best prospect for the city was for all the tenements to be consumed by flames, for all the lawless poor to be dispersed by heat like rodents in a forest fire, for the squalid quarters of the city to be fumigated, cauterised. 'Let's build again. From scratch,' he'd said.

Aunt and Victor were driven back along the street towards the bakery. Victor was crying from the shock and drama of the fire. He wanted Em. He wanted Mother now. He would not walk a pace, so Aunt was forced to lift him on her shoulders until the policemen judged that they had driven back the crowd to a safe and sterile distance. They turned and watched the smoke knit grey scarves above the roofs, with flecks of dying orange made by airborne sparks. Aunt asked those Princesses she recognised if they'd seen Em. They thought they had. They weren't sure. Yes, yes, they'd seen her standing in the street eating bread with Aunt and Victor just a while ago. Or no, they hadn't seen her, not for days. Em who? They didn't know her by a name.

Aunt did not panic. She was sure that Em was safe. She'd heard it said the building had been cleared. In any case, the fire had started in the attic rooms, and all the attic girls seemed well enough if not exactly dressed for shopping or a ball. Em would have had more chance than them to wake, to dress, to come downstairs, to go in search of her sister and her son. What could Aunt do except stay calm? She was the calmest woman on the street. She was just glad that she had remembered to put on her hat, her battered cloche. It's known that flames make snacks of straw.

The crowds were thickening, drawn by the smoke. Some men were trying to breach the line of police. They lived in houses close to the burning building. They knew that fire had legs and wings and that their rooms and homes were next in line. They'd only come onto the street to see what all the fracas was and, when they knew, to find a certain place of safety for their families. They'd found themselves expelled, pushed back from their front stairs, spectators to the colonising heat.

'Let's fight the fire,' they begged. 'At least let us go home and save a thing or two, before it all goes up in smoke.'

'Keep back,' the policemen said.

Their commandant did not organise a chain of buckets or send for nurses from the sanatorium, or for the water pumps. He sent instead for mounted policemen and another van of men. This was his district and he knew that trouble on the streets would be a black mark in his book.

It was not long before the word was out that the city councillor who'd recommended, just a week before, that tenements like these should be brought down to earth by fire, had got his way. How was it that the police were there, at dawn and in such numbers? Why was it that no one was allowed to investigate or to fight the fire? The police, the politicians, the nobs and profiteers who wanted all the city to themselves had come before the sun was up to make a furnace for the poor. It was not only hotheads in the crowd who now found cobblestones and staves or started pushing against the policemen's chests. The neighbourhood – in both respects – was now inflamed. They'd beat themselves like moths against the cordon of the law to get nearer to the flames.

If there was fighting to be done, then districts such as this were good for volunteers. Young men with little else to do got out of bed and ran into the street. Beggars, hawkers, prostitutes, the unemployed, the young, the criminals, the men and women with grudges and with principles, in fact the sort who had scores to settle with the city and the police, were glad to add their lungs and muscles to the throng. The crowds were driven from the rear by rumours and by the more mature of troublemakers who, hanging back, felt safe to bruise the air with threats and insults. Their curses and their slogans, lobbed at the riot from the rear, caused punches, cobbles, bricks to be thrown at the front.

Riots are like fires. They look their best at night. They smoulder and they flare with greater drama when the sky is dark. They beckon and they mesmerise. This breakfast riot was short-lived. The city had no need of it. It had its work to do, its schedules and appointments to address, its daylight hours to endure. Those men – and the few women – hurrying down the pavements at that hour on their way to work had only time to poke their noses down the narrow lanes where they could see the police and smoke and hear the curses of the neighbourhood.

If this had been at dusk, not dawn, with all the duties of the day dispatched, then only the most innocuous, the wariest, would pass the mayhem by. That's something every beggar knows – that breakfast times are dead, that crowds proliferate when work is done and time is no longer money. At dusk the riot would have spread out of the narrow lanes, beyond the burning tenements. It would have helped itself to food and clothes through the broken glass of windows. It would have picked on men in carriages or cars and taken wallets, watches, hats, and paid for them with beatings. It would have toppled tram-cars, and started new and spiteful fires in districts where the residents were rich. But it was dawn, and spite was still abed. The police soon gained control with their horses and their truncheons and their farmdog expertise in splitting herds and cutting out the single troublemaker from the pack.

Five buildings burned. The Woodgate district lost its wooden gates. But only Em was killed. The tiles and timbers of the tenement fell all around her like the trees had fallen once across her village lane, that other breakfast time when the winds had stretched the memory and bent the tallest, oldest pines beyond endurance. The sun fell onto the cobbles of the street for the first time in who-knows-how-many? years. The fire-shortened tenements had cleared a path for it. It thinly penetrated smoke and waltzed like light on water as the wind gathered, turned and spread the ashy air.

The crowd were now subdued. The ones whose homes were outside the police lines went home. The unlucky ones stayed put. And waited. They prayed the wind would settle down and let the fires die. The residents of the five damaged buildings would be happy now to see the wind and flames whip up so that their grief could spread itself throughout the town, so everybody would know what it meant to wake at dawn in purgatory, and without blame, and with no hope of heaven as reward. But there is no patterned justice to the wind or rain. And rain there was, quite soon. It made the timbers steam. It dampened spirits. It cleared and cleaned the streets, so that the rivulets of rain which sped along the gutters took off the ash and dust which had so recently settled.

Em had been roasted and then dusted by the ash. The rain was her undertaker. It showered her. It made her cold and shiny almost, as ready as she could ever be for her discovery two hours later by, at first, a pair of dogs and then a sergeant in the police. By noon they'd brought a box for her. It was not easy to lift her body from the rubble. She was too well cooked. Her flesh was falling from the bone. They wrapped her in a blanket then and lifted her. They kept her in the city morgue, in ice, and out of sight. But no one came and so they gave her earthy eyelids in the common grave and put her on the register as 'Woman, unidentified'.

Aunt still was calm. She knew where she should *rendez-vous* with Em. The market place, of course. Em's place of work. Her pitch where she had sat with Victor on her breast, palm out and up and heavy with coins.

'You have to walk yourself,' she said to Victor. 'I'm not a donkey. Walk!' She made him stand. She held his hand. 'Come on. She's waiting for us. Walk a little way, and then I'll let you have a ride.'

Victor was shocked. Not by the fire, and not by fears of losing Em. But by the clutter and the hardness of the streets, by the smoke and horses, by the anger and the weeping, by his Aunt's strange mix of harshness and attention, her calmness and her urgency.

When he was eighty and looked back, it seemed to Victor that this was his first unfettered image of the town, that up till then he'd only glimpsed the city streets. At most he'd seen those dislocated country views of fruit in carts, of vegetables displayed on stalls, of shoppers, traders, bar loafers, from the waists down. He did not like what he was seeing now. He clung to Aunt's hand and her skirts. His cheeks were wet. His chest was shaking, partly from the morning cold and partly from the bubble sobs which he could not suppress. He walked – a little gawkily, of course. He was still young. He was not strong – and wished that he could be elsewhere. His head was full of countryside; the snoozer snake, the falling fruit, the little king returning home in a carriage made for melons, the burning, lucky candle on the step, the birthday chair that's legs were saplings, that's back was green and woven like a wreath.

7

WHEN VICTOR WAS AN older, richer man, a twenty-six-year-old with property and prospects and – already – half a grip on all the riches of the Soap Market, he found the time and sentiment to search the city archives for the bound and brittle volumes in which the local newspapers were preserved. He knew the year and month that Em had disappeared. He knew there'd been a fire and still retained the snapshot memory of being lifted to Aunt's back and watching flames and scarves of smoke across her shoulder.

It was a morning's work to find the thumbnail news item, amid reports of city trade and gossip and a world gone mad with war: 'Five tenement houses frequented by itinerants, prostitutes and beggars were fired during dawn disturbances yesterday in the city's Woodgate district. Several rioters were detained and charged with assault and theft following attacks on police, fire officers and local trading premises. The disturbances were initially occasioned, it is reported, by rivalry between criminal groups. The body of an unidentified woman was removed from the debris.' The single-column headline WAS BREAKFAST ARSONISTS DETAINED.

But at the time Victor had no apprehension that his mother might be harmed. His aunt had said, 'Come on, she's waiting for us.' His only fear was that he would be obliged to walk too far, before his aunt rewarded him with the donkey ride she'd promised on her back. He tugged her hand, so that his walking dragged on her. But she was tough and unlike Em. His tugs earned harder tugs from her. Her grip on his small hand was only soft if he matched steps with her. The instant that he slowed or faltered she bunched his finger bones. 'Keep up,' she said. Or 'Quickly now'. He had to run to keep in step. Four trots of his to match her single stride. He'd rarely run before, except in play, and then the distance had been little more than wall to wall in their small room. He hadn't realised the urgency, the clumsiness of speed, or how painful it could be.

Who knows what ants or termites feel when boys or bounty hunters kill the queen? Their structures fall apart. The soft, iron magnet lets her fleshy filings go, so even those far from the nest who have not witnessed the sacking of the royal chamber or seen the assassin's needle impale the queen, go listless-haywire at the instant of her death. Looking back, it seemed to Victor that the world that day was a pandemonium of ants, and ants without a queen. How else could he make sense of city streets, or cars and trams and carriages, of random, indiscriminating sounds, of pavement anti-patterns in which bodies flocked and fled like cream turned in a whisk, of Aunt once madly kind and now so rushed and unforgiving?

Aunt was quite certain, as she dragged her nephew by his finger to the market place, of two things – that Em was waiting in her usual place, that Em had perished in the fire. Or else a nightmare mixture of the two – that they'd find Em, her blackened palm outstretched, her thin, charred back propped up against the usual snag tree on the edges of the Soap Garden.

If they'd found Em, alive and well, their future would

have been the past. They would have gone back 'home', to the countryside in May. At worst the springs and cushions of a swelling hedgerow are better bedding than the embers of a city fire. But his mother was elsewhere, and Aunt was not nostalgic for the pains and pleasures of the earth. She sat cross-legged all day at Em's worn pitch. She'd give her sister till the night to resurrect herself and then she'd set about the task of finding once again a nesting box. Aunt did not try to put her nephew to the breast, or beg from passers-by. Victor was left to shuffle in the garden and the market place at will. At last. He loved and hated what he saw. He felt like we all feel when we're first left at school – condemned to a freedom that at first seems narrower and more enclosed than the cell that's family and home. The market paid him little heed, except to bruise and buffet him, and startle him with noise and colour.

His aunt was not a callous woman. She guessed the worst when Em did not show up. Her eyes were damp despite herself. But nor was she the sort to mope. If Em had disappeared, had died, was lost, had fled without her son, was lying in a pauper's ward scorched and bruised by smoke and truncheons, then still the world went round, and breakfast followed dawn, and shitting followed food, and life went on. She gave her old straw cloche a whirl. She primped its dog-eared dog-rose sprigs in felt. She made its deep brim curl and grin and made a face herself to match. She wiped her eyes and, dutifully, checking one last time for Em, she went in search of Victor; and then, her nephew clinging to her back, she headed for the town.

Street luck is what the city excels at. Aunt's hat (a little *passé* now), her smile, the boyish burden on her back, attracted comment from the livelier of the men she passed. One followed her – a man about her age, but dressed much older and in the bar-room style with patent shoes and collar studs, a soft homburg, trousers with a centre crease, a jacket of the latest cut with sloping pockets and long revers.

'What's that you've got on your back?' he asked. 'The kid must have seen that hat and thought he'd take a donkey ride!' She answered cheek with cheek. She said the kid was paying for his ride. She was a human tram. 'Jump up, if you can find the fare,' she said, (and winked). 'There's room inside for a little one.'

'There's more to me than meets the eye,' he said, matching winks with Aunt. 'Want to see? Hold on a bit . . .'

'What bit exactly should I hold?'

'Your tongue!' he said.

They called him Dip, though he was known by many other names. His speciality was crowds. He'd dip a hand and make off with your purse and the most you'd feel would be a sense of loss and an unaccustomed lightness in the pocket. He could unclip brooches, take watches out of fobs and replace them with stones of matching weight, remove a banknote from a billfold and then put back the fold, swap a necklace for a length of string, steal (it was said) the glasses off your nose. Hard luck the lady who took a helping hand off Dip, who let him take her arm to cross the street or welcomed his assistance with the too-high step to board a tram. One hand at the elbow left one hand free to browse the handbag or the purse. Tough luck the well-heeled man who hovered in the street when Dip walked by. It only took the slightest nudge from him, a stumble, an apology. The man would never guess his pockets had been searched and emptied, his tram fare and silver tie-clip stolen, his saint medallion removed.

At first, Dip's interest in Aunt had been professional. A woman forced to give a piggyback to a tired child might have an unattended purse or, perhaps, an outer pocket which he could open up with just one brushing cut from the pivot blade of his pig-sticker. He'd been surprised when she drew close how young she was. And poor. And to his taste. He liked these country girls, their jollity, their give-as-good-as-take, their duelling repartee. This one was plump and scruffy, it was true. Beneath the disguise of the broad-rimmed cloche, her forehead and her upper cheeks were dry and pocked like grapefruit skin. But she had level eyes, a playful face, a comic angle to her chin, and – Dip, like every other man, had fantasies too strange to name – she satisfied his liking, his desire, for girls in hats. He'd never met a woman before who wore her hat with more flirtatiousness than Aunt. One glimpse of that had put his rhubarb up.

'Please let me help,' he said. 'I'll carry him. Where to?'

She shrugged: 'Who knows?'

'What's your boy's name?' he asked.

'Victor . . . and, anyway, he isn't mine. You go and tend your own potatoes. It's not your business who he is.' That's what she said, but what she thought was something else: This man is sent to us to take the place of Em. She let Dip take the boy from off her back and lift him in a flying angel onto his shoulders.

'Where to?' he asked again.

She told him all about the fire and Em and what their life had been; and telling it, she buried it, still warm. Life was too blunt and short to waste it on the dead.

Dip was enthralled by how Aunt span her hat whenever

she was lost for words. He held his breath, as if his lungs were as fragile as frost, when she recounted how the men in bars had tossed their coins in her hat-brim to win themselves short glimpses of her legs. Here was a woman, he was sure, who was a gift from heaven and from hell. He jangled stolen coins in his pocket and hoped that he would get a chance to toss them too.

His room, he said, was near. So near that he could smell the market fruit from it. He offered her some floor.

'And what about the kid?' she asked.

It's true, he thought. The kid is in the way. But then, he's small and young. He'll sleep. And when he sleeps? Who knows what might occur?

They put 'the kid' to sleep, and then they set to work. Aunt did her best to seem experienced though, truth be told, she'd never suffered this intimacy before. She knew about it, naturally, but only in the way of comic patter, the sexual flirting that it took to beg some coins from a man, the flush and stillness that settled on them when her legs were on display and she was trading winks and innuendo.

Some Princesses – the prostitutes, the opportunists – had kept them all amused one night with stories of their clientele. How one old boy had paid good cash to watch a girl spit on his feet. How others wanted armpits licked ('My wife would never kiss me there!') or asked for entry by the tradesman's door, or took their pleasure spiced with oaths the like of which would shock the guardians of hell. How the teenage sons of bourgeoisie were brought by uncles, godfathers, family friends to girls like them to 'taste the fruit' but more often begged for mercy and their innocence; or wept; or failed 'to stiffen the worm'; or changed their minds when they found out what, how and where, it all involved; or came into their underclothes before their trouser buttons were undone; or wet themselves.

Aunt was prepared for oddities. She was prepared, in fact, to be amused. Hilarity, it seemed from what the Princesses had said, was the stablemate of making love, and Dip had shown that he liked fun. But she soon found herself more startled than amused. Dip's kisses were the colonising kind. His hands – those hands so used to slipping gently and unnoticed into pockets, tucks and folds – seemed suddenly to lose their expertise. His fingers – adept in crowds at unloosening, unfastening, unbuttoning – were trembling at the strings of the nightcloth which she still wore beneath her coat. He seemed uncertain how to deal with the clips on his braces. He tried to pass his hands through solid cloth. He seemed unable, or unwilling, to push his trousers down without Aunt's help. His breathing had become so uneven and so laboured that Aunt began to think that they had better stop before the poor man had a fit and her new dream of moving in with a good and handsome city thief was ended with a death. His temperature was fluctuating. His face was red. His levity, his measured confidence – those two characteristics which had made Dip so attractive to Aunt – had disappeared. Instead here was a man who did not seem able to form a simple sentence, but was behaving with the blunt and charmless urgency of a child denied the breast. Indeed, quite soon his mouth was partly on her breast, and partly chewing on her cotton undershift. One hand pulled her heavy coat and nightcloth to her waist; his other hand was pushed too tightly – and was trapped – beneath his trouser band, beneath his underclothes.

One gentle shove from Aunt would have sent this Dip toppling like a trussed piglet onto the bare floorboards of his room. But Aunt was in no mood to shove. Despite her bafflement, she was at least gratified to be the centre of attention, to be the focus of Dip's *ballet buffo*. It kept the grief of sisterhood at bay. She let him slide onto the mattress, his sinking head pressed to her chest . . . her abdomen . . . her stomach . . . her crutch . . . her thighs . . . her knees. She let him put his tongue between her toes. She laughed and laughed. No wonder prostitutes were such a jolly breed.

'Undress,' he said. 'But not the hat.'

8

Now do you see the charm of cities? None of this adventure could have happened on the village green where Aunt and Em had first played tip-and-kiss with boys. There were no flirting, pocket-picking strangers to encounter there, in patent shoes and collar studs, with private rooms. The only available men were cousins all. Or neighbours' sons. Or daft. They were as solid and as passionate as trees, as heroic and original as farmyard hens. That is to say they were all dull and without sin; their only privacy was sleep and shit. But city air makes free – and country pullets can become street cockatoos or fighting birds or songsters once they've shaken hayseed from their wings. So, Aunt and Dip, two village souls gone free and wild in city streets, could no more pass each other by than cats can pass a dish of cream.

The dipping and the begging became less urgent. They lived on love and bed. These were sufficient for a while. So when they woke, curve-wrapped on their mattress like two bananas on one bunch, Dip breathing through the filter of Aunt's hair, Aunt folded like an infant in his arms, it was not often long before they found themselves embracing face to face or delving in the blankets for a breast, a testicle, a pinch of fat. Sex was breakfast for these two. It fuelled them for the day. Sometimes they breakfasted at leisure, no stone unturned. At other times Aunt merely turned away and let

Dip wriggle into her, to puff and quiver, for a minute at the most, at her buttocks and her back. Aunt did not care for breakfast much. Her appetite for love grew with the day. But she was content to let Dip make use of her after dawn, so long as – in the afternoons, at night – he'd do what she desired.

Each day they washed with water from a jug which Aunt had filled from the public fountain the evening before. They dried themselves on air. They dressed in their best, only clothes, and walked out into town not like the cockroaches they were, but eagerly and hand-in-hand. They had to eat. Aunt dealt with that. She knew which market men would happily part with bruised fruit, which bakeries threw out collapsed or wounded loaves, where trays of eggs were stored and could be reached by someone small and agile like herself, where it was easiest to snatch the bread or chops off diners' plates in restaurants.

They needed money, too. Youth and love are spendthrifts both. Here Dip's expertise gave them an undulating income. One day he'd lift a wallet with enough inside to last the week; and then a week would pass and all he'd get would be 'blind purses' containing buttons, tokens, keys, *eau-de-Cologne*, but not one coin. Dip did not choose his victims well. He'd rather pick their pockets comically so that Aunt – his witness from across the street – would be amused. He did not concentrate. He was on show. He took it as a challenge to remove a worthless glass and metal brooch from the lapel of a stern-faced, clucking woman, and lost all taste for lucrative yet humdrum theft. Aunt satisfied the predator in him. The time would come when he'd insist that she stayed in the room when he went out to work. He'd say she soured his good luck. But in those months when they first met he did not care if business was not good. A note or two, some silver change, would be enough to reunite their hands while they, leaving Victor in the room with blankets for his toys, went off to find a bar.

Aunt had a liking for the clear, cheap, country spirit known then as glee water, but now, of course, tamed and bottled by the drink barons and marketed as Boulevard Liqueur. It did not take a lot to make her drunk. One shot, and she would lay her hat and head on Dip's shoulder, her hand upon his knee, her foot on his. Two shots, and she would press her lips against his ear and say what they'd do to pass the time when they got home, if Victor were asleep. She'd be a 'Princess' and she'd let him buy her for the afternoon. She'd be as hard as nails for him. Or else they'd make imagination manifest: 'Let's sit apart and masturbate.' Or else, 'Let's buy some honey, Dip. We'll put it on and lick it off. I'll put some on my breasts and you can feed off me . . .' Or else, 'Do you want to do me in my hat? I'll do a show for you. You toss-and-pitch and watch. For every coin that you land inside the brim I'll take something off.'

Once, when she had watched Dip lifting purses from the smarter ladies of the town, she asked, 'Why don't you try to burgle me?': 'Just like we're in a crowd,' she said. 'You come up and dip your hands inside my clothes and try to find my purse.' For Aunt the narrative of sex, the scene, the characters, were seldom twice the same. Her passions were theatrical. She cast herself in parts in which the heroine was more slender and had better skin than her, in which she was in charge, desired, insatiable, amused, in which she could transcend herself, become any one of those grand or glamorous women on the street.

The Princesses were wrong. *Hilarity* was not the word, though laughter was a part of sexual pleasure. *Euphoria* was what she felt. When she and Dip were making, staging love, it seemed the real world could be kept at bay. She could have kept the world at bay all day! What was the hurry? What was the point in hurtling, like men, through such sustainable pleasures to the brief and unreliable moment when the bubble shudders, bursts? She could not understand how Dip, at breakfast time, was so easily, so speedily, so undramatically relieved. That was his word, 'Relief' – 'Give me relief,' he said. For Aunt not-making-love was not the absence of relief, but a muting of that part of her which found its best expression in the gift of love.

They'd put 'the kid' to sleep when they'd first met and kissed. Of course, tired and dispirited though he was, he did not sleep for ever. For Aunt and Dip to live the life they chose, to play such parts each afternoon, to spend those hours drinking glee, they needed privacy, the privacy of two, not three, bananas to the bunch. A child of Victor's age was old enough to inhibit anything beyond a kiss. Both Aunt and Dip had understood, the day they met, that if their passion for each other was to boil and whistle like a kettle and not steam and simmer like the water in an open pot, they would require time to themselves.

'We'll put the boy to work,' Dip said, when he had suffered inhibitions for long enough. 'He's missing his mum and this'll give him something else to do.'

What kind of work? Aunt raised an eyebrow almost to her cloche's brim.

'The boy can hardly walk,' she said. 'And I won't have him begging on his own. Besides, he's just a baby, though he's big. He's hardly weaned . . . He isn't bright enough. He isn't tough . . .'

'I'll fix him up,' said Dip. 'The streets are full of kids like him, and doing very nicely, too.'

'But doing what?'

Dip hadn't thought it out, but now he had to find a scheme and find it quickly, too, before he lost his patience with the boy and showed it with his fists. He settled for the first idea that came. The boy could build a future out of eggs.

'What eggs?' Aunt asked.

'The eggs you steal from out the back of that big storehouse.'

'Then what? You think he'll build a nest and hatch them out?'

'We'll boil them up, what else?'

'What else? It's juggling that you have in mind, I guess. Or sulphur bombs.'

'We'll boil them up. Get the kid a little bag or tray, some twists of salt. He'll have a business on his hands! When I was little, that was lunch at harvest time, or if we had to travel anywhere outside the village. One boiled egg. The only salt we had was sweat. My grandma used to tell our fortunes from the broken shell. The shell could show how long you'd live. Perhaps the kid can trade in fortunes, too.'

'He's hardly seven years of age.'

'Seven's an old man in this town.'

So it was that Victor first became a marketeer, a soapie at the age of seven. Aunt was his wholesaler. She crept into the storehouse from which she'd stolen – but more modestly – a dozen times before. It was late at night, after the fresh eggs had been brought from the railway station, sorted, placed in straw-lined trays. She lined a muslin bag with paper, lifted the one loose wallboard which provided access from the city lane at the rear of the building, and crept into the midnight room.

On that first night she was afraid. She'd stolen eggs before, but only one or two. A watchman, catching her, would not call on the police or his employer for what it took a hen a day to make. He'd settle for the lecture he could give or, at worst, demand some other recompense.

But on that night she wanted fifty eggs at least, more hen's work than could be shrugged off as 'breakages'. If she was caught and put away then Victor would be orphaned once again. She did not trust her Dip – left as a sentry in the street with Victor sleeping on his shoulder and her hat in hand – to give the boy a home or love. She'd never seen them touch affectionately. Dip was the sort who having never been a cared-for child himself thought touch and tenderness were simply trinkets with which men could flatter, soften, win their women. But Aunt – persuaded now against all reason that Victor would be *happier* left on his own, the boiled-egg sales-man of the market place – had made herself the promise that he would 'always have a beam above his head at night'. If she could guarantee that he was safe and warm at night, then she could put him out of mind by day.

She was the cheerful type. What was the point in brewing guilt? Who'd benefit if she and Victor caressed and hugged all day, and let their empty stomachs shrink and pucker in the cold? It seemed to her, as she gained entry to the storeroom, that stealing eggs for Victor was the greatest gift that she could give because these eggs would free Em's son from her, and leave her free of him.

That night the storeroom was not entirely dark. A late

winter moon turned the skylight window-panes a liquid silver and made the room look colder than it was, as if the ceiling had been tiled in translucent squares of ice. What light there was picked out the thousand brittle, bony skulls of eggs. The shells absorbed the light, reflecting none onto their bedding straw, like button mushrooms butting into oxygen from earth.

Aunt walked as gently as fear allows between the egg trays and the light. The odour was strong, and reminiscent too. The chicken dung, the straw, the timber of the room, the salt-and-semen smell of white and yolk, the moonlight dressing, was farmyard simplified, was field. Aunt took just five eggs from each tray and – counting in a whisper as she worked – filled her bag with sixty eggs. They were the size and weight of perfect plums. The only sounds she heard were Dip whistling in the lane outside – his warning that there were passers-by – and, far away, the midnight alarums of the drunks and revellers amongst the final trams and scuffles of the night. There were no rats to alarm her. The watchman slept on undisturbed. But still she was afraid. The eggs were ghosts. They looked like souls or sins encased in sculpted skin. To steal these icy eggs at night made Aunt feel like a grave-robber. Each one was someone dead and someone loved. Which were her parents? Which were the villagers who'd been alive when Aunt was born? Which one was Em?

She could not move. Dip whistled without cease, suspiciously and tunelessly. Perhaps there were policemen on the street – then whistling would only bring ill-luck to Dip. But if he stopped?

Aunt crouched beside her bag of eggs. A moth flew up from God-knows-where. A bat-moth, black, grey and red. It

landed on the back of Aunt's right hand. It closed its wings
and rested on her warmth. No great weight, no manacle, could
have rendered Aunt more still or breathless than that one
moth. Then Victor woke. She heard Dip curse, then whistle
once again – a slower, sleepy version of the dance he'd been
attempting before. But Victor would not settle to this bogus
lullaby. His thin crow voice was raised in protest at the
pressure of Dip's hold, the darkness of the lane, his orphan-
age. 'Shut up,' Dip said. But Victor knew the power of his
lungs and screamed. Nothing would make him happy now.
He was alone, at midnight, in the city. Tomorrow he would
earn his living – a marketeer at last. But for the moment, but
for ever, Em was dead, the eggs were stolen, packed, and Aunt
was crouching in that brittle-mushroom field, transfixed. She
was not certain what had pinned her there – the screaming or
the whistling or the moth. She only knew what everybody
knew who'd come from village into town, that midnight is a
lonely and ungenerous time when streetlamps blanket out the
stars.

She held the bat-moth by the wings and put it on the
eggs. She had to take the chance of climbing back into the
town. Victor's screaming, Dip's slow dance, were loud and
strange enough to bring the army out. She lifted the loose
wallboard and looked outside. It seemed safe enough. She
clambered through the gap and reached back into the storeroom for the bag of eggs, and then replaced the board to
disguise her entry. Dip had seen her now, and stopped whistling. Victor screamed. Despite the hour the lane was busy.
Men, mostly alone, were making for a brothel-bar where
drinks and women could be bought until dawn. They passed
between the distraught child and the woman thief without a

comment or a glance. Crime and distress were the common starlings of the street. They could not give a damn.

9

A COUNTRY CHILD OF six or seven might work all day at harvest time. Hard work, too; helping with the stacks, or pulling roots, or climbing to the furthest branches for the remotest plums. At dawn it very often was the child who was sent out to slop the pigs or strip the maize for chicken feed. The youngest daughter had the milking stool. The smallest son was sent at dusk to gate the herd or flock, and if he came home empty-handed – that's to say, he'd found no firewood, mush-rooms, nuts – then very often supper was withheld. 'Empty hands, empty stomach,' was the village phrase. At lambing or when the fruit was in its fullest blush, some girl or boy would have to keep the foxes or the applejays at bay. All it took would be a fire, a scare-drum or a horn. A single child in every orchard or each field throughout the day or night would do the job at no expense, so long as they were vigilant and did not sleep. Nobody said, That kid's misused. How could you leave a child so young, alone, for such a time, with so much danger all around? Rather, their childhood seemed ennobled by the tasks they had. Work made them independent, healthy, spirited. Why, then, the fuss when city children worked? Compared to country kids the poorest city children – home-less, reckless on the streets – had an easy time of it. At least they pleased themselves. If they were bored with holding carriage horses for small change, or selling matches, papers, sex, then they could take the time to share a cigarette with friends or join the shoal of sprat-sized thieves and beggars in the Soap Garden. They could vie with pigeons for rinds of bread, or glean the market for discarded fruit, or splash around in the motherly and greying laundry water of the public washing fountain.

Philanthropists, of course, would do their best to net the shoal, to place the best and brightest of the girls in houses where they'd be taught to iron and make the beds. They'd do their best to separate the boys from their bad ways, their friends, their cigarettes, their threadbare clothes, by indenturing them to coachbuilders, factory men, or anybody wanting hard work for no pay. They thought a hostel was a better place for orphans than the street, yet could not answer why it was that once their orphans had a bed, a schedule for their prayers, once they had work and food, a change of clothes, they still broke loose to join the starlings again.

The answer's tough and simple. It is this: that routes to misery and hell are often much more fun, more challenging than routes to virtue and well-being. Why else, how else, would children such as those who thronged the Soap Garden and the Market, then and now, embrace the destitution of the city streets with such audacity and such appetite? We should not grieve too much for little Victor, then. Not yet, at least. The market was a warm and busy place, more cheerful than a four-walled room, more sociable, more nourishing than the four dry, sweet breasts that had sustained him till the fire. He was bereaved, twice over. He was not strong. Or wise. But he was young enough to mistake mischance for the natural order of his life.

He sat, contented, resigned, before his tray of eggs, exactly in the place – where else? – where he had sat and suckled for so long with Em. His back was set against his mother's tree. It was a home of sorts. And though his face was not well known (how could it be, pressed up against his mother's flesh and shrouded, swaddled from the light?), he knew enough about the tricks of trade to turn his thin mouth up and advertise his wares with what appeared as undesigning smiles. Indeed he was amused. What boy, a few weeks short of seven years of age, would not delight in sixty eggs of which he had sole charge?

Aunt and Dip were his first customers, pretending to be casual passers-by. They dropped their coins in his hand and made the most of choosing a well-boiled egg. They smelled the shells. They tapped the shells and held the oval echo to their ears. They ate their eggs exactly where they stood, stooping down theatrically to help themselves to salt.

'Sweet God, these eggs are good,' they said, to anyone who caught their eye. 'Go on. Buy one. This kid has got the cheapest breakfast place in town.'

Victor was glad to see the back of them. It left him free to turn their coins in his hand, to wet his finger for a plunge of salt, to stare into the ranks of eggs, to study all the cracks and stains that came from boiling them, to wait in vain for some-one else to stoop and buy.

It was not until he left this home-of-sorts to wander on his weakly and untutored legs amongst the café tables and the market panniers that he began to sell. He did not even have to smile. He did not have to cry his wares. 'Boiled eggs! Boiled eggs' was a less eloquent sales pitch than the silent, hardened eggs themselves. Besides, this was a market place. No need to state your business here. Display was all it took to do the trick.

By late lunch-time, on that first trading day, the fifty-eight remaining eggs had been reduced to three. The salt was gone. Victor's pockets hung like udders with the weight of cash. It was not much in value but volume matters more to kids than value. They much prefer the playfulness of coins to any paper note.

Victor ate the last three eggs himself. He was not skilled at taking off the shells, and had to spit the bony flakes onto the cobbles and flagstones of the Soap Market. He turned to make his way back to the garden, to wash his mouth out in the fountain water. But first he was seduced by the clanking, twig-thin man who sold fruit juices out of spouted cans and called out what was seasonal: 'Berries, honey gourds, oranges. Fresh juice. Fresh juice.' Victor pointed at a spouted can. He could not tell what juice it held. The hawker rinsed a glass with water from a skin. He shook the glass dry and clean. With practised shrugs he tilted the can and filled the glass with bluish berry juice. He took a coin out of Victor's hand. Victor stood, struck motionless. He was rejoicing in the simple algebra of buy-and-sell which had so quickly and so effortlessly transformed his boiled eggs into juice.

The street kids did their best, with threats and brittle charm, to make Victor one of them. They had their gangs. The Moths. The Dross. The Market Boys. The Fly-by-Nights. If Victor meant to limp with his burden of eggs between the market pitches or sell them to the café customers in the Soap Garden, then he at least should make his peace with those tough boys and girls who were the gangland chieftains or their generals. They seemed so competent at everything from marbles to manslaughter that, surely, they were the natural allies of any child out on the streets alone. But Victor had been buried for too long. He did not understand the courtesies of life amongst the pack. He did not wish to speak with his contemporaries, or take on board relationships which were not trading ones, which were not serious, which did not earn. These were the sort of boys who made their cash like tough old men, and blued it all on sweets, and toys and cigarettes, not eggs. Victor thought these urchins far too trivial.

At first these gangsters – that's the word – just circled him and nudged as if he were a goldfish in a tank of orfe. They helped themselves to eggs and pelted him with what they couldn't eat. They kicked his shins. They found a name for him. They taunted him with 'Vic the Prick', or called him Goose because he walked unsteadily, and had a lot of eggs. They said he had to join the gang, or pay, or leave the market place, or else. Or else? They pressed their fists into his face. They burned his wrist with Chinese twists. They knocked his tray so that his eggs cracked on the cobblestones. They meant to illustrate what else might happen to a boy, alone, who did not court the approbation of the gang.

Victor did not understand what blows or twisted arms or threats with fists and knives were meant to signify. Their language was not his. What did their violence mean? He only understood that there was chaos on the streets more urgent than the protocol of gangs. Each day had its uncertainties: that it might rain. That nobody would want to dine on eggs that day. That there might be some pointless kindness from a marketeer who'd give away a damaged pear, or pay for eggs with too much cash and not require the change. That there'd be holidays when no one came – the market would be closed, the cafés shuttered, the cobbles and the sky laid close and listless, like sheet and mattress on an empty bed. He took it all. His job was selling on the streets. The eggs passed through his hands like worry beads. No Chinese burn, no punch, could deflect his armoured single-mindedness. He did not understand the power of cash yet. He was content that when he went back to Dip's room at night his pockets were turned out and all the change removed as 'payment for tomorrow's eggs'. He had to learn a stranger and a tougher algebra of trade than the one which fed him berry juice – that is that all his patience and hard work upon the street could be so quickly and so effortlessly transformed into beer and other treats for Aunt and Dip. He was the middle-man, the trading lime – and he was being squeezed.

Of course, Aunt no longer crept at night into the storeroom to steal the eggs for Victor. It had only taken three days for the packing foreman to observe that random eggs had disappeared, and that they disappeared at night.

'You think they're hatching into bats?' he asked. 'Or are we being robbed?'

He and the watchman found the loosened board and set a trap. They sat on stools behind the entry board with sticks upon their laps. They shared a bottle of *aqua vitae*, and suppered silently on pork and bread. One dozed while one kept watch.

At midnight Aunt arrived, a little slowed and fortified by drink. She had no appetite for foraging amongst the oval ghosts. But it was easy money, and Dip was far too tall and dandified to forage for himself. They'd been amazed how much their little Vic had earned on his first day. He'd made enough to win himself not-quite-a-hug from Dip. It was not enough to buy good clothes or meals in restaurants. There was enough, though, turned out from his trouser pockets, (the country phrase, again) 'to oil their throats and grease their bums'.

Aunt was too hurried to remove her hat. Her battered cloche, much loved, clove to her head as tightly as an acorn cup. Dip signalled that the lane was clear. Aunt freed the loose board with her foot and pushed her hat and head straight through the gap. The packing foreman, full of self-esteem and pork, woke up in time to see the watchman's stick make contact with the straw. Aunt's hat fell off, but – good friend that it was – it broke the blow. Her head went back into the town. She tore her chin on wood. She stood. She ran. Though she could have just as safely strolled away. The loose board was too narrow. The foreman and the watchman were twice Aunt's size and had to satisfy themselves with that one battered trophy, that old straw cloche, that disembodied gaiety.

What should Dip and Aunt do now? What could they steal? Where were there eggs to boil for the next day's trade? Aunt took the money that Victor had brought home. She did her sums, and showed Dip how it worked with matchsticks spread out on the floor. They'd buy the eggs from a poultry-man like blameless citizens for such-and-such each egg. Cheap eggs perhaps, not fresh exactly, but not green either. They'd boil them up, and dispatch Victor to sell them in the market place for such-and-such and such-again. Ten matches spent earned fifteen matches back. And fifteen matches made more than twenty-two. It was safe and legal – and lucrative, so long as eggs were à la mode. If only Aunt could recover her old hat or buy another one, the pair of them would be content again.

So it nearly was. At first they provided and prepared the eggs, and Victor sold them on the streets. But soon they were too bored with boiling them, four at a time, in their one pot.

They said to Victor, 'It's your job.' And so he got them from the poultryman himself. He learnt to count the money out and pay. He begged for charcoal or found wood to feed the stove in Dip's one room. He boiled the eggs himself, and took more care than Aunt or Dip had ever done to keep the shells intact and clean. They shared the profits, but he kept his merchandise well out of sight. They hardly spoke. They hardly met. When Dip and Aunt came back at night, Victor was curled up with stomach pain and sleep. The eggs he ate each day had made him constipated. His guts were pumped up with wind. They were as hard and bilious as sated snakes. His farts were counter-tenor monotones, as noisy and as regular as chimes. This was the fiercest smell. But there were others too – the eerie odours that the eggs released when they were boiled, the badger-pungency of souring, broken eggs, the mawkishness of shells. The three of them had sulphur nightmares, sulphur in their clothes, brimstone breath. They might as well have slept on Etna or inside the crater of some *soufrière*, decapitated like a breakfast egg. The smell was sweet and hot and aggravating. Victor's guts whined like unpunctured sausages in coals. Aunt did not snore, but puffed and hummed all night as if she did not dare to taint her lungs with inward breaths of air.

Dip hardly slept. He stayed out on the streets all night. He longed to push his hands in strangers' pockets once again. He had no appetite for sex with Aunt, or drink with Aunt, or hatless Aunt. One evening he did not return. He'd make his fortunes in some other part of town. Then Aunt – her judgement blurred by reckless loneliness – found some other man. Her sister's boy? She left him with her baggage, unattended, in what had been Dip's room and now was his. These were the first days of a life alone.

When Victor was eighty he could not recall his mother's face, or Aunt's, or Dip's. He could recall the parasol, the broad-brimmed cloche, the patent shoes, the collar studs. He could recall the painted cart piled high with greens and melons which Em had promised would one day take him and her out to the city edges where the trees began. He could recall his father's greying candle stub.

He did not talk about these things – though the bricks and cobbles of the town and market place stored all his early life like walls store moss, and the osmotic gossips of the city had taken in his life and passed it on to anyone with time to spare. Victor himself, when he grew to be a man of consequence, had just one public story from those days of poverty and waifing eggs. It was the story that he told when he could not escape the duties of the business millionaire and was called upon to make a speech to the Commerce Club or talk to someone from the radio or the financial press, or write a foreword for the little magazine his staff produced.

They knew he started life with eggs. But then? What was it drove him onwards, up and out of eggs, apart from cramp and flatulence? How was it that a boy so young could have the vision to diversify from eggs to eggs and fruit and bread and cheese, to upgrade his tray with decoration, then with wheels until he traded off a barrow? Where did he find the energy, the business zeal, to strip his barrow when the trading day was done and hire out himself and it for bringing produce cheaply from the station, until he had two barrows, five, and twenty-five, and ten boys in his pay, and fruit stalls of his own, and packing firms and farms, and, finally, before his fortieth year, the Soap Market itself?

Why not stop when he was crowned the Fruit King of the

city? Why battle on to set up Import/Export firms, and truck-
ing companies, and canneries, to build Big Vic, to spread his
fortune round the city and the world so that each lemon
squeezed for tea by anyone in town would have been pack-
eted as seed, and grown in soil, and harvested in plantations,
and sent in trucks and trains and boats, and invoiced out of
offices, and sold on market stalls that Victor owned?

'You tend your tree. You get good fruit,' he used to say.
Or, 'I was born a countryman – and country people always
reinvest their seed.' These were both phrases he had taken
from his man called Rook. But that single story from his past
was not Rook's work. It was Victor's own: one evening – he
was nine or ten, Aunt and Dip were gone, and he was still
surviving on boiled eggs – he ended up as usual in the cafés
and the bars of the Soap Garden. Boiled eggs went well with
mugs of beer – but he had learnt there was no point in
offering boiled eggs to those who drank the favoured clay-red
wine or ordered coffee. Malt and eggs do not do battle in the
mouth – but eggs with coffee or with wine destroy the taste
and smell of both.

There was a man who nearly always bought three eggs
and ate them, without pause, whether he was drinking beer or
wine or coffee-and-a-shot. He paid a little extra to have his
eggs unshelled by Victor. He did not take a plunge of salt. He
dipped his eggs instead into the sugar pot. He halved each egg
longways with his teeth and then consumed each half open-
mouthed and without much regard for the spectacle and mess
he made. It was not clear what kind of man he was. He sat
alone, though everyone who served or passed by deferred to
him. He was so fat that he walked with a stick, not because he
lacked the strength to bear his weight, but simply as a means

of maintaining lift and balance should he need to sit or climb a stair, or – rarity indeed – to step aside. His walking-stick was tarbony and topped in silver, not ostentatious but smart, and as sturdy as a cudgel. The scroll etching in the silver was made bold in its recesses by city grubbiness and verdigris and – who could doubt it? – dried blood.

They said he was a landlord of some sort, a pimp, a man who'd been a consul in the tropics and had made a fortune out of gold or slaves or running guns, an impresario, a counterfeiter, an operatic star who had not sung since some scandal or some love affair had silenced him, an undercover cop. He hardly ever spoke a word. He took his usual seat, at the margins of the nearest café. It was a seat which did not require him to negotiate the narrow spaces between tables, chairs and customers. He drank his drinks. He ate his eggs. He read his paper or his magazine. He made a note, occasionally, inside a grey-bound book. He held his stick as if he were a shepherd eager for the chance to drive away a raven or a dog. He staved off fullness with excess.

'We never knew his name, or what he did,' said Victor. 'The only certainty about this man was that he was worthy of respect.'

So Victor was fastidious. He made certain that the eggs he sold to him were fresh and free of shell, and clean. He placed the three shelled eggs, as usual, on the metal bill-and-tip which the waiter had positioned next to – that balmy night – a glass of beer, and waited for his payment in small change. There was always a wait. A fat man finds it difficult to fish his purse or coins from his trousers or his coat. His right hand was trapped inside his pocket when someone knocked him from behind. The table shuddered. And the beer? It spilled a little and would have fallen from the table had not the fat man, with the speed and delicacy of a lizard's tongue, shot out his one free hand and steadied it. He turned as best he could. His body did not turn, just his head and neck. His chair and back received another blow and this time the beer and glass were on the ground before his hand could move. The eggs began to slide and arc across the table-top, their passage eased and oiled by beer. They jostled at the table's edge like nervous bubbles at a drain, fell off, and then were split and knocked as tasteless as the cobblestones.

The fat man did not feel the third impulse. Two fighting men, one pushing with stiff fingers and a spittled mouth, another walking backwards and attempting to defend himself with kicks, sent the table spinning on one leg, then sprawling, legs aloft, above the eggs and beer. So far as one could tell from the stream of threats and imprecations they exchanged, their differences would not be solved without the death of one.

They were two market traders, partners, neighbours, old-time friends – and what they'd fallen out about wasn't worth a bead of phlegm, let alone the lungfuls that the two of them, now out of fighting range, were looping at each other through the air.

The younger of the two had wisecracked with the customers of the older man, the one whose fighting fingers were so certain and so stiff. He'd teased them, half cunningly and half in jest, that his neighbour's produce was not fresh.

'He's selling fossils and antiques today,' he'd said. The neighbour swore this foolishness, these lies, had cost him trade. And more. And worse. He knew for sure that, while his back was turned, the younger one pocketed the cash for onion clumps which they had purchased as partners and whose profits they should share. He did not listen to his friend's defence – that 'while my back was turned' meant 'while I filled myself with drink, while I let the business, onion clumps and all, slide into hell'. There were a hundred other microscopic aggravations between the men that, in the sudden heat of anger, seethed and thrived like viruses. 'Go dine on shit,' one said. The other held his little finger up, a gesture meant to show disdain, and said, with feeble dignity, 'I'll never talk to you again.'

The fat man filled his lungs and put some pressure on his stick. His knuckles whitened. It looked as if he were about to show how he could slay these two with just one etched and silver blow. But he was only holding tight so that he could stand. Once up – and once the two adversaries had quietened and were watching him – he dipped his hand into the inner pocket of his coat and pulled out a wallet. He took out one banknote. He unfolded it and held it up, theatrically, for all to see. A blue five-thousand note. A two-month wage. Enough to purchase a good horse, enough to buy a thousand eggs. The fat man folded the blue note in two, lengthways, exactly as he halved his eggs, and tore it carefully along the crease. What was he then? A conjurer? Would he set fire to those two halves, or chew them up, then make them whole again? Was this a good note? Was it counterfeit?

There was no movement in the Soap Garden. Even waiters, trays aloft, were frozen where they stood. Victor was not the only one who'd never seen a note as large as that before. What kind of man would tear such wealth in two?

The fat man flung out and spread his arms, a half note in each hand. His voice was both bourgeois and everyday. It

165

was, surprisingly, for one so large, a little reedy too.

'One each,' he said. He shook the worthless halves impatiently. 'Come on. Step up.'

The younger man was the first to step forward. He did not look the fat man in the eye. He concentrated on the half-a-fortune and the walking-stick, expecting there to be some finger trick or some low, crippling blow. He need not have feared. The stiff, blue piece of paper transferred to him with just the slightest reticence where the embossed printing snagged on the fat man's dampened skin.

The elder of the two was also reticent. He recognised the fat man's game. He had children of his own and knew how squabbles were resolved by parental trickery. You broke a ginger stick in half and let the children suck away their moods. Yet half a ginger stick had value on its own. It tasted just as good in pieces. But half a note? He could not formulate exactly what the trick might be, yet he was in no doubt, as he took in the fat man and his neighbour holding half a fortune in their hands, that he would be a fool to walk away. He might as well take half a note. To turn away would not look good or wise. Pride would not allow a market man to jeopardise just half a chance of making random, unearned cash.

He did not move. He put his hand out. Palm up. The cussed supplicant. Let Mammon come to him. The fat man was not proud. He did not mind that he would have to move a pace or two. He took three steps. He spread his weight across both legs and leant his stick against a chair. He rolled the half note in a ball, dismissively, with studied irony. He dropped it on the outstretched, flattened palm. And then he took the market trader's hand in both of his and wrapped the fingers round the paper ball.

'Now talk,' the fat man said.

Both traders felt more foolish than they'd done since they were adolescents. They did not hang around. They did not walk away, of course, arms linked, their two half lives already interlocked. They disappeared like cats, their heads and shoulders down, their ears alert, their fur on end. They would not talk that night – but who can doubt that they would trade weak grins the following day and then handshakes? They'd see the sense in being partners once again.

The fat man did not watch them go. He waited for a moment, on his stick, while three waiters put the chairs and table back in place, wiped up the beer, removed the mushy eggs. The proprietor himself brought out a replacement beer, the best. 'It's on the house,' he said, thankful for the damage and the mayhem that the blue note had thwarted and thankful, too, for all the rich absurdities which they had witnessed.

The fat man started on his beer, as unbothered, it would seem, by the spat which he had ended as by the money he had lost. The no-expression on his face said, Five thousand? That's a morsel for a man like me. I'd throw a hundred of them to the wind just so long as I can have my beer and eggs in peace and quiet. He looked up, then. The thought of eggs had made him lift his eyes and run his baby tongue along his lips.

Victor was standing where he always stood. Hypnotised. The fat man held three fingers up. Victor selected three more eggs. He cracked their shells at their thick ends and peeled them white and bare. He brought the sugar from another table. He stood and took the coins from the fat man's hand. He hoped that he would tear a note in half for him as well. He was not old enough to fully understand what he had witnessed: the fickle, slender contrivances, the artifices, the

stratagems of wealth, its piety, its fraudulence, its crude finesse. But – given time – he'd understand it all and make a
scripture out of it.

'The fat man taught me', Victor explained, to those who
wished to hear or read the complex moral of his anecdote, 'that
money talks.' He did not know that such an insight was old
hat and crassly simple. Or that his variations of this insight –
such as 'Money is the peacemaker' and 'Money's muscle' –
were simple complications of the truth. What the fat man had
displayed was cynicism, if cynicism is the trick of seeming to
engage with chance and danger but without taking any risks.
Money has no moral tact. It's true, the rich have power to
intervene, to heal and damage as they wish. Toss money in the
ring and see the drama that it makes of other people's lives.
But, more, they have the power, if they choose, to stay more
silent and discrete than monks. The rich – and here was
Victor's unacknowledged dream – can simply make a wall, a
fortress shield of wealth, beyond which the dramas of the
world can run their courses unobserved.

Victor so far – he was nine or ten – had led a life not free
of drama of the tragic kind. The misfortune of his father's
death. The journey into town. The nights beneath the parasol.
The fire. The days with Aunt and Dip. The liberation and the
tyranny of eggs. His was a moral tale, an exemplar of how
miserably the small fry of the world can fare. Someone could
write a book on his first years and make it stand for all our
city's woes. No wonder, then, that Victor now wished for
something more mundane than poverty. He wished to be a fat
man, too, protected from the city by what his wallet held. In
this, he sought what Joseph, decades later, sought. And that
was privacy. He saw himself, an older, wealthy man, alone

and dining in a public place. At times it was a city restaurant, at other times a trestle in the countryside, with chickens and with trees. There was no noise, except the sound of cutlery on plates. He was quite calm and unafraid. No one around was close enough to disappoint him or betray him. A waiter, paid to do his job, was all he needed. He did not need or want a family, or friends. He did not need the warmth of company or conversation, or the reassurances of praise. No one could come and give him Chinese burns. No one could let him down or disappear. There was no comfort which could not be bought. There was no problem that he could not solve by tearing notes in half. What is more eloquent and reassuring than a shield of private wealth?

So Victor now – and almost by design – became an undramatic boy. He had his room, his job, his street routines. He had ambition, too, but nothing to make good grand opera from. He set his sights painstakingly on targets within reach – more sales of eggs, a market stall, an orchard and a field, a motorvan, some staff, some ledgers and a desk . . . He told himself that when he was more safe and certain, he would test the magic of the torn banknote. Not five thousand, naturally. He was the timid sort. A hundred note perhaps. But that day never came, despite the money that he made. Because he never felt that he was safe or certain? Because he was mean and unadventurous? That was the judgement of the town. No one expected such a man – and so late in life – to lower his defences for a while and toss his money in the ring.

PART THREE
VICTOR'S CITY

1

IT WAS THE MONDAY after Victor – pent up all his life, between the nipple and the purse – had celebrated being old with a birthday lunch of coddled fish, fresh air, accordions. It was the Monday after he became engrossed in his last, his first, his only *civic* fantasy, to publicly display his private wealth at last by building a market worthy of a beggar woman and a millionaire. A damp and windy morning, just short of nine o'clock – and Victor the Insomniac, a boss who normally was at his desk a little after dawn, was nowhere to be seen.

Rook, with Anna at his side, walked the two kilometres of cobble, stone and asphalt between his apartment and the tunnel below Link Highway Red. Her hand was on his arm. They seemed as fearless as lovers half their age, made adolescent by the comfort – unexpected, overdue – of flesh on flesh. No one would think these two – this sparrow-chested, greying man, this woman, warm and pouchy as a pastry bun – were husband and wife. Such wooing, binary displays belong to fledgling romances. Maturer ones are more abashed, less startled and enraptured by the luck of love. These two fledglings on the street were not the married kind. Their circumstance was clear: here was an out-of-season *grande affaire* between two people almost old enough to be too old, too sleepy for such public love. 'Sleepy' is the word the growers use to specify a pear, and other soft-fleshed fruits, which have

173

matured but, though they have their colour and their shape, will soon begin to brown and rot and lose their flavour and their bloom. To taste such fruit is to taste the gamey pungency of middle age.

As they cut diagonally across the town, between the rush-hour traffic and the crowds, beneath the ochre-coloured eiderdown of clouds, Rook and Anna seemed misplaced, late Sunday revellers caught by the Monday morning light. The hastening single people in the street, tooth-paste and coffee on their gums, a day of labour summoning, a desk, a loom, a till, gave way to them, as if a couple so engrossed and casual had passage rights, like yachts, to an unhindered channel at the pavement's crown. We all defer to couples, do we not? A man and woman hand-in-hand can make the toughest of us step aside, can stop a tram.

This couple were not rushed. They were not hungry for their desks or eager for their colleagues and their phones. They held each other by the hand, the upper arm, the elbow and the wrist. They held each other's waists. And when they reached the walkers' tunnel – just at the spot where Rook had used his keys and fists and where the mugged and flattened laurel leaves still lifted in the draught – they took advantage of the solitude and gloom to kiss. Once they reached the windy mall, however, they separated by a metre, and walked in parallel. The weekend spent in Rook's apartment had been refreshment for them both. They'd hardly left Rook's bed by day, and then at night they'd taken to the streets and bars to fuel themselves, with the reckless alcohol of crowds, the aphrodisiacs of drink, for more love-making. Yet now they walked demurely, chastely, along the coloured marble flagstones. It was not wise to love too publicly. Who knew who might be watching from the greenhouse on the 28th, or through the tinted windows of his office suite? Who knew if Victor – that unimpassioned, loveless man who seemingly had never tried the luxuries of pressing skin to skin, who could not understand the pleasures of the thigh, the tongue, the abdomen, the breast – might take against two lovers in Big Vic.

The mall was cunning preparation for the lobby of the office block. It cooled and shrank pedestrians. It echoed with the click of heels, and the heavy doors of taxi-cabs, and sighing ventilation ducts. The shiny brick-veneers, the mirrored colonnades, the fish-trap cloisters leading to the finance palaces and the trading brokerages which were the tenants there, did not invite ill-discipline or dawdling. The mall's misanthropy struck Rook and Anna dumb, just as the deep, cool shade of conifers will silence those who exit from a field. They did not speak. They even blushed a little, as if they guessed their weekend intimacy could not be hidden here. Their entry to Big Vic was self-conscious, too; Anna's face a little too composed and Rook's – unanswered – greetings to the lobby staff, the uniformed commissionaires, too hearty for the time of day. They shared – a shade too clumsily – a segment of Big Vic's rotating doors. They shared the lift for twenty-seven floors. But once they reached the office lobby they headed for their desks as if the only love they shared was love of work.

Rook was in the best of moods, and with good cause. He was relieved to find his desk was, for the moment, clear. Normally by that time on a Monday, Victor would have sent his Fix It list – a sheaf of notes, queries and instructions, recriminations. Victor himself did not like to deal with people on the telephone, or even speak to clients face to face. What was to blame for that? His hibernating temperament? His hearing aid? His shield of wealth? He read reports. He scanned accounts. He watched the share and stock prices dance banking quick-steps round their decimals on the office VDUs. If there was anything to be *done*, then Rook could do it. He had younger legs and ears. But on that Monday, there were no tasks for him, no estate manager to intimidate by telephone ('We note that field beans are a trifle mean this year. And late'), no groundless tension to diffuse amongst the market traders, no thin letter of regret, refusal, to be composed and sent, no group executive meetings to be called and chaired while Victor claimed some old man's malady as pretext for staying in his room or on the roof.

Such liberty! It suited Rook. He had his own plans for the day and these involved a little horse-play at the office desk. He was used to having sex with Anna on his bed. A day or two of anything is time enough for it to seem routine. It had been fun – exhilarating fun – but not adventurous. His sexual needs were escalating. Making love to her at work was what engrossed him now. Big Vic's solemnity was more a stimulation than a restraint. The need for stealth and speed and stiflement would blunt the appetite, you think? Think twice. Lovemaking is at its best when it transgresses social ordinances and strays far from the trodden path into the briars of the undergrowth, where risk and lust run neck and neck.

Rook wanted something more subversive than bedsteading. He wanted intercourse with Anna in the place where he had sat for months and contemplated her. He wanted office sex, with all the office work continuing, and all the VDUs alight, and these two colleagues, ankled by their underclothes, and pressed together like a pair of angler's worms. No one would think it odd if, later in the day, he called Anna to his room for consultations. She'd come, an innocent. He wasn't sure that she would share his eagerness – but from the appetite she'd shown for making bed-top love he had an inkling that she might.

He draped his jacket on his chair and then – with nothing else to do so early in the day – he went to Victor's office suite. The birthday throne was still outside, its plastic foliage evergreen and fresh. It seemed so foolish now that he had wasted so much effort on this birthday gift, for a man who had no appetite for sentiment. He pulled the foliage with its sticky tape free from the wood. He'd get someone to take it to the atrium and reconnect the stems where he had snapped them free. Or else he'd put them in a pot, a comic bouquet for Anna's desk – a teasing prelude for the courtship that he planned for her in his own room, at his own desk. But first – the bouquet in his hand – he knocked on Victor's door. He knocked again. And tried the handle. The door was locked. The old man's growing soft, Rook thought. He's slept through dawn for once. Rook bent to peer through the key-hole in the door. The inner key was in the lock.

'No signs of life!' he called out cheerily – and inanely – to the company accountant who, carrying a steaming coffee and a bank of ledgers, was passing through the lobby, tip-toeing through, in fact, as if he wished to keep his presence secret.

'Where's Victor, then?' The accountant shook his head and seemed unwilling to meet Rook's eye or match his cheeriness. 'Where's Victor, then?' Rook asked again.

'He won't be down today.'

'Why not?' Again Rook had to settle for the shaken head.

The accountant went into his room, and slammed the door shut with his heel.

Rook took his bouquet to Reception. The women there were busy at their desks.

'Where's Victor's schedule for today?' he asked. Again he had to ask the question twice.

'It's cancelled.'

'Oh, yes. Why's that?'

No one could say. No one seemed keen to even talk about this rarity of Victor absent from his desk, his schedule 'cancelled' for the day. It was perplexing that the staff were unforthcoming and morose when here was opportunity for them to waste a little time with talk.

'What's going on?' Reception shrugged and held its tongue.

'Why so grumpy, then?' Rook asked out loud. 'The Monday miseries? Too much to drink on Sunday night? Cheer up, cheer up. It's only a job. "Work not shirk is life's best perk. So join my harem, said the Turk." '

Their smiles were thin and stretched. Something embarrassed them. He waited, unsure of what the problem was, but certain that these three women, hired for their public charm and cheerfulness, were ill-at-ease. At last he said, unflippantly, 'What's up with you three, then?' Still, there were no volunteers to look him in the eye. At last the eldest of the women said with a voice that quavered in and out of key, 'It's not for us to say.'

'It's not for us to say.' In other words, this was a private thing, too personal and intimate for them to comment on, despite Reception's reputation as the building's bourse for rumour and hearsay. Rook no longer was perplexed. He guessed what caused their awkwardness, their blushing jealousy. Some office spy had spotted him and Anna out on the town on Saturday, perhaps. Or walking hand-in-hand towards Big Vic. The word had spread. The word 'Romance!' For some reason he could hardly understand this out-of-office liaison was not approved. You'd think this was some tutting medieval monastery, Rook thought (seated for the moment at his desk). Was this just jealousy, or sullen irritation that he'd breached an office code that those in charge and close to Victor should be as continent as him? Or was secrecy the culprit? Did Reception and Accountancy and, come to think of it, the uniformed Commissionary at mall level, resent that Rook had kept his tryst with Anna to himself for one weekend?

'Ridiculous!' He spoke the word out loud. It *was* ridiculous. Unlikely, too. The men and women in Big Vic were magnetised and not rebuffed by any hint of scandal or of secrecy. They loved the ribaldries of life. Particularly the trio at Reception. They wore their grandest, most libertine of smiles when there was gossip to be shared and prurience to trade. They would not drop their voices and their eyes, and act like undertakers' clerks. They would have looked Rook in the eye and said, 'What's this I hear?' or 'You had a nice time Saturday! A little pigeon spotted you and Anna rubbing noses in a bar . . .'

What then? What could the problem be? He went through Friday in his mind in search of irritants. What had he said, or done, to set this Monday morning frost? He'd seen that everyone had shared the fun with champagne and cakes. He'd been his usual self, the Prince of Irony and Idleness. What had he done to give offence? Something was irking them, no doubt of that. And, truth to tell, something was irking him as well. His conscience was not entirely clear. Again he ran Friday through his mind and recognised exactly what it was that had stained his day. The subway fight with Joseph. The viciousness of fists and keys. The parting kick. The pleasure that he'd taken in such a squalid triumph. Yet these were private acts, less public than the time he'd spent with Anna. Who could know and disapprove of what had happened out-of-sight and underground and to an ill-dressed clod who had no contact with Big Vic? Why would anybody care?

Again Rook shuffled through the Friday pack. The pretext that he'd used to get down to the Market Place. The orange that he'd peeled. The tugging and the ripping of the laurel stems. The shaming bout of asthma in the presence of those men. The creaky birthday lunch. The gleeful coda to the day: Anna laughing on his bed, delighted by his mordancy, his teasing hands, that clowning routine with his underpants, 'Ourselves, Ourselves, Ourselves'. And yes, (I raise my head above the parapet again) the mocking column that I, The Burgher, wrote about the taxi and the boss's coddled fish. All the workers in Big Vic would have seen and laughed at that . . . and thought, perhaps, The Burgher's source was Rook? For that was just like Rook, to feed the babblers of the press. So, then – they would not look him in the eyes because they thought he had betrayed a fishy confidence? Again, 'Ridiculous!'

A firmer possibility occurred to Rook. He need not search his diary or his conscience any more. Of course! The staff's solemnity could have only one cause. By God, the old man's dead! he thought. 'No sign of life' indeed! Rook almost felt relieved, as all that morning's oddities were now explained. The missing Fix It list, the closed, locked door, the empty schedule, those phrases, 'It's been cancelled . . . He'll not be down today.' What apart from death, or at least a major stroke perhaps, would keep Victor from his work? If he had tumbled, say, and cracked a hip, his memos would be flying plumply from his bed like pigeons from a loft. While there was air left in his lungs and sufficient power in his arm to hold a pen, nothing would stop him orchestrating his affairs.

So that was it. The stick had snapped at last. Victor had died, and no one on the staff was senior enough to let Rook know. Or else, perhaps – this was a possibility – they thought he knew and were embarrassed by his lack of gravity or grief, his flippancy. 'It's not for us to say,' the women on Reception had insisted. And they were right. Rook had been the boss's eyes and ears, his fixer and his messenger. He was as close, as intimate, as anyone could be to such a cube of ice. No wonder nobody could face him with the news. No doubt the Finance Manager or the Group M.D. would come up from the floor below to inform Rook personally that there had been 'a sad event'. Or Anna, even. She was senior enough. Rook sat and waited, hoping it was Anna who would come. He closed his eyes and dropped his chin onto his chest. He felt – for the first time since the Friday night – that he would benefit from sleep.

Rook's door was open. There was no need for Anna to knock so formally on the stained veneer. Yet she was wise enough to knock and wait. He woke from his half-sleep and waved her in. Already he had prepared an elegiac face; already he was searching in his mind for what the death of Victor meant to him. Advancement? Displacement? Something in the Will? At least it meant that this was no time to close the office door and push his hands beneath the bands of Anna's skirt and blouse.

Anna did not look at Rook. Her expression was the same as those worn by the Reception staff, by the accountant as he hurried to his room, by the commissionaire who had ignored Rook's airy greeting as he had entered Big Vic from the mall. Now he was sure he had identified the truth. She looked so shocked, so drained, so unlike the face upon the pillow. 'Come in. What's wrong?'

'Bad news,' she said. She looked as if her knees would give. He held her in his arms. It didn't matter what the staff might think. Her tears fell on his jacket and his tie.

'Sit down. Sit down,' he said. He wished to cry himself. He felt so nervous and so powerful. He could not focus on the old man's death.

'What's wrong?'

She took deep breaths, and then she looked him in the face at last. 'I wish it wasn't me who had to tell you this,' she said.

'I know.' And then, 'No need to tell me, Anna. I can guess.'

'Guess what?'

'It's Victor, isn't it? He's ill. He's dead.'

She shook her head. She almost laughed. 'He isn't dead. You'll wish he was. It's you . . . It's us!' She wiped her face, and took deep breaths until she found her usual even voice: 'He says you've got to go. He seems to know that we've been meeting out of work. How can he know? It's not his business anyhow. This isn't sane!'

She handed him an office memorandum. Victor had put it on her desk, unsealed. Some office rubber-neck had read it and spread the news. It only took one prying clerk, one internal phone call, to circulate bad news throughout Big Vic, from the atrium to the 27th floor. Victor had written the memorandum – in pencil – late on the previous Friday night, his birthday night. It instructed Anna to tell Rook: 'His out-of-work contacts and activities are not morally compatible with the trust invested in him. They have no place in an organisation such as mine where relationships between all members of the office staff, producers, clients, and customers, should be based on propriety and honesty. He is dismissed. Please inform him that he has until midday to clear his desk, and that there can be no further contact between us except through the mediation of lawyers.' There was an envelope for Rook – a formal note of termination.

'He's mad,' she said. She understood the comforts of hyperbole. 'He's old and mad and wicked! He's shut himself away up there like a gutless little kid. Does he think he owns us all? Can't we have "contacts, out of work" without the nod from him?'

But Rook was in no doubt what Victor meant by 'contacts and activities'. Someone – he hadn't got an inkling who, not yet – had spilled the beans. Victor knew now all about the pitch-money which the soapies had paid each quarter and which had made Rook so rich and careless.

'He isn't mad,' he said. 'And this hasn't got anything to do with you, or us.'

'We'll fight for you! Come on!'

She was prepared to head an office strike, to draft petitions, risk her job, give Victor merry hell. She was prepared to burrow into Rook, and make a warren at his heart. Rook shook his head. Why fight to lose? Who'd be his ally when the word got out about the scheme he'd run, the money that he'd made, the cynicism of his office jocularity. If he made merry hell, then Victor or his lawyers might make hell of some less cheerful kind. They could inform the police and then the charge might be Extortion or Embezzlement. He'd end up in a cell. The old man hiding in his room had struck a distant deal with Rook that robbed him of his work but not his liberty.

'Anna. Please,' he said, and shook his head. 'No fuss.' That's all he had the heart to say. Already he was letting work and Anna go. He only asked for dignified retreat. He almost packed a bag and just walked out. But Anna would not understand. She stood her ground.

'Do something now,' she said.

Her pluck – and innocence – put Rook to shame.

'Alright. I'll make him talk to me.' He thought there might be just a chance of changing Victor's mind. He'd find a way of justifying the unofficial payments he'd received. The payments were in Victor's interest after all. They kept the traders quiet. They guaranteed Rook's role as intermediary between both camps. 'I had to take their money,' he could say. 'They wouldn't trust a man who wasn't in their pay.'

He knocked on Victor's office door again. He tried to call him on the apartment's internal phone, but the day-valet merely repeated that his boss could 'take no calls until the afternoon'. The truth was that Victor was hiding in the greenhouse on the roof, exterminating aphids once again and primping plants and looking out through glass and rain and wind on distant neighbourhoods. What was the point in facing Rook himself, when he could deputise dismissals, and Rook could just evaporate before the afternoon and leave no trace?

Well, Rook could not co-operate. He could not disappear, at least while Anna was around. He could not clear his desk and leave no trace. He planned, instead, to sit it out. He'd stay exactly where he was, his feet up on his desk, his door ajar, his room a mess of plastic leaves, until Victor tired of hiding on the roof. Let him descend. Let them discuss it face to face. Let's see, he thought, if Victor has the strength to be a tyrant other than by deputation or by memoranda. Might something, then, be salvaged from the wreck?

At midday Rook was still inside his room, alone and looking out across a rain-lashed city. Already cars and buses drove with full headlights, and the neon on the streets was liquid and intense. The coloured awnings of the market place could not be seen and certainly no hills or woods or parkland greens, no shafts of natural light, lent any gaiety to what he saw. The city was as grey and formal as an office suit. Rook heard, but did not recognise, a man's voice ask for him by name. He heard a secretary whisper something in reply, then footsteps to his room. Two men, in uniform, one from Security, the other a commissionaire, his face familiar from the entrance hall and atrium, stood at the door.

One coughed. 'Are you ready, sir?'

'Ready for what?' asked Rook. Was this the summons from his boss?

'It's midday, sir.'

'And so?'

'And so we've come to escort you . . . outside.'

Outside! The word was a kidney punch; it winded him. Outside. Out in the cold. Out on his arse.

He shook his head: 'Not yet.'

'It's midday, sir.'

'Not yet.'

They came into the room. 'Come on,' they said.

'I haven't done my desk.' Rook opened up a drawer to
show he was not ready yet, and rescued his nebuliser from
amongst the pens and calculators. He sucked on the mouthpiece. He could feel the spongy alveoles tightening in his
lungs.

'We've got our orders, sir. It has to be midday.'

They offered him some help. Was it his breathlessness, or
were they simply being firm? They lifted him by his elbows.
They pulled his chair clear, and shut the desk drawer. They
might have been from the Ambulance Brigade, they were so
mild, and Rook so pale.

'You'll have to leave your Staff Pass with us.' Rook put his
hand into his pocket, to do as he was told. He was resigned to
going like a lamb. He fumbled for the sharp edges of his
laminated Pass, and found instead the old flick-knife, the
bunch of keys. How long was it since he'd put Joseph on the
ground? Here was an opportunity to use his fists again.

He found and gave them his Staff Pass. He would have
ripped it into two if laminated plastic had been more biddable
and if he could have controlled his shaking hands.

'We'd better go,' they said, and led him through the
offices to Reception and the lifts. There was no sign of life.
Even Anna had disappeared. Someone had had the cruel sense
to ask the staff to keep away while Rook was led 'outside'. He
let them take him to the lift. He let them walk him to the
tasselled rope and join him – three to one segment – in the
automatic door. He let it sweep him into the rain and wind
beyond. He wrapped his fingers round his keys, key tips
protruding through his knuckles, so that his punches when
they came would do the greatest harm. But the moment never
came. Such moments never do, except in books and films. His

warders were too proper and too big to fight.

'Thank you, sir,' the commissionaire said, deferential to the last, as he watched Rook pass from the dry into the wet. No one offered to summon a company Panache, or a taxi. He was expected now to take his chances on the street. He was of less importance than a perch.

He knew, he felt it in his water and his bones, that already Victor was at work, no longer hiding from the world. Security would call and say, 'He's gone!' and Victor could count it safe enough to come downstairs and sit behind his desk as if he had no hand in all the harm that had been done, and would be done. Would he miss Rook? What should he miss? His fixer's willingness to serve? His care and knowledge of the market place, his intimacy with vegetables and fruit, his office cheeriness, his social skills? No, Victor had the wealth and power to replace these things, to find another yet more honest Rook, who would be glad to be old Victor's aide. He hardly gave the man another thought. He was too old and crammed.

Beyond the tinted, toughened glass of Victor's suite the wind was fast and strong and sharp with rain. Big Vic was swaying slightly at its top, and whistling. Victor's coffee moved inside its cup. His office door fell open, then fell shut. A paperweight shaped out of polished serpentine slid across the old man's desk. And Rook, once more, was out upon the canyon floor, between the gleaming, swaying, whistling cliffs of glass and steel and stone.

2

WHAT WOULD YOU EXPECT of Rook? That he would decompose without the frigorific regime of the working day? Most city people – men at least – are wedded to their jobs, and when you take those jobs away they soon become as empty and as brittle as blown eggs. Work is for the idle. It gives a chaptered, tramline narrative to life; it empties suburbs and estates and provides the displaced, liberated residents with dramas structured by the clock. It then provides the wages note, the cheque, the cash, the banking draft which, more than where you're born or live, is what it takes to be a citizen. A salary can make an interloper feel at home; 'An empty purse', or so the saying goes, 'makes strangers of us all.' But no, Rook, weak and self-indulgent though he seemed, was not the sort to crumble like dry pastry. He was – like everybody else with any sense – too selfish and too vain to sacrifice himself. He spent three days indoors, bereaved. He would not answer Anna's calls from work, or let her in when she came round to the apartment in the evenings, or respond when she delivered a snapshot of her – younger – self, inscribed 'Let's meet and talk'. What was the point? He did not even read the baffled notes which she left in his letterbox to reassure him that 'whatever Victor does can make no difference to us'. Rook knew better. She would not seek him out once she had learnt exactly what his 'contacts and activities' had been. Why nourish love when it was bound to fail? He dared not think of her or quantify his loss. He needed first to concentrate on how he could excrete, transmit, the anger that he felt. He was consumed by malice, but none of it was turned upon himself. What had he done, except to be a cheerful pragmatist who'd seen a chance and taken it? He blamed the cheerless millionaire. He blamed the hide-bound traders in the Soap Market. He blamed the coward who had gone behind his back to blab. Who blabbed? Rook did not find it very hard to know who told and when. It must have been one of Victor's cronies, one of the five arthritic soapies who had shared the birthday lunch. Which one? He could not tell – so, for the moment, he would blame them all.

He'd once seen a film – *One Deadly Kiss* – in which an English lord had hunted down, one by one, the five male passengers on a country post-chaise bound for London. His motive? One of the men – and only one – had 'kissed and robbed' his wife as she slept in the cushions of the coach. 'Better that all five die than that one blackguard lives to taint again the honour of a lady,' the Englishman had said, in those vaulting, vowelly tones that English gentry, and English actors, used to have. He bribed the coachman, richly, to reveal the passenger list, and set off across the country in wild and righteous pursuit. He did not know, as he dispatched another with a pistol or a knife, that all five men were guilty of some other, capital offence – arson, murder, treachery – and so 'deserved' to die. He did not know – how simple these films are! – that none of the five had touched his wife. The rapist was the bribed and silent coachman, free, as credits roll, to kiss and rob some more!

The English love these ironies, and Rook took pleasure in

them, too. Rook dreamed the film, but in his dream the
passengers were greengrocers, the coach was Victor's birthday
lunch. Rook became a younger man, the firebrand dressed in
black. He hunted down and polished off the five. They fell
amongst their fruit. They died on beds of spinach. Who was
the coachman, free to sin again? Rook's dream was crowded
out by deeper sleep before the credits rolled.

By day, Rook fantasised; and in these angered fantasies he
would avenge the noon indignity of being thrown out, a
vagrant, from Big Vic. He would be the English lord, though
more heroic and less mannered. His weapon would be Joseph's knife. He practised with the blade, and mimed the
damage he might do. He punched the bathroom door. He bit
off the nails on both his hands. He masturbated, but could not
hold the image of a woman in his head. He lay in bed too
long. He stayed up late, and drank too much of the Boulevard
Liqueur he had bought for Anna during the weekend. His
breathing became laboured, first with nerves, and then his
asthma took hold in his right-side chest, brought on, intensi-
fied, by his loss of work and income and the anger that he felt.
He nebulised more often than he should. He grew light-
headed and unsteady from the alcohol and medicine and from
the cheap narcosis of his dream.

At last – for wrath's a sprinter and soon tires – he became
more calm, less frantic. Bruised, he was, discoloured by the
blows that he'd endured. But it slowly dawned on Rook, the
self-approving optimist, that he was not weakened as a man,
but made more potent. He was persuaded now that Victor had
freed him from a curse. The job that Rook had lost was no
great loss. Good riddance to it. He'd paid for it a dozen years
before, with . . . what word is there to use but 'soul'? The

moment that young Black Rook had taken Victor and his cheque by the hand he'd dropped the sanction of the street, he'd lost the casual chatter of the market place. The city sparrow had spread its wings to rise on cushioned thermals beyond the pavement commonwealth and join the austere governance of hawks. Now he was back on earth again.

He felt too sick to eat, too shaky in the hand to lift a fork or pour a cup of coffee, but now at least he looked ahead as much as he looked back. What could he do with this new potency, this rediscovered soul? He was too old to start a fresh career. But, surely, he was rich enough to set up a modest business of his own. He checked the balance of his savings. He counted all the currency notes which he'd amassed. He had no debts, no obligations, no family to maintain. His situation could be worse. To be a rich man without work was not the meanest fate of all. There was no rush. He'd take a month or two of rest, and keep his eyes peeled for . . . for what? A bar, perhaps? A shop? He was alarmed by the dullness in prospect. Could he afford six months of rest? Or nine? He deserved a little breathing-space to plan his future years. At least the spare time on his hands could be good fun. He'd please himself and no one else. His tie could hang loose all the time. He need not wear a tie. He need not wear a suit. That was the uniform of servitude. He need not hasten through the city streets, his coffee hardly drunk, to be at work on time.

Now he was ready to go out. He searched his wardrobe and he found the black leather jacket he'd once worn. The skin was scuffed and greying and the cuffs had split, but still it fitted, and the zip was good. The leather smelt a little of the market place, and the lining was stained beneath the arms and in the middle of the back from working sweat. He did not have the working trousers or the shirt to match – but he had dark and casual office clothes, and these he wore. He felt transformed. The jacket set him free. He had resurrected the man he'd been a dozen years before. He transferred his keys and wallet, his nebuliser, the Joseph 'nife' from his suit into the zipped pockets of the leather jacket. He tidied the apartment, read the notes that Anna had left, put her snapshot on the mantelshelf, and went into the town.

It was just a week since Victor's birthday lunch, a week in which he'd rediscovered love, and lost his job, and soared and plummeted, one hundred metres, twenty-seven floors, onto the street. All-in-all he felt winded and invigorated, like some shaken boy who's just stepped safely from a switchback ride. He set off for the Soap Market. The sooner he was seen amongst the stalls and soapies the better for his shaken self-esteem.

He walked between the banks of vegetables and fruit without a greeting or a glance. He was not snubbed. He was not recognised, at first. His leather coat was a disguise. It made his walk more bear-like, from the shoulders, hands in jacket pockets, collar up. The suited Rook had seemed a little taller, more loose-limbed, and walking from the hip. But once he sat amongst the traders at a bar in the Soap Garden, his face was known. He heard the whispers, and caught the glances and the nods. The waiter was his usual pleasant self, but waiters do not count. The market workers – the porters and the salesgirls – did not speak to him, but then they never had. He'd been too grand. He'd been the old man's *nuncio*, his Representative on Earth.

Rook did his best to seem relaxed. But he was not relaxed enough to hold his cup steady with one hand. He shook so badly that the sugar for his coffee trembled in the spoon. He wished he had a newspaper with which to shield himself. He wished that he could hide behind a cigarette, without the smoke occasioning a fireball in his chest. Part of him feared that he would see one of the birthday guests, some arthritic merchant on a stick, and feel obliged, compelled, to make a scene. But mostly he feared what the market men might do to him now that he was stripped of office. He feared their jeers, their ironies, the jabs and punches they might give to him, and with good cause. Those modest tithes, those sweeteners, which Rook had levied every quarter and for which he'd guaranteed clean access to the boss's ear, were now revealed as money down the pan. Rook was further now from Victor's ear than any soapie in the market. He was the only one whose contact with the boss was limited to 'the mediation of law-yers'.

Mid-morning, though, is not the time for arguments or scenes. The market was too busy and the traders too immersed in chalking prices for the day to spend much time on Rook. It was no secret, naturally, that he had lost his job – but no-one there was certain why. The five old men were keeping quiet. Old men have enemies enough, and take more pleasure out of secrecy – their greenhouse secret with the boss – than spread-ing tales amongst the market *hoi polloi*. So Rook was noted, but not judged. The men who never cared for Rook, did not abhor him more or less because – or so the rumour was – he'd lost his job. Why would they like him any less because he was dismissed? The traders did not know the social protocol. His misfortune was, perhaps, good news for them. It might save them money. Who could tell? But then, there'd be new Rooks, and tougher ones whose pitch fees were less modest. They'd rather stick with their asthmatic. He was not loved but he was witty in his way and had the common touch. He had, at least, sprung from the market place. He'd robbed them, true, but done no lasting harm. Such is the vagrant logic of the street that Rook was almost popular with his old foes, just as a bully's popular when he releases captives from his grip.

Those who'd been on good terms with Rook and considered the pitch payments to be bribes initiated by themselves, felt just as proprietorial now about their 'man at Victor's ear', despite the fact that their man had been sacked. Indeed, they even felt a little guilty that their market cunning might have been the cause of Rook's dismissal. They felt a little fearful, too. What might the old man do? They judged it best to wait and see. But there were one or two – the younger ones, the ones who'd had less coffee and more shot – who went across to Rook. They shook his trembling hand. 'A bad business,' they said, inviting Rook to reveal exactly what had occurred with Victor. And then to end the silence, 'Let us know if you need any help.' Or they put a shot down on the table and invited Rook to stun his bad luck with a little drink.

So Rook still had a welcome in the market place, somewhere to pass his time while he decided how to spend his life. He came each morning, exchanged a repertoire of gestures with Cellophane Man who stood as usual at the market edge directing people, trollies, vans, and sat amongst his allies there. If they enquired, 'Come on, what did you do to get the push?', he told no lies. But neither did he tell the truth. He was good at keeping quiet and hinting with his mouth and eyes that he was innocent of blame. Within a few days the market men behaved as if he'd never been their go-between, or in their pay, or they in his, and just enjoyed his dry sarcasm and his cawing, nasal laugh when he told stories of the boss amongst his cats and insects on the 28th. Market memories are short so long as debts are settled fast. A lasting grudge is one that's waiting to be cashed.

Rook wandered through the alleys and the lanes of vegetables and fruit with fresh eyes now. He need not be as watchful as before, noting prices, faces, infringements of the market code. He need not be prepared to take pitch payments, surreptitiously, or listen to complaints about the price and quality of olives or pears. If he pushed through the crowds to the peaks and canyons of a citrus stall, no fruiterer would simply click his tongue and shake his head to signify 'No need to pay!' He was the public now and he was ruled, like anybody else, by the market creeds which one trader – tired of scrumpers or being asked for credit – had chalked up on his stall: 'No Loot, No Fruit', and 'We take IOUs, but only in cash!'

Rook was content to be a simple shopper, thumbing, like all the other shoppers there, but with more blatant expertise, the skins of fruit to check their readiness. Or plucking one leaf from pineapple tufts and judging by its reticence the softness of the core. Or testing whether pod-beans would snap or bend between his fingers. Or lifting melons to his nose and knowing, from the smell, the reasty from the ripe. Or scratching new potatoes with his nails to see how well the blistered skins would lift. He knew the trick of listening to cabbages: the hearty ones were silent in the ear. He understood the colours of the carrot, and how the reddest roots were soapiest and only good for stews. You could not confuse him with a waxy pear, or with mushrooms 'dirtied' with a spray. A butcher might make a fool of Rook with some false cut, some trick with bone or fat, but no one in the Soap Market had greater, wider skill with fruits and roots and leaves.

Why waste such expertise? Why couldn't he return from whence he'd come – the smart son of a marketeer – and become a marketeer himself, a soapie for the second time? Because of Victor? Because he was a snob, who having laboured at a desk was not prepared to rise at five to bend and lift and sell? Because he was too old to mend his ways? He was not rejuvenated by the thought of merchant Rook, his thin and greying head peering from behind a gleaming splash of fruit, his fortune measured out in paper bags. But neither was he much seduced by the alternative – a Rook with nothing much to do except to sit and age and spend. If only he could find the heart – and shamelessness – to lift a pen, a telephone, and answer Anna's calls to him, then, maybe, having nothing much to do but spend would seem less mournful.

Rook hoped to meet her on the street, by chance. He was alert for her, for any word of her. Anna's was the only face, he thought, from which he could get pleasure. For sure, he did not hope to see his mugger once again. The boy – whose 'nife' he still possessed – had no importance in his life. Yet, on the morning of Rook's tenth visit to the market bar, he encountered Joseph for the second time. The youth was barrowing red sacks of onions, three at a time, from an open truck which was parked amongst the vans and cars at the market edge. Rook was not pleased to see these two adversaries of his in such a partnership, with Joseph working for the man who'd always treated Rook with cold disdain. He was perplexed at first. He could not think what chance, what scheme, what machination, had brought these two together. But his confusion could not last because the moment that he focussed on the strangeness of it all, he realised the truth. Rook did not need to draw himself a map. The mugging and the sacking of two weeks before now made full sense. Details that had escaped him returned in trusses and in clusters. Rook remembered now how Con had shaken the sealed envelope of pitch money so tauntingly in his face, a challenge on his lips. Then, within two hours at the most, Joseph – armed with a photograph, a knife – had tried . . . tried what? Tried at Con's behest to resecure the envelope. And having failed to resecure it with a knife, what had Con done? He'd made a call, or sent an unsigned note, that afternoon to Victor. And here was Joseph, still in Con's employ. And here was Rook, disinherited, without a job to do. Those five, blameless party guests! Those harmless, dry old men! Rook found it grimly comic that he'd dreamed of tracking down and wiping out such innocents. So now he knew who'd caused this chaos in his life. If he had half a chance he'd see to it that Con was sent the bill.

But, for the moment, it was Joseph on his mind, not Con. He'd beaten Joseph once before; he'd beat him yet again. So when a few days later Rook spotted him in the Soap Market, he determined they should speak. It was quite late and dark. It was that summer's warmest night and the city had its sleeves rolled up and could not sleep. For once, Rook had outstayed the waiter's welcome at the market bar. The Soap Garden was becoming his back-yard. He and three other men had played domino dice until all the other empty chairs and tables had been stacked and the bar staff had changed into their own clothes.

The barman closed the shutters and rinsed the final glasses and left the four men in the midnight July gloom to finish off their game. Rook was the last to leave. He was not skilled at dice and he had chanced his stake on one hot throw. He'd won, against three lukewarm throws from his companions. They'd settled up in thousand notes, and Rook had ten of them, folded in the pocket of his leather coat, as he set off for home.

The sweep-jeeps and the men with hoses had been at work and what had been a dusty, waste-strewn space, cluttered with dismantled stalls and flattened produce boxes was now as gleaming and as scrubbed as a spray-washed shingle beach – except that night-time beaches reflect the white lights of the sky, and smell of medicine, and perform a nocturne, made from water, wind and stone. This washed place smelt more of soup. It honked the jazz of traffic horns and voices in the summer night. It was lit by the yellow, oblong constellations of distant windows in offices and rooms where no one had the energy, in such a heat as this, to pull the blinds or go to bed.

In the summer there was hardly space for all the dispossessed and homeless who came to roost in the dripping troughs and crevices of the Soap Market. Why sleep indoors, in derelicts or hostels or up against the bricks and tiles of bridges, subways, underpasses? Why squat in dark, abandoned flats – your only privacy an unused mattress up against the window or the door – when it's July and there's no rain and the sun has been so fierce by day that all the midnight, city air is swollen with the heat?

There was no need to light a fire from packing debris, but there were fires because the poor are always cold in spirit and need the optimistic mesmerism of the flames to take them through the night, to help them kindle just a little desperate joy amongst such misery. Some of the fires would not last long. Their purpose was to shed a canopy like bulbs shed light, making rounded rooms with walls of melting night for children who could not sleep without the fantasy of 'home'. Some fires would burn till dawn, topped up by sleepless residents whose thirst for alcohol could not be blunted by their desperation or fatigue. One fire gave light for noisy games of cards. Another was the fire where spuds and sweet-corn, gleaned from the market floor, were ember-baked on skewers made from cycle spokes. Another warmed the singers' throats – the singing broken up by coughs, those two most humble sounds of human life becoming tangled in the mouth. In this, their simple warmth and light and sound, the night-time soapies were the closest citizens in town to the earth's enduring elements. They understood what every moth must understand, that flame is enemy and friend. Some found in it good cause to smile, but others were expressionless or else astonished beyond words by the scalding visions that the flames revealed. But mostly people sat or slept alone, disgruntled, shamed, made volatile and distant by a life which cast them as the rootless, parasitic clinker weeds amongst the steady stems of native bedding plants. Some slept on cobbles, statuesque, their heads upon their knees, their arms looped round their legs. Some curled on cardboard mattresses with pillow-sacks, or nested in the timber and the canvas of the market stalls. Women – rarer, older than the men – looped their arms through plastic bags of clothes and dozed, or pretended to. To seem asleep was their frontier against the raids and sorties of the town. It gave them some respite from their pain – their swollen feet, necrotic toes, their boils, and coughs, their migraines and their chills. Men talked in voices that were stripped to wire, or muttered madly to their chests, or carried their misfortune squarely, cleanly, without shame. Until they slept, that is. Who could tell the shameless from the lost, when all of them seemed just as thin and innocent and urinous beneath the duvet of the night?

Rook walked as quickly as he could between the starvelings and the vagabonds, the gangrels and the drunks. He was an easy target for their wit or for the begging hands which waved at him or tugged his trouser cuffs, or for their savage mutterings. He did not like the market when the awnings and the stalls were felled, and when the ripe and appetising daytime colours of the crops were replaced by the moistened greys of night. He did not look when he heard oaths or offers. It was not wise to be waylaid by their ill-luck. If he gave cash or time to one, then all of them would rush to him like mallards in the park, pecking for a crust.

Ahead he spotted three young men, as awkward on their legs as day-old foals. They called him to them, but he did not go. He could not quite unscramble what they said. But he was certain he knew what they held inside their paper cups, their shallow plastic trays, their makeshift dishes. These were what people nicknamed the Taxi Cabs, clumsy, noisy, slow and fuelled by petrol. They sniffed whatever petrol they could steal. They did not care that nowadays the petrol contained an Anti-Sniff. 'Danger' warned the stickers on the petrol caps. 'Ethyl Mercaptan'. It smelt of skunk. So what? The boys smelled just like skunks themselves. It did not dull their appetite for fuel, not even if the Anti-Sniff made them nauseous, hyperactive, violent. It blocked their tongues, and caused them to tremble like crones and greybeards made helpless by a stair or kerb.

Rook did not lift his head to face the Taxi Cabs; or even to trade signals with Cellophane who was still on his feet and summoning Rook, 'This way. This way. Then right. And straight ahead,' as if Rook were a van that's passage blocked the market place. He chose a route which took him to the market's edge, near the house where he had lived when young. He liked to walk those streets and look up at the cluttered windows of the carpet salesmen. Was that cracked glass the same that he'd pressed his face against, what? thirty years ago and more? for private, hawk-eye glimpses of the local girls? His mind was already set on women. The July heat, the weeks since he'd last slept with Anna, made him wonder what he'd do if some young woman bedded down on polythene amongst the cobblestones asked for money in return for sex. He did not trust himself. He was afraid.

He walked a little quicker now, the touch of panic and arousal at his heels. He almost stumbled over Joseph, sleeping at the market edge amongst the padlocked carts and barrows. The mugger's face was busy with its dreams. It was not proud or shy in sleep, but blinked and gaped and made no secret of its missing tooth, the cherry birth-stain on its cheek, the pitted craters on its nostrils and its chin, the meagre, ill-advised moustache, the crusty scar above the eye where he'd been wounded by a key. The skin was just as cracked but not as bronzed as it had been when he'd fled the countryside by Salad Bowl Express. The city life had whitened him. He looked as harmless and as dull as bread.

What made Rook feel again as tough and sentimental as a movie star? Was it the triumph of his fists, that time so long ago? Was it the residue of how he felt about old Victor, Anna, Con? Or just his dreadful appetite for girls transformed to violence when he saw the sleeping boy?

He thought he'd wake him with a kick. But what if Joseph
yelled? The mob would come. He'd have a tottering circle
made from drunks and Taxi Cabs. Rook was tempted to drop a
coin in the open mouth and creep off to watch the boy awake,
or choke. Instead, he searched his pockets for the knife. He
sprung the blade and squatted at Joseph's side. Just like a
father with an oversleeping child, he squeezed Joseph's ear
lobe, a parent's trick to open up the eyes. He waved the knife
across his face, and said, 'It's Joseph's "Nife" – without the K.
Is this your property?' He lay the flat blade on the young
man's nose.

'Don't move,' he said. 'We owe each other favours, don't
we? Don't shake your head. Don't move. I gave you that.'
Rook pointed at the scar. 'And you've scarred me. I ought to
hand you over to the police. At least you'd have a decent place
to sleep . . .'

Joseph sat up. He recognised Rook's face at last, despite
the lack of tie and suit. He was not frightened by the knife or
anything this thin-faced man might do. His own face was
wide enough to take more scars. He did not care. He'd snap
this man in half for waking him. He'd punish him for being
rich when he was poor. Rook stood and backed away, the
knife less certain in his hand.

'Have you got money?' Joseph asked.

'What's that to you?'

'Or cigarettes?'

Rook shook his head. Joseph put his hand out, palm
upturned. 'You woke me. You'd better watch it, mister. I know
you now. You'll pay for what you've done . . . Come on, give
me some money for some food.'

'Go to hell.'

'Piss off yourself!'

Rook was nervous of the threat that Joseph posed. He knew how strong the young man was. He'd seen him tossing onion sacks as if an onion grew fat and ripe on helium. He should have turned and walked away. Or run. But Joseph's words, 'You'd better watch it, mister. You'll pay for what you've done!' convinced him that the two of them should now negotiate for peace.

'All right,' he said. 'I only meant to give you back the knife.' He pressed the blade into the handle and gave it to Joseph. 'Hold on!' He found a crumpled nest of notes inside his jacket pocket. He pulled them out one by one, looking for a fifty. But the first ten were thousands, his winnings from the dice. He smoothed them out and held them in his left hand. He found the fifty, let it loop and float onto the cobblestones at Joseph's feet, and then spread out the ten one-thousand notes. He'd put them to good use.

'How'd you like to earn a wad like this?'

'For doing what?' Joseph was certain now that Rook was looking for a man to share his bed. He'd been approached before, but not for so much cash. For money of that kind he'd take a chance. To make a living he would do 'bad things' – his simple phrase for kicking down a door or kicking in a rib or letting some dull man pay for his touch. Whatever Rook was offering, there was bound to be a way of cheating on the deal. Ten thousand? What might that buy? What might a man like Rook expect for such a fee?

Rook himself had not yet formulated what he wanted Joseph for. But he was market-wise. He knew that Joseph could be bought, by Victor, Con, by anyone. Rook knew he had to purchase this *On the Town* before he went elsewhere.

Here was a bargain too tough and useful to be missed. Buy in haste, use at leisure. He'd take his time dreaming up some useful task for this hireling to *commit*, something to damage Victor, Con, or anyone.

'I'll speak to you again, be sure of that,' he said. 'Do what I ask and this little bunch of notes is yours.'

Joseph was not pleased. ' "If and when" don't butter bread,' he said, but for an instant he saw himself as the well-dressed model in the catalogue, his pockets stuffed with one-thousand notes. He would – with Rook's fat fee – sit at the bar and hold the barmaid by the wrist. He would drink muscatino from midnight till midday. He held his hand out for the notes.

'Just wait!'

'I'm sick of waiting. Give me something now!'

Rook arranged the ten one-thousand notes so that they made a perfect sheaf. He folded them in half.

'Give me the knife,' he said.

The knife had danced between the pair of them so often now that one more time was neither here nor there. Joseph returned the knife. The blade was sprung. Rook slipped the knife inside the notes and cut along the fold.

'Money is the peacemaker!' He mimicked Victor perfectly. 'One half for you. One half for me.' He put one set of severed half-notes in his pocket, and gave the matching set to Joseph, wrapped round his knife. 'So now you know I'm serious.'

'I can't spend this.'

'Nor can I!'

'So what's the point?'

'The point, dear Joseph, is that we will have to talk again.

As friends. I've got a job for you. Don't ask me what. But
when that job is done, I'll add my half to yours.'

3

VICTOR WAS FLATTERED BY the courting of the
architects, their optimism. He liked the language that they
used; the ease with which they sang of pits and peaks and
galleries and foliage travertines and moduled trading canyons,
as if the market buildings which they had conceived were
ancient caves, or forests, mountains, landscape parks, as if
they were importing countryside to colonise the city's heart.

In November – five months after Rook's dismissal – building plans which were jostling for the privilege of standing at
the ancient market site were presented to Victor in his offices
by men who looked like poets or composers dressed as restau-
rateurs. Expensive suntans, casual suits, the glistening, barra-
cuda eyes of those who live by their imaginations and their
wits. Not one contested that the existing market was diseased.
Their diagnoses matched. They were agreed on its ill-health,
its pathology, what treatment it should get, what surgery. The
old Soap Market was a tumour at the city's heart and had to be
removed. They prescribed the chemotherapy of the bulldozer,
the radiation of the great iron ball. 'Reduce the little that is
there to rubble. And rebuild.'

These architects were far too grand for schools and
houses. They boasted of the museums, marinas, hotels and
concert auditoria, the bank HQs, the city halls, the celebrated
malls, that they had built elsewhere in the city and elsewhere

in the world. In Tokyo. And Amsterdam. And Barcelona. And Zagreb. In tedious, smaller towns which they had placed upon the map by squeezing in a white-walled university where once there'd only been some fields, some woods, a run-down neighbourhood.

Great swathes of greased paper with lightly pencilled plans and elevations spread across Victor's desk, and draped his chairs. Scale models, computergrams and video enhancements presented new Soap Markets all of which the architects espoused like stage evangelists. Axonometrics in 3-D lifted up the draughtsmen's lines and made them real.

Victor had no eye for shape or form. He assessed the buildings by the words that were used for their promotion. He'd heard it said – and liked the phrase, despite its false extravagance – that architecture was frozen, geometric music. He judged the tone and rhythm of the plans by how the architects could sing their wares, what bafflegab they used. Once he'd made his mind up, then he would allow the managers, the financial planners, the development engineers, the accountants in his pay to take command.

Anna made arrangements for the eleven men and one woman to visit Victor in his office suite. She met each of them at the entrance from the mall and during the journey through the twenty-seven floors she gave them strict instructions that they should stay no longer than forty minutes and that they should not be 'overtechnical'.

'Victor is eighty,' she explained. 'He's not patient. His hearing isn't good.'

One architect – the first to audition – said his building had the swagger which was fitting for a market place. A forum for the sale of food, after all, deserved a confident demeanour.

No need to skulk like banks or barracks do. No need for bashfulness. A market 'hall' could be ambitious, energetic, optimistic, noisy, rash, hi-tech. And here his presentation sketch showed all the anorexic shamelessness of modernism on a spree, the veins, the innards and the entrails, the ducts and pipes, clinging thinly to the building's black glass skin.

'Too varicose,' was Victor's judgement, though he, or more exactly Anna, expressed this view more blandly in a letter of regret which was delivered to the architect that same afternoon.

Others presented plans in the post-modern cocktail style so favoured by hoteliers and out-of-city shopping magnates: a dash of Empire grandeur, two shots of common sense, a slug of metal rhetoric, all sweetened and made palatable by twists of pastel ornament.

The woman architect – from the practice which designed The Wall Memorial in Berlin – was a no-nonsense pragmatist. She had no time for curves. Her inspirations were tombstones, bookends, freight containers, washing powder packets, the square black holy Kaaba at the heart of Mecca, the Pentagon, matchstick boxes, wooden packing cases, dice. She most admired the tall, straight democratic canyons of Manhattan. She wished to put up on the market site 'a bold and simple slab, free of ornamental flippancy, in which the dogma and perfection of the rectilinear design confronts and challenges the inevitable disorder of the market place – and, incidentally, doesn't jeopardise your profit margins'.

'Let's not disguise, but celebrate, the probity of rectangles and cubes,' she said.

One handsome local architect, a young man much adored by social columnists for his daring disregard of public taste and of the women in his life, called for buildings which were visual metaphors, the city's aspirations made tangible in bloated glass and stone. The metaphor which he'd prepared for the Soap Market was most visible to God. Viewed from above – from a helicopter at a pinch, or even the roof-top garden on Big Vic – its shape was cruciform, a square-winged bird in flight. Its split swallowtail was, for the people on the ground, two tapering wedges which welcomed and embraced its clientele. It guarded them from wind and sun, and led them to the market doors at the swallow's rump.

'This building holds a dialogue with the people passing through,' the architect proclaimed. 'Its language is the language of the street.' Victor was deaf to what it had to say. If he had wanted metaphors for God he would have built a church.

He was more taken and more patient with the esperanto architects whose Shanghai-Aztec market halls were decorated with façades which owed their haywire debts to Marrakesh and to Mondrian, or to pyramids and pagodas, or to the paint-by-numbers graveyard classicism of Rome and Greece and Père Lachaise, or to the Hanging Gardens of Babylon and the IBM Garden Plaza on New York's 56th and Madison, or to spas and fairs and paddleboats. It was amusing to be guided through these global 'theme' environments, to hear of screens in bamboo and in steel, and roofs in metalthatch, and market 'trading modules' whose veneered marble counters were friezed and plinthed like tombs.

But there was never any doubt who'd win the contract once Signor Claudio Busi arrived and told the old man that his creed was this: 'My allegiance is to what you want. Great buildings such as this must glorify the vision of the man who pays. I quote dell'Ova and I say, "The tallest buildings throw the longest shadows. Thus great men make their mark." '

He'd done his homework, God knows how, for Victor's passions and aversions were not documented, and Anna, in the ascending lift, was tempting but not helpful. Or perhaps this Busi simply had the gift of insinuating images into an empty head with flattery. But, by luck or cunning, everything he had to say was pleasing and on target.

Claudio Busi was a stringy man of sixty-nine, the eldest partner in a practice celebrated for its taste and pragmatism. It was Busi who designed The Riggings, the waterfront development at Port St Phillips which had been laid flat by Hurricane Eduardo two years before and had not been rebuilt. The wrought-iron Exhibition Hall in Amsterdam was his work, too. And so was the Curtains Project in Milan which won the UN Prize: 'A stunning engineering adventure'. And the Centenary Centre on the lake in Michigan. His book, *The World Beneath a Single Roof*, had started a short-lived vogue for 'space as playground, building as event', and had established Busi as a charming, architectural pundit at colloquiums and on television shows. A lady's man, they said. He had the kind of peachy voice that could soften stone.

His younger partners had to treat him with respect – but they had largely forced him from the drawing-board. He had become too careless, too *passé*. He did not understand the functional obsessions of the modern clients who wanted 'splendour out and squalor in', that is to say, huge entrances, but offices as cramped and mean as prison cells. He travelled in his olive suits between their studios in New York, Paris and Milan much like a bishop travels his diocese, with great pomp but little power or control. He was a figurehead – and just the man, his partners judged, to win for them the Soap Market contract. A man of eighty could both patronise and trust a man of sixty-nine. So Busi was dispatched from Milan, to be their mouthpiece – and to give them all a break from his phrase-making and his charm.

Signor Busi would have preferred to be the spokesman for his own designs – but he had convinced himself that this task was his because he was considered by his colleagues and his rivals 'a philosopher amongst journeymen'. (A journalist had once described him thus, though with the nuance that, per-haps, Signor Busi talked more convincingly than he per-formed, with buildings and with women, too.)

He took a room at The Excelsior and spent a day looking at the Soap Market and its garden. The team of three from the Busi Partnership who had spent two months on site earlier that year, had warned the Signor in their briefing papers that the market was 'cheap, inefficient and artificial'. Busi thought so too. 'Squalid' was the word he muttered to himself. His taxi had abandoned him to walk – all very well in precincts and pedestrianised streets, but here was chaos, a nightmare for pedestrians. To cross the market by foot was to volunteer for service in the bruising labyrinths of an ants' nest. It was – for sure – neither beautiful, nor functional; neither playground nor event. It failed the Busi litmus test. It turned the simple task of buying fruit into an expedition. He marvelled at the depth and animation of the crowd and at the patience of the traders obliged each day to erect their stalls, barrow in their produce over cobbles, and then to box and barrow out each night the unsold residue, to end their day dismantling the stalls again. Inane. Insane.

Signor Busi ended up exhausted by the place, his suit dishevelled, his shoes discoloured. He rested in the Soap

Garden but was not happy with the coffee and the pastry that he bought, or with the waiter who was too hurried and lacking in finesse. He tried but could not find his way back to a traffic street. The market was not logical. It had no signs, no thoroughfares. A man in cellophane had sent him deeper in. He had to pay a boy to guide him to a taxi rank. He was elated that the Busi Partnership of New York, Paris and Milan might be the ones to introduce some Order and some Uniformity. A modern, regulated city should be governed not by the impulses of crowds but by the dictates of its tramlines, pavements, traffic lights, timetables, laws. A modern, regulated city would not allow such squalid topsyturvydom.

When at last they met, Signor Busi complimented Victor on Big Vic and on the mall which was its artery.

'It is gracious and it is legible,' he said. 'I applaud you that you wish to extend such geometric harmony into the ancient centre of the town where, evidently, legibility and graciousness are out of fashion.' He waited for an instant to allow Victor an opportunity to respond to these pleasantries. But he saw at once that Victor was no conversationalist and would be silent but attentive, too. He unzipped the black portfolios of draft proposals which he had brought from Milan, shook his body in his suit, and fixed his merchant client with his finest 3H smile.

'We have nostalgia and we have experiments,' he said. 'But you are not the man to like such things. You are a man of *now*. So let's not waste our time with these survivals from the past.' His hand dismissed his rivals' plans. He lifted the corners of a design by the Ultra Studios and raised his eyebrows: 'And let's not bother either with science fiction. It is dated just as soon as it is built. You see my Ultra colleague –

should I talk behind his back? – has designed another Centre Lyons-Symphonique for us, all pipes and tubes and vents, but this one is for cabbages and not for culture. He thinks it's witty to put a building's guts on show, to put the inside on the outside. But this is what I have to say to you: you are a man of eighty, this I know. Witty is not what you want. You want a little dignity. You want a market place which comprehends and celebrates your business intellect and not the artful vision of an architect. I'm right, I think. So, we dispense with inside on the outside. For you, for this great market place, we put the outside on the inside, we bring the outdoors indoors.'

He spread the drawings over Victor's desk. His partners had had the sense to keep them small and simple, at one-five-hundredth scale, so that the spirit of the group's proposals was more evident than their complexity. For Signor Busi, the outdoors which they planned to bring indoors was more than just a scheme to shield the market stalls from wind and rain and temperature. The 'outside' meant the countryside as well, the world beyond the margins of the town.

'What is a market anyway, but country brought to town?' he asked. 'Let's give the people a country walk right at the city's heart.'

He pointed to the 'conceptualisations' which had been sketched in ink and artist's wash.

'Please, pick them up and take a look,' he said. 'What do these elevations recall for you?' He smiled, but furtively, while Victor shook his head. The design was called the Melting Glass Meringues by colleagues in Milan. Four spectacular glass ovals which seemed both like cakes and the domes of viscous mosques filled the Soap Market. Nine tapering barrel-vaulted aisles – spaceframed in wood and steel, spaceglazed – radiated from the centre without geometric logic but in the pleasing, balanced way that surface roots spread out from trees.

'Here is a landscape at the city centre,' Busi said. 'There are no straight lines in our design, no matching planes or pitches. Instead we have the horizontal disunities of the natural landscape. We give you hills and plains and ridges made from curving sheets of glass. We look for coherence. We look for harmony. We let the natural city light, which is absorbed by brick and stone, pass through our glass and flood the building in the way that light can flood and warm and make fertile a country greenhouse. The inner walls are mirrored, and all the framing is constructed out of reflecting steel or polished wood, so that the journey of the natural light is not truncated. We have a greenhouse, then. We have the temperature and air control to maintain the perfect environment for plants and shrubs and trees. The walls are breathing walls. Outside, the city; countryside within. We have glass-bottomed elevators rising on a scenic ride through the foliage. We have nine trading corridors in human scale. And then the scale is more divine – four domes, the largest fifty metres high and visible from far away. It is a sculpture made from glass and greenery. It is a living carapace frozen in metal. It is . . .' (and with a flourish Signor Busi revealed the project's title) '. . . Arcadia. But modernised. Climate-controlled. Efficient. Accessible. Contemporary. Defended.'

With this last word, Signor Busi spread his hands, the saddened pragmatist: 'Arcadia must be defended. Of course! We must admit the truth. If it is your wish to lure into Arcadia those better citizens who have good taste and incomes to dispose, then we must promise them security from . . .' Again he spread his saddened hands. '. . . from the city itself. You see we have provided surveillance cameras, anti-theft shutters, suicide netting, commissionaires. The building is a fortress. A hand-grenade would only shake its glass. It can survive the full impact of an intercontinental airliner. But this is not enough. We owe it to your customers to keep out drunks and tramps and demonstrators and people who do not come to spend, but simply wish to shelter from the rain, or sleep, or cause unpleasantness. Arcadia – as you will see – is far too good for them.'

He took Victor on a tour, beginning with the two-storey basement, cushioned in poured concrete and served by a delivery ramp concealed by lines of trees. He showed where refrigerated storage pods kept produce fresh, where ripening units brought on bananas, apples, mangoes, to the colours judged best and most tempting for shoppers. Here were the offices, the basement studios, the service workshops, the market courtyards, recapturing – intensifying – a medieval market atmosphere, with coloured awnings, painted signs, terrazzo flooring, augmented natural light. And beds of shrubs, and greenhouse trees, and displays of bedding plants, with ivy, vines and bamboo stands.

The four meringues were joined inside Arcadia by a central hub much as the four seed-carpels of nasturtiums cling fatly to their stems. The hub supported terraces and balconies, with views through foliage of the heads and hats of shoppers, and the 'authentic' coloured awnings on the fixed-site stalls. On the lower terraces there were bars, a restaurant, an open concert arena. The upper balconies were almost out of sight. Below them stretched netting. It hung across the higher chambers of the domes like the billows of a Tuareg tent. Above and beyond the white and green patterns of the netting, there would be the largest aviary yet built in which the Busi Partnership envisaged cockatoos and cockatiels and minah birds, who finally, would learn to call like traders. 'All fresh today. All fresh today. No loot, No fruit.'

'The centrepiece!' Signor Busi produced a final sketch. 'You see, we are not charlatans. We have respect for history. We have not torn the medieval washplace down. We have given it new life.' The sketches showed what careful restoration could achieve, how medieval gargoyles could be rescued by the heroic dentistry of modern masons, how old and pitted stones could have the plaque removed, the cavities disguised, the broken tops replaced. There'd be new fountains, waterfalls, where previously the flow had been fitful and controlled by taps.

Signor Busi showed photographs of the bludgeoned washing basins where soap and stone and cloth had for so long made slapping music with the water. Then his new designs: the renewed basins were transformed by lights and plants. They were kept full and busy with piped, pumped, filtered and circulating water, which tumbled from hidden faucets into sculpted pools and then ran into channels to troughs of plants. At night, the air-conditioning, the concourse lights, the water would be turned off and floodlights would shine onto the four meringues. They'd make the innards of Arcadia warm and fathomless with the haywire shadows of pot-bound trees.

'I am a Milanese,' said Signor Busi, 'but even so I must admit that here we have a building which will be as beautiful and functional, more functional perhaps, than the Galerie Victor Emmanuel II in Milan. You share a name. You are Victor III, perhaps. You share a place in history as well, if you allow the Busi Partnership to make these drawings come alive.'

Signor Busi spread his arms and laughed. 'No more to say.' He left the plans and drawings where they were and put out both hands to Victor. 'I am at your disposal until Sunday, naturally. *Tante grazie, Signor Victor.*'

Victor summoned Anna. She took Signor Busi to the boss's private lift and travelled with him to the atrium and to the exit on the mall. He was ebullient and playful like an actor who has triumphed on the stage. He liked the woman at his side. Her perfume and her plumpness and the crowded intimacy of Victor's lift loosened him. His wife was far away. He laid two fingers on her wrist. He said, 'I think that your employer will give to me the contract for the Soap Market. Perhaps I ought to celebrate tonight, and you should be my guest at my hotel.'

Anna shook her head. 'It's very kind,' she said, 'but far too early for a celebration yet, don't you think? Victor has another three to see.'

'My dear,' said Signor Busi, letting go her arm, 'I feel it in my blood that we shall win. Our plans will be preferred.'

'Perhaps Victor will decide to preserve the market as it is.'

Busi laughed. 'There's nothing to preserve. There's nothing there. There is nothing to demolish. Of course there are the cobblestones to lift and lay again more cunningly. And there are those unkempt small bars and restaurants which cluster round the Soap Garden. Those we have to level off. And then we start from scratch! So we will speak again, I think. And many times.'

His car drew up and Signor Busi left Big Vic a happy man. Above him, on the 27th floor, his plans were strewn across the desk and carpet. Victor stood amongst them, a reference dictionary in his hand. *Arcadia* – a rustic paradise, he read. *Arcadian* – of pastoral simplicity. *Arcade* – a covered row of shops.

Signor Busi waited at the Excelsior for three more days, and on the fourth he received a call. Anna spoke for Victor. She was pleased, she said, to let him know that the Busi Partnership had secured the Soap Market contract. A formal letter would be sent, and Victor would be grateful if Signor Busi would extend his stay for three more days so that a press conference could be arranged and the timescale for construction plotted. He would, too, be sending Signor Busi sketches of a small statue which was a birthday gift to Victor from – how appropriate! – the leading market traders. It was a mother and a child and should be incorporated into Arcadia.

'A small statue? This we will give pride of place!' Busi told Anna. And then, 'So, please let me give you pride of place at my table at The Excelsior tonight. Now I think it is not too soon to celebrate.'

4

ANNA ATE VEGETABLES LIKE anybody else, but she was not an habitué of the Soap Market. She lived a little way from town – ten minutes on the bus, a forty-minute walk. She did not count herself so poor or so energetic that she need queue at market stalls and then transport her purchases by bag and bus. Within a hundred metres of her home there was a delicatessen with a fresh-products counter and an unhurried clientele, and this she used. Of course there were those times when she preferred to shop in city streets for clothes or shoes or presents for her nieces. Once in a while, after work, she set off down the mall towards the boutiques and the studios, determined to spend money on herself.

On the evening that Signor Busi first met Victor and then ventured to hold Anna by the wrist, she had felt so glad to be herself, so glad to be admired and flirted with (if only by a creaky clothes-horse from Milan) that she went looking for a treat in town. She'd seen a brooch that she wanted, hand-made, a galaxy of silver stars, a single moon of pearl. She'd need a darker jacket, too, to suit the brooch. Some Belgian chocolates, perhaps, could keep her company that night. She'd take a taxi home.

The jeweller had her workshop-studio beneath the timber galleries in Saints Row. Anna walked there by the quickest route. She was a little anxious that the galleries might close before the larger stores. But there the owner was, at work on a bracelet, a flight of copper geese. Anna could not see the brooch she wanted on display. She went inside. She asked. The jeweller did not lift her head, or take the magnifier from her eye. She said, 'I sold it. Weeks ago.'

'Do you have something similar? Another galaxy?'

'I don't do stars and moons, not any more. What I do now is birds and butterflies.' Anna waited for some helpful word, for some expression of regret, for some polite farewell. Instead the jeweller, clearly not prepared to talk, instructed, 'You could try elsewhere.'

Anna was too vexed to look elsewhere. What kind of businesswoman had such contempt for customers that she could not be bothered to raise her head or lift her eyes. Anna regretted that she had not gone home by bus as soon as work was done. She did not need a darker jacket now. She would not treat herself – and just as well, perhaps – to Belgian chocolates. Or take the taxi home. Instead she'd catch the bus back to her sewing and her television set, and spend the night, as many single women do, as silent and as self-possessed as quails. But first, she thought, she'd take a look at the Soap Market. It was so near, and on the way to her bus-stop. Her contacts with the architects and with their plans had made her curious to see exactly what Signor Busi had meant that afternoon: 'There's nothing worth preserving there.' She'd buy some salad for her sinless evening meal.

Anna had, a month before, turned her back on pasta, bread and rice, and hoped to make her peace with lettuce and with beans. Her only lapse was chocolates. Those times that Rook had pinched her at her waist, the hoop of flesh too loose between his fingers and his thumb, had made Anna discontented with herself. She used to push his hands away. He called it teasing. He thought it was a pleasing intimacy to draw attention to her loss of shape. She counted pinches of that kind as bullying. Men, it seemed, were never satisfied for long with the details of the women that they loved. And that was heartless, was it not?

When Rook was sacked and had ignored her visits to his apartment and the notes she'd left, Anna had found cause to blame herself. She'd frightened Rook with too much passion. She'd slept with him too readily. She'd been the secret cause of his dismissal from Big Vic. Her 'details' were not right for him. If only she was slim and thirty-five, then Rook would leave his door ajar for her. Yet he was just as middle-aged and lined as her. At least she was not dry like him. She was not greying, yet. She could breathe without her chest trembling – though it was true that her chest would pout a little less if she shed three kilos, say. She'd learned to blame her weight, and not herself, for losing Rook. She never thought to blame and hate the man himself.

Quite speedily, she'd lost some weight and, if not trim, she was more statuesque and confident. She bought new clothes that fitted her. She had her hair shortened and razored at the neck. She exercised each evening on her *phaga* rug. Now that she was just a trifle lighter and more disguised by what she wore, she felt unburdened. But nothing that she did or ate could take away the pouching underneath her chin, or recompense her for the sudden, hurtful loss of Rook. What use were mottoes such as *Yes-and-Now-and-Here* if *Now-and-Here* were desk and home and bed without her Rook?

She was surprised, however, on that broochless night, how cheerful she was feeling amongst the shopping crowds and how seductive were the market stalls. One soapie dealt only in roots, the gormless starches of the fields. His carrots ranged in colour from the red of mutton steaks to the pink of carp; he had carrots as round and bright as fairy lights; he had them straight and long like waxen stalactites; he had them double-limbed. He had potatoes, too – all shades, all shapes, and kept apart in separate buckets. He had whites, yellows, reds, pinks, scrapers, bakers, boilers, friers, cocktail spuds, Idahos, Egyptian, Old Andean, starchy, seedy, sweet. He had potatoes which were grown organically and were presented with the soil intact (to mask the blemishes). He had potatoes slightly greened by light. These were good in salads, raw and shredded with some mayonnaise.

Anna burrowed deep into the Soap Market. She passed the ranks of oranges, the monsoon fruit, the chicory, the sea kale, the Valentino pears, the commonwealth of apples, and came into the cooler kingdom of the leaf. She wanted just one lettuce, but she was teased by choice and colour. She rummaged at a stall for a garden lettuce with a tight rosette. She'd never noticed how they smelled before. The salads at the produce counter of her local delicatessen were odourless. But here, banked up in such profusion, the leaves were acrid almost, funereal. Their odour was precisely that of damp clay newly turned to take a coffin. The lettuce that she chose was tight and heavy – an early Wintervale. Its leaf stems were white. The leaves themselves were strongly ribbed and shaped like scallop shells. These were the lettuce leaves that the Spirits of the Field would use as plates at midnight feasts when they were standing guard against the pinching frost. The soapie dropped the lettuce in a bag and took Anna's payment as if the Spirits of the Field had yet to visit him.

Why did she not go now to catch her bus? Because she was seduced by all the multiformity of food? Because she was confused by colour, noise and crowds? Because Cellophane directed her on some detour? Or because a woman who had just detected death in lettuce leaves could have no difficulty picking up the smell of Rook as he sat with his coffee in the Soap Garden?

Rook spotted her as she negotiated chairs and customers. At first he watched her idly, thinking simply that she was a woman to his taste, a trader's stylish wife, perhaps, or the elegant and tempting boss of some boutique. Then he recognised her, just in time, as she saw him. His chest grew tight. His trousers, too. The lovers had not spoken for five months. Or touched. So Rook felt doubly cornered, both by the brutal carelessness with which he'd treated her and by the meanness of his sudden concupiscence. He wished to be a thousand miles away; he wished to be ten metres closer, so close and wrapped that he digested her, took from her mouth the salty sauce and fillet of her tongue.

'You've changed,' he said. 'You've cut your hair.' She seemed embarrassed. She reddened when he complimented her on how she looked. Was that the red of anger or delight? She did not speak, but put her lettuce on the table, and sat down facing Rook. Let him speak first.

'Am I to take it that there is another man?'

'Why should there be?'

'The way you look, of course.'

'Like what?'

'You've blossomed since I last saw you. Is there a man?'

'Of course there is,' she said, quite truthfully.

'And who is he?' Rook looked as if his face had lost its
bones.

'An architect,' she said. 'He's asked me back to The
Excelsior, no less. To celebrate.'

'And what is there to celebrate?'

'The end of all this!' Anna spread her arms and flapped
her hands, as if she were an illusionist who could make the
real world disappear.

To some extent she was exactly that. Most women are.
They are illusionists, at least when they are young. They have
the trick of making clocks stand still for men, of making clocks
run fast, of lowering the temperature a trace, of raising it, of
being so desirable that all the world beyond the bubble of
themselves is distanced and diluted. Their narrow heads, their
scent, the scissored hairline at their neck, the leafy rustling of
their skirts, become bewitchments. So Rook was netted and
engulfed, and Anna gloried that she was not too old or large
to hold this man in thrall. She laid her hands upon his table.
He had the courage and the shame to hold her by the wrist.

'Just like my architect,' she said, and then her story
tumbled out, how secretive the boss had been, how plans had
been passed off as something else, how nine architects – so far
– had been escorted up to Victor's suite like prisoners in
custody and not allowed to share a lift or chatter with the staff.
She told how Victor was obsessed by plans, and how his
books on greenhouse pests had been pushed aside by models,
elevations and projections for the Soap Market. She told how
Signor Busi had – that afternoon – seduced the boss with
sculpted words and how she was convinced – like him – that
Busi would be the man to 'start from scratch'.

'I could have stopped him. I *would* have stopped him,'

Rook said, more energised and focussed than he had been for a dozen years. 'But now I've gone, who is there to give him good advice?'

'So, that's why you got the sack? He didn't want you in the way . . . ?'

'What does Victor say?'

'What does Victor ever say? He hasn't said a word. When does he ever say a word? You know what he's like, out of sight, out of mind . . .'

She put her one free hand on top of his so that the three arms on the table made a *bas-relief* of flesh and fingers. Rook felt reprieved. Anna had not learned about his market fraud from Victor. The ice-cube had not revealed the truth. Nor would he. Rook raised his head. He squared his shoulders. He was a cockatoo, all squawk and feathers now, all strut and peck and preen.

'Come home with me,' he said. 'Let's celebrate.'

'I've called round at your home a dozen times,' she said. 'I've written and I've called. Not one reply.'

'So come home now. We'll put it right.'

'We'll see,' she said. 'You're not as fancy as my architect.'

'Ah, the Italian, yes.' Rook took his fingers out of hers. He held the edges of her coat. 'If he wins, I'd like to see his plans.'

'He'll win. I'd bet on it.' Anna's voice had lost its resolution. She held her breath. She watched his fingertips.

'When will you know?'

'Next week, officially. There'll be a press conference and a presentation of the scheme when the contract is awarded.'

'And where?'

'Big Vic.'

225

'I'd like to see the plans before next week, before the press. Can you do that?'

'Do what?'

'Give me a preview of the scheme that wins.'

'Why should I take that chance?'

'Because I want you to,' he said. And (he thought) because the old man plans to put an end to all of this. Because there's no one in Big Vic to stand up for the soapies and the market place.

Rook spread his arms and flapped his hands in mockery of her. But there was no illusion at his fingertips – no desire to see the real world disappear, no wish to interfere in the bustling kinship of the citizens who went about their business in the Soap Market with the fitful, browsing innocence of weevils in a cake.

'What can I do?' Anna said. 'Victor keeps his room locked. And anyway, those plans aren't small. They're tablecloths.'

'And what about your fancy architect?' Rook let her repossess his hand.

'Who? Busi?'

'Yes. He must have duplicates.'

Anna nodded, shrugged, as if to indicate she had no access to this man.

'I think', said Rook, his hand pushed through the buttoned vents of Anna's coat, his palm upon her slimmer waist, a finger tucked beneath her belt, 'that it might be a good idea to let the signor take you out to dinner. At The Excelsior, no less.'

5

ROOK WAS A JUGGLER. He held and tossed five
lives. He had to spin and mix them in the air. He had to pitch
them so that they arched and fell into his hands with just the
angle and the impact he required. Rook had to space the five
lives in his grasp, ensure they did not meet or touch, for he
was keen to settle scores – deftly, speedily, undetected. He was
ready and impatient now to pay off debts and make amends,
with Busi, Joseph, Anna, Con, but, most of all, with Victor.
Quite what he ought to juggle up, Rook was not sure, though
at their simplest and their meanest his intentions were to
punish Con and Victor for the job, the private income from
pitch payments, the self-respect they'd robbed from him.

The uniformed expulsion from Big Vic tormented him. He
had to torment in return. This was unadorned revenge, and
revenge is next to lust in its single-mindedness, its self-regard.
So Rook did not care that Busi, Anna, Joseph and yes, Con and
Victor, too, were mostly innocent of blame for the malfunc-
tions in his life. He'd still be on the 27th floor and welcome in
the Soap Market, sweet with Victor, Anna, Con, if he'd resisted those envelopes of cash, that money in the palm, those
bribes. This is something that country people understand
more readily than townies. If you sow thorns, then you get
thorns. They don't need watering. They flourish and they
snag.

Rook would not admit his pettiness, that what he wanted most was some wounding, simple recompense. He fooled himself that there were nobler motives driving him. The fiction that he made was this: that his months of leisure, free from Victor and Big Vic, had resurrected an old self that had ideals and principles worth fighting for. How could he forget the man he'd been a dozen years before when the produce boycott had been organised? They'd listened to him in the market then. They'd cheered. He'd stood on a platform made from crop boxes, dressed in clichéd black, and made that speech that all the papers had reproduced in full.

'This Soap Market', he had said, 'is here to make good salads and fruit pies. To put some muscle into stews, some zest in cake, to keep the city fed. It is not here to make men millionaires. So we traders should let the market die before we let the prices outstrip the common people.' They'd flocked to that – and they'd held out on strike for seven weeks. A stirring time. The world turned upside down, with market customers bringing cake and cheese and bread to feed the soapies, and every stall and awning dismantled, and not a scrap of lettuce to be seen.

The striking soapies had given Rook the mandate to negotiate. They'd trusted him. But Victor knew the trick of tearing notes in half. 'Why let the market die?' he'd asked, made loquacious by the seven weeks of damage to his wealth. 'You only harm yourselves.' His agents and his managers had offered Rook a compromise. You lift the boycott, and trade according to the prices we have set, they counselled. And in return we freeze the market rents for two years, maybe three. You traders save a little cash for . . . okay, you win, let it be frozen rents for the full *three years*. You save the market place for good.

Rook had said he was only a mouthpiece, that was all, but that he doubted his colleagues would betray their principles. Victor had spoken again. 'How much are principles?' he asked himself, but he said out loud, 'It would be democratic, don't you think, if my, our, colleagues in the market had some constant spokesman at my side to represent their principles.' He had not looked at Rook, but had written a sum in pencil on a memorandum pad and slid it across his desk so Rook could see. 'That is the kind of yearly sum that we would pay for such a diplomat.' Rook had shaken Victor by the hand and had taken the stipend of the diplomat.

So now Rook felt he had the chance to make amends, to piece together once again the man that had been raised within the odour of the market place, that had been schooled in radishes and rambutans, that thrived in clamour and crowds. He'd save the Soap Market. He'd be the champion of marketeers. He'd climb up on the platform once again and 'represent their principles, their fears'. But then, once he had sobered from the fever of the phrases in his head, he thought again, more clearly. Platforms were for innocents. Speeches only waylaid passion with fine words. The player with the strongest hand, the running flush, was not required to show his cards. So it was in politics – for, yes, Rook was now so inflated with the altruism of his mission that he'd cast himself as a man in service to the citizens. In politics you did not need to spout or strut or speechify if you could quietly slip behind the scenes to sabotage, to juggle, and to complicate. He had a plan, unformed but irresistible, which would deliver Anna to his bed, and damage Con, and punish Victor, and introduce that muscly Joseph to the truth that brains and money are more powerful than youth. He'd cause a little mayhem, too, for Signor Busi of Milan – and leave himself the hero of the market place.

So, four days after Rook and Anna reconnected in the Soap Garden bar and on the day that Signor Busi won the contract for Arcadia and once again invited Anna to his table, they walked to The Excelsior. They'd been together every night and had slept so deeply, back to back, that the dreams and snores which celebrated their resurrected passion did not wake them. They were refreshed by the affection that they gave and got, and Anna took the change in Rook, his liveliness, his youth, to be a sign that he returned her love. Why else would she, a careful woman wedded to her work, agree to dine with Busi and to chance his busy hand so that she could, for Rook, become a common thief?

Rook had been careless. He should have let Anna walk the final metres to The Excelsior on her own. But she was nervous – as she had a right to be. Dining with a stranger in a hotel such as this would make the toughest of us tremble. Rook had let her hold his arm until they reached the polished marble steps of The Excelsior.

'Aha, my dear. You've brought a companion?'

Signor Busi was standing at the carpet edge, spying on the women in the street. Anna let go of Rook and, at once, wondered why. She held his arm again.

'He's a friend,' she said, but had the sense to give no name.

Rook was disadvantaged by Busi's height, his clothes, his age.

'I was just passing by,' he said. 'Have a pleasant evening.'

He walked away, but slowly enough to note how Signor Busi had a voice that was as carpeted and marble as the hotel steps.

Rook would never know what happened between Anna and Busi that night, and she would never learn how Rook had passed his time. Though they, of course, would tease each other with alternatives.

It was quite clear to Rook and Anna that they were tethered to the ardour of the night. As they parted, both were charged with the sexual static implicit in the triangle that they formed – the ageing, elegant seducer; the apprehensive woman in her finery (bathed, perfumed, bangled, silk-dressed in gold and black); the thin-faced breathless lover transformed to thin-faced, breathless pimp as he dispatched his paramour on her – on his – assignment; the dining table set and waiting with its single rose, its silver tub of ice, its candlelight and its connivance in the creed that all is fair in love and trade; the hotel bedroom with the balcony and matching lampshades, curtains, bedspread; the salacity of wintertime.

Rook had said to Anna, 'Do what you can to get a copy of those plans. Do anything. It's up to you.' He had not said she ought to sleep with Signor Busi but, then, he had not asked her not to. He was excited, that's for sure, by the power that he seemed to have. He liked to enmesh her in his intrigues and to allow the notion, if not the fact, that she would sleep with Busi if instructed so. How sensual it was, how riggish, how sportingly loyal, how grandly stimulating that she might do this thing for him. What would she not do, now, with Rook in his own bed, on his own floor, if she could be so dutiful as to serve him with another man?

Anna, for herself, had not contemplated for too long what Rook had meant by 'Do anything. It's up to you'. She took his meaning, but she took it as a joke. She did not want to think that Rook, despite his recent protestations of affection, would use her as a bribe, a trinket. She had no wish to be his representative in Signor Busi's arms. But Rook had spoken with such passion and such verve about his mission to save the Soap Market that she had redefined herself as a woman who, by surrendering and making servile her love for Rook, could consolidate his love for her.

Of course, she would not, when it came to it, allow the architect to touch a centimetre more of her than the pale, unsensual flesh around her wrist. But she had fooled herself into believing there was no insult in Rook's evident indifference. She did not say, 'If that old smoothie has the nerve to try it on with me he'll get my dinner in his lap,' or 'If you're so keen to get a copy of these plans why don't you go and sleep with Busi yourself. He doesn't seem the choosy sort. And nor do you.' She did not say, 'I'm not a prostitute.' She simply let the atmosphere between them stay a little warmed and moist with the licence he had imposed on her to 'Do what you can to get a copy of those plans'.

So she had bathed and dressed for The Excelsior in clothes which she had brought from her own home to Rook's apartment. As she dressed before the mirror, arranging belts and tights and underclothes, and testing scents and bracelets on her arm, Rook sat and watched. His breath was shallow, his tongue was dry, his heart beat fast. Not asthma – but an ailment which nearly every man is martyr to, the subjugation of all sentiments and resolutions to the tyranny of sex. He smelt of badger. He felt his penis lengthening inside his trouser leg. He had to shift his leg and readjust his clothes. He was not slow to help her with her zip or take the landlord opportunity to wet her neck with a kiss and press himself into her back.

'Not now,' she said, and rubbed his trousers with her hand, proprietorially. He was transfixed, entranced, by the prospect of the night. But he had lost the chance of giving full expression and relief to the promptings and the tensions that he felt. He'd happily see the market torn down, and Victor triumphant and untouched, and Signor Busi left to dine alone, if only Anna would agree to turn around and put her face to his. He'd happily – but for how long? – relinquish mission and revenge for five demented, silken, musky minutes in her arms.

She was putting on her shoes, and smoothing down her dress, and searching for her toothbrush in her bag. And they were descending to the street. And they were walking arm in arm like married couples do, respectably. And Rook was looking up at Signor Busi on the hotel steps and saying, 'A pleasant evening to you both.'

Rook walked down to the Soap Garden and found an isolated chair where he could sit in privacy and think. And drink. What were the diners doing now? Had they reached dessert? Anna liked sweet things and Signor Busi would insist she had exactly what she wanted. No doubt she bubbled; it did not take much drink to make her gamey. No doubt the old Italian was urbane and courteous, and lightly anecdotal in the way that men who are not young must be if they want to charm their juniors. Rook pictured Busi as he lightly put his hand upon his guest's bare arm and called the waiter to the table so that his intimacy could pass as etiquette. Perhaps he asked if she required a *digestif*. A Boulevard Liqueur? Did she stay still? Did she encourage him to leave his hand in place?

To stroke her arm perhaps? To take her hand in his?

Rook shook his head, and rearranged the dinner table once again. This time the architect was silent and Anna was urbane and cunning. She kept the conversation light and tempting. She flattered him, his suit, his taste in wine. He boasted of his fame as an architect, the work he'd done to shape the new Arcadia. She said, I'd love to see those plans myself. He said, They're in my room. She said, Why don't you order some nightcaps and we can take them up.

Again Rook cleared his head. He'd conjured up a harpie, out of character. Anna was not a predator. She'd have to be cajoled upstairs, unwillingly, but with her task in mind, to borrow, steal, a second set of plans. Perhaps she'd asked to see the plans. Busi said, You'll have to come upstairs. He let her know that dinner was not cheap and that Victor would not wish his architect to go without affection in his town. Rook could almost see the plans upon Signor Busi's bed. He saw the look on Anna's face as Busi hung his trousers, creases straight, across a chair, and turned to watch the black and gold on Anna loosen, crumple, drop. Rook saw her, Busi watched her, hold her stomach in as she pushed down her tights and underclothes and stood, in nothing but her slip. Signor Busi cleared the plans and elevations from the bedspread and then pulled Anna to him by her wrists. 'My name is Claudio,' he said.

Now Rook, if he had been a younger, fitter, more dramatic man, would have run between the Soap Garden and The Excelsior. Not out of anger, nor jealousy. He was not fool enough to be jealous of these chimeras. But out of lust. He wanted sex; he wanted intercourse. He wanted to express himself before he burst from lack of it. He could not hold his coffee cup. He could not halt himself. He walked unsteadily, a little drunk on his imaginings.

He found a girl – not more than seventeen. A country girl who'd never kissed a man she loved. She took him to a third-floor room two streets behind the house where he was born. She pulled her blouse apart. She pulled her denim skirt up to her waist. She wore no underclothes. She was as thin and unprepared for city life as Anna was mature. Rook said to her, 'My name is Claudio.' There were two grey patches on the mattress of the bed, where ten thousand knees had been before. Rook put the money on the chair, and did as he was told.

'Undress,' she said. Then 'Wash.'

The water on his penis sobered him, but he was drunk again when she came to him with a sheath and rolled it on. She lay down on the bed. She removed her watch and chewing gum and, pressing the gum onto the watch face, dropped them to the floor.

'Okay,' she said. 'It's up to you.'

She might have been a country girl, but she was as nonchalant and passive in her work as any city labourer or clerk or factory hand. It paid the bills. She held a steady course between professional cupidity and personal disdain. She was wise enough to forge a little interest in the man who paid. The bread won't rise without the yeast. She shook her head or nodded as required. She matched a dozen groans of his with one of hers.

They always looked the same, these men, when they were done – a little disappointed, eager to depart. She retrieved her chewing gum. It was still moist and almost warm. She watched him search his trouser pockets and then the pockets of his leather jacket. He found his handkerchief and wiped his nose. He pressed a spray into his mouth and sucked on it, as if he wished to blast away the taste of her with Pine-'n-Chive. His face was red, but weren't they all, and with good cause? But this one did not rapidly turn pale. His breathing was not free. His chest was quivering as if his orgasm was trapped and heading for his lungs. She did not care. He'd only paid for fifteen minutes and time was up. Another girl would want the room. She picked his trousers up and put them in his hand.

'You'd better get some fresh air,' she said.

She waited by the door until he put his spray away and pulled his trousers on. She went alone down to the street where she had friends and where her face and chewing gum could stretch and soften in the darkness.

Rook had cleared his mind at last. He left the street and market area. And as quickly as he could – in other words not speedily at all, but chin upon his chest and hands upon his lungs and phlegm upon his lips – he returned to his apartment.

He lay on his bed and shut his eyes and could not disentangle Anna, Signor Busi or the prostitute. They coiled like anglers' worms so that it was a puzzle where they ended or began. He slept and trod the waters of a shallow dream. Too much nebuliser. Joseph wore the uniform of a commissionaire. He threw Rook out of doors, apartment doors, office doors, and doors to gloomy bars. He slept with Anna, and Anna slept with Victor, and Signor Busi slept with Rook until the bed became a market stall turned to leaf and root. The prostitute was in his bed and would not leave, and Anna's feet were on the stairs. And she was not alone. Now someone joined them in the bed and put a hand upon his chest. 'You don't look well,' she said. Her breath was garlic and cigar. Her perfume was Boulevard Liqueur.

She sat in front of the mirror and let him wake. She took her bracelets and her earrings off and started on her eyes and cheeks with cotton wool and rose oil.

'How did it go?' he said.

Anna was too satisfied to tell the truth. How easy it had been, with Signor Busi keener to secure her admiration and her rapt attention than to lure her to his bed. He had not touched her once. He seemed afraid that he might go beyond the point where he impressed her. He was adept with wine lists and cigars. Waiters were polite with him. The chef – a fellow Milanese – came up and shook his hand. He thrived on conversation. He could talk and eat and drink as neatly and amusingly as a juggler with five balls. He flattered Anna charmingly. He could let her go without seducing her and do his reputation not a jot of harm. But if he tried his luck with her? What then? At best he'd take her to his room and she would see how papery he was beneath the suit and how his posture – tall, erect – was aided by a spinal truss. It took him minutes to remove his jacket. He had to shake his shoes and trousers off. To see him climb onto his bed, undressed, was (he admitted it himself) to watch a scene from *Marat-Sade* or witness anti-ballet of the kind danced by the chorus of the dead in Przewalski's 'Crematorium'.

So there they stayed, at table, in public safety. He was, he said, excited by the prospect of spending a few months in town. His junior partners were good at seeing ideas through, but not so good at nurturing the building itself. He was the old-fashioned sort of architect, he said. He liked to have a love affair with everything he built. He let this slogan do its work, and then he threw it out before it did him harm in Anna's eyes: 'Excuse an old man his absurdities. I promise I'll be less extravagant at the press conference. No gibberish, I think, for journalists.'

'Ah, yes, the conference,' said Anna. 'Victor will need another set of plans . . . before the conference.'

'Of course, my dear.' (He had not used her name or even asked her what it was.) 'I'll send them over to him by courier.'

'I'll take them now, if it'll help. That'll please Victor. I'll feel I've earned this splendid meal.'

'They weigh at least ten kilos.'

'I'm stronger than you think.'

Signor Busi was not keen to go with her to his room, or, indeed, to do the round trip all alone. It was too far. He was too tired and full. He called a bell boy to the table. He handed him his key. 'Be so good as to go up to my room and fetch a yellow file. It's this thick and so high.' He mimed the file. 'You'll find three of them leaning up against the window bay. Just bring me one.' He gave the boy a hundred note, and then embarked upon an anecdote about a client's file that he'd once lost in New York, in a cab. The telling of it tired him. He lost the thread, and was relieved when the boy came back with the yellow file. He could not fight a yawn.

'I'll let you get to bed,' Anna said.

Signor Busi stood and slowly straightened. His stomach squalled. He took her hand. 'Good night, my dear,' he said. 'It has been a great pleasure.' He watched her leaving for the line of taxis in the street, the bell boy and the file of papers at her side. She walked triumphantly.

'She really is the most enticing woman,' Signor Busi thought as he began the journey to his room.

Rook was now sitting up in bed. 'How did it go?' he asked again. Anna pointed to the bedroom door. A yellow file, fat with plans and papers, leant against the frame.

'Have faith in me,' she said. Why should she tell him any more. Let him imagine what he wished. Rook did not betray his lack of faith in her. His conscience was not clear but smudged with two grey marks where he had placed his knees.

They sat in silence for a while, Anna at the mirror, Rook in bed, each with secrets to preserve, but only one of them felt sure enough to smile.

6

ROOK SMILED AT CON. 'Let's talk,' he said.

'What for?'

'Because, unless we talk, your market stall will fall to bits.' His arms were up and stretched. 'All this will disappear.'

'Get lost.' Con smiled at Rook, but his smile was lipless. It did not crease his eyes or pack his cheeks. It was tight. It elevated 'Get Lost' from curt indifference to chilling malediction. The smile dismissed Rook as a man not worthy of contempt. But Rook was not dismissed. He put his hand out to stop Con packing for the night. He had counted on Con's hostility. He'd hoped for it. It would not do if Con was a conciliator who preferred *What's done is done* to the bald *Get Lost*. Rook rubbed a finger and a thumb to mime the crumbling of a solid into dust.

'Get lost,' said Con. 'I've work to do.'

'But not for long,' said Rook. 'You'll soon be out of work and rattling round the streets like me. Except you won't have the savings I've got to make your unemployment pleasant.'

'You're farting through your mouth,' said Con, but he was enticed enough to stop his efforts with his stall and turn to look Rook in the face.

Rook had prepared his speech: 'Pay attention,' he said, as if the trader were a six-year-old. 'Don't be a fool. We've more in common than you think . . . and I'm not blaming you.'

'Not blaming me? For what?'

'For that stupid scuffle with the country boy, and all your poke and squeak with Victor. For losing me my job. What do you think?'

'You can blame yourself for that,' said Con. He'd not bother to deny that he'd launched Joseph on the fumbled attempt to repossess his pitch payment. Why should he? It was reclamation, just and fair. He did not understand what 'all your poke and squeak with Victor' might be or why he should be blamed for Rook's dismissal. Nor did he care. Rook was despicable, he thought, but as harmless as a snake that having lost its venom makes do with hiss. It did not matter what Rook knew about that farce with Joseph in the walkers' tunnel. How could Rook damage Con now that he was, by all accounts, truncated from his boss for good?

'You had it coming, and you got off lightly,' he said. 'I should have sent four boys, not one. You'd be on crutches now. Why should I feel guilty? I'm only sorry I wasn't there myself.'

'Don't play the hero,' said Rook. 'If I was holding grudges I wouldn't be here at all. I'd fix you privately. I'm here to help you out. Not that you deserve my help.'

'Get lost.'

Rook wrapped his fingers round his keys. How he despised this man, his smell, his clothes, his tight and unforgiving face. But Rook had to persevere. His only route was Con. He put the yellow file of duplicate designs from the Busi Partnership on the trader's stall, amongst the bruised fruit and the waste that Con would jettison. He took the top drawing out. There were the melting glass meringues, the starfish corridors, the indoor trees, the relocated cobblestones in wash and watercolour. There was the legend: 'ARCADIA – a sketch'.

'What's this?'

'It's what dear Victor has in mind for you.'

Now Rook was free to make his speech. He told how Victor was not satisfied with profits from the market place, how he'd been prompted by his bankers and his strategists to build, how Signor Busi and Arcadia had won the old man's ear – and eye. An easy task because Victor was demented with old age, indigestion, and his obsession with a statue of some kind: 'A mother and a child, would you believe. And not a statue of himself!'

Rook made the most of his regrets that he was no longer in Victor's pay. It was his view, he explained with patient irony, that since the one man who knew the Soap Market 'from the inside out' had been removed from Victor's side, then Victor had been free to run amuck.

'I protected you,' he said. 'Maybe you didn't like to pay for that, but I protected you – and see what's happened now that the Soap Market has got no one to speak for it inside Big Vic.' He punched the drawings. 'There's a press conference in three days' time,' he said. 'They think they've got the only set of plans. But your man Rook has earnt his pay and got a second set.' Rook recalled for Con the chilling boasts of Busi, 'There's nothing to preserve', 'We level off and take away', 'We start from scratch'.

'I don't hold out much hope for you or this, unless you organise, unless you defend yourself. Yourselves,' concluded Rook. He'd said enough. He pushed the file of papers towards Con.

'Why me?' asked Con. 'Why not one of those old wind-socks you hang out with in the bar?'

'Because they're windsocks, like you say. Limp when things are fine, and when it's stormy full of air. But you, you're not a windsock; you're one of life's malcontents. You're not afraid of fights. You were the only one to give me any trouble over payments for your pitch. The only one from what? . . . from two hundred and eight stallholders. You're one in two-o-eight. You, Con, are a natural troublemaker. And may you be in Heaven for an hour before the Devil knows you're dead.'

'All right, so I'm a malcontent. Then why not you? You're the maestro amongst mischief-makers. You've got the plans. You know the innards of the man. God knows, you've got enough spare time to organise a global war. Why me?'

Rook spoke with passion now. He was not obliged to equivocate with abstracts. He spoke of his damaged reputation in the market place, how he might still be seen as Victor's eyes and ears, as some double-agent whose loyalties were as brief and unpredictable as shooting stars. Or else the word would be that the sacked factotum of the millionaire, disgruntled, venomous, was using marketeers to settle his own scores. The press and television would make a meal of that. They loved bad motives. They preferred an intrigue to the simple justice of a cause.

Or else no one would trust him. The older traders would not forget how Rook's brinking leadership a dozen years before had been so readily tranquillised by Victor's cheque. His appeasement had impoverished everyone but himself. Unless they were as forgetful and forgiving as chastised dogs they would suspect him.

'Besides,' said Rook, 'I've got to stay out of sight. That architect has seen me with . . . the person from Big Vic who

stole the plans for you. I can't name names. The less you know
of that the safer she, or he, will be. With luck they won't trace
the leak. But if Busi sees me with the plans he'll make connec-
tions. He's slow and foreign but he's not stupid. Our routes to
Victor and to Busi will be blocked and our informant will get
sacked, at best. As things stand our sharpest weapon is surprise. What do you say?'

Con did not say a word. He gathered up the papers on his
stall. He pushed them in his bag together with his newspaper,
his change of shirt, his takings for the day. He'd sleep on it.
Then, next morning, he would call a meeting of the marketeers
and take directions, not from Rook but them.

He set to work dismantling his stall. He was dispirited by
what he'd heard, though, normally, when work was at an end
and home was near, he felt at his most contented. He wished
that Victor's man – he could not think of Rook in other terms –
would take the hint and leave. He'd said his piece. He'd mixed
his poison. He ought to disappear. But Rook seemed keen to
stay. He was smiling even; the same smile with which he'd
burdened Con before they spoke.

Rook took the end of Con's stall and helped him lift it
from the trestles. He packed the produce boxes to one side. He
unhooked the green and yellow awning and began – inexpertly, incorrectly – to fold the canvas. His hands and fingers were
as soft and clean as soap. Con took the bulky canvas and
unfolded it. He stowed it once again, so that it made an almost
perfect square. He stood on it to clear the air. 'I don't need
help,' he said.

Rook shrugged. 'We all need help.'

'Get lost,' said Con and, as he had his back to Rook,
allowed himself the briefest smile, but one which packed his

cheeks and creased his eyes and put his lips on show. It was true what Rook had said. He relished fights. He was the one in two-o-eight.

7

VICTOR AND SIGNOR BUSI were taking breakfast on the 28th when Con and his two hundred colleagues set out from the Soap Garden. Press cameramen and a television unit from the local studios were there to film the marketeers' procession to Big Vic.

Rook, in his role of unacknowledged puppet-master, had made the phone calls to the press on his own initiative. Even though he was not fool enough to join the demonstrators, he watched them from his usual café table and was pleased. Two hundred out of two-o-eight was good, though not all the men and women there were stallholders. Some were porters, some were soapie wives and sons. Others represented the cafés and the bars that Victor wished to level to the ground. There were some customers, too – a dozen men and women from restaurants and small hotels in the Woodgate district who bought fresh produce from the Soap Market and liked the cheaper prices. They all feared change. Yet they believed that change could be confronted and repelled. Remember how the residents of Stephens Well, a small and wealthy suburb, had beaten back developers, or beaten them down at least. They'd forced the architects to lop three storeys from the top of their new office block because it cast a shadow on the suburb's private park for forty minutes every day. That contravened the ancient Law of Light. Consider how the city's conservation groups had stopped the widening of roads when widening would bring down trees. Trees of that age and size were protected by the Sylvan Ordinances of 1910. The market place had trees and light as well. So there was hope.

Rook drank his coffee, and peered at everyone who passed. His newspaper was spread out across his lap, unread and wet. It did not matter what the headlines were, or what the world was coming to, or that, if NASA got it right, an asteroid, one kilometre in width and travelling at 74,000 kilometres per hour, would 'wing' the Earth at noon, missing the Soap Market (also one kilometre in width) by an astronomically narrow half a million kilometres of space. His mind was focussed on the detail of his life and not Eternity. Here – within a stone's throw – he and the soapies were confronted by a danger they could witness, understand and quantify in human measurements. Here was a space they could protect.

Of course the market did not close. The marchers all had partners, deputies or family to defend them from a trading loss. Each stall was open and the crowds were much the same as on any other day, at least on any other day that rained as hard as this. The demonstrators used their placards as screens against the rain. They pulled on hats. The television unit clothed its camera in a plastic hood. Someone had thought to bring a drum and he was ordered to the front by Con. They set off through the market place a trifle sheepishly, routed and regrouped by Cellophane. He'd never known such ordered crowds, such unity, before.

It's difficult to concentrate on grievances when all around are friends. Con had a dozen leafleters. The Soap Fund – a reserve to pay for traders' funerals or help out widows or support those injured at their work – had provided money for paper and printing. The leaflet showed the Busi sketch in ink and wash of Arcadia. Its black and gothic banner was 'Arcadia? Who pays?' – and then it listed, with more regard for impact than for grammar, '*You*, the shopper . . . *Me*, the trader . . . *Us*, the citizens . . . *Them* that value history and tradition.'

When they had regrouped, at the Mathematical Park, to enter Tower Square and curve round with the traffic into Saints Row, the leafleters set to work, walking in the road to press their message on to drivers, dodging through the pavement crowds. The crowds, in fact, had slowed to let the traders through. They had no choice. Their umbrellas made it difficult to negotiate a passage through the squints and alleys of a throng. It only takes a drum to cause the gawpers in the street to stand and watch, or to make those drivers with a little time to spare twist at their steering-wheels to see what the drum might signify. Once a few had stopped to look, then everybody slowed. The usual speeding lava of the streets had cooled. Then there were horns and tempers. Pedestrians, blocked on the pavements by the ones who stopped to watch, spilled out onto the street and tried to hurry on between the cars and vans and gusts of rain. A courier motorcyclist bumped up on the pavement, and tried to clear a passage for himself.

The soapies could not find an easy way. Only the drummer, whose pulse and drumsticks seemed to threaten anyone that blocked his path, proceeded with much speed. The camera crew and the photographers walked backwards through the traffic. Their lenses squared the scene and transformed this hapless chaos, unintended and short-lived, into an act of scheming anarchy. Marching in a traffic jam to the formal beat of drum and to the blatant discord of car horns, the protest had undermined itself. It could hardly move. The rule of modern cities is that wheels and legs must keep on moving or keep out of town. At least they should keep separate. They should observe the segregations of the kerb.

The police arrived – a single officer, already wet and robbed of patience – and there were comic scenes adorning both the evening and the morning television news and the front pages of the daily papers, showing the drummer and policeman eye to eye. Both had their sticks raised in the air, both were intent on beating skin. The policeman, though, had been discreet and brought his night stick down upon the drum and not the drummer. The drummer was less restrained. He beat a tattoo on the policeman's hat. In the photograph, two traders were stepping forward through the jam of cars to intervene. They held placards as if they meant to chop the policeman down. One placard said, They Shall Not Pass – ironically, in view of all the chaos in the street. The other exhorted, Save our Market from the Millionaire. That was the picture that the city saw. Those were the slogans that introduced them to Arcadia.

The traders were elated. Now they understood that, for a while at least, two hundred citizens could bring the city to a halt. They formed a crowd, a laughing, animated crowd, at the top of the steps to the tunnel beneath Link Highway Red. Soon they were chanting slogans with one voice, walking unencumbered except by wind and rain down the centre of the mall. Their voices ricocheted wetly off the office glass and stone and sounded like a bullet sounds when it is shot in a ravine and lodges in the buttocks of an elk. They were loud enough to summon Signor Busi and his host from their breakfast to the parapet of Victor's roof-top garden, and to crowd the tinted, toughened windows of Big Vic with staff, including Anna on the 27th floor.

The mall had not witnessed noise or passion such as this, not since the builders had removed their huts and debris and left the buildings clean and free for business. The architecture said *Don't raise your voice, Don't run, Don't hang around.* Office workers, coming, going, did what they were told. The mall prepared them for the obeisances of the office desk just as the aisles of churches subdue their congregations between the door and the altar. But the procession of greengrocers was not intimidated by the prospect of a desk. Encouraged by the cameras, the echo and the camaraderie of rain, they bellowed slogans down the mall. The closer that the soapies got to Big Vic, the unrulier they became. To see their faces you would think that they were mutinous and angry. In fact, these men and women were having fun. What is more fun than making noisy mayhem in a place where you're not known but, yet, are flanked by a company of friends? For once they felt like crusaders instead of selfish middle-men in trade. This day enriched them. Indignation and a drum would save their market from Arcadia.

They lined up with their placards outside Big Vic, unprotected from the rain, ennobled by discomfort, emboldened by their fears of being driven from their stalls. What then? No one had thought to make a speech or send a deputation in or lobby for support and signatures from Victor's office staff.

'They only need to see us,' Con had said. 'And hear us too.'

So they stood firm and wet; and they began to chant and clap and jeer and offer leaflets whenever anybody passed them by to enter Victor's fort.

Just before eleven the architectural press began to arrive for Victor's conference, but there were other writers too, from papers and from magazines that would not normally concern themselves with building schemes. Rook's phone calls, Victor's press release and invitation, the early radio reports of trouble in the market place and streets, had stirred the news editors and the diarists to send their representatives. The Burgher himself had come (again my face is hoist above the parapet), and I was keen to follow up the anecdote of Victor's coddled fish with something else to make the rich seem ludicrous. I noted what the placards said – Save Our Market from the Millionaire – and when I took their leaflet, saw what comedy The Burgher could construct from Signor Busi's pregnant domes. Already – and without, as yet, much cause beyond an appetite for mischief – the traders had a champion. The Burgher loathed those men who gained their power and wealth from trade.

'Who are these people?'

Signor Busi was glad of an excuse to leave the breakfast table and look out on the mall. An hour of non-business conversation with Victor had obliged him to sit silently, engaged in food, or else – his choice, in fact – to hold a monologue. As Victor showed no sign that he was either bored or entertained, the monologue was free to range untrammelled and, perhaps, unheard, amongst the pleasantries of Busi's intercontinental life. He talked at length about New York, its obesity. Did Victor know New York? No? So Busi spoke about Milan, the town he loved and loathed the most. It was more Celtic than typically Italian, he believed. Did Victor realise that London was closer to Milan than Sicily? Victor had not realised, but seemed prepared to accept Busi's word.

Now the architect was stuck. The more he said, the less he had to say. So he was happy to stand and help the old man to the parapet and relay – his eyes were sharp – what he could see; the banners, the picket line, the drama in the mall. No, Victor did not know what all the distant noise was for. He sublet twenty-three floors of Big Vic to fourteen different companies, so there were fifteen possible reasons for demonstrations at the door.

When Anna came to lead her boss and Signor Busi down to the press conference, she said that there would be delays. They had expected just five writers at the most and perhaps an agency photographer, but there were thirty journalists in all, including a film crew and two people from the radio. The meeting room was far too small. They'd have to find a larger venue.

'Then use my office suite,' Victor said. 'You might have guessed there'd be wide interest.'

Anna thought it prudent not to detail the width of interest that had gathered in the mall. She replied to Signor Busi's urbane bow with a ceremonial smile and left to fetch the press.

Both men were pleased to launch Arcadia to such an eager group. The cameras were put to work as soon as the two men came down by Victor's private lift. Anna distributed plans and paperwork. Each file contained an architectural brief, a plan, a sketch, an article from the *International Gazette* about the Busi Partnership. Big Vic's Publicity Manager introduced the two men to the press. Signor Claudio Busi, he explained, would say a word or two, and then there would be questions and photo-opportunities and wine.

Signor Busi embarked upon his second monologue that

morning, but on this occasion he had come prepared. The speech that he had already made to Victor would do for these people, too, except that now there was no need 'to glorify the vision of the man who pays'.

'My work is familiar to you, I think,' he said, implying that the new Arcadia was all his work. 'I have been called . . .' (here he laughed, to demonstrate his lack of vanity) '. . . a guru of design, a philosopher amongst journeymen. I introduced the notion, as you know, of "building as event". That is to say, that when we use a building we should experience narrative and drama in the way that on a mountain walk we experience the textures and elements of landscape.'

As yet the pens and pencils of the press had made no mark. What were they building in the market place? A planetarium? A Disneyland? An operatic set? A wildlife park? Mont Blanc?

'We have nostalgia and we have experiments,' he continued. 'We also have modernity. I think it will be clear to you – if I can now invite you to open up your files and look at the impression of Arcadia – that we have opted for modernity, that is to say, for this city of today we replace the chaos of a medieval market with the harmony and dignity of a modern one.'

He held his larger illustration of Arcadia up against his chest. 'What does this recall to you?' he asked, and gave no time for anyone to make a guess. 'Here is a landscape at the city centre,' he said, and then – encouraged by the smiles that greeted every word – Signor Busi added 'an amusing confidentiality': 'Something to make us laugh. My colleagues in Milan have called Arcadia the Melting Glass Meringues. You see their joke, I think?' I held The Burgher's pen. It went to work. Busi had given me a comic heading for that evening's diary. He had surrendered his confectionary Arcadia to my cartoonist and to my irony.

'Meringues? Are these cakes known to you?' asked Busi, unnerved that no one seemed amused.

Victor hid behind his desk, his eyebrows making Ms and Ws. Perhaps he wondered whether this Italian was entirely sound, or else was blinking back his mirth.

When questions came, there were the usual queries about budgets and timescales which Signor Busi and the Publicity Manager handled with unnecessary detail. Then the tougher questions came, 'What consultations have there been with the street traders currently at work in the Soap Market?' and 'What provisions have been made to protect the interests of the marketeers?' The PR man made reassuring noises. It was his opinion that the building scheme was in the interests both of the city and the traders. 'Why, then, are there a crowd of soapies demonstrating in the mall?'

The Burgher rose upon my legs. I held the market traders' leaflet up and read the question that it posed and then the answers that it gave: 'Arcadia? Who pays? You, the shopper. Me, the trader. Us, the citizens. Them that value history and tradition.'

'There are placards at this very minute at the door which call on us to help protect the market from the millionaire,' I said. 'I see the millionaire himself is silent. I wonder whether we can ask him to reply to what the traders say?'

Victor did not stand. He did not want to speak, but had no choice. Old men can take their time, and not seem slow. He looked down at his hands. It seemed he would not speak at all, but then he raised his head and looked, not at the people in the room, but at the rain which swept into the window-panes.

'The market's getting taller. That's all,' he said. 'When I was small the traders put their produce out on mats. You had to bend to make your choice. Then we brought in raised stalls with awnings on which bags and tresses could be hung. You had to stretch to take your pick. So now we have Arcadia with steps and lifts and balconies. The market's like a plant. It grows and flourishes, or else it withers. There will be no problems with the marketeers. Arcadia will make them rich.'

'The traders at the door do not share your optimism,' someone said.

'They will,' said Victor. 'I'll speak to them myself.'

Quite what he meant no one was sure. They stood and watched him as he turned his back and went into his private lift, with Anna at his side, his papers in her hands. Would he go up or down? He could have said to Anna, 'Phone the commissionaires and ask them to select a couple from the crowd who are presentable. I'll talk to them. And phone the police to clear the others from the mall.' Instead he said, 'Let's get it over with.'

'What? Up or down?'

He pointed at his shoes.

It was simple, icy curiosity, not pluck or duty, which determined Victor to descend. His earlier roof-top view of what was happening below – even with Signor Busi as his sharper eyes – had not been satisfactory. It all had been a little out of tune, a half turn out of focus, just as the television was these days for him, for all old men. Words and images had frayed for him. Their selvages had gone. When Signor Busi had spoken for so long that morning, over breakfast, Victor had simply stared, uncertain when to nod or laugh or show concern. His hearing-aid was temperamental. It worked more clearly in shuttered rooms than in the open air. Weak light was a thinner filter for the sound. It left the consonants intact. It did not squeeze the words. At breakfast there was too much light, and too much accent in Signor Busi's speech. At times, it seemed to Victor, the architect had retreated into Italian, or else was speaking seamless prose in which the pauses were as crammed with words as the sentences themselves. Was that a question that he asked? All Victor did was shake his head – a gesture which he hoped would be appropriate. The animation of the younger man was tiring. What kind of dilettante was he that he chattered while he ate? What sort of breakfast guest was too insensitive to match his host's own reticence?

Victor had been relieved – though startled for a moment – when Signor Busi had so suddenly left the table to peer down on the mall. 'Who are these people?' Victor had not got a clue. It seemed to him the tide was going out and beaching him with failing faculties. It ebbed, it ebbed, it ebbed. Quite soon the only sounds and images which were defined would be those troubling ones – of Em and Aunt and eggs and fire – which were his memory.

Now that he was in the lift with Anna, though, his hearing-aid was working perfectly. He heard the whisper of the steel hawsers, the detonation of the papers which Anna was tapping on her leg, the brittle timpani of his own bones. He even heard and felt the air grow thicker as the lift went down. How long since he had last been to the lobby? How much longer since he'd passed through Big Vic's revolving doors? Three months at least. How long since God had last descended from the heavens to stand with mortals on the ground?

The power of the speech that he had been obliged to make for the journalists, the felicity of the words that came with such simplicity, had fired the old man with sufficient self-esteem to think he could anaesthetise the crowd with 'Arcadia will make you rich'. He was not nervous in the least – except, perhaps, that he was uneasy in the lift. It had dropped through twenty floors and more and seemed to travel at a speed and with a purpose that was reckless. He had to steady himself on the lift's steel walls, and then on Anna's arm. He was not sorry when his first journey for three months at least came to an end. The single door drew back and Victor looked out on the foliage of the atrium. All the ground-floor staff – receptionists, security, commissionaires – were looking out onto the mall where marketeers were drenched in rain and indignation. Victor pushed his hair back – needlessly – with his hand. He buttoned his coat, and walked across the atrium and stood, the shortest, oldest man, behind the crowd who blocked the exit doors. No one gave way. No one deferred. No one noticed him. He did not pass through these revolving doors each day on his way to work or on his way back home. The man was not familiar.

Anna tried to clear a path, but did not have the voice or strength to cut into the crowd. But when the press arrived a minute or so later, packed into Big Vic's main lifts, the crowd was soon pushed back and Victor was identified by camera-men and journalists who wished to winkle from him some idea of what he meant to say to the soapies on the far, wet side of the revolving doors.

Now Security did its work. It cleared a path. It made the staff give way. It made the pressmen step aside, and let Anna, Victor, and the breathless PR Manager whose face they knew, proceed towards their confrontation on the mall. Rank, age and power, and the circling quarters of the automatic doors – too fast and intimate for more than one high-ranker at a time, or so the doorman judged – conspired to send the old man, first and singly, into the rain. The Taxi Captain knew his boss's face. He'd been at Big Vic since the start. He hurried over with a black umbrella and followed Victor as he crossed from private territory into the public domain of the mall. There was no sudden wind. The sun did not break through to mark this unaccustomed meeting between the subjects and their distant king. The rain was democratic and it fell as dully everywhere – except that Victor was not wet. He had his canopy, and now a retinue of three – Anna, PR, and the umbrella man.

The stout commissionaire – the one who had escorted Rook out of Big Vic with such inflexible diplomacy – took it on himself to block the building's exits. If the boss was on the mall, then it became Victor's private place and no one could presume the right to go outside and join him there unless they had appointments to do so. The newspaper and the television cameramen had to press their lenses to the rain-splashed, tinted glass, while the soundmen and the scribes stood by helplessly or made the best of their imprisonment by inter- viewing Signor Busi.

Victor's hearing suffered in the air and light. He was surrounded by the banners and the slogans of the marketeers, but he could not make sense of what they said. The news that he was Victor had somehow spread. It rippled every placard there. It made each demonstrator briefly vehement in prepara- tion for the quiet they knew must come. They crowded him. They waved their placards and their leaflets – and, one or two, their fists. If only Victor could have separated sound from sound he would have understood the essence of their anger, that a man who lived in grandeur in an office penthouse on a business mall could, by decree, destroy their livelihoods, could build on them, could sweep them up and bin them out like worthless market waste.

'Who speaks for you?' he asked.

They pushed Con forward and made him stand square on to Victor so that the rain which ran off the black umbrella splashed at his feet.

'You have been misinformed,' Victor told the man. 'You've been misled.' He took the leaflet from the trader's hand. 'I don't know how you got hold of this.' He pointed at the illustration of Arcadia, taken from Busi's confidential plans. 'But had you been more patient you would have heard the good news that we have prepared for you. "Arcadia? Who pays?", your leaflet asks.' He put his finger to his chest. 'I pay. Who else? Sixty million US dollars it will cost, but not one dollar of that comes from you. I take the risk. I tremble at the bills. And who will benefit from this? Who will have dry and permanent premises? Who will no longer need to put up and pack away the stalls each day? Who will no longer need to barrow in the produce from the market edge, but will have storage space and access for the lorries and dumper lifts to bring the produce to the stalls?' He spread his arms to encompass everybody there. He promised them that he would not betray his 'market friends'. He spoke of meetings where all the details would be hammered out and all their worries could be voiced. He suggested there should be liaison every week, and a trading parliament inside Arcadia on which the marketeers could have their representatives, their ministers.

Victor looked around to check there were no journalists, and then he spoke again the words that had worked so well earlier that day.

'The market's getting taller, that is all,' he said. 'I'm eighty years of age. I've seen it grow. When I was just a kid and your fathers and grandfathers were the traders there, they put their produce out on mats and sat like Buddhists on the cobblestones. When we brought in raised stalls, the sort you use and seem to love today, your fathers rioted. They said they were a modern curse. They said no one would buy from stalls. But market stalls have made you wealthier. And now we have Arcadia with all its beauty and its benefits. Everyone will want to buy their produce there. Not just the poor. The wealthy too. Why else would I agree to invest so much in you? To make us all as poor as our grandfathers were? My friends, have faith. Arcadia will make you rich.'

Now Con was saying something in reply. Though Victor could not make out all his words, he knew the mood had changed. The placards were gripped less resolutely. After all, the boss himself had come out. He'd treated them as colleagues. He'd promised them meetings, safeguards, parliaments. And what he said made sense. Why would he wish to damage market trade? Their business made him rich.

Victor made a show of shaking hands, and then he turned about with Anna and the umbrella in his wake and re-entered Big Vic. He would not talk to journalists. His publicity manager (now surrounded by the traders) was paid for that. He felt immensely tired and disconcerted. It was not age, but anger that such private plans as his should suffer from such scrutiny, from press, from public, from market traders, and that despite his eminence and wealth he had to barter in the open air as if he were a boy of seven dependent on a tray of eggs.

He shared the lift with Anna. He said, 'Now I suppose you'd better see to it that meetings are arranged. We must be democrats.' He held up Con's leaflet for closer scrutiny. 'Those plans were confidential. Someone's leaked.' He looked at Anna. Looked straight through her. 'Find out who leaked,' he said. 'Give me the name, it doesn't matter who, or what it costs. He gets the sack.'

For a moment Anna almost gave the boss a pair of names, her own and Busi's. Would the old man reward her for her honesty? Would he send Busi home, Arcadia and all? She doubted it. But then, why should she take the blame? There was another name, a guilty name. Rook was the man, and he was safe from anything that Victor might do. You cannot sack a man when he is sacked. If she was ever cornered, then Rook would be the name to help her out, to keep her safe, to earn rewards. 'I'll ask around,' she said.

Victor ordered sweetened tea and waited for it, standing at the window of his office suite. The mall was almost clear. A broken placard lifted slightly in the wind. A few of Con's blue leaflets were plastered to the marble flagstones by the grease and rain. Unhurried soapies stood in a circle by the fountains, as unimpassioned in their manner as a crowd of football fans discussing their team's uninspiring draw.

The evening paper ran the photograph of comic revolution on the streets, the policeman and the trader beating skins. The Burgher, on an inside page, led with some gossip about a writer and his wife. His seventh item had the heading, 'Victor's Glass Meringue', and comprised one, long-winded feeble joke – I must admit – at the expense of cakes and architects and millionaires. But the front-page headline read

'You have been misled'. The newspaper group for which The Burgher worked had financial interests in Arcadia and the trading wings of Victor's companies. It did not wish the old man any harm.

8

THIS IS THE SORCERY of cities. We do not chase down country roads for fame or wealth or liberty. Or romance even. If we hanker for the fires and fevers of the world, we turn our backs on herds and hedgerows and seek out crowds. Who says – besides the planners and philosophers – that we don't love crowds or relish contact in the street with strangers? We all grow rich on that if nothing else. Each brush, each bump, confirms the obvious, that where you find the mass of bees is where to look for honey.

The conspiracy is this, that we – the seemly citizens – obey the traffic lights, observe timetables, endure the shadows and the din. We do not cross, or park, or push, or jump the queue, or trespass, except where we are ordered to. We wed ourselves to work and tickets. We ebb and flow with as much free will as salt in sea. Yet we count ourselves more blessed, more liberated than the country dwellers whose tumult is a tractor and a crow, whose ebb and flow is seasons, weather, meals. And why? Because we townies are the only creatures in the universe to benefit from chains, to make our fortunes from constraint, to wear the chafing, daily harnesses of city life as if they are the livery of plutocrats.

Who is more harnessed, then? The docile banker whose life is squared and mapped and calibrated, or the vagabond? Which of these two is more blessed with power and with

wealth but is most likely to observe the bulls and firmans of
the street? Who is the lag and who the libertine? Yet who
would be a vagabond by choice? What ploughman would not
hope to be a trammelled plutocrat? We flock in to the city
because we wish to dwell in hope. And hope – not gold – is
what they pave the cities with.

So Joseph, then, was happier than Rook. His life was more
uncomfortable, of course. But he was rich with hope. He had
more empty years ahead, more possibility, while Rook now
knew that he was in decline. Rook's harnesses had been
unloosed. His city held for him few promises, few hopes.
What was he but an unemployed, unmarried and unhealthy
man, a firebrand turned to ash? Who'd take him on? What
woman, what employer, what company of friends, what
neighbourhood? He looked for sentimental comfort now, the
first quest of the middle-aged. His life orbited round Anna,
her gossip, what news she had of Victor and Big Vic. He was
resigned to witnessing Arcadia.

Of course, he spent each morning at his table in the Soap
Garden, drinking fewer coffees than previously, but more
spirits and – foolishly – even smoking a cheroot. You could
count on him to join in cards or dice or dominoes, and to win
or lose more recklessly than most. He rested on his bed most
afternoons, but did not sleep. He took no pleasure in the radio
or television. He did not read (except the evening news). He
rarely cooked a meal more complicated than some soup or egg.
At first he met with Anna every night. She slept with him. She
had her own drawer and a suitcase in his apartment. Her
blouses and her cardigans shared hangers with his trousers.
She used his razor on her legs. He used her perspiration
sprays. They talked of selling both their homes and pooling

what they had to buy a quieter, larger place a little out of
town. They'd buy a car with the profit. They'd take a holiday –
in Nice or Istanbul or Amsterdam. He'd look for work, he said,
but did not look. He promised he'd bring brochures from the
travel firms, but he forgot. He would not visit valuers to
discover what the flat was worth, or what sort of home the two
of them could buy on the outskirts of the town. He only *talked*
of how their life would be if they lived as a pair. His only act
of union was in bed.

Within a month or two, Anna felt she needed more time
on her own. She was too tired after work for Rook's invasive
restlessness. She enjoyed, instead, the short bus journey to her
own home, the respite of the empty rooms, the opportunity to
sit alone in casual clothes with no demands beyond the television set. So she took to meeting Rook only on Wednesday
nights and at the weekends. Rook was not pleased, of course,
but Anna's half-time absence suited him to some extent. It left
him free to drink and smoke and gamble at night as well as
day.

In time Anna's Wednesday visits became less welcome.
She wanted only to relax, to recuperate from work, to cook,
make love impassively, sit up in bed with silence and a
magazine. She did not wish to go out in the streets, take
snacks in bars, make love more frequently, more rapidly, more
testingly. The sexual hold she had on Rook was episodic and
capricious. To indulge it was to end it. The moments of their
greatest unity – their mouths and chests and genitals wrapped
humidly together, their hands spread on each other's backs,
their legs in plaits – were the moments, also, when Rook
became absolved of her. That is the turpitude of men and love.
Rook's orgasms unharnessed him. They transformed him, in

an instant, from a man obsessed with Anna and the universe of bed to one impatient to pull his trousers on and walk, alone and passionless and free, out into town. He'd leave her less rewarded than a prostitute. At first, she would get out of bed with him, to wash and dress and rush outside when all she wanted was a massage and some tea, a shower and some sleep. But Rook always led her to the Soap Garden as if it had the only bars in town.

'Why don't you sleep out with the beggars and the alcoholics in the market?' she asked. It appeared to Anna that Rook was obsessed, but not with her. He only wished, it seemed, to woo the Soap Market and its garden before they disappeared for good.

If Anna had been more certain of herself she could have taken charge of Rook. She could have gripped him by the wrist, as if he were a child, and led him to the valuers or to the travel firms or to employment agencies. She could have banned him from the market bars. He was weak enough to do what he was told. Instead she made do on his half portions. What choice was there? She made excuses for him.

One Wednesday night, he would not settle down to sleep, despite embraces on the counterpane and the post-coital sedative of sheets. He dressed again. He said he had to buy some milk. He needed some fresh air. He couldn't breathe. She waited for him, but could not fight off sleep. When he returned, the broken noise of traffic from the street made clear that it was long past midnight. She did not need to ask him where he'd been.

She did not come on Wednesdays any more, and he was glad of that. When all the bars were shut he liked to join the vagrants in the market place. He liked to stare into their box and carton fires and share with them a song, a cigarette, a cob of roast maize, a throat of wine, a curse. They did not guess from how he dressed – his leather coat was old and bothered – that he was rich. They merely counted him as one of those, down on their luck but not yet down-and-out, who drank with them when all the bars were shut. They did not know, they did not care, what happened to him when he left. For all they knew he had a niche not far from theirs. In a corner of the market place, perhaps. Or in the sink estates – a tram's ride out of town – where what had not been vandalised had never worked, where ground-floor flats were tinned up with corrugated sheeting, where staircases and lifts were urinous and dangerous and dark. No one among them knew about Arcadia. When Rook described the changes that would come it did not move them more than any other drunken, midnight speech. Why should they be alarmed? The distant future made no difference to them. They only waited for the bottle, still half-a-circle from their grasp. They only hoped the wood would last till dawn.

By day, Arcadia was much discussed among the marketeers. Of course. Surveyors were at work, and questionnaires were circulated. Inspection ditches had been dug across the grass in the Soap Garden. Women wearing ID badges sat on stools to monitor and graph pedestrian usage of the different market sectors. Outline proposals and planning certificates were displayed – as law decreed – at focal points. The marketeers were bemused, but flattered, too, by all the attention they received and by the consultation meetings and the Soapie Parliament that Victor promised them. They had agreed amongst themselves that there was little point in fighting progress with more demonstrations or with petitions. What power had a line of people or a list of names against the will of money to be spent? No, they would be modern citizens. That is to say, they would suppress their passions and hope to profit from their pragmatism. The boss had given them his word. The demonstration on the mall had winkled Victor from his lair. He'd stood amongst them in the rain and what he'd said had been a challenge: change your ways and prosper.

They imagined working under glass: warm in winter, cool in summer, dry and windless, weather-free. There'd be the same old camaraderie but air-conditioned. The fruit and vegetables would survive, be crisp and firm, be sellable, a few days longer. There would be less waste, and what waste there was would make a profit, too. Pig farmers on the edge of town would pay a fee for each full bag. The soapies saw themselves driving freely in vans. They'd save on porters' fees. They'd save on time. There'd be disruptions, naturally. How would they manage during building work? But, all in all, the traders were buoyant. In fact, they were impatient. They were tired of being soapies: make us Arcadians, and quickly.

Rook's bitter auguries did not alarm them. It did not matter how disgruntled Rook might be. Con was the man to listen to, and he, though cautious, shared the view that they had less to fear from progress than from torpor. Rook had fooled him with his jeremiac prophesies, 'All this will disappear', 'You'll soon be out of work and rattling round the streets like me'. Con now was more inclined to trust the word of Victor. It angered him that Rook was such a fixture in the market place and in the bars. Had he no self-respect? Had he no tact? If Arcadia would put an end to Rook, then that was fine by Con. Rook preached his words of warning, but anyone could see, and smell, that his views were distilled in alcohol and flavoured with the bitters of regret. The time would come when all his kind, the night-time nestlers, the parasites, the idlers, would be swept away. Welcome the day!

It took a little less than twelve months for the Busi Partnership to complete their plans and raise a Bill of Quantities and put out the building tender. Architecture is a bureaucratic art – and *Markitecture*, as some comic christened the attempts to marry art and trade, was doubly bureaucratic because each detail had to satisfy the pocket and the eye, the aesthete and the businessman.

Victor provided offices in Big Vic for Signor Busi's younger colleagues. The Philosopher Among Journeymen was not involved. He'd been persuaded to spend the winter in New York; the weekends in Manhattan, the weekdays upstate at Cornell where he had been appointed Comstock Visiting Professor in Art and Design. He gave sermons there on the Italian Masterbuilders – Giovanni Michelucci, Franco Fetronelli, and himself.

Busi's colleagues wished he had not promised to make space for Victor's birthday statue. They were the modern school and saw no point in statues that were, they said, 'as sentimental as Capo di Monte figurines, but without the benefit of dwarfishness'. They wanted something glass or plastic, something steel, something big and time-honoured in concrete, a symbol of Arcadia. But they were stuck with *Beggar Woman and her Child*, style 1910, in bronze.

Victor had insisted on where the statue would be placed: at that entrance to Arcadia which was the closest to the Woodgate district, halfway between where Em had begged and died.

'Perhaps we could persuade a builder's truck to back up

and wreck it,' one architect suggested. 'We'd have a modern sculpture then, *Flattened Woman and her Child.*'

My God, how they were bored by meetings, and evenings spent in their hotels, and all the budget-bullied cutbacks from their plans which were required, and which themselves required new plans, new calculations, work. They did not like our city. Newcomers seldom do. They are not literate in what leads where, or how and when. These architects hoped they'd never need to know our city well. Their main desire was *Do the Job, and Home.* They set a day, the first day of the year, when building work on Arcadia – two years of it – would start. So New Year's Eve would close the market and the decade down.

There was a problem. You did not need to be a space–time engineer to spot a two-year gap between the closure of the Soap Market and the opening of Arcadia. Those rash and early promises that builders and merchants could work in concord, the market stalls amongst the scaffolding, trade amongst construction, could not be kept. Were they naive, or mischievous, these undertakings? How had anybody ever thought that tomatoes by the kilo could be compatible with six-tonne shovels and ballast lorries and men in safety hats? No one on site! That was the builder's sensible demand. It only needed some old lady laden down with cabbages and onions to take a fall or take a bruise from building work and she'd be shopping for a lawyer and for damages before her bruise was brown. So Victor's managers were told they had to relocate the market stalls for at least two years.

Victor himself was sent a memorandum – but what did he employ managers for? Besides he only had to look out of his window to see the perfect and the only answer to the two-year gap. There were open fields of tarmac, parking for the mall's nine thousand staff and more for visitors. Two areas, three hectares each, were underused. They were too far from offices, and windswept, dirty from Link Highway Red which passed close by. Blue whisker herb and smog-nettle had taken purchase in the tarmac, making do with lime from the painted parking grids and puddled rain for soil. At night this was where lovers came and prostitutes who traded from the kerb, with rocking cars and peeping Toms parked asymmetrically for privacy. By day it was as empty as a prison yard. With access from the highway and, for pedestrians, by tunnel, this was the perfect place for market stalls. Good news for everyone involved. Or so Big Vic would have the world believe.

People are ready to be fooled. That's optimism. 'This is the price you have to pay for Arcadia,' the stallholders were told, when they were trying to make light of their predicament, their exile to the carpark. 'If you want your share of wealth then you must expect to take some risks, to suffer inconvenience. We're talking business here, not charity.'

Who told them that? Why, Rook, of course. He was amused to tease them with their foolishness, their gullibility. Why had they ever thought that Victor's plan was some crusade to make them more secure and wealthier?

'Con led you down a *cul-de-sac*,' he said. 'You may be sure *he*'ll turn out fine. They'll keep him sweet and quiet at any cost. The last thing that they want is trouble on the mall again – so Victor's men will take good care of Con. He'll get prime site, you'll see. But what about the little traders, the ones who don't make noise but just scrape by, selling from the backs of vans? Or those who've got five kids to clothe? Or those . . .'

Rook was drunk and smart enough to make an endless list in which the only one who showed a profit from the move into the carpark site was Con.

No one doubted Rook was mischievous. He'd ducked and weaved too many times before. He'd broken free and re-aligned too frequently for any of his alliances to count for much. But it's a fact that even fools and drunks and liars can sound alarms. What does it matter who shouts fire, or how, so long as there are flames? Here, then, was the Soap Market in its final weeks. It seemed the same as it had always been. There were no closing sales. No bargains to be had. Fresh food has a shelf life of a day, a little more in wintertime. There were no stocks to clear because in produce markets stocks are cleared each day and replenished overnight. But there was something stale upon the air, more pungent than the market waste or the odour of too many people in one place. This was the putrefaction of resolve, the enfeebling of that prod-and-nudge which got the traders from their beds each day at five to bargain with the wholesalers, which gave them pride and pleasure in the stall-top patterns they could make with what they had to sell, which made them cheeky, cheerful, quick with repartee. Now they did not wake with an appetite for work. They did not relish the day. They were offhand with fruit and customers. It did not matter which of these were bruised or handled without care. They left the business in the hands of sons and nieces and stood in circles, hands dug deeply into pockets, shoulders down, to hear the latest rumour or hard news about their prospects between the market and Arcadia.

The bars and restaurants which fringed the Soap Garden had most to fear. There'd be no place for them in Victor's carpark. They'd been promised leases in Arcadia, and there was compensation to be paid, negotiated by lawyers from Big Vic. They'd have to look for premises elsewhere. But for two years? What landlord would let his premises for just two years? Theirs was a quandary impossible to solve – to move, to stay, to wait and see? Yet, as the new year drew closer, so the market mood transformed again. Business boomed at all the bars. The marketeers were thirsty all day long. They stayed at tables, stood at counters, found perches on the weathered stones around the medieval washing fountains. You'd think they had no work to do, and had no end of cash. You'd think they were in celebratory mood, the noise they made, the bottles that they drank. Theirs was a carnival of despair, the despair of those whose rafts draw closer to the weir and see both the tumbling dangers and the placid pools beyond. No one is fool enough to swim, yet none looks forward to the rocks.

Of course, they played the game of *If*. What if they moved as docilely as lambs and did their best at what they did the best, that is, sell fruit and vegetables to people in the town, no matter where? Would carpark profits be the same as those made in the Soap Market? By spring, would they be smirking at the fears they'd had and wishing, secretly, for Arcadian delays so they could stay and flourish in the carpark? What if, what if they'd stood their ground and said, We Stay!? These cobblestones are ours. We don't want risks and challenges. We want the market as it is. What if that Rook, that braggart Rook, that told-you-so, had not been sacked and still held Victor's ear on their behalf? Would he have stopped Arcadia, as he now claimed? What if old Victor had not lived to be so old?

Rook was Cassandra now, the unregarded prophet whose

truth was trash. He and Anna were no longer friends. A woman of her age does not need ballast of his kind. She kept away, and when she thought of Rook she flushed with anger not with love. As he grew freer of Big Vic so she became more part of it, more loyal to work which now she thought of as 'career'. She wished the boss to favour her and so, of course, ambition ruled her tongue.

'I have a name for you,' she told Victor. 'Remember what you said? The name of who it was leaked Signor Busi's plans. You said I should enquire. I'm certain it was Rook, the day that he was sacked. He went into your room, I'm sure. He used the photocopier . . . I have informants in the Soap Market. They say he boasts about the theft.' She knew the timing made no sense, that Rook had gone before the plans arrived. But she guessed – and hoped – the old man's memory was logically unsound. He'd not know one month from the next when both these months were over one year old.

Victor rewarded her with nods. He was content to believe the thief was Rook. He would not have to endure the awkwardness of sacking someone else.

'That's good,' he said. 'We harmed him more than he harmed us, I think.' He was ready now to turn to other matters. But Anna knew that silence would not earn much from Victor. She had betrayed a one-time friend, at no cost to that friend, perhaps, but still, it was a real sin and sins should stir up wind: 'Rook's workload has transferred itself to me in this past year. I've worked here now for seven years. I wonder if . . .'

'We'll see,' he said, but it was clear to him what he would do. Anna, when all was said and done, was already Victor's eyes and ears. She did what Rook had done, except she knew

the innards of Big Vic more closely than she knew the Soap
Market. What could that matter now? He'd send a memorandum to her, giving her Rook's job, Rook's salary, Rook's desk,
Rook's access to his suite, his apartment, his roof-top hermit-
age. He almost gave her the news right then, by word of
mouth. But he resisted such intimacy, and asked that she
present the cheques and documents to sign. He was not fond
of gratitude. Gratitude was not the same as debt. You could
not settle gratitude by cheque.

So Rook and Anna were lieutenants in opposing camps.
So what? They did not meet again, or even glimpse each other
on the street. Their streets were not the same. And Rook
would soon be off the streets for good. There was bitterness
between them, unexpressed. Rook saw that Anna's name was
where his name had been, on letters to the traders from Big
Vic, on market documents.

'Don't trust that woman,' he warned them, shocked at the
ease with which he told such lies. 'She's loyal to no one but
herself.' She was the one, he said, who'd given Busi's plans to
Con. What should they make of that? The woman who had
chanced her job by stealing documents was now promoted to
Victor's personal aide, the old man's buffer and his fixer. In
Rook's version, everything was clear. It had all been a plot.
'Don't underestimate that man. He planned your demonstration on the mall. He had the press on hand. He had his speech
prepared. No doubt that PR monkey laboured over it for
weeks and rehearsed each word with Victor. "The market's
getting taller"? Oh, yes? And who is standing there out in the
rain while Victor makes his pretty little speech and promises
to make you rich? Sweet Anna, that is who. His parlour-maid.
Who was it chaperoned old Busi at The Excelsior? Who was it,

actually, who sacked me from my job? Who's now ensconced in my old chair? Anna goes from strength to strength while you, poor fellows, pack your bags on New Year's Eve for two years' hard labour at the gulag carpark in the frozen wastes of New Town.'

Rook sketched for them a future made from rotting unsold fruit, and yellow leaves, and roots gone soft and pliable. No one would last the two years 'in the wilderness', Rook said. That was Victor's masterplan – to shed the soapies so that he could have Arcadia himself. But Rook was talking to nobody. His bitter punditry, his ironies, made people turn their backs, and seek out less bilious company. And company like that was not in short supply. By mid-December the market place was frolicsome. For once the centre of our city was in vogue. Perhaps it was not paradise, but then neither was it hell. The soapies knew of better places and much worse. Who'd volunteer, they wondered, to live, along with twenty million others, in Mexico City in ghettos so dirty and so packed that roaches fled to countryside and pig ticks came to town? Or in Hong Kong where, it was said, apartments were so small and public space so scarce that should you wish to twist around in bed at night you'd have to take the ferry and twist around in mainland China? Who'd spend a single night by choice in London? Half the population there could only sleep with pills. Who'd want to breathe the air of Tokyo – where the holy mountain of Fuji was no longer visible through the smog? Or drink the waters of Detroit, where the Rouge River was so thick with effluent that, in infra-red satellite pictures, it showed up as solid ground? Who'd swap our modest traffic jams for those great constipations in LA? Compared to these great towns, the unromantic modesty of our city centre was cause for gratitude.

As December drew to its end so everybody in the city came to see the market for the final time. They brought their children. They blocked the streets with cars. They bought their token vegetables, their memento fruit, and wandered in between the stalls remarking how engaging market places were. Cellophane directed them. They did what they were told. They treated him with more respect than he had ever known. They stood transfixed to watch him swing his arms or block the passage of a wayward van.

The soapies loved this valedictory clientele, this slow and gawping audience who bought bad fruit and never asked the price, who swallowed every tale a soapie told. One trader – asked a hundred times how he'd lost the last joint of his little finger – winked at his wife and told how he had found, the month before, a fruit snake in a tub of peaches.

'It was no longer than my hand,' he said. 'But those fruit snakes are poisonous. One bite and you're dead in thirty seconds. That's if you're fit and strong like me, and have the heart to last that long. What could I do? I took this bill hook and cut the finger off there and then before the poison reached my heart.' At other times and other tellings, he carried out the surgery not with a bill hook but with a banana knife, a piece of glass, a razor blade, an axe, a coffee spoon. And once, 'What could I do but hold my finger up and let my wife here bite it off? She spat it out. It landed in that carrot box. We haven't found it yet.'

One apple trader, a man who kept a bottle by his till, lectured as he sold: 'To bite an apple is to taste the world's most scientific fruit. It was a falling apple that gave us gravity – though none of mine have fallen from the tree. They've all been picked and packed without a bruise. And here's the apple tempted Eve. You see the blushes on its cheeks? And here are cooking apples like the ones that Einstein used in his experiments. It's got the mass, it's got the energy. It's very good with cheese.'

Another found a *bon viveur*, or nectar bug, amongst his fruit, as swollen by juice as a ripe green grape. He held it up for all the customers to see – and, spotting children watching him, he did a sleight of hand and swapped the bug for a real grape. He tossed it in his mouth. It popped between his teeth. He poked his tongue out at the children. Squashed green flesh lay in the ladle of his tongue.

This new, naive and richer clientele could not conceal its pleasure. Was this a circus or a market place? If only parking was a little simpler or the journey from the suburbs not so long, they'd do their shopping in the Soap Market every time. The fruit looked better free from cellophane. You had a chance to touch and choose exactly what you wanted. And so much choice. And much more fun – if less convenient – than the bright and covered stores they usually used, close to the office, a short walk from home, two minutes in the car. What a gift, as well, to find this patch of greenery at the market heart. There were such cheap cafés there – and bars like country bars with slatted tables, trees for shade in summer and protection in the winter, waiters and waitresses who were neither servile nor imperious. They could test the strangest drinks, and eavesdrop on a tumult of conversations, profanities and propositions like they'd never heard before.

The buskers came, like wasps to beer. They played old songs and standards from America. It was so crowded that the gipsy with the concertina could hardly stretch and squeeze his notes. The waiters had to carry trays of beers above their heads. The fact that Rook sat preaching doom was only further evidence that here, in this grassed and cobbled relic, life was ripe.

Some stayed all day, most of the night. In fact, in that last week between Christmas and New Year, the night took over from the day. The alcohol replaced the fruit. Trade gave way to pleasure. Some single traders ceased to trade. They did not rise at dawn to fidget over crops or fuss with decorations to their stalls. They got up late. They stayed up late. They drank like camels. Who gave a damn what fortune and the carparks held? There was a party to attend. A wake? A christening? Or both? No one had time to wonder or to care. Even those five men who'd been with Victor at his birthday lunch and were too old to take much pleasure out of noise and drink were not allowed to go home sober. How could they refuse a toast to 'Ourselves'? And then another toast to 'All these years we've shared'? And more: 'To all our loyal customers'. 'To the new year and the old'. 'To Health, Wealth and Women'. 'To Arcadia'. Quite soon they had the gipsy and his bewitching concertina at their table and were dredging for the words and tune of

'Are you for sale, sweet market maid?
(And if so, can I squeeze you?)
How much a kilo of your breasts?
(I'll take a pair, so please you.)
How much for thighs?
And how much eyes?
Oh, tell me that you're merchandise.
Sweet maid, I long to lease you.

What is your fee?
That's fine by me!
Now settle down upon my knee,
before my missus sees you . . .'

These were nights too good to end, so full of sin and yet so blameless and so virtuous. The celebration would not last. On the morning of January 1st the market would be cleared. The hoardings and barriers would go up. The diggers and the trenchers would move in. The soil beneath the stones would be on show, flints and shattered cobbles blinking in the light for the first time in six hundred years.

Rook wished to save the cobblestones. And himself. There was no place for him in Victor's carpark, or in Arcadia. They'd not marked out a site for him, where he could trade on having been the Woodgate boy, the firebrand of the market place, the boss's right-hand man, the soapies' champion. On New Year's Day his world would be reduced to the four small rooms of his apartment. He'd be the undisputed king of walls and furniture. He'd have no reputation on the streets. Unless, that is, he took this final chance to make his mark, to take revenge, upon the town.

On New Year's Eve there was no room at his usual table in the Soap Market. Young men and women he had never seen before, and all the residents from thereabouts, had joined the traders, porters, drivers to celebrate year's end and mark the closing of the Soap Market.

At seven, the mayor had come, with cameramen, representatives from the Busi Partnership, and Victor's development and trading managers. The police had cleared a path and set up metal barriers so that the city mayor could be the first customer to shop unimpeded in the Soap Market, without the pressure of a crowd. The route which he would take was set, as was the stall where he would pause, the conversation he would have with the chosen soapie, the single orange – already washed and wrapped by a town hall official – that he would buy and peel and eat. There'd be a photo-call ('Please bite the orange, Mr Mayor. A wider mouth. Smile!'), an interview, a walkabout, a hasty departure to give a speech to city businessmen at their annual dinner. A secretary made a note that in two years' time, this mayor, or the next, would need to buy a second orange and eat it for the cameras to mark the opening of Arcadia.

So much for the proprieties. Now the traders were free – and glad – to dismantle and to stow their market stalls for the last time. They did not pack them in the usual way, or lay them down for rest on their trading pitches, but followed the instructions which had been sent to them from Anna in Big Vic. They folded their awnings and their trestles, packed and boxed their unsold fruit and vegetables, fixed on a numbered label, inked in their names, and carried their trading rigs to two collection points behind the bars. Victor's lorries would arrive at dawn to take the stalls across Link Highway Red to their new carpark homes.

For once the cleansing teams could be as careless as they wished with their sweepers and their hoses. They washed the cobbles wet and black, removed the daily waste, and left the market clean for its dawn clearance. The traders joined the party in the garden, their grimy aprons and hats persuading people in the crowd that they were soapies and should be let through and served at once, much in the way that funeral crowds defer to family mourners.

The cobbled oval which surrounded the garden and the bars was emptier than it had ever been. The new arrivals took advantage of the space to park their cars close to the bars. It only took one car to brave the medieval cordon of the cobblestones, for a hundred, then five hundred more to follow. You did not need a ticket there. You parked for free. There was a short-lived symmetry in this – a carpark lost to marketeers below Big Vic, a carpark gained in market space at the centre of the old town.

The Soap Market gleamed. The windscreens and the roofs of cars caught, tossed back, the street and building lights. The cars were silky, sated beetles, nesting on the corpse while it was wet and warm. The wise drivers put their windows up, retracted their radio aerials, locked their cars, before they headed for the bars. They did not like the look of those men and women who hung around, the beggars and the drunks, the homeless, jobless, feckless, hopeless, ancient men, the ones who counted cobblestones as bed, the petrol sniffers overawed by such a choice of petrol tanks.

Where would the night-time soapies sleep that night? Where were their nests? Where could they light their fires? They called to Rook, the ones that knew his face. 'What's going on?' they asked. The quieter ones just walked around between the cars with nowhere else to go. Some tried the handles of saloons. Some pulled off petrol caps and dined on vapour. Some sat on bonnets passing bottles, bothering the passers-by for cash or cigarettes. It was too late to think of somewhere else. This was a home to them, and they were as nervous and volatile as if they were bereaved.

Rook stood and watched, debating with himself whether now was the time – before he grew too troublesome – to go

back home, to see the old year out, soberly, alone, in bed. He
was not well. The evening damp was sitting on his chest. His
head was crammed. He felt close to tears. Then he saw Joseph
for the fourth and final time. The boy was sitting with his
back against the smaller pile of stalls, asleep. The only sleeper
there. Rook could not resist the opportunity. He leant to wake
the boy.

'It's me,' Rook said, the Devil shaking Faust. Joseph's nose
was running. His eyes were wet. He smelt of alcohol and fuel.
He could not hold his head up straight. His breath could
bubble paint. 'I've got a job for you.' Rook searched his
pockets, found his wallet, and produced the ten half-notes.
'You have your halves, I hope? I'll give you my halves tonight.
I'll make you rich if . . .' If you can shake a wand and make the
market whole again. If you can mug me back my job. If you
can kidnap Anna from Big Vic and place her in my bed. If you
can trick the lines to leave my face, the grey to leave my hair,
and make me young and dressed in black again. If you can
stop the city in its tracks.

'If what?' asked Joseph, half awake. Rook tapped the stack
of trading stalls with his toe.

'We'll have a bonfire, eh?' he said. 'To end all this, to see
the old year out.' He produced a book of matches – free from
The Excelsior – and dropped them into Joseph's hand. 'Set fire
to all this wood and canvas. And then the other pile as well.
That's all you have to do. It's money for nothing.'

'What for?'

'Just do it. Either you burn that or I'll burn these.' He
flexed the ten half-notes he held. He put them back inside his
wallet. 'Wait ten minutes. Do your job. Then find me here
tomorrow. Start the new year ten thousand richer than today.'

Rook would not go home to sleep soberly or alone that night. He wished to see what mayhem he could cause. But he would need an alibi. He must be seen, a noisy innocent, when the fires began. He made his way between the cars. He pushed a passage through the crowds until he reached the scuffed winter lawns of the Soap Garden. He got himself an empty glass in time for midnight, and as the toasts for Health and Wealth were offered to the crowds Rook was the noisiest respondent, like the worst of sinners at a mass. He called out madly. He made ironic toasts for Victor, for Arcadia. He stood on tables, made a nuisance of himself with women, traders, young men in garish clothes. He let them know his name. 'I'm Rook, and this is my back-yard.' He was unforgettable. No one noticed that there was orange dawn rising from the west, with clouds of smoke. And no one turned to sniff the old and woody smell that comes from country hearths and bakeries and forest fires.

The first to warm their faces and their hands upon the flames were the market's night-guests. Their nests were going up in smoke, but they were cheerful with the light and colours reflected in all the windscreens of the market place. They squatted on their haunches with their bottles and let their faces redden with the drink and heat. They cheered as flames collapsed the tepees made from wood and canvas. The heat compacted and sent its front-row audience back down the aisles of cars where it was darker, safer, less intense.

The crowd was growing. Late arrivals who had parked on pavements in the Woodgate district and who were too elated by the date and time to go back home, were making for the market bars when they were blocked by smoke and fire and crowds. They were not alarmed. The midnight fire was not a threat to them. It only marked the closing of the market or the closing of the year. It gave a cheerful touch to New Year's Eve. The drunks and beggars pestered them for cigarettes and one or two lit up their cigarettes with embers from the fires.

The fire itself was changing mood. It spat. It was exasperated, and trapped. Fires by their nature sink and spread. They smoulder at their edges and colonise the land around. But cobbles do not burn. They kept the fire at bay. The heat grew angrier, but it could not do much except startle everybody there with the pistol shot of cobbles splitting underneath the fire and timber detonating.

There's a winter city wind we call the Midnight Wheeze. The night-time warmth of city life is dragged up by the moon, and colder country air is sucked in underneath, along the pavements and the alleyways and the tram routes, and blows till dawn. It and the fires made *rendez-vous*'s. They waltzed. Their gowns flew up and sent out puffs of heat. The flames were animated now. They dipped and reached, they stretched, recoiled, as the wind shadow-boxed the night. The smallest of the fires had stretched the furthest – and, at last, it held on to the leafless twigs of two snag trees which grew behind a bar. It turned them black. The flames had hardly touched. But those who watched saw fifty airborne smokers draw on fifty cigarettes as the twig tips drew in wind and glowed as redly as an owlet's eyes. The cigarettes caught fire. The flames now skipped like elves amongst the branches, feasting on the bark. The revellers in the Soap Garden looked up to see two trees on fire and giving voice to wind as trumpets do. Already twigs were falling onto roofs, and roofs were chattering with debris and shrugging noisily at the sudden warmth. Already insects filled the air. And there were rats and bats and cockroaches that sought to flee the flames.

The wind now turned. It let the trees collapse. It blew back on the market place where the crowd had grown quieter, less amused. The fires hissed. Flames curled like Chinese waves and broke onto the bonnets and the windscreens of the nearest cars. A tongue of heat blackened, shrank, a linen football flag that some young man had tied to the radio aerial of his creaky van. It scorched the chrome on ancient bumpers, drew acrid smells from new ones moulded out of plastic.

Rook saw the trees go up, and he was gripped with guilt and fear and exhilaration. He ran, when everybody ran, to see what happened. He joined in the panic, whipped it up, agreed with, echoed every shout from every trader who read conspiracy in every flame, in every car, in every stranger's face. 'They've burnt our stalls!' Too late to recover anything. Too hot and dangerous. 'They've set fire to us now,' though who 'They' were, they did not say. 'They' were the mayor, and architects, and businessmen, and Victor. 'They' were the men who came at dawn to 'start from scratch'.

Who was the first to overturn a car? Not Rook. He was too small and breathless and had no comrades. Some young men who loved their cars had tried to back them out of danger, reversing into spaces where people stood, pressing their bumpers against the bumpers of the car behind, attempting three-point turns where there was not sufficient room to turn a hand-cart. Some drivers at the front tried to clear a path at the fire's feet. They blared their horns, were more concerned for paintwork than for flesh. They found themselves enclosed by men. Their cars were rocked and turned. They had to scramble free. One young man – his back tyres melting smoke, his windscreen smashed – sought reparation with a flaming stick. He'd kill to save his car.

The Soap Market did not have enough exits for all the vehicles that were parked. Besides, the narrow roads and pavements which led away were blocked by other cars and more crowds, drawn to the place by noise and light and smoke. What chance then for the fire brigade? Their engines could get no closer to the fires than the hydrants at Tower Square and on Saints Row would allow. The hoses that they ran could not reach the market rim. The firemen did not care. This fire was self-contained. It could not leap the cobbles to the town. Besides, at dawn, as everybody knew, the demolition would begin. So 'Let the fire burn out,' the police advised. 'We'll clear the market place of people. We don't want injuries.' But try to separate a drunken crowd from fire, or owners from their cars, or market men from what was left of all their working lives. No one would budge, though the captain of the district police made announcements with his megaphone.

It did not take long for those two trees to burn. The flames climbed down the trunk and sped along the ground. They jumped like cats across the roofs of outhouses and drink stores and kitchens at the back of bars. The drinkers and the beggars took their chance to loot before the fire drank all the beer and wine. They dragged out cases, smashing open bottles. They helped themselves to anything to eat or spend or sell. They fought the fire with German lager. They egged it on with Scotch and rum and wooden chairs. The bars and gardens had no time to bargain with the flames. There was too much wood. Only the burgher laurels were reluctant to join in. Their leaves seemed proofed, their branches far too flexible for flames. But when they burned at last, their molten marzipan hung in a cloud of country cooking which settled on the night like frost on fields.

The city police are not as patient as their country brothers. It seemed to them that this was a market protest which had gone mad. They well remembered what the market traders had done to the traffic when they marched on Big Vic, and – years before – the mayhem of the produce strike. The soapies had a reputation for independence, for cussedness. The police had little time for marketeers. And they were not fond, either, of the 'dross', the down-and-outs, who slept out there. Now these two groups were teaming up with young drunk men. A fearsome trinity. And there was fighting, looting, fires. Already there were pockets of disturbance on the streets beyond the Soap Market. Young men attacked big cars, blocked trams, uprooted shrubs in the Mathematical Park. They took revenge on everything and everyone as if violence was the only way to make the city notice them. They knew instinctively that they were invisible unless they rioted and smashed and stole. And then their faces made the television screen.

The local police – exhausted, shocked – did not need a permit from a priest or mayor to draw their truncheons, raise their shields, and bruise the crowd. What was the point in holding back, in softening their blows. If they did not put an end to this disturbance now, then who could tell where it might lead and what it might achieve?

9

SO FAR, SO GOOD. A little local trouble, nurtured at the festive chest of New Year's Eve. But though the cobbles held the flames at bay, the heat and passion spread. Emptied bottles soon were filled with fuel from cars and stopped with rags and lit and thrown. What had held beer arced through the night like fairground comets, falling short on cars, exploding in the air, or showering the firemen and the police in flaming rain. In other times the older traders would have called for calm for fear their pitches might be destroyed, their customers abused. But what had they to lose now that the market place was stripped, their trestles and their canvas already up in flames, their stomachs full of drink? 'It shouldn't end like this,' they thought, but not with sufficient certainty to interfere. Instead they raised their arms and voices with the mob. Midnight made them brave, eloquent and loud.

What wisdom caused the captain of the police to radio for help? Why did he lose his nerve? Was he alarmed he could not stop his men from cracking heads? Was it the flaming bottles? Was it the cars? Or was he simply calm and procedural, judging that his men were now outnumbered by a mob and that diplomacy and night would not damp down its fire?

He radio'ed for help at five-past one on that first, smoke-filled morning of the year, though what he said to his superiors is in dispute. The public inquiry that was held could not unravel truth and lies. But this is sure, his plea for – so he claimed – another fifty policemen at the most, disturbed the brandy and cigars of the city's powered notables. The Chief of Police, the mayor, the owner-publisher of all three city newspapers (my remote, rotund boss), three of the city's four leading financiers, (no Victor, naturally), their partners and their consorts (my boss's blatant wife), had all been top-table guests at the businessmen's annual dinner. They'd made their annual speeches, dispensed their annual handshakes and their pledges. They'd joined in the choruses of New Year songs. (Once more the buxom sisters of the Band Accord were wheezing music for a fee.) And now they were alone, except for waitresses and cocktail staff, in a private suite.

The Chief of Police was trying hard to understand an anecdote the mayor was telling when a waitress brought him a folded note on an enamelled Persian tray. He read: 'HAPPY NEW YEAR, and to celebrate the occasion there is organised rioting in the market area. Briefly: arson, vehicles and property destroyed, incendiary devices, injuries (fatalities?). The district captain is flapping like a scorched moth. Requests urgent help. What action?' The ornamented B.L. below the note was the signature of the Chief's uniformed aide.

'At last, the Revolution,' the Chief said, and read the note out loud.

His wife raised her eyebrows. 'I suppose this means we have to leave,' she said. 'Who'd be married to a policeman? I never get to finish meals. Or drink. Though duty never calls so loudly during working hours. Oddly.'

'We stay,' her husband said. 'That is my resolution for the New Year. Never leave a party before you've smoked the butt and drunk the dregs.'

'And what about the Revolution, dear? That starchy little man who calls himself your aide won't give you any peace until you've done his bidding. I'm never sure who works for whom.'

The Chief preferred his wife when she was sober, and out of sight. He passed her comments off as family jokes. 'I do not need to leave the room to settle this,' he said. He took a ballpoint from his jacket and added just two words to his aide's short note. 'Deploy URCU.' His signature, attempted with a flourish, pierced and tore the paper. He held the paper up dramatically.

'That should do the trick,' he said. 'Revolution ends before cigar, I think.'

On public holidays, such as New Year, he explained, it was not easy to solve problems of this kind. District policemen, it seemed, were in short supply at such a time. The ones that were not working on the New Year's shift were either out of town or drunk or celebrating on the street. But there were young men in the barracks who'd been on duty all night long, denied a drink, denied cigars, denied festivities. Let loose a bored detachment from the Urban Rapid Control Unit, the Chief assured the other guests, and there would be – he sought a phrase which could be both manly and dispassionate – 'sudden order on the streets'. How simple it felt, amid such comfort and such company, to settle revolutions with a phrase. He called the waitress. He placed his two-word note upon the tray and sent her off whence she had come to activate his aide and URCU.

The district police had been extempory. Their blows had been offhand, and improvised. Their strategy was unrehearsed. They were the jazzmen of the law. But URCU were the classicists, contrapuntal, harmonised, notated, drilled. Their last note was implicit in their first. And their first note was this: a barrack klaxon call that in less than four minutes filled the barrack yard with two hundred and twenty men, selected for URCU duties because their deference, their height, their eagerness to please suggested they were loyal to orders and to masters rather than to class. Kitted out in Impact Hats and blue-black riot overalls and keen to stretch their limbs after an evening spent crouched over dominoes, letters home and boot polish, they listened to instructions ('Suppress, contain, arrest') with the queasy eagerness of footballers at a pre-match briefing. Defenders had been issued with long, transparent, perspex shields. The strikers, divided into eight snatch-squads of six, had short shields, night-sticks made out of toughened PVC, and lighter boots for running swiftly and for kicking with numbing accuracy. The Specialists had short-barrelled weapons, or plastic-baton launchers, or canisters of gas, or dogs – and – perks for the élite – hip-flasks of rum to keep them warm and reckless until their specialities were called upon. Someone set up the URCU 'anthem' beating on his shield, the unforgiving sound of PVC on perspex. In seconds every shield was shivering in unison. Dum dum dum-dum-dump. Dum. Dum. Dum-dum. Dump!

URCU rode across the city in their Sweepers – blue-black riot coaches (to co-ordinate with overalls), their fish-net windows grilled, their foremost fenders prowed and aproned like snow-ploughs. Soon there would be field toilets, civilian back-up units, refreshment vans for officers and ranks, the paramedics, the parasites. Already trams and traffic had been stopped from entering the older parts of town. Already marksmen with infra-red night-sights were seeking out the attic rooms in those offices and homes which looked down on the fringes of the Soap Market. Camera crews, from police and television, buzzed and hovered like carcass bees. Police radio wavelengths were as overloaded and as chattering as a telephone line sagging with its swifts and swallows on summer's last warm day. Here was a city at full-stretch, able – as only cities are – to Suppress, Contain, Arrest the chaos of the human heart as if it were as fettered and as mindless as a tram.

So when the URCU came, what could the soapies do, that undrilled coalition of beggars, fruiterers, revellers, ne'er-do-wells? Disperse? They were 'bottled up', to use the phrase preferred by the URCU foot-soldiers to the euphemistic 'contained' of their officers. Where could they go but back towards the flames? Those few who sought to leave by calmly walking at the police were driven off with dum-dum-dump, or driven back by water jets, or knocked onto the cobbles by boots and sticks, or told – if they were too old and smartly dressed to be struck or kicked or drenched – 'Get back in there. You don't come out until we say'.

The market drains – muzzled already by the leaves and peel of fruit – could not cope with the water from the hoses. The drains were hydrants, tumbling with water and not removing it. They soaked and drowned the cobblestones. What flames there were found ducking, orange twins to dance with in the flood, and there were silver floodlamps for the dancers, too, from police and TV helicopters whose rotaries sent frowns across the water.

The wisest men and women stood at the market's heart, ankle-deep in water, breathless and demoralised in the smoke and clamour. Rook was there. He held his chest. He held a handkerchief to his mouth. He felt exultant and dismayed.

Who now could doubt the power and the patience of the rich?
They held the ground. They held the sky. The city was all
theirs. Had Rook not told the soapies so? He looked towards
the conifer of lights which was Big Vic at night. Was Victor the
Insomniac looking down upon the Soap Market? Was his
permission sought before the URCU squads were sent to put a
cordon round his tenants on his territory? Whoever'd given
Victor his first name had chosen well. Who was the victor
now?

Rook found his nebuliser. He held it to his mouth. He
sucked on its fine mist. It was no match for damp and fire and
night. He wished he had a desk on which to rest his head, or
Anna's chest. He wished he had the skill to rise above all this,
say twenty-seven storeys up beyond the smoke and noise and
danger of the street. If Rook was silent at the centre of the
storm, then Joseph was at the typhoon's active edge. His jacket
top was thrown off. His sleeves were up despite the time of
year, despite the hour. He pulled at cobblestones. He helped
with flaming bottles, upturned cars, with threats and challenges in the puddled, twenty-metre showground between the
people and the police. He took his work-shirt off. The smoke
from the wet fires was just as gelid as the steam and vapours
of the train, the Salad Bowl Express, in which he'd bared
himself at home, when he had raised the produce boxes to his
head and steadied them, his face well hidden, his body on
display. Now he did not hide his face, and what he hoisted
overhead and shook were fists. The noses and the foreheads
pressed to glass were not rich women's or their daughters' on
weekend shopping sprees but those of URCU; unpowdered,
unpampered noses and foreheads, unpainted mouths steaming up the perspex of their shields and waiting for the order to

Advance-dum-dum, Suppress-dum-dum, Arrest-dum-dump.

It was Joseph who found the stacks of unsold fruit and vegetables, as yet untouched by fire. He held a mauving loose-leafed cabbage in his hand, as light, for all its size, as a can of beer. He was a child. He had no self-control. He ran out in the showground, hoisted the cabbage in the air with all the might that comes from years of lifting sacks. Many were the times when cutting cabbages he'd found a damaged one and, just for fun, had launched it in the air to reach the hedge or scare the girls or break the boredom of the work. His training helped him now. The mauving cabbage held its own against the pull of earth and seemed to hang inside the helicopter searchlight from above as if it were a pastel moon that had till dawn to land.

The men of URCU watched the cabbage arc towards them through the night. Not one amongst them knew what threat it posed, but certainly it looked more menacing than cobble-stones or petrol bombs. What escalation did it represent? How would their shields withstand a missile that was so large and pale and full of flight? The line of long shields tensed. The squad knee-ducked to halve the impact of the foliage bomb. The cabbage, dropping now, unnerved them more than stones or flame. Four men from URCU, directly in the cabbage path, fell onto the ground in preparation for its blow. The cabbage struck a shield square on. It hardly made a sound. A chicken's egg could make more noise and do more harm. The cabbage fell apart. Its leaves were sheets, were flakes. The target URCU fell onto his back and, if blushes weighed as much as stones, he would have died beneath the load.

The laughter and jeers from the Soap Market were louder even than the helicopter blades. Now everybody ran to arm

themselves with fruit and vegetables. Never had shopkeepers
and shop-lifters been in such harmony. They knew – this is
the lesson of the insurrectionist – that ridicule and laughter are
more subversive, more disarming than bullets. What can a line
of soldiers do against a fusillade of cabbages? Put down their
shields and face the leaves? Hold up their shields and face the
jeers?

Quite soon the air was thick with greengrocery. Potatoes
were quite damaging and could be thrown further than even
cobbles or bottles. Apples, pears, and avocados beat tattoos –
dum-dump – on shields. Tomatoes blooded them, or burst on
blue-black overalls or overpolished boots. The comedians sent
bananas through the air. 'Like boomerangs,' they said. Indeed,
some did return. You can't control the tempers of young
URCU men who're made to feel like village clods. They sent
bananas back. An URCU officer was uncapped by an aubergine. A courgette caught a policeman in the corner of his eye.
A TV cameraman took on his cheek the full deceit of a peach:
first the tight and rubbery impact of the skin, and then the
sticky embrace of the flesh, and finally the wrinkled bullet at
its heart. The peach stone split. It cut his cheek. His blood was
peach juice, and his juice was blood.

Joseph indulged himself. He was a citizen at last. He held
the front of stage, and worked his way through fruit. The
snatch-squad leader noted him. 'We'll have him first,' he told
his men. 'The comic with the birthmark on his cheek. We'll
give that bastard birthmarks, head to toe.' The police and
press took Joseph's photograph. They had a picture of him
with his fists high in the air. They had him holding cobbles in
his hand. And cabbages. And Ogun melons. And pomegran-
ate hand-grenades.

At 1.45 a.m. the senior officer sustained a chest wound from a sugar beet. It struck him between his heart and epaulette and knocked him to the ground. What could he say, to all who'd seen him tumbling on the cobblestones, except 'Enough's enough. Go forward. Clear the market. Let them know who runs this town.' So they were beating shields again. Each blow upon the perspex shields took the URCU cordon one step closer to the produce bombardiers, the upturned cars, the scorched remains of trees and stalls and bars, to vaunting, topless Joseph, and to Rook.

'This is the classic public order manoeuvre,' explained the police PRs. Undermine resistance with a show of strength and noise. And then send in the Short Shields to arrest the troublemakers. And then send up the canisters of Green Grief, the gas that blinds the rioters and dyes them green and makes them weep and grimace like Picasso's Cubist lovers. And then mop up.

They griefed the centre of the market first. The police – though they had masks – did not wish to gas their own advance. Rook kicked a canister away. His legs and shoes took on the airborne moss. His skin turned ghostly, apple-white, while Grief, as light and volatile as gnats, rose to his waist, his chest, his throat, his eyes. It was a pity all the lemons had been used as missiles. Lemon juice, rubbed on the face, is some protection against gas.

Rook felt for safety. He found a car. He crouched. His eyes and chest were tight. Rioters should not mix drink and gas. Asthmatics should shun crowds. He clutched the front tyre of the car. He alternated handkerchief and nebuliser at his mouth. He coughed. But coughing did not clear his chest. The sticky sputum that landed on the cobblestones and on the rubber tyre and in his hand was lining from his lungs. Its release left him raw. It hurt to swallow smoke and Grief. It hurt to barter oxygen with CO_2. His bellows wheezed and tightened if they were opened wider than a crack. He had to pant as quickly and as shallowly as marsh frogs do, his chest distended, his lungs migrating to his throat, his upper orifices strung like candle-tops with waxy phlegm.

The country people say a dying man is concentrated in his thoughts. He sees the heights and depths of life ranged before him like coloured beads on a Chinese abacus. He's deft and concentrated, accounting for his faults and triumphs. 'The dying never lie,' they say. But Rook was lying to himself. His abacus was ranged only with the whitest beads. His thoughts were hardly concentrated. His brain was in his throat, buffeted by outer, wicked air and inner, pinioned breath, now damp with bubble blood and overladen with the weight of mucus. His tongue and nails and lips were blue. He sweated and he trembled as he sank from sleep into coma. But then, perhaps, he was not dying after all. The rain, the breeze, the slight protection of the car, the gas-repellent sheet of water which cushioned cobbles (and in which he now fell forward, his cheek and ear submerged) might dampen down the asthma and save Rook from the suffocating embraces of the air. Perhaps he stood a chance, for help was close at hand.

What did the market look like, now that the police had broken ranks and were intent, like running boys with flocks of seagulls on the beach, to cause disordered flight amongst the trapped and agitated crowds? Helmets moved amongst bare heads. Soapies grouped, regrouped, broke up like antelope before the snapping jackal truncheons of the police. It seemed that URCU – far outnumbered by the crowd – were deadened men who had no pity and no fear. They went to work as if their orders were to complicate the mayhem of the night, not bring it to an end. Joseph was fleeing for his life. He'd already taken blows to his bare shoulder and his back. The Short Shields had him marked. They knew his face. His torso had been photographed. He was the prize stag in the herd. 'Get the one without the shirt!' He ducked and dived between the people and cars as lightly as he'd done when he'd played tag with other boys between the orchard sheds and trees when he was young. His life had led to this. He had a plan: to find an open car and force his way, between the springs and cushions of the rear seats, into the boot. Where else was there to hide or go? The URCU had the soapies bottled up, their clothing steeped in green, reduced by Grief from revellers to snivellers.

Joseph had tried two dozen doors before – exactly this – he stumbled over Rook. He recognised the face, the cough, the leather jacket that he wore. He sat Rook up. 'What's up?' he said, too dull to find dramatic words. Rook did not speak. His eyes were shut. One ear was full of water. The other one was stained with Grief. He was unconscious now. The best of luck to him. To be unconscious is God's way of settling the lungs. He did not fight the inner or the outer air. He breathed more shallowly, more evenly, less frequently. Joseph placed him with his back against the wheel arch. Rook's head and chest fell forward. His diaphragm forced heavy air into his upper lungs. By chance, his breathing pipes were tipped at just the angle for recovery. Joseph beat him on the back. The blows expelled damp sods of air.

'Come on. Wake up,' said Joseph. 'I want my money now.' He slapped Rook's face. The colour of his cheeks had turned from green to pink.

'Give. Give,' he said. 'You've had your bonfire. Now
you've got to pay for it.'

Rook was peaceful now. Too comfortable to wake and
speak. He made a noise that found a passage through his nose.
It was the noise that athletes make when marathons are run. It
was a snore of restitution. It repaid the debt of oxygen.
Joseph's slaps and blows – who knows? – had saved Rook's
life.

Joseph had no time to spare. He heard the heavy boots
close in, the cries of pain, the lifeless impacts made by sticks
on men and cobblestones on shields. This place of safety by
the car's front wheel could not last long. He tugged on Rook's
coat. It would not shift, not speedily at least. He took his 'nife'
from his trouser pocket. He placed it at Rook's stooped back.
He did not say a word, but opened up the leather purse of
Rook, along the jacket's backbone seam, the woollen shirt
beneath, as if this were no man but some slain goat. The knife
cut from the inside out. It meant no harm to Rook. He was not
hurt, just robbed. Joseph pulled off the left half of the jacket
and the shirt, by the sleeves. And then the right half too. He
checked the inner pockets, found the outline of Rook's wallet,
and would have cut the pocket out, but Short Shields were too
close. He stooped and ran again – and as he ran he pulled the
two half-jackets with their half-shirt linings on his arms and
round his shoulders. His leather jacket had a stripe of flesh
down the centre of his back. His muscled torso had only partly
disappeared. He looked like some stage-punk, prepared for
surgery.

Rook was not aware that Joseph had come or gone, or
what he'd done to save his life. He felt the cold of New Year's
dawn and all the fires put out and no shirt or jacket on. He

shivered when he became conscious. He was startled by the
noise and by his semi-nakedness. He almost stood, and as he
almost stood two URCU saw his lack of clothes. He was the
one without the shirt. They pulled Rook up. They hit his legs
and then his back with swinging blows. They put the handle
of their batons in his ribs and pressed. They kicked him in the
face and testicles, their boots scooping water from the ground
and skidding on Rook's skin. They were well trained. It was a
rule that policemen who were obliged to assault a suspect on
the street would not arrest the man, but leave him to be found
by other officers. The two that roughed up Rook were wise
enough to roll him on the ground and disappear.

Joseph, split in two, Rook's wallet on his heart, found a
car at last of which the window could be forced. It took him
half a minute to get in. Another half to squeeze into the boot.
He was appalled at being trapped like that, but hoped that he
was safe. Indeed he was. No one was checking boots, while
there were people still free in the market place. Joseph curled
up in the darkness. Once he felt the car rock violently as
someone outside was thrown against the frame. He heard one
cry. But mostly he heard nothing, except the pulse inside his
ears, his nervous breath. He did not hear, six cars away, the
cough and splash as Rook rolled over for his last time, his
dead face half-submerged on market cobblestones.

10

WHEN JOSEPH HEARD THE ambulance siren, he re-emerged from the warren of the boot. He squeezed into the rear of the car, and peered out on semi-darkness. Dawn was a narrow silver bar across the windscreen. Already it had reached the edge of town and was advancing with the first trams along the boulevards. The upper storeys of Big Vic could not be seen. Low cloud enclosed them. New Year's Day would be a rainy one.

The few officials and the policemen that remained in the Soap Market had their backs to Joseph. They did not see or hear him open the passenger door and step out onto cobble-stones. A pulse of icy light was flung out by the ambulance like an irrigation sprinkler watering a field. Joseph ducked each time the beam swept by, as if he feared a drenching in the light. Joseph thanked St Joseph, the Patron of the Holy Corpse, the Undertaker of Our Lord, that he was well enough to leave the market place by foot and not by ambulance. He'd made it through to the new year without the beating he deserved. His only bruise was in the muscles of his shoulder, from throwing too much fruit.

There'd been a thousand injuries between the midnight and the dawn, though some of those had been administered at police HQ, in the privacy of cells. But there had only been one death. The corpse had not been found until the market-site

302

was cleared of drunks and revolutionaries. They might as well pump air into a brick as try the kiss of life. Rook would have blushed at being caught like this, flat on his back in water, naked from the waist up, his chest a splintered prow, his stomach just a touch too plump for one so slight and vain. The market boy had died the market death, his back on cobbles, green from Grief, discarded like a bruised courgette, and looking now as dull and common as the stones which were his mortuary. Here was a most unlikely Martyr for the Cause – though, as time would prove, his name was good for martyr-dom. Not easy to forget. We all remember Rook.

Joseph recognised the face, but did not wait to see the body wrapped inside the body bag. He stole a broom which had been left leaning on the side panels of an URCU truck. He soon became just one of dawn's sweepers, brushing up the missile debris for little pay and less respect. He was invisible. He swept his way across the cobblestones, past URCU men, reporters from the papers, gawpers on their way to work, young men returned to claim (they hoped) their unburned cars. He swept towards the market edge, towards the exit where the banana vans had been but were no more. He joined the early morning New Year crowd, his severed clothes hardly noticed by the late-for-work, the late-to-bed. He made his way through the squints and alleys of the Woodgate district, uncer-tain whether he was rich or poor. Perhaps Rook's death had been a cunning way to keep the two halves of the banknotes forever separate, as disunited as the clothes upon his back.

Joseph found a place to stop at last, a graveyard in a *cul-de-sac* with high tombstones and cypresses, and two plane trees, the perfect citizens surrounded by the sloughed-off litter of their toxic bark. There were no spectators, except for pigeons, and a pack of feral dogs. He pulled Rook's wallet from Rook's jacket and went through the spoils. He laid them out before him on cold stone. A photograph of Anna, inscribed 'Let's meet and talk'. A set of keys. The ten odd halves of the ten one-thousand notes. An ID card with a photograph of Rook, a grainy square in grey and black, expressionless, with – below – Rook's home address, his status 'Single Male', and his signature in neat green ink. A folded advert from a catalogue, the model on the stool, the barmaid in his grasp, the suit, the unattended glass. Five untorn fifty notes. A contraceptive. Credit cards. A throat spray of some kind.

Joseph only kept the money and the keys. He lifted up a slab of stone and put the empty wallet and the rest beneath. If ever he had need for contraceptives or had a customer for stolen credit cards then he could find this stone again. He memorised the mossy name upon the stone, but the feral dogs would snout the wallet out as soon as he was gone. Already he had memorised the address on Rook's ID card, and set off looking for a bed and an inheritance.

He'd seen that Rook was 'Status: Single Male' and knew there was a chance that Rook's home would be undefended. What better way to spend the dawn on New Year's Day than use the dead man's keys, and find some shelter, warmth, some food, some sleep between four walls?

He found a parcel of deliveries in the entrance hall of Rook's apartment block. He tucked the parcel under his arm and took his time upon the stairs. What could be more normal at that time of day, than deliveries? If anybody met him on the stairs they'd take him for an errand boy, a scruffy, docile errand boy of the usual kind. He met no one. He found Rook's door and tried the keys. Two locks. Two sets of teeth unclenched. The locks obeyed the keys. He was inside. This was the dream he had when he was loading produce onto trains: the day would come when he came home to his apartment in a city. He closed the door on everything. He'd never known such perfect carpentry or such a calm as this. He went from room to room. He opened every cupboard, every drawer. He looked inside the fridge. He did not touch, or eat, or steal. That could wait. He knew what he was searching for. A roll of clear tape. He found it in a wicker basket with some scissors. He sat down at the table and, breathing through his nose for better concentration, made for himself, from twenty half-notes – his and Rook's – a fortune and a future.

The police would say they found him looting Rook's apartment. Already he had stolen, it would seem, a parcel of antique books intended for the collector in the attic rooms. They said that every drawer and cupboard had been opened and all Rook's valuables had gone. They said he planned to strip the place, that his accomplices would come with vans to take the furniture, to make off with the fridge and television set, the knick-knacks that were Rook. Who knows? Joseph was not a saint, though in a way he'd been a hero of a kind, for half-a-night at least.

They had his picture in the first newspapers of the year, but not for burglary. Not yet. They had him semi-naked on Page One, his arms raised up, an aubergine in hand. He was 'The Face of Discontent', 'The Market Rioter'. He shared the page with Rook. The headline was 'Man Dead in City Violence', and underneath reporters reproduced what they'd been told by police, how 'groups of Trotskyists and Anarchists, trained by foreign radicals and at secret camps in Germany, have been identified as orchestrating the disturbances'. The dead man's name had not been learnt officially, but on the street the word had spread that URCU men had bludgeoned him to death. He was an 'activist', an innocent, a man who simply wished to voice his fears. The police had hit a thousand heads the night before. They'd hit this one too hard.

No statements came from URCU. They were beyond the press. But police PR was doing what it could to give the corpse a name, to find the cause of death. They had their answers by midday. The market place had witnesses. A trader had seen a semi-naked Rook go down and not get up. He'd seen the URCU pair run off. The police had rioted, he said, 'not us'. He made his statement to the radio and to a journalist from the sentimental left-wing press. So Rook became a martyr to the cause. The man who'd been top-brass in Victor's palace; the man who'd left Big Vic on principle because he feared for the Soap Market, the man who had fought off-stage against Arcadia, the man who was a trader's son himself, this market boy, had been brought down – 'assassinated' was the word – by police clubs and boots. Coincidence? Wake up! They'd sought him out, the rabble-rousers said. They'd marked him down for death.

The Chief of Police had hardly slept. He and the mayor and two financiers had celebrated the new year long after their wives had been driven home. They'd smoked the butt and drunk the dregs. Their waking tempers were not sweet. Their throats were raw with talk and smoke and spicy food. The Chief was nonplussed by the headlines in the morning paper. Where was the 'sudden order' he'd requested in the night? He'd sobered up to find a scandal on his hands. A middle-aged man was dead, and rumour on the run. How long before some busybody asked, 'Where was the Chief of Police when his men were clubbing citizens to death?' He took some comfort from hurried medical reports that the 'victim' (a mistake, he thought, to have used that word) had died from respiratory failure – 'asthma, possibly'. But there were broken bones and bruises, too. His ribs had sixteen fractures. His testicles were torn. His back and legs were ribbed and grilled with bruises. His scalp was peeled by blows from boots. There were sole marks on his cheeks. His nose was pointing east-south-east. A vehicle had crushed the corpse's knee. If this was asthma then this man's lungs deserved a trial and punishment, and we all courted death each time we sneezed.

'Come up with something better,' the Chief of Police instructed his aide. He was in luck. The officers who went to Rook's address to tell his next-of-kin, if he had next-of-kin, found Rook's apartment violated, the keys left hanging in the lock. They found the ne'er-do-well asleep, his elbows on the table, his birthmark cushioned by the newly reunited notes. They recognised the face – the boy in all the photographs, the crazy anarchist from German insurrection camps. Within a day they had the evidence that they required. Two witnesses had seen this Joseph kneeling at Rook's side. One swore he'd noticed blows rained down on Rook, slaps to the face, punches to the back 'consistent with the bruises on the corpse'. The other said he'd seen a knife. He thought it was a knife. It gleamed. But, no, he could not be certain there was not something blunt as well. A cobblestone, perhaps. The ground was strewn with broken cobblestones. A broken cobblestone can tear a testicle and fracture sixteen ribs.

What chance had he? He was the one in the photographs, assaulting policemen with vegetables and fruit. Just the sort to pick on someone middle-class, respectable, like Rook. Perhaps at first he only sought to steal a jacket for disguise, but then – ever the feckless, opportunist thief, so everybody from his village claimed – he'd seen the wallet and he'd killed for it. The prosecution case was clear. Here were two men who'd seen it all. Here was the stolen jacket and the shirt, in halves, on Joseph's back. Here was a 'nife'. Here were the black field boots with which he'd bludgeoned Rook. The muddy imprint from them marked the victim's face. Here was the accused man, fresh from the murder, in Rook's home, a fortune in his hands. And his defence? Joseph only had deranged and far-fetched explanations – the mugging in the underpass, the severed notes, the lighting of the fire – to show why he and Rook weren't foes, but partners.

VICTOR, AS USUAL, HAD not gone early to his bed on New Year's Eve. His night-time wanderings from room to room in Big Vic had distorted fitfully the perfect conifer of lights. Just short of midnight he had gone out on the roof to clear his lungs by jettisoning and melting phlegm in the potting compost of his plants. The country people always cleared their lungs on New Year's Eve: 'Spit out bad debts,' they used to say if they were merchants, or 'Last year's spit for next year's spring,' if they were working on the land. The merchants spat like pellet guns; the farmers dropped their phlegm onto the soil like bakers adding egg to cake.

Victor was not obliged to spit alone on New Year's Eve. He could have chosen company. There'd been the usual annual invitation to be the mayor's guest at the businessmen's banquet. But Anna had sent off Victor's annual regrets and his donation to the Widows' Fund. He said he was too old to celebrate the passage of another year.

'You're there in spirit,' Anna said, flourishing the widows' cheque for him to sign.

Yet being on his own as all the city clocks struck twelve was not entirely to Victor's taste. He had been tempted to suggest that Anna ought to stop behind and join him for a drink – but why embarrass her. She was not family. Her duties ended at the office door.

On the twelfth stroke he'd almost gone down in his lift to shake the hands of those tall men in uniform who kept Big Vic secure right round the clock. He need not hold a conversation with these men, a modest gratuity would satisfy. For once, he felt regret that Rook had gone. The man was neither honest nor efficient, it was true, but he was more like family. A flippant nephew, say, determined to amuse. And he was skilled – Victor acknowledged this – at catering for veterans. That birthday meal that Rook had organised had been the highlight of the year, just like the village parties he had known and never known. He hummed the march from 'La Regina' which Band Accord had played that early summer's day upon the roof. The coming year would make him eighty-two. Would he be there to celebrate?

The midnight roof was cold. But then old men are always cold, like fish. It's heat they cannot bear, and noise, and sudden movements close at hand. He shivered but was glad to be outside – almost the only 'outside' in his life, these days – liberated from the humming equanimity of air-conditioners. The wind snatched at his spit and tugged his dressing-gown. He hurried through the darkness to the greenhouse door and found the switch to light two meanly powered orange bulbs, the 'forcing lamps' of market gardeners. The orange light expelled the night. The glass leaked wind. It moaned and chattered in its frame. Two liquid-gas heaters kept the winter greenhouse warm. They kept his specimens alive and made the winter temperate for succulents, for palms, for greenfly and for bugs.

He found low staging for a stool. He found the brandy bottle, amongst the liquid feeds and aphid sprays. He spat again. He spat for spring. And then he filled his mouth with brandy from the bottle. Its fierceness numbed his mouth. He drank more manically, determined to gulp down the medicine, the sleeping draught. He held the bottle up against the light. It looked like melted beeswax. He took his medicine until the brandy was lower than the bottle's label. Enough to make him moan and chatter to himself in unison with window frames. Victor was neither hot nor cold. He was the temperature of plants. He pressed his nose upon the glass, staring out at first towards the outskirts and the hills. There were no stars, just damp and glass and greenhouse algae acting as a screen against the night. He heard the fire sirens at his back. He turned to see the flames, the incandescent trees, the unprecedented sight of car-lights on the market cobblestones. At first he could not place the flames. He could not place them geographically or in time. The oblongs of greenhouse glass made the distance two-dimensional. It was a film, a flaring, fading early colour film, the print besmirched by water, algae, fumes. Here was a scene brought on by sleeplessness and drink. Here was a scene that was familiar. He dared not blink. He had to concentrate to bring the memory back. The flames were old and watery. But, at his bidding, people had appeared, and sound. There was an old straw hat. The smell of bread and urine. The disconcerted snufflings of sleepers on bare boards. The sirens were his mother's screams, the screams of Princesses on fire, of people separated from their homes, the screams of rain-soaked timbers made dry and hot too swiftly by the fire.

He drank more brandy, finished what was left. He stood and looked more closely at the market flames. He wiped the glass clean with his dressing-gown. The film was three-dimensional at last. The flames waved and beckoned to him –

the ancient and dramatic call to warmth that is so eloquent at night. The fires seemed close when viewed through dewy glass, so close, he thought, that they could have been candles mounted on the roof-top parapet. Victor blinked the candles into distant fire. He sent them off. He brought them close again. Now he saw his mother in the glass, packing her possessions in a canvas bag and strapping her only child across her chest with a shawl. She threw some grains of maize across the doorstep of their country home. She lit a single candle and left it – for too short a time – standing at the centre of their wooden table. She closed the door.

When Victor focussed once again, his mother's table was alight. The door was orange flame. She could not keep the fire away. She could not stop the timbers cracking. She called for Victor. He was gone. She went down on her hands and knees. She could not breathe. She curled up in the smoke and flame. She did not know if he was safe or dead. They'd find her well-cooked body in the morning, the rain its undertaker. They'd find a blanket for her, a morgue, a box. They'd give her earthen eyelids in the common grave. Victor blinked the fire back into candle. He blinked up tears, but then old men are used to having water in their eyes without good cause. It's part of growing old. Besides, the heating of the greenhouse let out fumes, and fumes are just as sure as sentiment to make men weep.

By now the helicopters were aloft. Their searchlights left Victor in no doubt – once he had wiped the past away and focussed on the night – that there was trouble in the Soap Market. The helicopters sobered him. They were a match for brandy and self-pity and for the apprehension that he felt. He left the orange bulbs to burn. He chanced the roof-top wind

and made his way to bed. For once he slept quite readily. He
did not dream or need to wake to urinate. When dawn came,
his body on the mattress formed an arthritic question mark,
his right ear on the pillow, his torso curved, his knees and legs
brought up for comfort. His question was – Why do I feel so
scorched and dry?

It was New Year's Day and – not for the first time in his
life – Victor was plagued by an anxiety which he could not
name. Who's dead? What's dead?, he asked himself. What
could the fires and helicopters mean? He had a hollow in his
chest that only getting out of bed could displace, that only
going out into the town and seeing for himself could fill. He
tried to conjure up his mother's face, but failed. He saw his
aunt. But more than Aunt he saw the market as it was when
he was young and poor. He sat cross-legged upon the ground.
A tray of eggs at his feet. There were no customers. It
seemed that this imagined market was piled with produce –
but, when he looked more closely, the sacks and bags, the
spuds and watermelons, turned to corpses. There were a
thousand bodies on the ground. The cobblestones were
corpses too, as still and stiff as graveyard flesh, as implacable
as eggs.

So it was, when Anna came on New Year's Day to re-
hearse his duties for the week, Victor was prepared.

'You've heard the news,' she said. He shook his head. She
showed the morning papers and the police reports. Joseph
straddled the front page, 'The Market Rioter'. And naturally
there was an unnamed corpse. A man of middle age, stripped
naked to the waist, softened, bruised and split like an old
banana by the beating he'd received.

'I had a dream like this,' he said. 'I dreamed this death.'

'It's not a dream,' she said, unnerved that he should mention dreams. 'It's pandemonium downstairs. The phones are smoking – traders, press, the police, the architects, the building contractors. Arcadia will have to wait a day. I don't think we can go in with clearance gangs until they've buried that poor man at least.' She pointed at the sub-heading, 'Man Dead in City Violence'.

'Condolences are due, perhaps,' he said, 'if he has family. Please organise a cheque for me to sign.'

She made a note. 'It's all in hand,' she said, 'though there are problems to be solved.'

'Please specify.'

'Such as, the market stalls. They are all destroyed. What will the traders use tomorrow when the carpark site opens? The city must be fed.'

Victor did not seem alarmed. It was his view that merchants have to cope. They did not need their trestles to do trade. They were the sort who'd sell fruit off the floor or from their vans and be content so long as money bruised their thighs. He might have been alarmed, perhaps, if fire and riot had reduced Arcadia to rubble on the ground. Yet no damage to Arcadia was done, or could be done. Not for a while at least. The riot was benign as riots go. A riot on an empty building site could do no harm.

He shrugged at Anna, as if to say, Don't worry me with trifles. But what he said was this: 'It would be diplomatic, don't you think, if I went down to show my face?' The shrug was meant to hide his awkwardness.

'Down where?'

'To the Soap Market. Where else?' And then, 'I feel I ought to demonstrate concern. But privately, you see. No need for fuss. Or press. I simply want to satisfy myself, with my own eyes, that all is well.'

It was the early afternoon when Victor's black Panache was backed up to the entrance to Big Vic. 'The old man's going out,' the chauffeur had been told. He hardly had the time to air the car, to polish off the dust. Security held the rubber-neckers back as Victor came out of the lift, with Anna at his heels. Her new winter coat was black and long and astrakhan. His coat was alpine wool, and grey and fifteen years of age. They knew how cold it was on New Year's Day, and how the wind could grip the knees and thighs, how rain could bounce off paving-stones, how colds and rheumatism were unforbear-ing muggers on the street.

Anna had already lost the final kilo of the three she'd targeted, and so she felt the cold more keenly than before. She wore a business suit beneath the astrakhan, the same creamy colour but a more expensive cut than Joseph's *On the Town*. It did not tug across the chest or pinch the waist. Her hair was short and razored still, though her hairdresser had added 'just a little fire' by lightening her quiff. She was not the jolly Anna any more, and glad of that. Jolliness is a despairing refuge for women of her age. It tries to take the place of youth and looks, and is not dignified. Anna was now as solemn and as trim as the clothes she wore. She'd had enough of men, and she had vowed, for this New Year, to do without their oily approba-tion. She would not seek their sexual patronage. She would not be their carrion. Let them fear her for a change. She held the keys to Victor now – and anyone who sought the chance of sitting at his desk, enveloped by his cheesy old-man's breath, must knock upon her door.

The doormen did not wince a smile at her as they'd once

done, as she followed Victor onto the rainy mall. They almost called her Sir, she was so manly in her self-regard. And she herself no longer had the need to smile from 9.00 to 5.00, or be polite, or defer to the men in suits and uniforms. Promotion had redeemed her from the curse of growing old. She had an office of her own, an office staff, the power of command. She'd use that power to the full. She'd not be loose at work like Rook had been, his feet and cake crumbs on his desk. She'd not emulate his lack of *gravitas*, his office improprieties, his open door. She'd not be Rook, or Mrs Rook. She would, though, welcome just one chance to see the man again, to let him know how disengaged she had become from him. To let him see – and rue – her power and her sleekness and her pride. She'd have him on his knees. He'd be like Victor, like a child.

The old man now was in the car. His door was closed. His face was purposeless and spoiled. He needed her like no man ever had, that is to say he had no need for love or touch. Where should she sit? Beside the chauffeur? With the boss? The doormen knew the protocol. They opened up the front and near-side door so that she could sit in the servant's seat, where Rook had sat on those rare occasions when he'd shared a car with Victor. But Anna walked round to the driving side, emboldened by her freshly minted resolution for New Year. The chauffeur was too slow to open up the far rear door. She opened it herself and sat down on the same bench seat as Victor, one upholstered metre between their hips. He would not try to hold her hand. He would not try to touch her knees, or even look at them, despite their newly nobled shape, now that they sat as colleagues side-by-side. She tapped the glass behind the chauffeur's cap and they set off into the city. When they cleared the mall she spoke for Victor into the intercom.

'We're going to the Soap Market,' she said. 'We'll need an umbrella when we're there.' Then no one spoke. The chauffeur hid behind his cap, disturbed by the breach of protocol which placed a woman at the boss's side. The old man closed his eyes and mouth, in disapproval, surely. The chauffeur could not see him breathe or move.

Anna, sitting with her fingers laced across her lap, sucked on a granny mint to make her breath and stomach sweet and anodyne. What would she do if she saw Rook where Rook was bound to be, amongst the soapies in the market place? She let herself imagine he was standing there, among the idlers on the cobblestones, with nothing else to do but watch the limousine, with Victor getting out, and Anna hovering behind. She'd look him in the eye if he was there, if she had pluck enough to lift her head and face the crowd. She'd have no need or time to smile. It was too windy and too wet to smile. She closed her eyes and mouth to match the old man at her side. The windscreen wipers sounded like an oxygen machine, pumping air into their lungs. If it stops raining we will die, she thought. Her heart-beat matched the wipers. It pulsed beneath the astrakhan. The black and courtly limousine advanced through the rain. There was no haste. They were like mourners in a hearse, composed, embarrassed, fearful for themselves, grey-eyed, but from weariness not grief.

When Victor's chauffeur took the car through the Woodgate district to the edge of what had been the Soap Market, all appeared quite well. Much of the debris had been removed, and nearly all the cars that had been parked were claimed and driven off. Already work had begun on the wooden palisade that would enclose the empty oval while Arcadia was being built, and city labourers were taking down the hazardous charred remains of bars and trees. For the first time for six hundred years the fountains and the gargoyles of the ancient washing place were unattended. They were as disused by the city now as pyramids. Soon the trenchers and the labourers would come to harvest cobblestones and box them up like sugar beets for their deployment in Arcadia.

The police had cleared the site of everyone but the workmen and themselves. Detectives had set up a caravan at the market edge to interview those witnesses who volunteered to speak. They looked through the rubbish for evidence of organised disruption and put the charred and broken bottle-bombs in plastic bags together with examples of the fruit and cobblestones that had been thrown. They interviewed the last few young men who came to claim their cars. A fixed-frame canvas shed had been erected above the spot where Rook had died, but no one stood on guard. Inside, placed on the cobblestones, were six or seven lighted candles and a spray of greenhouse blooms, making the inside of the shed a warm and makeshift corpseless shrine. Who'd put the candles there no one was sure. But they'd been left to burn themselves into the ground.

Two uniformed policemen controlled all access to the market site. They hesitated when they saw the black Panache, but were persuaded by the chauffeur's cap and the imperious flashing of the limousine's front lamps to lift the makeshift barrier. Victor and Anna were driven a further twenty metres. Then they stopped. The chauffeur's umbrella matched the car and Anna's coat. Now Victor and his female aide were thigh to thigh beneath the chauffeur's outstretched arm. She took her boss's elbow to help him walk. He was no longer used to cobblestones or hazards such as broken glass, wet leaf mush, splintered wood. She let him lead the way, but he was lost.

There were no markers in this empty space for him to recognise. Where had the women sat with their shallots? Where had
he stood with eggs? Where was the thoroughfare of stalls
which seemed, by day, as ancient and as permanent as a
Roman road? Who'd start a fire, who'd die, to save a place so
empty and so dull?

Victor was not the sort to share his memories. He seemed
just like the old, rich man he was – too grand to feel the rain.
So this was his diplomacy, to shuffle on the cobbles for a
while, and not share what he felt with those two aides who
kept him dry and upright. They walked, this threesome, to the
public washing square. The trees and shrubbery which had
been there were reduced to blackened stumps. The lawns were
stubble, stiff and dead and black. But fire could not harm
stone or water, and the medieval fountains, with their gargoyles and their pitted scrubbing stones, were just as they had
been the week before, the century before. The fountain water,
augmented by rain, was like all mountain streams, like
every brackish spring, indifferent to every living thing on
earth.

They watched the water for a while and then turned back
towards the car, but took a slightly different route, enticed by
what might be beneath the canvas of the blinking, well-lit
shed.

'That man died here last night, I guess,' said Anna.
'They've made a shrine for him.' She knelt and re-arranged the
flowers so that they made a neater shape between the candles.
'It's sad.'

The two men did not speak, so Anna rose and spoke for
them. 'He's someone's husband or son or dad. Or else he's one
of those no-hopers who sleep out here. Perhaps they'll never

find out who he was. They'll put *The Unknown Soapie* on his grave.'

'My father's buried over there,' the chauffeur said. 'In the Woodgate cemetery. My mother, too. We used to live round here. I've soapie blood . . .'

They stood like tourists in a foreign church, familiar with the funereal intimacy of candlelight, but ill at ease with dispositions they'd not met before: the flapping walls; the cobblestones; the rhythmic catechism of the rain on canvas. The weather worsened. They could hear it growing sullen. The candle flames curtseyed in the damp, cold air which pierced the fabric chapel. Water made its way between the cobblestones and crept inside to puddle beneath their feet. They might have been upon some Afghan plain, three hundred years ago, pinned in by space and sky and frost. The office blocks and tenements which circled them, though distantly, invisibly, were ancient cliffs, shrinking in the cold and wind and rain.

'I'll bring the car,' the chauffeur said, glad to leave the candlelight. 'It's raining pips and pods.'

'Exactly,' Victor said to Anna after they had stood still and silent for longer than made sense. 'It's pips and pods. Just listen to the rain. I never hear the rain inside Big Vic. It's pips and pods. She used to use that phrase. You can hear exactly what she meant.'

'Who meant?'

Victor did not dare reply. He did not wish to make himself seem foolish as the chauffeur had, weak with sentiment. He crouched as best he could to look into the candle flames.

'I think,' he said, 'we'll take a lighted candle with us when we leave. The fellow who died here won't mind.' He broke the waxy seal which fixed a candle to its cobblestone. 'A country ritual, that's all. You take a lighted candle from the old place to the new. That way you keep the goodwill of the past.'

'I'll carry it.' Anna held her fingers out. Just as she'd thought, the boss was like a child.

'No, no.'

'What "new place" will you take it to? Arcadia? That candle isn't long enough to burn for two years.'

'We'll take it to the carpark site. It's just a symbol.'

Anna's nod displayed her patience and obedience, but not a sign of understanding.

'It's true you don't grow rich on sentiment – not in the market trade,' said Victor. 'Hard work is what it takes, and common sense. But ritual has its part to play. We should not underestimate . . .' He did not finish what he had to say. He was an undramatic man.

'Alright,' he said. 'You carry it.' He held the candle up for Anna to hold. 'Take care the wind and rain don't put it out. A rain-soaked wick is bad luck for a hundred years.'

* * *

Who phoned The Burgher? I can't be sure. I did not take the call. The chauffeur, maybe. Anna? No. The policeman who controlled the barrier and let the Panache pass into the squints and alleys of the old town? A worker at the carpark site? Some restless, spying spirit of the town? There's always someone in a city with a tale to tell, and there are always Burghers to dress it up and publish it. Prompted by the memo on my desk from this unnamed source, I wrote a paragraph for The Burgher column. They ran it on the morning after Victor's market pilgrimage on the usual inside page of the edition which had pictures of both Rook and Joseph on the front. The headline was 'Soapie Rioter Charged with Murder'. Rook was described as being 'an executive assistant in the produce market industry, until his recent redundancy'.

By nine o'clock on the morning of January 2nd, when Anna walked down the mall and entered Big Vic, Rook's name was known throughout the town. Office workers in the atrium pored over copies of our newspaper, regretting, relishing the fate of one so popular as Rook.

Anna sat before her untouched desk. She breathed as evenly as her tightened ribcage would allow. Could she now make more sense or less of what had happened in the canvas shed, of the strange journey in the car protecting that small flame as they sped through the town? The day before, the words she'd used had seemed too strong. 'It's sad,' she'd said. But now 'It's sad' took on a fugal note. She could not find the words to go beyond 'It's sad'. She could not comprehend the burden of the news expressed so solidly in print.

The Burgher – steered by me – took the lighter view, of course. 'It's rare these days', I wrote, 'to see Victor, the city's octogenarian Vegetable King, out on the streets. But if you could see through the tinted glass of limousines you might have spotted the old man in the recently truncheoned Soap Market yesterday afternoon. No doubt he came to creak his respects to Rook, his one-time accessory, who was struck to the ground in the small hours of New Year's Day.

'Sharp-eyed citizens report that Victor did not come away empty-handed. The greenhouse recluse who is not, you will recall, averse to transporting fish fillets to his table in a taxi, departed from Rook's market shrine with a lighted candle in his hand. The candle made the journey across town by chauffeur-driven limousine. Of course. Who says the rich aren't ludicrous?

'My colleague, our religious affairs correspondent, tells me as he passes between the city's clubs and bars on some lifelong mission of his own, that "candles light the darkened alleyways through which we all must pass when time is up, and all our bottles emptied to the dregs". Is it the fashion in these straitened times to pay respects to recent employees by *removing* candles from their place of rest? Victor's "spokeswoman" could not say when I phoned on your behalf to put that simple question. She only knew the price of beans.

'I'm sure a man as practical as Victor will find a use for Rook's half-candle, if only to grease the elevators of Arcadia. The old greengrocer might, too, like to pillage the cemeteries and morgues of our city for further spoils. Gravestones make good foundations. So do bones.'

PART FOUR

ARCADIA

1

TODAY THE PRESS CLUB Buffers have their monthly lunch at Victor's-In-Arcadia. We have the private room, beyond the mezzanine restaurant. There the finest produce of the market floors is served *al dente* for the city's swiftest, trimmest, smartest clientele: I am not one.

The female *maître d'* of Victor's-In-Arcadia – 'Madame' to us, but Sophia to the younger men – conducts me past the rising stars, the upstart businessmen, the skipjack currency kings, whose mobile phones and calculators share tablecloths with button mushrooms *à la grècque* and vegetable brochettes. I pass the inner bars, and then the Conversation Pits where men and women half my age strike deals and attitudes in easy chairs. This is not the populace at lunch, and these are hardly citizens at all. They are – forgive my want of charity – Invulnerables, protected from the town by bottled water, parking permits, air-conditioned cars, and by the jaundiced deference of waiters, commissionaires, receptionists, the police. Their tables are reserved. Their clubs, their tailors, their dentists and their apartment homes are 'Private and Exclusive', meaning they are closed to those who are not dignified by wealth or birth or fashion. They seldom need to queue or step onto the street, but organise their lives through fax machines, credit cards, and home deliveries. Or else they delegate these tasks to secretaries, adjutants and housekeepers

JIM CRACE

who are employed to keep the world at bay. No wonder that, despite the stresses of the street, their faces are so cool, their suits and skirts so crisp and clean, their tempers so dispassionate. No wonder I am tempted to topple bottles into laps as I pass slowly by.

Our room is on the highest level of Arcadia. Sophia leaves me to go alone upstairs. She is too busy to escort those Buffers whose hearts and lungs and legs are so abused and slack that they climb slowly. Not one of us is less than sixty-two. What journalist, at sixty-two and more, could climb a stair at speed? What journalist would climb the stair at all unless there were good food and drink and gossip at the top? Not one of us is so required at work that he – yes, every Buffer is a man – cannot take time away from his desk to lunch with fading comrades. We're of an age, when we toast 'Absent Friends', to mean those colleagues who are dead, or those few and tough successful ones too busy to be there – the managers, the editors who've grown grey and powerful like grizzly bears, while we are as grey and powerful as pigeons.

But us, the Friends too idle to be Absent? We undertake the stairs at Victor's-In-Arcadia unburdened by wealth or status or by energy. We're winding down our working lives. We're dining out on what we were, before they took our offices away, before we were reduced from editors to columnists, from publicity executives to small-ad men, from roving correspondents to custodians of the Letters Page, before our bylines were removed.

The Burgher now is someone else. A younger woman has my job. She is not interested in the fate of millionaires or city councillors. The power that she follows is power of a different kind. She spends her afternoons in bars and restaurants and hotel lobbies. She writes a column cast with television hosts, and dance club managers, and rich men's sons. The term 'Invulnerables' is hers. She never misses trysts or *tête à têtes*. She lunches out on indiscretion, celebrity tantrums, scandal, flagrancy. Her sources are the city's *maîtres d'*, the waiters and receptionists, the hotel boys who take the breakfast trays to guests.

I'm bitter, naturally. What trickery of physics allows the world to spin, yet leaves me motionless? They've moved me sideways to the Waiting Room, their mordant description of the office where the older, *valued* men like me are asked to wait until, at best, our underfunded pensions turn us out. I'm known as Back-End Editor. I have the weather and the law reports in my control. Obituaries, as well. You see how comic these professionals can be with words? And grimly accurate? Of my four predecessors three have died of heart attacks. The fourth has cancer of the throat. The Back-End Editor? The Waiting Room? The Press Club Buffers? My laughter thins and hastens as I grow fat and slow.

Today I am the first Buffer to arrive, and glad of it. I have the chance to catch my breath and fuel myself with drinks. We like to formalise the lunch, to listen to each Buffer give his news before the meal. Today I'll tell them what I know of Victor, the man who built Arcadia and gives his name to this restaurant and bar, the man who is too old these days to interest my substitute. His ninetieth birthday passed by, unremarked by her.

Why Victor? Here's the news which almost gives a skip to my edgy pacing of the room. Six months ago I prepared the old man's obituary for the Pending File. I turned – the well-trained journalist – to the trusted testimony of the cuttings

files. What could I learn of him from what's in print? I
searched the archives and the only items on the man, apart
from industry and trade reports, were those I'd written up
myself. He'd brought fish by taxi for his birthday once, from
the station to Big Vic. He stole a candle from a colleague's
grave. Enough to deepen interest in the man, of course. But
not much of an epitaph. I phoned Big Vic. Anna, his deputy, a
woman in her fifties now, sharp-faced, a little overdressed, but
winsome still, did what she could to help. And then – when
she had checked the accuracy of the obituary – she said, 'He's
looking for an author to prepare a memoir. Might you be
interested? . . .' And so I am the one retained to write his Life.
Luck has landed me a paying task for my maturity. A contract's signed, and already I have spent some – mostly silent –
time with him, though he has told me anecdotes of a fat man
in the Soap Market and he has talked a little of his childhood.
Is that the word? Is 'childhood' not too innocent for how he
passed his urchin years, for how he says his mother died in
flames? The old man had a mother, yes. Her name was Em.
He's not the product of a melon and a cucumber after all. I
have, through Anna, some access to the files, her private
memories, and – more crucially – some pointers to the old
man's early life which seem to bear his story out. But Anna
much prefers to talk of Rook, and of the boy who murdered
him. She has procured court depositions for me to study, and
can arrange, she says, for me to visit Joseph on the prison farm
(he's working in the fields again!) where he is serving Life.
She mistakes me for a detective-journalist, a Woodward or a
Bernstein, and wants me to investigate what truly happened
all those years ago to Rook. I have asked her more than once to
dine with me, to socialise about the book. But she declines.

She gives more thought to Rook, it would appear, than she gives to her boss's Life. She shows no interest in his childhood or his youth. For evidence of Victor in his later years I have no need to search. I only have to look around – at our hired room, at our refurbished town.

I'm in a tree-house made of glass. On two sides there is stretched netting screening off the market concourses below. The netting supports creepers, cycads, vines. They are the building's drapery. They grow from elevated beds, together with other hot-house plants such as philodendrons and spider palms which can breathe and neutralise the atmosphere. It is their task – for nothing here is idle or unplanned – to filter from the air the carbon monoxide, the benzene and the formaldehyde, the fumes and vapours, the leakages and pungencies of Arcadia.

The plants define the frontiers of Signor Busi's 'largest aviary yet'. One hundred cockatiels, one thousand finches, sixty pheasant doves, a throng of budgerigars, and cockatoos and parakeets and minah birds, a petal storm of buntings, are billeted up here. They seem to like the glass and framework of Arcadia better than the trees. They make their nests and perches on the tops of the suspended humidifiers which – under the direction of a computer christened Zephyr – blast compressed air into the tropics of the aviary. The birds shuffle on the metal girders and the arching glassmounts, pecking at the paintwork made loose already by the eczema of the rust. Rainforests cannot keep rust at bay. But glass has kept the day-hawks out. They hover at the transparent domes of Arcadia, like children at sweet-shop windows, hopelessly drawn to candied parakeets.

Imagine what so many birds can do to glass. They settle

331

on the window frames and jettison their chalky waste in reckless, heavy streaks which provide food and habitation for lime flies, silver thrips, and fleas. What architect could plan for that? What glazier could outwit birds and coprophagous parasites? What scaffolder could foresee the territorial conflicts that take place above Arcadia's trading concourses, its restaurants and bars? I look out through the room's streaked glass to see what causes such raucous purpose amongst the rainbow flocks. A small brown interloper from the city streets, a sparrow in its business suit, has found its way inside Arcadia. Busi's 'hermetically sealed megalith' is no match for a hungry sparrow. It has squeezed through the cavity of an expansion joist, and then found passage through the ill-docked heating duct. The bird now seeks to feast on sunflower seeds, mixed nuts and grain put out in feeding trays by the custodians. The doves are beating at it with their wings. A cockatiel has caught the sparrow's underbreast. Down in the folds of netting which separate the people and the birds, a dozen corpses can be seen. Dead sparrows that have reached this dripping, heated heaven and have died.

The third side of the room has unstreaked glass. No birds. My view is unrestricted, except by bamboo leaves and vines and slight myopia. I look down on the building's centrepiece, its hub: the garden court to which the trading corridors and halls, the stairs, the patios, the terraces and balconies defer. I spend a little time watching the light-show on the fountains, its blushes and its loops, exactly like the blushes and the loops which decorate the chamber music being played by three young women and a man on the concert podium by the open brasserie. The entertainment's free all day. Six Africans will play their drums this afternoon. A girl will juggle with some market fruit. The Band Accord, those ageing sisters and their friend, will squeeze out melodies for tea.

The tourists take their coffee and their photographs, with views across the rebuilt medieval washing place towards the thickest foliage of Arcadia. The camera with a narrow lens can take a photograph which shows just water, washing place and leaves, a flash of cockatoo, a beam of sun. Arcadia, so framed, could be a part of Yucatan or Abyssinia. It's true the tourists cannot sit and pose amongst the resurrected gargoyles or the repaired stone, or trail their fingers in the water as they smile on film. A man in uniform is there to see they don't. 'What next,' he'll say, if they protest. 'Let people touch the water, then they'll want to wash their feet in it? Swim in it? Piss in it?' He's down there now. I see him prowling at the water's edge, a two-way radio reverberating in his hand. He helps and points, reproves and redirects. He shows where handicapped visitors can find the Courtesy Wheelchairs, where children can be left in the Jungle Crèche while parents or *au pairs* shop and take a snack in the Picnic Basket, the Texas Pantry or the Hunger Monger. No eating on-the-hoof, of course. It is not done to take an apple or an orange from your bag and munch it as you browse. There's pith and skin and core to clear. No dining on a sandwich that you've bought outside. There's paper then, and crust. No cigarettes, except inside the bars. This is the price you pay.

Yet, Arcadia is a triumph. Let's admit it. It weathers as I watch; it settles in. There is no complacency, just the swagger and ambition that cities flourish on. I'd stand here happily – glass in hand, alone – all day, and not be bored, and not grow tired, and not be stifled by its flamboyant uniformity, by its recreant geometry, by its managed cheerfulness. Give me the chance. Give me the time. Give me the bottle and the glass. I'd sooner look upon Arcadia than anything in town. Yet I'm obliged to socialise. The room is filling now, and we are making phatic conversation, amongst the vines and birds. We put the world to rights. We are as vehement about the rain as we are sanguine and ironic with politics and trade. We do not merchandise our gossip, yet – not till our sixth or seventh glass.

When we have eaten, swapped our formal news, we leave the table and our muddied plates to stand in groups about the room, to stand in pairs in conversation as we look out through the bird-stained glass at birds or through the cleaner glass at Victor's earthly paradise. What must we look like, standing here engrossed in our last drinks? I press my nose against the glass, twenty metres up above the market concourse, and watch those citizens, those purchasers below. I look, no doubt, like Victor looks, up on the roof-top garden of the twenty-eighth. I look like every suited grandee looks: untouchable, untouched. Yet, this I know, as I grow older, I must descend the stairs and join the populace before my day is done. The city claims its citizens before they die. The taxi-cabs are full of younger men. The trams – soon to be replaced by subway trains – are slow with pensioners who cannot find their money or their step. The streets these days are for the old and weak and poor. I'll leave no monument to me. No bar or restaurant, no market hall, will bear my name. My book, if I survive to see it done, will have my name in print – but think how big my name in print will be compared to Victor's name, a banner on the cover. My labours print his mark more deeply on the town. His labours press me deeper in.

So the lunch is done, and we go back to work or home, a

little drunk and overfed. I've time to wander in Arcadia. I fool myself this is research, that everything I see is Victor manifest. Certainly it is not dull, though Victor-manifest should be more dull than this. It is a work of art and industry and arrogance, but, then, where would our city be without these three? We'd be a village still. Arcadia hunches its four backs against the town, the sky, the world. Who, passing through its halls, its barrow-vaulted sub-lit aisles of glass, can tell or care if it is night or day, or north or south, or spring, or windy, wet or bright? Arcadia is – that word again – Invulnerable.

I take the route, along one trading corridor, which would have led from the old bars to the edge of the Woodgate district. I am besieged by colour and by smell. There is no wind or cold, and any sun that filters through is bounced by angles, shed by glass, and spread by glossy walls as if it were the bogus light of theatres. The music and the smells are piped: fresh bread with Paganini; oranges augmented by the quintets of Osvaldo Bosse. I cannot hear the birds. Even the humidifiers – roaring in the heavens of the building's carapace – are silent at ground level. The fountains cast their strands of water as quietly as a jug pours milk. The traders do not shout. They do not cry their wares. They have found out what only now I discover for myself, that – removed from wind and open air – man-made sounds are quails. They cannot fly. They cannot travel far. They tremble on the ground. No screeching indoor parakeet can pierce a flight path with its cry. Any raucous marketeer evangelising fruit would find no echo to endorse his claims. At best, the sound he'd hear – if he were close enough – would be the sullen impact of his voice on toughened glass.

Though the noises of Arcadia are flat, the fruit and vegetables have never seemed so polished and so uniform. The traders, beneath their matching awnings, seduce the passers-by with produce of the gene-bank and the science farm, enhanced by Spray-Dew, Frost-Ban and by packaging. Recessed orange lights warm and flatter every radish, every grape, every hybrid superfruit. Together with the onions and the swedes, are Kingquats, a kumquat bigger than a plum and every part of it – the peel, the pith – is edible. And there are orange grapes, and bananas from Barbados shaped like avocado pears. And avocado pears without a stone. And lab-grown lettuces (red or green or white). And glasshouse broccoli with flower-heads as big and tight as cobblestones, achromatic rhubarb force-grown under fluorescent lights, and bio-technic aubergines which some chemist-gardener has artificially bloated in dioxide pods. Young men in search of romance can still buy their loves a Courting Quince, just as before, but more romantically presented in a silver nest with a heart-shaped, perfumed top. Each purchase has its plastic bag, each plastic bag its coloured logo for Arcadia; each coloured logo is a dancing apple with a hygienic, grub-free smile.

If I were rich I could buy jewellery and suits from boutiques which trade side-by-side with salad stands. If I were ill I could select a dozen cures for my maladies from the fresh herb shop; some adder buckthorn for my bowels (recalcitrant), some juniper for failing sight, some camomile to help me sleep, some cuckoopint to keep alert my hope of finding love, some mistletoe as sedative, some poisoned laurel sap for the new Burgher's gin. If I liked fungi (I do not) I'd have the choice of fifty sorts from Mycologia, The Mushroom Shop. Should I prepare a *fritto misto* for my supper from an edible bolete? Or should I select a honey mushroom or a chanterelle?

If I were looking for a gift, a set of gaudy stamps from the philatelists might take my fancy. A first edition (slightly stained) of dell'Ova's *Truismes*, complete with margin notes by Pierre Loti's bastard son. A pair of hand-made gloves. A pastry-house with stucco-marzipan and flaked walnut tiles. A tee-shirt printed with my name, or any name I choose. A postcard hologram of Arcadia. Or I could light a candle for the birthday of a friend. The Market Chapel is a shop and pays the usual rent, so needs to sell as many candles as it can. Nothing is cheap, of course. Don't rummage for your bargains here. Arcadia is built to shake out pockets, unzip wallets, cash cheques, debit bank accounts. It is a monumental Dip. Victor has created the perfect cash machine. The traders pay, on top of rents, percentages to Victor, too, like feudal peasants paying 'overage' on everything they sell. You see, Arcadia observes tradition after all. Something medieval is preserved intact! (If I were still The Burgher, there'd be a paragraph in this.)

Is there not cause to celebrate this new diversity, this innocent variety of goods, despite the claims of oracles and pamphleteers who say our city's in decline – and money is the force? Yet how could those greengrocers who once traded out of sacks and boxes in the Soap Market meet the rents and standards of Arcadia? They had to modernise or close up shop. Every shop that closed was taken up within a day, by businessmen whose visions were much looser and much wider than the soapies they replaced. Who needs so many outlets for a grape? One grape these days is much like all the rest. It makes good sense to let a market such as this diversify.

You only have to see the crowds to know these changes work. See how the middle classes flock from shop to shop, a bunch of parsley in their bags along with a batik headscarf that they've bought, and a piece of blue goat's cheese. See those valet-attended dowagers braving arthritis and discretion in the *couturières*. See how the bars and restaurants are packed with men and women who never used the windswept bars in the old Soap Market for fear of chaos and antipathy. See the foreign faces here; the tourists who have come to witness what Fodor calls 'the city's triumphant fusion of modernity and tradition, order and spontaneity, Life and Art, business and entertainment'.

Of course, you will not see the night-time soapies here. The bye-laws say there can be no loitering, no Unlicensed Trading, no begging, no entertainment without a permit, no vehicles (including skates and skateboards), no animals (except for guide dogs), no unrestricted access to the sort who clutch a bottle or whose dress and cleanliness would strike a sour note. 'Shop in Safety at Arcadia', the adverts say. 'Attended parking for two thousand cars'. There is no need to taste the city air at all, for those who drive, then shop, then drive. But who's so fearful of the city air that they dare not venture into the open forecourts which surround Arcadia? Here an open market still survives – three stalls of fruit (no vegetables), with staff in rural uniforms of dirndl skirts, straw hats and clogs. There's a take-a-number, wait-your-turn lunch stand. There are greenstone benches, and official buskers more impromptu and eclectic than the bands and string quartets inside.

I browse amongst the pushcarts there. Their tenants are the city's fireside artisans. I have the choice of jam or wooden beads or necklaces or cameos. One man sells woven bags. A woman and her dog have candles of a thousand kinds. Another deals in landscape prints and postcards of the town. I have the choice of riding on the garish carousel (restored from an original) or touring the old town by pony and trap, or visiting, with a bag of feed, the pigs, rabbits, goats and llamas of City Farm. I also have the choice of sitting here, bathing in the bounce-light of Arcadia, or going back to work. I would return to work, except that life is comforting here, and entertaining too. It's fun to watch the browsers shop, to watch the drama of the doorstaff turning back a drunk or turning out a bearded man with leaflets and a coat weighed down by badges. It's better fun than work to watch the 'flamingoes' operate their upturned litter scoops so that the market site is clean enough – if it were not against the market law – to sit upon the ground and doze.

It is, of course, the spirit of research and not distaste for work that takes me strolling round the wind-stroked, whistling outer rim of Arcadia. The Glass Meringue indeed. The Lobster Trap. The See-through Octopus. The Pumpkin. It has a hundred names. But one has stuck amongst those people rarely let inside or rarely rich enough to browse and buy. They call the place Fat Vic. It's Big Vic's plumper sibling. One stands, one squats. They are the city's strangest twins.

I come at last to Victor's birthday gift, the statue cast in bronze, commissioned by the merchants of the Soap Market. The move amongst the bleeding hearts, some time ago, to pull it down and put a statue up for Rook, has come to nothing. Victor's birthday gift survives. A woman sits cross-legged before a bowl. The artist has welded real coins inside. The woman has an infant at her breast. Its eyes are open wide, and fixed upon Arcadia. There was a time when children clambered over her, when office-workers used the plinth for lunch, when young men wrote the names of their sweethearts in felt-tip along the woman's arms, or coloured in her nipple, darkly. But, pretty soon, they railed her and her infant in. The statue's called *The Beggar Woman and Her Child*, but we all know it as *The Cage*.

So this is Em. And this is Victor, an infant at the breast. They are so still, you'd think their abject happiness could never end. Yet end it did. In flames. And here she – resurrected – is. Too rigid now to take the painted cart, piled high with melons – honeydews, casabas, cantaloupes, and musks – and far too late to set off, as she had promised, towards the city hems where blue fields match the sea-blue sky, with her small son her only passenger. I have the first line of his Life: 'No wonder Victor never fell in love.'

2

I'M IN THE MOOD to take my time. I walk across the last few patterned slabs and cobblestones of Arcadia and head off into town. The Woodgate pavements are old and cracked and buckled. They are ideal for puddles, weeds and saunterers. I peer down squints and alleyways. They seem more festive than they used to. Perhaps the presence of Arcadia has enlivened them. They are not back streets now, but brisk with bars and antique shops, and second-storey studios.

You cannot park. The wardens and the police make sure of that. How can they stop the soapies though? At first it was just one or two – disgruntled fruiterers who'd been displaced from Fat Vic's corridors. They had to work and feed their families, and so they set up shop in backs of vans and parked across the kerbstones in dead-ends, blind alleys, *cul-de-sacs*, providing low-grade, cheaper fruit for those in too much hurry for Arcadia. Quite soon there were a bunch of makeshift stalls, some coloured awnings set up at the backs of vans, some trays of produce set out on the pavement. You've never seen such rugged mushrooms, such unselected fruit, such tattered sugar-snaps, such unwaxed oranges, such blemished pears, such unwrapped chard – poor man's asparagus – and mulberries and radicchio still moist with country rain, already past their best, so cheap.

Quite soon, of course, the displaced market had a name –

Soap Two, just like a film. You think its characters are dead, and then the sequel comes along, as lively as the first. So now we see that it's not true that 'cities swallow up the small', that 'soufflés only rise the once'. The pygmies flourish on the street. I used to think that buildings were all that could endure in cities. But people, it would seem, endure as well. They hang on by their nails. They improvise. They kick. They leave a legacy which is not brick or stone.

The first to come and trade are well established now. They have their clientele, their daily pitches, their regimens. Some clever spark has improvised some light for dawn, and after dusk. Soap Two trades into the night when Arcadia is shut and under guard. The soapie trading light is pilfered from the streetlamps, by an illegal wire connected and undone a dozen times a day as uniforms approach. Who'll get the bill? Who cares! Not Cellophane. He does not give a damn. He is untouched by bills. He's shielded by the corset of his cellophane. He waltzes, as sheenily as a stage sardine, through the market all day and all night long. Sometimes he takes it on himself to direct the traffic as it squeezes past the stalls. Sometimes he lies down in the street to block the passing cars. He begs. He steals. He shouts obscenities. I've never heard such words before. He kicks the windfalls from the trading stalls. He's always at the market's edge, a cellophane commissionaire. As Soap Two expands then so he moves out from the core, to summon people in. It does not matter what their business is, or if they have no cause at all to pack into the streets. He simply hopes to share – and complicate – the ecstasy of crowds.

Now the Woodgate district, once so lifeless and depressed, is as noisy and congested, lively and unsafe, as the

Soap Market used to be. Merchandise is stacked in piles which
challenge sense and physics – towers of potatoes, conifers of
oranges, trembling with every passer-by. The makeshift market flourishes on noise and filth and rain. It would even
flourish – and it does – on poverty. 'All Life is Here', according
to the market chauvinists, a claim no one would make for
Arcadia, with its policed doors, its creed of Safety from the
Streets, its ban on pimps and tramps and tarts and bag-ladies,
street vendors, rascals, teenagers, drunkards, dogs. All life is
here, despite the wind, the rain, the airborne dust, the litter at
my feet.

The New Age meal I ate at the Buffers' lunch has left me
hungry still. I buy one sleepy pear. Its skin is bruised and
weather-beaten like a ploughman's face. The trader comes
down from his perch on the bonnet of his car. He leaves a
conversation with a friend, and his meal half-eaten on the
metal, his teeth-marks in the boiled egg; the ripped white loaf,
the plastic flask of over-sweetened coffee. He wipes my one
pear on his trouser leg to take away the marks of harvesting.
He pirouettes it in a paper bag. He twists the paper bag a pair
of ears. He takes my cash. I take the fruit. I'm free to eat it
when I want. I eat it now. My chin is wet. I cannot walk and
eat efficiently. I stand back from the crowd, against a wall
between a bistro and an odd-job shop to watch the man in
cellophane cause mayhem with the cars. I cannot say where I
prefer to eat, Soap Two, Fat Vic. The prospect of them both
seduces me. I'm free while there is sap inside my legs to make
my choice. I am not Invulnerable. Thank God for that. I am not
Victor and too old and dry to be at ease down here. He'll have
a book (perhaps) to celebrate his life. Arcadia. A statue, too.
But all his pears, I guess, are brought by train and taxi to Big

Vic. He takes Life on a plate. He has a serviette. He cannot simply – as I do now – toss the sodden paper bag which held the pear to the ground and find a warming corner for himself.

There is a little sun which falls directly on my face, my shirt, the damaged pear. I eat it now. I eat it now. The eye, the core, the stalk are given to the pavement, and flattened by ten thousand feet, as everyone is flattened by the town when they are done, when they are waste.

The sun is fully out for just an instant. It is radiant, then it is gone. The blocking bollard which has kept the weather dry has moved before the wind. The time has come for it to rain. It's hard and sudden as it always is in our city. It drizzles in the countryside but here the rain is bouncing berries on the roofs of cars. The squints and alleys cannot cope with this. They flood. They overflow. Their drains are blocked with cabbage leaves, handbills, discarded pith and peel. The pavements turn to green and slimy rinks of foliage. To walk on them is to gamble with your bones. What should we do but huddle underneath the awnings that are there, but gather in the doorways to the shops, or sit in cars, or seek refuge – and a drink – inside a bar?

I cannot quite escape the rain, despite the umbrella which my neighbour holds. My suit is sodden at the shoulder. My socks and shoes are wet. My forehead sweats with rain. The entertainment never ends. The weather is a ballet for the streets. But then there is a more substantial dancer too. Cellophane is kicking water in the air. He thinks we're going to throw him coins for the show. He bows. And as he bows the rainbow arches up, connecting the old town and the new. It is a bridge beyond the wit of architects reflected in the glass of Big Vic and Arcadia. The rainbow relishes windows. There is no need to draw conclusions though. We all know rainbows start and finish everywhere, that they are simply sun, shining from behind to trick the light from falling rain, if we look east in the middle afternoon towards the clearing shower of the day. They are not omens – but they are signs that it is safe to walk onto the streets again. The rain has almost done.

My face and eyes are wet. I have to frown and squint for focus as I pass between the glare and darkness, as I cross streets and circumscribe the puddles, as I avoid collisions with people and with cars. So many people with so many purposes. Too many people to know well.

I would not wish to be too grand for streets. To be removed from them is to lose the blessing of the multitude. The tallest buildings throw the longest shadows, it is said, by those who spend their lives in contemplation of their monuments, and those for whom the shadow life is better than the real. But most of us who live in cities die and take our shadows to the grave. We don't outlive the masonry or glass. It's said that great men have the grandest tombstones, too, and throw the longest shadows even after death. The cemeteries prove the truth in that. But I prefer to think that worms and damp and degradation are open-minded democrats which treat us all the same. We are all citizens at last. At least until we are all soil.

I make my mark upon the city, too. My living mark. I stretch my legs as best I can and set off slowly down the street. My rainy footprints on the pavement will soon dry, but footprints and the thousand sodden paper bags which held a thousand pears, the eyes, the cores, the stalks, the rinds of daily life, are more substantial – are they not? – than shadows. They swell the middens of the town.

There are people, wet and poor, who walk the pavements with a skip as if the puddles and the cracks are civic birthday gifts. And there are many whistlers around. My legs are old. That's all that holds me back from skipping on the spot or kicking up a puddled loop of rain. My tongue's kept busy by the scrap of pear skin lodged between my teeth. That's all that stops me sucking in our city air, and whistling.